A DOG IS BORN

JUNKYARD DOGS 2

DOMINIQUE MONDESIR

Copyright © 2022 by Dominique Mondesir

All rights reserved.

No part of this book may be reproduced in any form or by any electronic or mechanical means, including information storage and retrieval systems, without written permission from the author, except for the use of brief quotations in a book review.

This is a work of fiction. Any similarity to actual persons, living or dead, or actual events, is purely coincidental.

For my family without their support none of this would be possible.
Thanks to Cheynne Edmonton for the amazing cover art as always info@standoutcovers.com
And lastly thanks to my proof readers Martin Ohearn and Brandon Sommerville for making this book readable.
To my Grandmother, I hope you never read this.

1

The humid night air clung to my flesh as I stared out across the forest treetops. The only thing that gave off any light was the stars; with no clouds obstructing their brilliance they shone and danced putting on a show for the crowd below.

I leaned against the balcony railing and tilted my body as far as it could go over it.

Nothing but darkness could be seen below.

How easy would it be to just end it all, to just tip that much more over and tumble and flip all the way down, breaking bones on branches till I cracked my head on the forest floor? Would death be instant? Would I suffer? Would I cling to life, fighting for every breath until the darkness fully took me?

I shook my head and pushed myself backwards.

I could never take that path, not now. Not after everything that had happened. Not after everything yet to come.

I was to be a father.

Me.

I had been one once, but as I later found out the children weren't mine and my then-wife at the time had been sleeping with my boss for as long as we had been married, longer even. Although I loved them, they didn't love me back. They never saw me as their father,

My wife certainly didn't see me as her husband, but those issues had happened to a different person, in a different time.

In the time since I joined the Junk Yard Dogs, I had experienced life-changing events, which had changed me fundamentally as a person.

I had fooled my old company Xcorp into paying a fortune for a device which was nothing more than a computer virus, I had seen a mentor—friend—captain, die all because of greed and power, and I had unearthed a three-hundred-plus-year-old human-android genius who would very likely end humanity as I knew it.

I let out a deep breath and looked to the stars.

Even after all that, life still looked bright to me; the woman I loved more than life itself was carrying my child. Well, technically she wasn't a woman—well, she was, but not human, not in the "born by being conceived by a human" sense.

She was an AI humanoid, created by Alvis Bowman to be indistinguishable from any other human female. All the strengths, none of the weaknesses.

When she had told me she was pregnant I didn't believe her. Hell, who would? Yes, we had sex, but people had been having sex with every object they could find since man began walking on two legs; you still didn't expect your socks to become pregnant.

After she had finally explained to me how it was possible, puzzle pieces began to finally fit together. Alvis Bowman's desire to create a new race, the method and means of how he was going to do so, had finally become clear.

It was just crazy to think what his plan for Poppy was—no point in dwelling on that now. I had other matters to deal with.

Now I was in charge of the Junk Yard Dogs, I had unforeseen responsibilities I had to take care of. Making sure our ship had fuel, making sure we had enough supplies in the way of weapons, food, medical supplies, but more importantly making sure everyone got paid.

As Willis liked to remind me on a daily basis, if we didn't work, we didn't eat, and we hadn't worked for some weeks since coming back to Safe Haven. It wasn't that I didn't want to; it was once we got back out there, I knew what was waiting for us.

I had no clue if The Lady knew we were back on the planet, but once she did it was only a matter of time before she pulled us into her plans for planet-wide domination of Safe Haven, especially now she knew of Poppy's secret.

Then there was the matter of Alvis Bowman.

Poppy, Willis and Tuari had all contacted everyone they knew in regard to information or sightings of him, but Alvis had disappeared off the map. Poppy had an inkling he had gone back to Earth, but that was just a hunch.

I rested my head against the wooden railing and closed my eyes.

I felt a hand on my shoulder but I had failed to hear the footsteps that brought it.

"I hate when you do that, it's creepy. It reminds me of a ninja assassin coming to slay me in the night."

"Ninja assassin? I've been called many things in my long life, but that is a first."

"How about mother?" I asked, turning around and wrapping my arms around Poppy.

"I guess I'll get used to it after a while," she said.

"It's going to be weird seeing you with a baby bump."

"It'll be a lot weirder if you don't tell the rest of the crew, I know you said you need time, but they're going to find out eventually; it might as well come from you, their captain."

"*Their captain*. Now, that sounds weird to my ears. I guess you're right but it's a lot for them to take in—hell, it was a lot for me to take in and I'm the father, I am the father, right?"

She punched me on the arm as I chuckled in laughter.

"Ow, that's going to leave a bruise."

"Don't change the subject."

"Okay, okay. I'll tell them in a week or—"

She pulled away from me and narrowed her gaze.

"Fine. I'll tell them in a couple of days. By the way, when did you get so bossy? If this is a side effect to you being pregnant, I'm not sure I'm going to enjoy the coming months."

"And what's that supposed to mean?"

"Err, well..." I tried to think of something to say but my mind grew a blank.

She burst into laughter and kissed me on the lips, brushing my worries away, "Sorry, I just couldn't resist. Laughter has been so seldom heard around here anymore, I thought I would try and lighten the mood."

"I know what you mean, even Tuari hasn't cracked a joke in a while."

"It's being here, in The Jungle," Poppy said, gesturing to our surroundings. "The people from this area are all strict vegans and treat life as sacred, but with Tuari being a cook, he's finding it quite a challenge to prepare meals or—"

"I know. I know," I said with an eye roll. "If I have to hear one more rant about how a bowl of leaves and rice doesn't make a meal then I'm going to shoot someone. It's just a culture change. That's all. We just have to put up with it for the time being until we leave."

"And when will that be?"

"I..." I sighed as I brought her in close and kissed her on the forehead. A cluster of fireflies rose from the forest flowers that had intertwined themselves in the wooden railing of the boundary; they danced between us giving me a view of Poppy's naked form. "Is being here so bad?"

"No, I can see the charm. But like a vacation, you know it must end sometime. Burying your head in the sand will only work for so long; sooner or later there will be decisions you need to make, or those decisions will be made for you."

"I guess you're right, plus I don't know how much longer I can keep Willis from killing Samuel.

"To think those two are brothers boggles the mind—they couldn't be more different."

"They may appear different on the outside," Poppy said, "but they are made from the same cloth. Samuel has dangled from the edge by his fingertips; I've seen it in his eyes, he just hides it better than Willis."

"That may be true but I need them to get on tomorrow. Samuel has hired us to do a job for him."

"How come you never told me about it?"

"It's nothing really, just a simple trek in the forest to drop off some supplies for a settlement they have lost contact with. It shouldn't take longer than two days at most. I thought you could stay behind and put your feet—"

"Don't."

"What?" I said, lifting my hands up defensively.

"We've talked about this."

"I have no idea what—"

"You're treating me like I'm made out of glass now I'm

pregnant. I can punch through a brick wall, for god's sake; I hardly think a little trek through the jungle is going to cause me so much distress. If you feeble humans can manage, I think I can too."

"Wait, wait, wait. That's not the reason why at all," I said, lying through my teeth. "We have more than enough people coming along with us on this trip; it'll be Samuel and two of his guys and me, Willis and Tuari. Bringing anyone else is just going to be overkill to drag a couple of bags through some undergrowth. Plus, I want you to stay here in case anything happens—you're the best fighter we have and the most capable of dealing with any issue that arises."

She said nothing as she looked at me; I tried to keep my breathing and heartbeat as steady as possible because I knew she could read them whenever they spiked when I was caught in a lie. It was one of the disadvantages of being in a relationship with an AI.

I gave her a smile but she stepped back and shook her head, walking back through the bay doors that led to our room.

Damn it! I'd been caught out.

2

"I am sick and fucking tired of being sweatier than a miner's crotch, being eaten alive by bugs that make you sick, of having to take a shit in some hole and using biodegradable toilet paper that never gets your asshole clean *because it's safer for the wildlife, man*, of eating nothing but leaves and rice—"

"Hey," Tuari said, "that's not my fault."

"But most of all I'm sick of having to smell hippie BO wherever I go. There's something called deodorant! You smelly assholes! Use it. But most of all, you know what I'm sick of?"

"No, Willis," I said with a heavy sigh, "I don't."

"I'm sick and tired of complaining about this place. Fuck this place! Fuck this place!" he said, while repeatedly swinging his machete into the brush in front of us.

I looked towards Tuari, who shrugged.

"It amazes me a man as religious as you, little brother, has so little patience. Many *religious mystics* and zealots liked nothing more than to take a walk in the forest while they contemplated life. Most of the texts I have read on spiritual leaders has them spending an extensive amount of time in isolation in such a place as you are in now, but I guess that's why they are leaders and you a follower."

Willis's head snapped towards Samuel as he took a step forward, machete gripped tightly in his hand. The two men who accompanied Samuel took a step closer to his side.

"I am sure what Samuel was trying to say is, it takes a certain special someone to follow the teaching of a great spiritual leader instead of looking for spiritual fame and fortune themselves," I said, hurrying forward between the two. "Isn't that right?"

Samuel looked over my shoulder. "Yes, of course," he said finally.

"Funny," said Willis, "where was all this amazing insight when Mum needed you?"

Samuel opened his mouth but Willis had already moved ahead, machete swinging at anything that got in his path.

We had left the main city of The Jungle hours ago travelling by foot. At first the journey was pleasant, with the brush cut back and pathways laid out clearly before us. We had passed small settlements where large families or communities had chosen to live away from the main city, favouring an even more remote and bare-bones life than the simple city offered.

Most had gotten rid of all electronics and had lived off the land, using nothing but the tools they made and the clothes they had woven. The inhabitants of the first handful of settlements we passed greeted us with waves and smiles, as fruit was offered and village elders demanded as much information and news that Samuel could give, but those smiles and waves grew less and less the further afield we went.

As the hours stretched out before us with the sweat

soaking my shirt, the few settlements we saw were nothing like the first. The people who lived there didn't rush out to greet us, but instead crept out of doorways slowly with rifles pointed towards us. When they saw Samuel, shoulders relaxed but still, no smile was forthcoming.

Samuel held up his hand for us to wait and would always speak to them alone, sometimes entering their little hovel and not returning for half an hour or more. Some of the supplies we carried would always accompany him inside. I had tried to take a peek inside one of the bags but a stern hand from one of Samuel's men put a stop to that.

Whenever he would return the same worried expression was plastered on his face.

"Everything alright?" I asked, after some time hiking through branches and vines that pulled at our clothing and hair.

"Yes."

"You sure? Because we can't offer you our full services unless the client is truthful and forthcoming."

"I am not a client. You are doing The Jungle and in turn me a favour."

"Wait!" Willis shouted from behind us. "We ain't getting paid for this?"

"No," said Samuel, "you are not. Think of it as repaying our gratitude for all the free food, services and living arrangements we have given you and not asked anything back."

"You said, 'The Jungle is here to humbly serve anyone that is looking for rest and solitude.' Was that just some hippie bullshit?"

"No, Willis, my statement still stands, but The Jungle is low on... men such as yourselves, so whatever help we can get we shall take."

"*Men such as yourselves*—you mean killers?" Willis asked.

"No, I mean men who are resourceful," said Samuel, which made Willis snort.

"What's with the weapons? That's the first time I've seen anyone armed around here. I didn't even see anything resembling a weapon in the city," I asked.

"There are many things valuable in The Jungle, things people would pay highly for, things people would kill for; it is the sauce of all life. You can find anything here from medicine to combat headaches to cures for diseases such as cancer. There are even plants here that can open up the third eye and show you the true meaning of life, show you the inner workings of all things. The mother plant can illuminate your darkest desires; she can cure you of addictions of the soul. It's all here, my friend," Samuel said, brushing his hand along a flower the size of a dinner plate with polka-dot red and white leaves.

"It's all here. In the dirt we walk on, in the air we breathe, and in the plants we eat."

"What a load of bullshit," said Willis. "The only reason this place is so *important* to you and these people, is because of the drugs that grow in this region."

"That is but one—" began Samuel, but he was cut off by Willis.

"You may not realise this, Quinton, but The Jungle are the main distributors of drugs on Safe Haven and many other planets across the galaxy; they have a monopoly over everything from cocaine to opium. That is why they have the carefree attitude to life you see around you. Drug dealers can always afford a cosy life, on the foundation of everyone else's suffering."

"I wonder if you would be so confident of making such a statement if Zizi was here now. Yes, The Jungle distributes drugs, but we do not offer only the limited variety my little brother here knows. I have many teams off-world who use our planet's knowledge and funds to help out worlds less fortunate than ourselves, by giving them seeds to grow and knowledge to prosper.

"Human beings should have the right to choose for themselves what they want to take, be it psilocybin mushrooms or aspirin that comes from the willow bark. We should all have free choice.

"But large corporations, through ad campaigns, have demonised herbal remedies and natural plants because it affects their bottom line. Why take something natural and free when the pharmaceutical industry can offer you something made in a laboratory for triple the price with a list of side effects longer than your arm?"

"So you give away the drugs you produce for free?" Willis said.

"Well, err—"

"Thought so," Willis spat, pushing past Samuel.

The rest of the day had been uneventful, with us going deeper and deeper into the jungle. We had passed many animals and plants I had never seen before, large cat-like predators with shaggy black fur and green eyes that glowed; large carnivorous plants wafted a sweet fragrance which drew me towards them, but as I got closer I was stopped by Samuel, who threw a rock at one of the large leaves in the shape of a bell-like dome. The plant snatched the rock out of the air before it reached the ground.

It was now night and a small fire roared in the midst of

us, pushing away at the darkness but creating shadows demanding to be allowed into our nightmares.

Large bulbous vegetables crackled on a metal grill placed above a large pot that had some sort of vegetable soup brewing.

"I don't see why I couldn't have cooked us something," Tuari grumbled.

"We mean you no offence, but as you have rightly seen our dietary needs are quite complex," Samuel said.

"Complex! You cunts don't eat any meat or animal products, how complex can it be?"

Samuel looked to Willis' lips pulled in a thin line, I had hoped the pair would sort out their differences on the journey but it only heightened the sense of unrest between the two. At first, Willis hadn't wanted to come, but after I'd insisted his help was needed, he finally gave in.

"Thank you for preparing the meal," I said; "it's a pleasant change of pace to eat something different."

"Thank you," Samuel said with a nod.

Once the food was ready it was served amongst the group in wooden bowls and spoons, I dipped my spoon in the soup and brought it to my mouth. When I blew on it the scent of onions, garlic, carrots and another nutty spice I couldn't quite place enveloped my senses. Placing the spoon in my mouth, I closed my eyes and nodded my head in delight at the taste that danced on my tastebuds.

"This is superb," I said.

"You sound surprised," Samuel replied. "The journey we are on is taxing on the body, so we have added certain spices to this soup to help with recovery, and replace the minerals you have lost through your sweat. Eat up and get some rest. From here on out, the journey only gets harder."

A Dog Is Born

The embers of the fire crackled in the distance.

We had all retired for the night, after our meal. No-one was talkative after Willis had tried to get Samuel into a fight; he would poke and jab with comments that didn't appear to mean anything, but to them, the comments had deep roots in a long-lost history of hurt feelings and emotional scars. I had wanted to speak to Willis about what had taken place between the pair, but Tuari had placed a hand on my forearm and shook his head.

I had let it be, but if it continued, then as the captain I would need to step in before it became a major problem. We were short on allies, and alienating the last major player on Safe Haven that we could retreat to was not something I wanted to do. I had asked Samuel if he could give us any assistance in what was surely going to be a fight with The Lady and Alvis but he had declined, stating his borough's future was already intertwined with Isabella Ivanov and any betrayal on his part would lead to swift and violent repercussions against The Jungle, repercussions he wasn't sure he or his people could deal with.

I had offered our help, but he had once again declined.

We were a crew of four with a ship more suited to running than fighting. What help could we really offer him?

If I were in his position I would have done the same. It was always easier to back the winning horse than take a chance on the thousand-to-one favourite. Tossing for the hundredth time I stared up at the stars I could see through the foliage of leaves and branches and tried to settle my mind. Thoughts of what I had to do kept forcing their way into my mind and no matter how quickly I batted each away, another one would be right behind it to take its place.

One thing I knew was that Poppy was right, I couldn't stay here forever. This little haven I had found for myself would—

I opened my eyes. *I heard something. Of course you did, you idiot, you are in a jungle teeming with life. What did you expect to hear? The relaxing waves of the ocean?*

I forced my eyes closed again but less than a minute had passed when the same noise interrupted my sleep. Reopening them I got up to my elbows and scanned the darkness around me. Something deep in my DNA told me the sound was something I should be worried about, something that had sharp teeth and long claws and would like nothing more than to sink its teeth into my monkey ass.

I reached over to where my shotgun, The Peacemaker, lay, but hesitated. Even if there was something stalking us, the shotgun would cause too much noise and most likely scare everyone half to death, causing more problems than solutions. Retracting my hand I instead grabbed my small pistol and got up to a sitting position. No one else was awake.

I closed my eyes and listened again, but didn't hear the sound I had previously heard. Were my ears just playing tricks on me?

No. There it was again. Somewhere off to my far left. Getting up to my feet I held my gun out before me and faced the noise. The fire had burnt down to embers so the only light I had was from the few stars that pierced the overhead foliage; the sound came again to my left but another one soon joined it a few meters to the right. My head snapped back and forth as another sound came again to my left.

It sounded like the snapping of branches underneath claws.

Mouth dry I debated whether to wake the others; if it

was nothing then I would look like a fool, if I didn't I would place all our lives in jeopardy. The choice was an easy one to make—people had always seen me as a fool; if they did today then so be it. As I turned my head back to the camp and opened my mouth to warn the others something moved behind me. I turned around just as a shape leapt towards me. It didn't get far, as a gunshot rang out dropping it dead to the floor.

I turned my head and saw Willis aiming a gun towards me. Giving him a nod of thanks I turned back around as the camp sprang into life.

Another shape moved to my right and I brought up my pistol and fired. I missed. It melted back into the shadows.

Movement to my left swung my pistol that way but I was too slow to get a shot off. But I needn't have worried, as Tuari fired and hit it in the body. It didn't go down but it yelped in pain like a dog before it dived back into the undergrowth.

"Try not to hurt them!" Samuel screamed, coming up next to us. "Just fire some warning shots and that should scare them away."

Another body darted towards me. I fired off a shot but Samuel jerked my hand upwards forcing my shot to go wild. The animal kept on coming and only stopped when Willis put a bullet in it. The thing slid to a stop some metres away from us, its long body covered in dark fur with a tail to match. The absence of light didn't allow me to get a proper look at it, nor could I give the corpse my full attention as its brethren were still circling us.

Multiple snarls pierced the night.

"What were you saying about firing a warning shot and they'll scatter?" Willis demanded. "Seems to me your fluffy pets have dinner on their mind and we're the main course."

"I envy them, at least they get to die tasting meat," Tuari said.

"This makes no sense. Any creature in this jungle would flee than rather fight men with weapons. Yes, opportunistic predators have snatched children and on rare occasions adults, but—"

"Enough fucking talking!"

Willis pointed both his pistols, Sodom and Gomorrah, towards the darkness and opened fire. He switched them to automatic fire and I took a step back as they spat out their bullets at a rapid rate. The gun flashes illuminated the manic grin plastered on his face. Howls of pain filled the air as he spread his range of attack in a wide arc; this wasn't your classic pick a target and shoot, Willis was looking to do maximum damage by any means necessary and he didn't care what he hit as long as he hit something.

Both pistols ran out of ammo bringing relative peace to the campsite but it didn't last long as Willis reloaded and took up right where he had left off; he kept on firing until he was once again empty and was reaching for two more magazines when a firm grip from Samuel stopped him.

"I think that's enough."

Willis ripped his arm from Samuel's grip and took a step toward him. "You *ever* stop me in a live combat situation again and it'll be your ass that gets a bullet."

"Doing needless damage isn't going to solve anything! What happens if a stray bullet was to hit someone?"

"In the middle of the jungle? Don't be a dickhead all your life. Despite your insurances that those creatures weren't actively attacking us they obviously were, so instead of getting in my way you should be thanking me. Thanking me for saving your lives," Willis said, walking away.

Samuel watched Willis go and began to walk after him

but I placed a hand on his shoulder and shook my head. A brief spell of anger flashed behind his eyes but it left just as quickly as it came.

"Rebuild the fire," he said, turning to his men. "We will have to alternate guard duty, so the fire doesn't go out and nothing ambushes us again. I'll take first watch."

"Do you think," Tuari said, sliding up to me, "they would allow us to harvest the meat?"

"Of what?"

He said nothing but nodded his head towards the animal corpse that lay dead some feet away from us.

"I know you're the chef, Tuari, but I don't think that thing is edible."

"We don't know until we try."

"Wait till sunlight, before you start carving up anything, I don't want you to be snatched off in the darkness like Little Red Riding Hood."

"Aww, boss, you do care," he said, placing his hands against his heart.

I rolled my eyes and tried to push him towards his sleeping bag but his six-foot-four bulk didn't budge. "On second thought, I would be surprised if they could carry you off."

"Hey! What's that supposed to mean?"

But I didn't answer him as I made my way back to my sleeping bag and tried to reclaim the sleep I had lost.

3

The night had come and gone with no further incidents, but sleep had failed to embrace me in her grasp. With the sun beating down through the leaves, we all stood around one of the creatures that had attacked us during the night. It had the body of a wolf but was easily double its size. Coarse black bushy fur gave way to a body that was nothing but muscle; a square jaw with protruding front canines inches long rested below a nose as large as my hand.

"What is it?" Willis asked.

"They are only native to Safe Haven," Samuel replied. "Their original gene makeup dates back to the wolves from Earth, but their genes have been modified and altered over the course of the last couple hundred years to give you what you see before you today. They were created to be guard dogs for the rich in the Diamond Distinct borough, but their owners soon found out how wild and unmanageable they were, so like rich assholes everywhere they released them into the wild. They have found a home here, but this is the first reported case I have heard of, of packs actively attacking humans, even when shots have been fired."

One of Samuel's men bent down and parted the eyelid of the creature. Yellow colouration surrounded the outside of the sclera. He then parted the jaws of the creature and pointed to the same yellow hue, which coated the top of the animal's gums.

"It looks like this jungle wolf has been poisoned, or has come across something in its diet which shouldn't be there. No wonder the pack kept on attacking us. They must be suffering from something similar to rabies."

"How do you know that?" I asked Samuel.

"We.... had a similar case of this some years back."

"The cause?"

"Human intervention," he said as he double-checked the pack he carried and items on his person. "If we want to get to our destination by nightfall we shall have to leave now, and double our pace. I hate to say this about one of Mother Nature's creatures, but we need to be vigilant now we know the wolf pack that attacked us is infected."

"Do you think that was the only pack infected?" I asked.

"Jungle wolves operate like normal wolves in that only one pack will control a certain area, so it is highly unlikely other wolves have ventured into this area, but you never know."

"Are there.... other predators we should be worried about?"

Samuel looked to his men and something unspoken passed between them before he turned back to me. "Nothing we need to worry about," he said before walking off.

Willis and Tuari looked in my direction but I held up my hand stopping them before they spoke. I knew what they were going to say, but there was nothing we could do about it. We were a day's march from the city and even if we turned back now, there was no guarantee we would find it by ourselves. Our best chance of getting back to the city alive lay with Samuel and his men and keeping them from harm.

So we had no other choice but to see this through.

"The quicker we get this done, the quicker we go back home," I said, placing my pack over my shoulders and walking after Samuel.

The journey for the rest of the day had been uneventful, but that still didn't mean it was pleasant. From trying to get the sweat that rolled down my forehead from getting into my eyes, to preventing insects as big as my fist from attacking my body, I was in a constant state of discomfort. I pulled at my T-shirt, which clung to my body like I had entered a wet shirt competition, and grimaced as it flopped back onto my flesh.

I looked at Willis, whose red freckled face matched his beard, and tried not to laugh.

"Fuck this place," he mouthed to me, before hacking at a branch in his way.

A water bottle appeared in front of my face and I took it, giving Samuel a nod of thanks. "He really hates it here, doesn't he?"

"People of his complexion tend not to do so well in tropical climates. I'm surprised you chose to make this your base of operations," I said.

Samuel took the bottle back from me and took a swig himself. "Once you get over the heat and insects it isn't so bad; there's a level of suffering here I've come to enjoy. It keeps you honest. Doesn't allow you to become complacent with your lot in life. Makes your problems seem a little bit smaller."

"I get that; after nearly being eaten by wolves the heat doesn't seem so bad."

"Exactly, but the real reason I came here was because I was looking to escape. Like most people who come to Safe Haven—they are running away from something. That may be a crime, pain, heartache, whatever. The four boroughs have something for everyone. If you want to make your fortune or regain it the Diamond District is where you need to go; if you want to party or just find the answers to your problems at the bottom of a glass or needle, Paradise Lost is for you. You want the freedom of going anywhere you want and never setting foot on land, then The Floating City is for you, and if you want to get truly lost and never be found again, The Jungle is your calling."

"But it doesn't work like that, does it? How few really get to find the escape they are after?"

"Not many," said Samuel with a sad smile. "Maybe that was true of the first settlers who came to this planet, but now, everything you want here comes with a price. From paying Mr Lee's men for safe passage along the rivers, to not pissing off The Lady whenever you step a foot anywhere in her domain. I guess that's why I was drawn to this place; it was the last piece of untouched wilderness on this planet where the people were truly free, but I knew it wouldn't last for long if I didn't step in and take the reins. The people who call this place home are free spirits. They have no concept of money or power or the political murky waters that leaders of boroughs must navigate if they want their way of life to continue.

"So I stepped in and took control. There were a few

voices raised in objection at first, but when people saw what I was trying to do, that I was trying to save their way of life, then they embraced me with open arms."

I nodded my head in understanding.

"You must be the first person I have met on this planet who doesn't think about themselves."

"There was a time when that wasn't always the case. When I was younger I was wild. I made Willis look like a choirboy, and I paid for it. I paid for my selfishness with a price so great, I shall forever carry it across my shoulders."

"Your mother?"

He looked sharply at me but said nothing. We continued to walk behind the others for some time in silence, with me berating myself for sticking my foot in it. I tried to think of something to say but drew a blank. "Sorry for bringing up your dead mum" was hardly the icebreaker, and would most likely only insult him further.

"Yes," was all he said after a lapse of silence.

"Err, I'm sorry to have brought it up. It wasn't my place to."

"No. By all means, you have nothing to apologise for; it was me who shared the past with you. Like a forest fire I find it cleanses the soul to sometimes strip everything away so you can bare all. I...." He took a deep breath before he continued: "Like I said, I was wild, arrogant, brash, always looking for a fight. I didn't run with the wrong crowd, I was the wrong crowd. Everything was run through me and my gang, we thought we were kings of our little town on the outskirts of the city."

"Where did you grow up?"

"Sol."

"Never heard of it."

"Not surprised; it's a backwater planet which takes a

month to get to from Earth, and that's using FTL travel. The only thing Sol is known for is marshland filled with insects similar to mosquitoes. When it's not raining, it's misty, and when it's not misty it's cold. Those are the three things I remember most about home. Not the shouting or the fights or the violence, just always being in a state of permanent damp.

"Anyway Willis and I grew up on the outskirts of the city, too far to be called the suburbs and too close to enjoy nature. There wasn't much to do back then. Our father... he was a man constantly out of work and angry at the world; when he wasn't drunk he was hitting our mother and when he was drunk he was hitting us. Our mother was the kindest soul you could ever meet, taught me about nature, taught Willis about faith. It always amazed me how the most beautiful souls could end up chained to monsters who dimmed their light. Maybe it's nature's way of making sure they don't shine too bright, otherwise we would realise angels do walk among men."

He lowered his head, the corner of his eyes wet. We continued to walk; me saying nothing until he was ready to continue.

"As in sad hopeless stories everywhere I ran with the wrong crowd, until I was hardly ever home. Willis got the worst of it because of that, because of me. Whenever the authorities would come knocking, it was he who got my punishment. Until one day I came home and there was blood everywhere. It smelled so strong it was suffocating.

"I found my mother in a pool of blood barely breathing with Willis crying over her. My father was watching TV. I placed a bullet between his eyes."

The noise of the jungle sounded a decibel lower as the

only thing that made a sound was the sound of the undergrowth beneath my feet.

"With my father gone my mother recovered her full health, and peace had finally come to the Moors' household. You would have thought I would have learned my lesson after that—that I would have given up my wild ways and started life afresh. But life rarely works out like that, does it? So I went back to what I knew. Until one day I saw a rival gang leader drinking outside our local bar. He was by himself, or so I thought. It was the best time to get rid of someone who had been looking to take over my territory. I drove up and opened fire.

"I killed him but he wasn't alone.

"Members of his gang were inside the bar getting drinks; they stormed out and a firefight ensued. I got away. I thought myself lucky. I remember... I remember smiling; I was alive as I drove away. The thrill of the fight had left me buzzing.

"It wasn't until days later that I heard. My mother had been drinking in the same bar. She caught a stray bullet and bled out. The police were looking for whoever was responsible but I never came forward; I didn't want to know if the gun I fired matched the bullet that killed her. It didn't matter to me anyway; if it wasn't for me she would still be alive."

"I'm sorry—" I began, but he cut me off with the stare of a man with a condemned soul.

"Then and there I decided to end it all. It's amazing how quiet the mind gets when it knows life will be ending shortly. I left Willis a note about what had happened and I went out to kill myself.

"I tried three times. Three times, but I was saved where my mother was not. Three times I was on the brink of death but I was brought back by strangers. After the third time, I decided to use this gift of surviving I had for good. To only help others and never myself."

Not knowing what to say, I just walked, until the silence grew uncomfortable.

"The person I feel the worst for in that story is Willis," I said.

"I do too, even when he placed a gun to my chest and pulled the trigger. It was in that moment whatever bond we had as brothers died for good. It was also the day I knew I was born to do something great."

"Why is that?"

"Because I survived."

4

"We're here," Samuel said.

I looked around me and saw no difference from the trees and bush of the last few days to where we were standing now.

"Sorry if I'm being stupid—"

"Don't worry, we're used to it," said Tuari.

"But," I continued, "where is here exactly? Because all I see around me is nothing but trees."

"Good, if it was visible to anyone who stumbled across it then I would be worried," Samuel said, walking forward and placing his hand under the raised root of a tree. There was an audible click, then one of Samuel's men bent down next to the tree root in question and lifted up a trap door. Wooden stairs led downwards into the darkness.

We followed Samuel's crew into the darkness. The sound of dripping water along with our footsteps were the only thing I could sense. The darkness was so absolute I had to keep my hand on the person in front of me to stop myself from falling over.

"You know what this place is missing?" Tuari asked.

"A few more steps and you shall have it," Samuel replied, as fluorescence embedded in the walls around us came to life.

The lights reminded me of stars against the black rock that acted like a canvas.

"It is beautiful," I whispered.

"Yes, no matter how many times I see it, it still takes my breath away. The lights are created by worms that react to the sound and echoes of our footsteps."

We continued on for some time until I could see light from a cave opening. We approached it and got a view of a valley floor below. Trees lined a river on both sides and huts were dotted about here and there. I looked for a way down, but all I saw were sheer cliff trails that not even a billy goat would attempt.

"How do we get down?" I asked.

Samuel said nothing, but pointed to one of the cliff trails I had seen. My stomach dropped and my mouth dried as a rock came loose and rolled down the cliff.

"Did I tell anyone how much I hate this place?" Willis said, as Samuel and his men made their way towards the trail.

I would have loved to say it looked harder than I thought, but my body would have strongly disagreed.

Elbows and knees cut from more than one fall, fingernails bleeding and torn from clinging onto anything that I could while I tried not to fall to my death, and breath coming in sharp increments were what I had to show for my efforts.

Both hands on my knees, I looked to Samuel. "Whatever we're doing here better be worth it."

He said nothing but smiled and began walking towards one of the huts. I followed him as he picked a trail that followed along the banks of the river. I expected the water of the river to be clear, but chunks of mud and what turned out to be metal debris slowly floated by. I noticed sections of grass along our path scorched. A faint metal tang filled the air.

Blood.

I reached for my shotgun at the same time Willis and Tuari reached for their weapons. Samuel's men did the same before stepping in front of him. I noticed he was unarmed.

We continued on, slower this time, heads turning to scan every boulder or tree we passed. The sense of unease I felt only grew as we continued on walking. We came across our first sign of blood to the left of the trail path; it had dried on the grass and if we hadn't been looking for signs we would have missed it. One of Samuel's men bent down and scanned the area. He rummaged amongst the grass until he picked an item up.

It was a bullet casing.

Everyone tensed up as we continued and saw more spots of blood dotted about the grass; the bullet casings were evident as they littered the ground in some places.

My nose twitched as it picked up a scent. It grew stronger the closer we got towards the huts.

I brought my shotgun up, stabilising it as I scanned the area in front of me. One of Samuel's men crouched down and held up his fist. We stopped and waited until he gave us the all-clear.

As we got closer to the huts, I could see they were made out of dried mud and rough stone. Large banana-type leafs covered the roofs. Satellite discs stuck to the sides took away the home-made tribal feel.

The closer we got the more overpowering the smell became.

The door of the first one was closed. One of Samuel's men tried to push it open but something gave him resistance. When he put his shoulder to the door it finally gave way, releasing a torrent of flies and a smell that brought bile to my mouth.

I did my best to swallow what I could before spitting out the rest.

Bodies piled on top of one another covered the floor of the hut. Flies crawled across vacant eyes, and bloody head wounds that I could see through had long since bled out.

I tried to take a step forward but the smell was like a barrier I couldn't get past.

"Close it," Samuel whispered.

"I counted ten bodies," Willis said in a low voice. "How many people were stationed here?"

"Ten."

We all exchanged looks.

"I think the best and quickest thing for all of us to do is split up in groups of two and search the rest of the huts. Willis will go with one of your men, I'll go with the other, Tuari will accompany you," I said to Samuel. "You'll need a weapon."

"I do not handle weapons."

"Whoever did this could still be in the valley. You need to protect yourself," I said.

"I am protected. I shall not die here. My path is not yet finished."

Willis rolled his eyes and moved off with his man, leaving just the four of us.

"Fine. If that's the way you want it, Tuari protects

himself first and you second; you shall not endanger my man. Understood?"

"Understood."

I gave them a nod and moved west with my partner. He had a faint scar across one jaw and was about a foot taller than me.

"What's your name?" I whispered as we moved from cover to cover.

He looked at me but said nothing. In fact, I hadn't heard either man who was with Samuel speak.

"Fine, I'll call you Scarface," I said as we approached the first hut.

A bloody hand mark stained the door but apart from that, there were no other visible signs of damage.

We stood opposite each side of the door, weapons raised. He looked at me and I gave him a nod. I was ready.

He pushed the door open but there was nobody inside, dead or alive. We did a quick scan of the hut. Plates sat on tables with half-eaten rotten food, blankets were draped over chairs, bloodstains again coated portions of the floor.

We continued our search over the next ten minutes, looking inside hut after hut.

Some looked like the first we had found. Others looked remarkably clean and lived in.

Search done, Scarface and I stood at the trail to the entrance of a cave. Tower lights and generators stood to attention; metal ore had been collected in hover containers that sat idle off to the side.

"Is this your people's doing?" I asked.

He shook his head and gripped the handle of his gun tighter as he made his way forward. Footsteps could be seen in the dirt leading back and forth from the cave mouth. The sun pierced the first couple of feet of darkness inside the cave, but I couldn't see further than that. Grabbing Scarface by the shoulder, I pointed him to the left and I took the right.

It was too dangerous to approach the entrance head-on, not without knowing what lay beyond.

My heart felt like it was in my mouth. The sun burnt the back of my neck. Sweat trickled into my eyes. I did my best to keep my vision clear as I placed my back against the wall.

I held up three fingers so Scarface could see and I slowly counted down to one until I gave him the go-ahead to move. We leapt forward guns at the ready and were greeted by nothing but silence.

We moved forward in unison, searching the cave for anything of note but coming up empty. More hover containers lined the walls on either side filled with metal ore; tools lay on the ground and overhead lights had been hastily fastened to the ceiling of the cave. We continued on for some time but there was nothing of note to see until we came to a tunnel that forked in two directions. Scarface moved forward but I held him back and shook my head, pointing behind us.

He gave me a look that told me he wasn't happy with the idea, but the last thing I wanted to do was go cave exploring when the others didn't know where we had gone. Making our way back to the entrance we found the others waiting for us.

"I take it you didn't know about this?" I asked Samuel, pointing to the cave behind me.

"I knew about the cave—that's why this settlement was placed here—but all these digging tools and equipment are new. The tunnels this cave host have been untouched for centuries."

"Okay. Okay," I said holding my hands up in confusion.

"I've got a few questions and I want answers, otherwise me and my crew are leaving."

Samuel sighed but remained silent.

"First things first. Did anyone find anything important?"

"Just a bunch of uneaten shit," Willis said.

"Uneaten shit?" Tuari asked. "That's a first. Surely you have to eat something before it becomes shit, not the other way around. But judging by your breath, I can tell you must have taken a bite out of whatever you found."

"What was that, lard ass?"

"Enough!" I said, stopping the argument before it started. "Tuari, Samuel, you two find anything?"

"Well, yes and no," said Samuel. "Some of the huts look like they have been lived in a lot more recently than.... the killings that took place here, which makes me think whoever murdered my men have been also sleeping in their beds."

There was a shine of rage in his eyes and his hand shook.

"You good?" I asked.

"This is not yet the time for mourning," he said.

"Okay, the second question I have is, what is this place? It's obviously special, otherwise you wouldn't have posted men out here so far from the city."

"It's.... what I tell you here cannot be uttered to anyone, and I mean anyone," he said, looking me in the eye.

"You have my word and the word of my team."

He gave me a nod of thanks before he continued. "This cave is a treasure trove of gold, diamonds, precious gems and rare trace metals the likes of which I have never seen. Normally a cave and the tunnels it formed would have gold or diamonds or another precious gem, but never have I seen a tunnel system littered with so many rare metals. It looks like Aladdin's cave. Since we found out about it, we have vowed to protect it no matter what."

"Why?"

"Because a species other than human was the first to colonise this planet; there are cave drawings on the wall and the art is alien, and it dates back further than any recorded time in history."

"Are you sure?"

"Positive."

I passed a hand over my face and took a step back. If what he was saying was true, then this place would be crawling with everyone from treasure hunters to archaeologists. Humans had long thought they were the only sentient species in existence. We had visited countless worlds and had found wildly different variations of wildlife, but there had yet to be a discovery made about sentient life. Theories about why this was numbered in the thousands but proof had never been forthcoming; now that we had found it it would change everything.

"You know what this means, don't you?" I asked. "That all the gold and precious metals and gems in that cave system is next to worthless compared to those alien cave paintings. They would tear this place up just—"

Ah, now I got it.

"You see why this place has to remain a secret. I can't have our home, our way of life destroyed just to satisfy the curiosity of some scientists in lab coats."

"Do you realise the significance this has?"

"I do," Samuel replied.

"I don't think you do. This could change the course of history. Everything we thought about the galaxy is wrong. There were beings out there, on this very planet in fact, that were different than us. We owe it to humanity to explore that."

"When humanity explores they leave nothing but devastation in their wake."

"You can't just hide this forever," I said pointing back towards the cave. "Eventually people will come knocking either for the riches or the knowledge, and it looks like someone already has. The question now is who—"

A single shot rang out through the air. A single head exploded. I watched in horror as one of Samuel's men, now headless, collapsed to the floor as all hell broke loose.

5

"It's coming from the cave!" someone shouted, but in all the confusion I didn't know who.

I scrambled forward as bullets peppered the ground around me. Some of our party returned fire but the shadows in the cave concealed more than they revealed.

I leapt forward and gritted my teeth as rocks bit into my knees and elbows. Pulling myself forward I leaned my back against one of the hover containers and made my body as small as possible. Peering over the lip of the container, I ducked back down as a bullet pinged off the top of the container.

Everyone else had done the same thing I had and used the containers as cover.

I looked to see if anyone had been hit but they all looked OK, Scarface was still alive, which meant his friend had taken the bullet to the head—someone like Scarface who had never spoken and whose name I didn't know.

"Can you make out anything?" I shouted.

"Fuck no!" said Willis. "They've got us pinned down

good and proper. But if we don't push forward then they'll pick us off eventually."

"Are you out of your little ginger mind!" Tuari shouted as he fired over the top of his container. "I'm not rushing that cave mouth."

"I always knew you were a pussy."

Willis was right—if we didn't make a move then, it would only be a matter of time before one of those bullets found its mark, and retreating wasn't an option as it would leave us open. But I would be lying to myself if I had any heroic need to jump into the flames.

"Isn't there any other—" began Samuel, but a bullet cut him off as it hit and sparked inches from his face, ricocheting off his container and burying itself inches from Tuari's groin.

No one said anything as we all looked at each other open-mouthed.

"Fuck it," said Tuari.

"Fuck it!" said Willis

"Fuck ittt!" I screamed, getting up to my feet. I moved from object to object giving myself as much cover as I could, as I began pumping shotgun shells in the direction of the cave. I caught Willis and Tuari either side of me, as they too did their best to overwhelm our target. Samuel and Scarface brought up the rear.

I kept on pushing myself forward despite the knowledge that any moment a bullet would find its mark.

The return fire from the cave grew less the closer we got and I saw three men from the shadows turn and run. Knowing our targets had quit firing only spurred us on further.

A bullet caught one of them in the back of the head, blowing his brains out the front. Another tripped and fell, gun slipping from his grip. His colleague turned around but didn't stop as he continued to flee.

The fallen man hurriedly got up and dived for his dropped weapon, before he scrambled for cover behind a container filled with metal ore. He fired blindly at us and although his shots went wild we took cover ourselves in fear of getting hit.

I ducked my head down as a bullet blasted a chunk of rock off the wall above me—rock fragments landed on my shoulders.

"Hold your fire!" Samuel shouted, but either no one paid attention, or they couldn't hear him as the echoes from the gunfire reverberated against the cave walls.

"Hold your fiiire!"

This time the shooting slowly died down as the last word he shouted stopped reverberating against the walls.

Peace finally came to the cave.

"Thank you. To our attacker, I wish—"

A gunshot sliced through the air, cutting Samuel off. All eyes turned to Willis, who gave everyone a look that said he cared very little what anyone thought.

"What?" he barked. "I thought the fucker was going for his gun again."

"No, I wasn't," came a reply from our attacker. "That's a bald-faced lie and that ginger tosser knows it."

"Who you calling a ginger tosser, you pisswizard!"

"You! You ginger tosser, and I bet your mum's a slagbag too."

"You what? Come and say that to my face."

"Pretty big talk for a man who's backed by four men. I know men like you, all anger and big talk because their dick's no bigger than their little finger."

"How did he know?" Tuari not so subtly said in my direction.

"You piece of shit," Willis said, getting to his feet.

"Willis, enough!" Samuel said. Willis stopped in his tracks, glaring his brother's way. I was surprised he had listened, but more importantly, I was surprised he hadn't picked a fight with him.

"This will get us nowhere. To our attacker, I would like to know why you chose to kill my men based in this settlement. I would also like to know why you attacked us unprovoked?" Samuel asked.

"Isn't that obvious?" he asked.

"No. No, it is not."

"Resources."

"Resources?"

"Resources. We had long suspected The Jungle had a wealth of hidden natural resources that could be farmed, but we didn't realise just how much there was to be had. Gold. Diamonds. Rare trace metals. Not to mention all the other natural resources you tree fuckers have been keeping a secret. The opportunity was too good to pass up.

"It was by luck our scouts happened to find this cave. But now we have the secrets out of the bag. To think we wouldn't even be here unless a certain big-time backer funded us to find a type of rare metal that he needed."

"Do you realise what you fools have done?" Samuel asked.

"Yes. We've taken what was always ours."

"You have started a chain of event's that will cause war! And for what? For some piece of metal?"

Laughter sounded from behind the container. "War? They said the leader of The Jungle was a pussy but I didn't realise how much of one till just now. Do you know how powerful your borough would be if you used the resources around you? Instead of selling *homemade remedies,* like some shitty flea market. You could control all of Safe Haven. The gold from this cave system alone would fund it. But yet, like all small-minded men with no vision, you are happy to play in your treehouse and braid each other's armpit hair."

"Raping my home of its natural beauty, just to call myself king, is not a reality I want to live in," Samuel said softly.

"It matters little anyway," said our attacker. "By the time they find you under all this rubble there shall be no home to go to!"

Shit. He had just been stalling for time.

"Everyone! To me!" I yelled as I leapt over to the largest empty container and flipped it on its side.

Explosions rocked the cave as our attacker began laughing hysterically. Rocks fell to the floor as a cave-in began.

Willis and Tuari strained with me and helped me flip the container upside down.

"What are you doing?" Samuel asked. "Let's make our way to the exit."

"There isn't time!" I said as rocks began raining down in front of the cave mouth, Samuel looked towards us, then back at the exit and back to us, before he rushed over. We gripped the lip of the container as we all made our way inside it. I looked for Scarface but he was sprinting towards the exit dodging one rock after the next. I shouted for him to come back but a large boulder fell behind him, blocking him from sight.

He was on his own now.

I dived underneath the container and prayed that he had made it out alive, but reminded myself as rocks fell around us, maybe my prayers should have been better directed to our party as everything turned black.

6

The sounds around us felt like they went on for eternity; the bangs, crashes and rumbles shook our little sanctuary of safety as I held my hands over my head and thought of Poppy. I smiled as her beautiful face came into existence. I muttered her name over and over again, like a prayer, hoping it would ward off all danger that fell our way.

I couldn't breathe.

I tried not to panic.

With so many bodies under the container it grew hot and sticky. I felt sweat trickle down my face as someone's limb moved and dug into my ribs. How much time had passed? A tremor shook the floor underneath us forcing me to make my body even smaller. I didn't want to die like this. Hell, I didn't want to die at all. I listened to what was going on outside and heard nothing.

No tremor. No crashes. No rambles.

Someone else moved and another limb found its way into the small of my back.

I breathed out slowly and kept on listening to the

outside but there was nothing to hear. It was hard to tell if I had died and just not known it. The darkness was everything, the silence deafening.

"Fuck me! Will the dick weasel with his foot in my face remove it before I cut it off?"

No. I hadn't died, and if I had, it wasn't an afterlife I was about to enjoy. I was pushed in the back as a commotion began behind me.

"Will you stop pushing?" said Tuari. "There is only so much room for me to move."

"Yeah, tell me about it," said Willis; "your giant ass is taking up half of it."

I was pushed again but this time from the side.

"Well, we can't all be men of *average* height now, can we?"

"What is that supposed to mean?"

"Nothing. Nothing."

"If you've got something to say, come right out and say it. Don't think I won't punch you because we are under—"

"Shut up! Both of you!" I said as I closed my eyes and listened. "I think the cave-in has stopped. It will need all four of us to lift up one side so we can make our way out of there. Everyone manoeuvre to the left and after three I'll want you to lift with everything you have."

"What if a boulder larger than big boy over there has fallen on top of us?" Willis asked.

"You're a God-fearing man. Pray that it hasn't. On my count," I said, positioning myself, so I could get a solid grip.

"One. Two. Three!"

We strained and lifted with all our might and bit by bit the lid of the container rose and rose, rubble and rocks scattered off the top, and I thanked my lucky stars nothing large had fallen on top of us and trapped us underneath the container. With a final heave, we flipped the container back and emerged out of our prison.

Darkness and dust greeted us.

I coughed and sputtered as dust made its way into my sinuses. Someone slapped me on the back as I bent over on my hands and knees and tried to breathe. Wiping my mouth, I got up and scanned our surroundings but it was pointless. The only source of light—the cave entrance—had been sealed up.

"Ain't there supposed to be worms or some shit lighting this place up?" Willis asked.

"Yes, Willis," Samuel said, "worms or some shit should be giving us light, but if you couldn't tell, most of the ceiling of this cave has been destroyed, so if we want to be guided by their brilliance, we shall have to venture deeper into the tunnel system, where no damage has taken place."

"And how do we do that, Sherlock? When we can't see anything?"

"When I know I shall be venturing into these cave systems, I always bring supplies with me in case of this eventuality," Samuel said as a sound like plastic being snapped echoed throughout the cave, followed by a faint glow. He held two glow sticks in his hands and strapped them to his chest, before passing two more to each of us.

We did the same as he did after activating our glow sticks and strapped them to our chest. With the light of the glow sticks now illuminating the cave, I took in the damage.

The entrance had been sealed off. Rocks and rubble blocked our only means of escape so completely that no daylight penetrated through. Around us, the damage wasn't so severe and we had been lucky in that no rocks larger than a football had landed on top of us, while the rest of the cave floor was riddled here and there with impacts from the falling debris.

"Well, I'm all for shoving Ginger's ass through the rubble to try and see if he can get us any help, but I don't think he'll fit," Tuari said.

Willis gave Tuari the finger as we continued to scan the cave. "Do you think your man escaped?" I asked Samuel.

"If anyone could it would be him. But even if he has, it will take days for him to get back to the city and round up help and a couple more days till help gets back here. The soonest that help would arrive here would be four days, maybe three at a push, and that's if he has managed to escape, which is a big if."

"Which means...." I said, turning around and looking at the tunnel that led into the darkness.

"Yes," Samuel said, coming to a stop next to me, "it means that we have to find another means of escape."

We had been walking for hours taking one tunnel seemingly at random after the next, but Samuel said he knew these caves somewhat and although not an expert he should be able to guide us to safety.

That had been three hours ago; now he didn't appear so sure.

"Do you know where you're going or are you just pulling which way to go out your ass?"

"*Yes*, Willis. I am pretty confident we are on the right—"

"Pretty confident isn't confident now, is it?"

Samuel muttered something under his breath while he pushed ahead, I took in the sights around us and felt dirt poor, just by being in the presence of such wealth. Precious metals danced and twinkled under the light the worms provided overhead, gold flakes glistered under our feet, but the thing I noticed the most was the calming sensation the place had on me. I had expected to feel panicked at the possibility of being trapped in the dark, but none of those thoughts had any real effect on me.

"It's a metal called Iremía. We discovered it has properties that calm and centre the mind. We have mined some of the metal and sold very small amounts to people who suffer from anxiety and stress."

"I thought all that stuff about bracelets made of metal improving your health was bullshit."

"Apparently not," Samuel said, gesturing at the surrounding tunnels.

I said nothing as our feet echoed around the walls that surrounded us. Who was I to judge what was real or not? I was having a baby with an AI humanoid.

"I'm sorry about the people you lost at your settlement and I'm sorry about the two gentlemen you brought with you on this trip. I know one may not be dead, but the other who got shot, I can only give my condolences. They seemed to be good men although they never told me their names."

"They were. In regard to them not speaking to you, don't take it personally. Some people in The Jungle partake in a ritual where they don't speak for a number of weeks, months or even years. They had both begun this ritual when they started helping me out. I too don't know their names but sometimes you do not need to know a person's name to know the value of their soul. They shall be truly missed and I shall mourn for them, like all the others when the time is right."

"How do you do that?"

"Do what?" he asked, confused.

"How do you detach yourself from the situation like that? I mean, everyone feels, everyone is overcome by rage, depression, lust, love, happiness. But no matter what happens, no matter who dies, you always keep your head."

"Because this life is not the end. Never mourn the passing of what is lost, instead celebrate the new beginning that loss has brought. So when the time comes, we shall celebrate the passing of our lost ones and embrace the change their passing has left on our lives."

I pondered his words as we continued on. Thoughts of dying of thirst or starvation crept across my mind periodically, but I did my best to push them away. Tunnels like these always had more than one entrance; I just hoped we would find one before our bodies gave out.

"Did you suspect someone was mining these tunnels? Is that why you asked us to come along?"

"Yes and no," Samuel said. "Contact with the settlement wasn't daily, but we hadn't heard from them in long enough to know something was wrong. Normally it's just the storm playing havoc with the communications, but enough time had passed without word from them for us to know the issue was more serious. I brought you along just for backup, which was a wise choice as things turned out."

"Do you know who the men that attacked us worked for?"

"I have my suspicions, but I would rather keep them to myself for now."

"You borough leaders sure love doing that, don't you?"

"Doing what?"

"Keeping information to yourselves."

Samuel chuckled as he shook his head from side to side. "I can see you are new to leadership, Quinton, so I shall give you a word of advice. *Information is everything.* He who controls it controls nations."

I allowed his words to sink in before I asked the next question that had been bugging me since our run-in with our attackers.

"Where do you think he ran off to? The one attacker who escaped."

"That information I do not have. But we shall soon find out."

Six hours.

That was how long it took us to hear the voices of our enemy.

It stopped us in our tracks.

"I told you, Montel, those fools are flatter than your mama's titties.

"Why should I stay behind and double-check if anyone was alive? Fuck that! I ain't no low-level grunt. It was bullshit I got placed on this assignment anyway. Mr Diamond knows I can give more to the organisation than this."

"You dickhead! You really think Mr Diamond knows who you are? Or even knows you exist? No. Your orders probably came from one of his underlings. Either Mr Ruby or more likely Mr Pearl. You should thank your graces Mr Diamond doesn't know who you are because if he did... boy, oh boy, you would be dangling from your balls right now because of the fuckup that took place here."

"What are you talking about? How is this my fault?"

"Well, Rick, it was your idea to kill everyone who lived in the settlement. There was no need for us to venture so close to that cave mouth. We had miles and miles of unprotected tunnel we could have mined without anyone knowing a thing. That was our order in the first place!

"Mine the trace metals undetected and get it all back to base. Now those Jungle hippies know what we've been up to and there will be hell to pay," Montel said.

"Like fuuuck! Those tree fuckers haven't got a pair between them. It's all kumbaya and peace chants with those freaks. I don't know why Mr Diamond hasn't claimed this land as his."

"You know why. They've got backing."

"I say fuck it. It's about time someone put that bitch in her place," Rick said.

"Oh! Look who's Billy Big Bollocks all of a sudden. You feeling brave, yeah? Feeling like you can take on the queen of the slums and come out on top? All by your lonesome? Well, maybe I need to put in a word with Mr Diamond and tell him he has nothing to worry about, that Rick Gomez has all his problems sorted and that he can rest easy in that skyscraper of his."

"That's not what I'm trying to say."

"What are you trying to say then?"

"That maybe, just maybe, we are giving the bitch too much respect. The only reason Mr Diamond hasn't moved on her borough yet is because there was nothing worth taking there, and he was happy to let the low-level crews fight amongst themselves, but now she has stabilised power and is looking to expand, I say we halt her momentum before it really gets started," Rick said.

Nothing was said as we kept on inching closer towards the sound of the voices. I hid the glow sticks under my clothing to block out their glow and motioned for everyone to do the same. Creeping inch by inch forward, I watched where I placed each foot and leaned my back against the wall as I crept slowly round the corner, holding my breath as I did so.

I saw two men in the dim light of the glowworms looking at each other. One was tall and thin with a crooked nose, while the other was shorter and stocky and was the one who had fired upon us and escaped. Their body language was tense, fists clenched and eyes stared unblinking while either man stood frozen, not wanting to retreat.

"You want to know why Mr Diamond hasn't moved on The Lady, Rick?" said the taller of the two, a finger poking Rick in the chest. "It's because we lost men—more men than our borough would like to admit—against her—"

"What do you mean?"

"If you shut up and listen, then I'll tell you. I've been hearing rumours about squads departing on missions, scouting missions, missions to intercept her cargo and supplies, missions to disrupt her power base, and you know what we've been getting back?"

Rick shook his head.

"Nothing but dead bodies. At first, I thought it was just a rumour, but after a few of my buddies disappeared and I asked about their whereabouts, I got the same reply from higher up on each one. 'They decided to leave and explore other employment.'"

"But why would they want to cover something like that up?" Rick asked.

"Simple. Our borough is seen as the strongest and richest. It wouldn't look good if we've been losing this guerrilla war against a borough that doesn't have a pot to piss in."

"Is that why we've aligned ourselves with this new player?"

Montel nodded. "Seems to be."

"But what can they offer that Mr Diamond can't buy?"

"Whatever it is, it has something to do with all this metal we've been mining—" Montel's eyes widened in surprise as he caught sight of us; his hand went to the pistol on his hip, he brought it up with a quick flick of his wrist and fired it our way.

I dropped back behind the wall as chunks of rock blasted across my field of vision and the sound of gunfire echoed throughout the corridor. "Rick, run!"

As the echoing gunshots faded, the only thing that could be heard was feet making a hurried escape.

"Don't let them leave," Samuel shouted as he vaulted from his hiding place and took off after them.

7

"What is the idiot doing?" I shouted after Samuel's retreating back. "He isn't even armed!"

Willis shook his head and gave chase, as Tuari and I brought up the rear. The enemy had gotten a good head start and was sprinting down the tunnel firing over their shoulder as they did so; mercifully none of the shots hit Samuel as he had his head down and was slowly gaining on them. I raised my shotgun but in the limited space, with so many bodies in front of me, I was just as likely to hit a friendly as I was a foe.

Our feet pounded on the gold-glittered cave floor as we took one corner after the next. As I passed moss-covered walls slick with water, my feet nearly gave out from underneath me and I lost my footing. Tuari grabbed my arm and re-righted me as we continued our pursuit.

Finally catching up with Willis and Samuel, I could see our targets only metres ahead of us. With each step, we were closing in on them. They twisted their necks to see how far back we were and their eyes widened in shock, when they realised we were only metres behind them.

"We have incoming!" Montel screamed as he and Rick took a corner and vanished from view.

We continued to chase after them but had to dive for cover as we entered a large area that stretched for miles in all directions; I ducked and rolled towards a stone pillar and pressed my back against it as bits of rock was blasted to bits around me. The area we were in had everything from a subterranean lake to large rock stalactites hanging from the ceiling.

I looked around me in wonder, before pulling my head back as another chunk of rock flew into the air. *Right. Right. This wasn't the time for sightseeing.*

"Is everyone alright?" I shouted.

A chorus of yesses rang out between the sounds of gunfire.

"Can anyone see the shooters?" I asked.

"Two on the far ridge. One hidden behind a rock at two o'clock. Three to my left. Two loading a light cargo carrier with metal ore in a hurry," Willis said.

"We can't let anyone escape here!" Samuel said. "Nor leave with that metal."

I nodded my head as I took in the information and began to load shotgun shells; I looked towards Willis and Tuari and gestured for them to come out on the left while I would move from the right. Two swift nods told me they understood.

I lifted my fingers.

Three.

Two.

One.

We leapt out of our hiding spots and moved purposefully. I lifted my shotgun and aimed it at the ceiling above the ridge where the two shooters hid. The explosive shotgun shells rocked my body backwards, as the ceiling above the ridge blew apart and rained down rock onto the men hiding there. Screams tore from their throats but they were cut off as hundreds of pounds of rock crushed them to death.

I forward-rolled and tucked myself behind a boulder as a shooter behind another boulder opened fire. Sparks flew in the dim light as bullets bounced off the rock.

"John! Eric! No," the shooter behind the rock yelled, as he kept on firing my way. "John. Eric. Say something, for fuck's sake, answer me."

My heart went out to the man, but I had a job to do and so did he. It was either him or me, and I wasn't planning on meeting my maker any time soon.

"You asshole! You'll pay for—"

I blocked his voice out as I counted to five. Picking up a rock by my foot I threw it left as I leapt right. Coming to my feet, I switched the shotgun chamber so it fired regular shells and began unloading upon the rock he was hiding behind. Fragments shattered from the rock as I moved forward toward my target. I didn't let up on the pressure and knew it was only a matter of time before my target moved.

He tried the same trick as I had pulled off on him, throwing a rock in the opposite direction while he moved from his hiding space, but I was ready for him and shot him in the torso twice, spinning him around. He lay dead on the ground.

Sounds to my left drew my attention as I saw Willis and Co. make their way towards a small cargo ship, parked on a ridge directly in front of a cave mouth that opened to the night sky.

The men that had been loading the cargo were now

firing at my crew, while Montel and Rick tried to get the ship started.

I sprinted along a platform that ran parallel to the ship. The engines kicked into overdrive as the men that were defending the ship looked over their shoulders in panic.

One took a bullet to the head, while the other one turned and began running towards the lowered cargo bay doors. The doors rose as the man shouted and waved. I got a glimpse of Rick as he waved the man onwards, while at the same time repeatedly pressing the button that would close the cargo bay doors.

Rick, the piece of shit, was planning on leaving his colleague behind.

The last man remaining buried his head in his chest and sprinted with everything he had; arms pumping he ran towards a large rock and leapt from it launching himself into the air. One hand grabbed onto the lip of the cargo bay doors jerking it back down.

The cargo ship tilted to one side as the man hung from it.

Rick was screaming something over his shoulder while trying his best to stomp on the man's hands to dislodge him from the ship.

I kept the ship in my peripheral vision while I continued to move along the ledge I was on. Switching the shotgun chamber back so it would fire explosive shells, I saw up ahead where I would take my stand.

The ledge ended in a steep drop where it would bring me directly in line with the ship's flight path.

"Rick, help me up, you prick!" yelled the man as he shuffled his hands back and forth out of the way of Rick's descending feet.

"The ship's overloaded as it is," Rick replied. "We can't take any more weight otherwise we'll never gain altitude!"

"I went to your wedding! I gave a speech—"

I skidded to a halt as I came to the end of the path and tucked my shotgun into my shoulder as I took aim. The body of the ship passed me by and I fired a shell, aiming for the ship's engines. The shell hit, exploding against the body of the ship. Flames erupted out of one of the thrusters causing the ship to jerk violently.

A scream tore through Rick's throat as he was pitched forward and fell out of the cargo bay. He grabbed a hold of one of his colleague's legs on the way down, hanging onto him for dear life.

"Don't let go!" Rick cried, as his former friend tried his best to kick him off.

The ship turned to fire at me and I saw Montel's ugly face through the windscreen as he narrowed his eyes my way.

Pumping another shell into the chamber I took aim and fired. The ship pivoted to the left, its wing scraping against a far wall, sending sparks into the air. The shell exploded against its underbelly but didn't do as much damage as the first shell as that part of the ship had been reinforced.

I took aim once again but abandoned the idea as the ship swung round, gun turrets trying to get a lock onto my location.

I caught a glimpse of Montel's smug face as he opened fire. Bullets kicked up dirt and rock into the air as I turned tail and ran.

I sprinted with everything I had but I knew it was only a matter of time before I got hit. With no other option I ran towards the edge of the path I was on and leapt off.

Arms windmilling in the air, I yelled out as searing pain

tore across my shoulder. I watched as the ground came towards me and gritted my teeth at the impending impact. Bracing my legs, I tucked my body into a forward roll and was up to my feet in one fluid motion.

Shotgun up I spun around to see the ship making its way for the cave exit. I ran after it and fired two more shells, which exploded against the walls as it manoeuvred out of the way. The sudden shift in movement finally caused Rick's colleague to lose his grip as he and Rick plummeted to the rocks below.

I kept on running but came to a stop as the ship gained the right altitude and took off with a roar out of the cave exit leaving nothing but a condensation streak across the night sky.

8

We walked toward the mass of red that had been Rick and his friend. Both their heads had struck rocks and exploded like watermelons attacked with a sledgehammer, I looked down at the sight in disgust before turning away.

"Tut, tut, tut," Tuari said, leaning over the corpses. "What a way to go. You know how I would like to go, when it's my time?"

"No one cares," Willis said.

"I would like to be lying in a hammock by a beach, the sun just about to set making the water golden with a busty beauty straddling me, while she feeds me mango slices mixed with meringues and just as the last slice touches my lips we both.... Well," Tuari said with a sly smile, "you know the rest."

"Your soul is destined for hell. You know that, don't you?" Willis said with a shake of the head.

"Probably, but you'll be strapped in right next to me. Friends forever until the end of time."

Willis shuddered as he closed his eyes and shook his head.

"Well, this mission was a complete waste of time," I said ,looking around me. Digging tools clustered the area, along with the metal ore the men had been digging.

"It wasn't a complete waste of time, boss," Tuari said, rolling up the sleeves of Rick—or was it his friend? It was hard to say now that both men were headless.

"One of these men belonged to the Diamond District—I take it that would be Rick, if what he said about working for Mr Diamond was anything to go by."

"One, how do you know that and two, who is Mr Diamond?"

"See this diamond shape tattoo on his arm?" Tuari said, pointing to Rick's forearm. "Although a shitty tattoo and crew logo, it signifies these men belonged to Mr Diamond. Mr Diamond is the leader in control of the Diamond District. Much like The Lady in Paradise Lost, his word is law in that borough.

"The second chap," Tuari said, rolling up Rick's friend's sleeves, and showing a tattoo of a golden circle with a red dragon sitting on top of a mountain of golden coins, "works for Mr Lee, who we've had the pleasure of meeting."

Mr Lee—the leader of The Floating City, and a man who had cheated us into owning him money just so Edward Thomas could buy off our debt so we would be indebted to him, thus forcing us to work for him.

"Great," I said, rubbing my hands over my eyes, "just great. Now we have every single borough on Safe Haven after us, save one."

"Don't forget Alvis Boman," Tuari said cheerily.

How could I forget?

"I take it you knew Mr Diamond was behind this mining operation?" I said, turning to Samuel.

"I had no hard evidence, but I had a hunch. Wherever precious metals and gems are concerned, Mr Diamond's sticky fingers are normally grabbing whatever he can."

"I've never met this Mr Diamond before; what can you tell me about him?"

All eyes avoided mine, while no one said anything.

"Surely he can't be as bad as The Lady?" I said.

"The saying 'better the devil you know' applies here," Willis said. "The man is.... well, pray you never meet him."

I nodded my head.

"It appears Mr Diamond knew about this cave for some time, judging by the conversation between Rick and Montel. The question that needs answering is why did he decide to act now?"

"It must have something to do with this new client, who is paying him to mine this metal," Tuari said, tapping a lump of ore with his foot.

I bent down and picked it up, turning it over in my hands. I didn't recognise the metal nor did appear to have any amazing qualities at first glance.

"Does this look familiar to you?" I asked, tossing the metal ore to Samuel.

He turned it over in his hands, examining it closely. "I've not seen it before, but that's not saying much. Much of this tunnel system has not been explored by my people, and I've never even stepped foot in this place," he gestured around him, "but if Diamond is willing to go to war for it, whatever it is, then you can bet it's valuable. More valuable than all the gems in this cave, which scares me greatly."

I sighed as I walked towards the crystal lake centred in the middle of the cave and just marvelled. Rock formations covered in gemstones hung from the ceiling like necklaces; they reflected the dim glow of the cave worms and in turn, the light bounced off the surface of the lake. Paintings that looked like a crazed mathematician made them graced any wall smooth enough to house them. They were unlike anything I had ever seen, vaguely resembling computer code, but that was like comparing a Ford Model-T to the latest aircraft.

It... just wasn't human.

Even amongst the cluster of the digging tools, this place was just—

"Breathtaking, isn't it?" Samuel asked, standing next to me.

I nodded my head as I looked up into the darkness above me. Bat-like creatures fluttered back and forth and dived into fist-sized holes embedded in the rock, their beating wings echoing amongst the walls.

Before we were ready to leave we gathered a few different pieces of metal ore and Willis buried a tracker underneath some rocks so Samuel's forces could locate this section of the tunnel again.

I took one more look around me before I joined the others at the entrance of the cave. The night sky was like a black bejewelled blanket as I looked off into the forested darkness below.

"So, what now?" I asked Samuel.

"We make our way back."

I looked at him with a raised eyebrow before scanning the bowel-dropping descent in front of us.

"You know of another way, right?"

"No."

I took a step forward and peered downwards. There was something of a passable trail leading down into the darkness, but even so, one wrong step and we would be hurling ourselves to our deaths.

"We can't climb down that in the dark," I said, pointing at the trail.

"Normally I would agree with you, but we are out of food and water and I would like to get back to the city as quickly as possible."

"Why can't we just drink from the lake?"

"I believe the lake and the river that runs through the settlement to be contaminated; that is why the Jungle wolves we encountered attacked us with little regard for their own safety. I have taken a sample," he said, producing a bottle of water, "for my men back in the city to test. Whatever explosives, acids and solvents Diamond's men used have entered this section of the Jungle's waterways. I would like to know what it is, so I can stop it before it spreads throughout my borough.

"My people depend on the water and a sickness outbreak is the last thing I need."

His point was valid. The longer we waited the worse the problem would develop, but hiking down a cliff face and into a jungle at night was just a recipe for disaster. But without food or water the longer we waited the weaker we would become...making the journey that much more difficult.

Ah, I missed the days when the hardest thing I had to tackle was why my formulas were not working in my spreadsheets.

"OK. Glow sticks at the ready, we travel no further than an arm's length away from the person in front of us. I don't care how long the journey takes, but we go slow and steady. If anyone needs to stop, we stop. Any questions?" I asked, looking at the group.

Tuari raised his hand. "I don't think I'm going to feel comfortable taking a piss so close to Ginger Nuts over there. I don't want him to get penis envy."

"I'm going to piss all over your boots," Willis said, glaring Tuari's way.

"Well, I never," Tuari said placing a hand over his heart.

I rolled my eyes and looked to Samuel. "Lead the way."

The journey was as slow as expected.

We took each step with care allowing the glow sticks and the stars above to guide our way. We stumbled more than once but hands grabbed arms and held on as we found our footing. I couldn't tell you how many hours had passed, but it was long enough for my throat to feel like sandpaper, and my stomach to go from rumbling, to hungry, to feeling like it was eating itself, to a dull pain.

My limbs felt weary from lack of sleep and more than once I bumped into the back of someone, mumbling an apology before we moved off again.

"We made it," Samuel said, snapping me out of my sleep-deprived haze.

I looked around and saw we were finally at the foot of the cliff; I looked back up searching for the cave entrance we had descended from but couldn't find it. Wisps of mist curled along the cliff face, making the journey we had taken all the more daunting.

"Now comes the hard part," Samuel said, "making our way home. I would say if we pass by a body of water we should take a drink, but like I said before, we should exercise all caution when it comes to drinking water found in this region."

"Yeah. Yeah," Willis said with a wave of his hands, "we get it. Water bad. Now can we get a move on, as I would like to get back to a hot meal and a warm bed as soon as possible."

"How long do you think it'll take us?" I asked.

"Two days at most, but I'm hoping that we can do it in one," Samuel said.

I licked my cracked lips and tried to think how close to dehydration I would be before things started shutting down or becoming painful. We were in a Catch-22. The faster we travelled the more dehydrated we would be, but the slower we travelled the longer it would take to get the supplies we needed to stay alive.

"Alright," I said, looking around the group, "if anyone needs a rest, speak up. This isn't the time to be a hero. We've got a long march ahead of us and I would rather we all made it back alive. Now let's get a move on. We're in for a long ride."

Daylight had come and gone and night had returned.

We had travelled through the day pushing through the jungle, hacking at vine leaves, pushing through the undergrowth and slapping away bugs determined to drink our blood. The going had been slow, painfully so. We were sluggish in our movements. Motor skills not working as they should do, we did our best as we continued on with our march.

I had noticed that I wasn't sweating as much as I had been when I had first started this journey. It was a worry I placed at the back of my mind to keep an eye out in case anything developed. My lips had gone from cracked to painful but again, it was something I couldn't really do anything about and just had to suffer silently.

The option to stop for the night had been raised, but we all thought on it and couldn't bring ourselves to spend a night in the humid heat with nothing to drink or eat, while we tossed and turned trying to grab whatever sleep we could. The only thing that would accomplish would be to worsen our situation, so we opted to continue on.

Now, as my foot caught on a branch and I stumbled painfully down to one knee, I wondered how smart that decision to continue on had been.

"Did... did, did I ever tell you the time when the world-famous chef Soul Food stole one of my recipes?" Tuari said, just above a whisper.

"Like... like you knew Soul Food," Willis replied just as painfully. "Soul Food is a legend. Now I'm not saying your cooking isn't good, Tuari, but compared to Soul Food's? You and him are not in the same league."

"Have you tried his food?"

Silence.

"Well, of course not, the waiting list to attend one of his restaurants is two years, not to mention the price tag to eat there would cost a small cargo ship."

"If you've not tried his food then I would suggest you refrain from making judgements," Tuari said, with a hint of anger I rarely heard in his voice. "Soul Food is a good chef, do not get me wrong—some may even class him as a great chef—but to be put in the same category as legends such as Alain Ducasse, Georges Auguste Escoffier or Yoshihiro Murata, no, my ginger friend, he falls far too short for that.

"Soul Food relies on his name, charm, and the gimmick that he has created for himself in the media to push his style so the public thinks his food is more than it is. No, Soul Food is not legendary, just another celebrity."

"So why is Soul Food not legendary, but these other chefs are?" Willis asked.

"He doesn't create from the heart."

Insects called to one another and airborne creatures of the night fluttered their wings back and forth while they dived for their meal; all the while we waited for an expansion on Tuari's thoughts but none were forthcoming.

"That's it?" Willis demanded.

"What more is there to being the best at your craft, than creating from your heart?"

"I—" Willis began but stopped. "Fair enough."

"So what recipe did he steal from you?" I asked.

"It pains me to even say it now, but I showed the bastard a simple chicken soup recipe and you'll never guess what he ended up doing with it..."

"Not his Chicken Soup for the Soul?" Willis asked.

"Yes, he packaged it and created his whole career off that one little recipe I showed him. I thought he would improve and create something else worth talking about but everything he has developed so far hasn't had the same hit."

"You're telling me," Willis asked, stopping on the path we were on, and looking back at Tuari with narrowed eyes, "that you, you who I've seen bite his own toenails, are responsible for one of the greatest food dishes of our generation?"

"Pretty much."

"I call bullshit!"

"It matters little what you think, Ginger Nuts. I know the truth and that's all that matters."

"Dear God," Willis said, lifting his hands up to the air, "I'm sorry to disturb you at this late hour, but we need your guidance. Please give us a sign, any sign to show us this lying sack of shit is telling the truth."

Willis cupped his hand to his ear and looked left and right as nothing but insects buzzed about us. "Thank you, Father, for once again showing this asswipe's true colours. See, I knew you were full of shi—"

The forest exploded in howls forcing the hairs on the back of my neck to stand up on end. Willis's prayers had been heard, but I didn't think he would like the answer.

9

We all looked at each other, none of us moving as the howls vanished as quick as they came.

Nothing but our eyeballs moved as we made eye contact. The fear and panic mirrored on everyone's face was clear. We were all thinking the same thing; we were surrounded and the wolves that had made the noise were more in number than when we had first encountered them. My sandpaper-like tongue passed over my lips painfully while I scanned the jungle.

Nothing moved.

The insects and other wildlife had gone quiet, almost sensing the apex predators of the neighbourhood were home and it would be best for all parties involved to go back to their houses and slowly close the windows and blinds and lock the door.

It had been more than ten seconds, but still, the only thing I could hear was the pounding of my heart inside my ears. Maybe the pack had moved on. Maybe they hadn't noticed us. Maybe—

The howls that escaped throats vibrated through our

chest, but this time growls and snarls that sounded way too close for comfort accompanied them.

"Way to go, Ginger Nuts!" Tuari said.

"What the did I do?"

"Maybe you can pray for some locusts too while you're at it!"

"This isn't my—"

The rustle of leaves and the snapping of twigs had us all grabbing for our weapons. A monstrous head that was all canines and drool appeared in front of me from the brushes, its snapping jaws looking to latch on to whatever it could. Taking a step backwards I shoved my shotgun in its mouth and pulled, the thunderous roar blowing its head into bite-size chunks.

Another head appeared and leapt out of the shadows but I dropped to the ground and escaped its snapping jaws, the wolf sailed over me and landed a few feet away, its teeth reflected the dim glow of the stars overhead as it braced itself for another attack; it jumped but someone else fired a shot catching it in the side. It slid to a halt at my feet and tried to get back up, but I placed the barrel of my gun behind its head and ended its misery.

"Where did they come from?" Willis asked, but no one cared to answer as we did our best to fire at anything at moved.

Another beast leapt from the brush; I dodged its jaws, but its claws still found my flesh and drew blood. Willis filled it with holes before turning his attention to the next target.

I looked around and saw we had to move. Brush and vegetation surrounded us on all sides. We couldn't see where our next attack was coming from and soon it would only take a lucky attack from the pack to do one of us serious damage.

"Run!" I yelled as another head tried to take a bite out of my arm.

I led the way feet pounding on the path, energy-drained limbs doing their best to run but not picking up the speed I wanted because of the lack of water and food I'd neglected to give my body. Footsteps behind me told me that everyone else had followed my path. I urged my legs to move faster but they wouldn't listen.

Howls in the foreground told me that the pack was on the hunt.

My heart felt like it was going to erupt through my chest, but I forced myself to keep going.

"Isn't... running from a wolf pack... the worse thing you can do?" Tuari asked, words coming out laboured.

"We need to find an area that gives us..." I slapped my chest as the last words felt stuck in my throat, "...a better view of what is coming."

Howls and snarls came from the vegetation on either side of us. I pointed my shotgun at the brush on my left and fired off a round that caused something to yelp.

"Samuel, does anywhere like that come to mind?" I asked.

Eyes wide in shock he stared through me and didn't say a word. His body was covered in blood but I couldn't see any wounds.

"Are you hurt?" I asked.

"We shouldn't be doing this. These poor creatures have only gone wild because of the Diamond District's involvement in my mines. The poor creatures are just in pain and scared."

"Look, fuckface!" Willis said, grabbing him by the shoulder as they ran. "I give two shits about those wolves—if it was up to me I would kill the whole lot of them and sell them as rugs, but it's not. The only thing I care about is getting out of here without getting a piece taken out of my ass. Now wake up and think! Where is the best place we can hold off these rabid mutts?"

"Less than half a mile up ahead, there should be a clearing."

I gave him a nod of thanks as we kept on pushing the pace. I knew we could never outrun a pack of wolves, but if we got to a defensive position where we could hold them off for long enough, then maybe, just maybe, we might survive this.

A snarl and the breaking of brush took me out of my thoughts as another monstrous head come towards me. It didn't get very far as I blasted it before it could leap in the air.

Heavy wheezing sounded behind me and I looked over my shoulder to see Tuari struggling to keep up. His six foot four frame, covered in slabs of meat and muscle, wasn't designed for long-distance running. I saw the pain behind his eyes as he tried his best to keep running, but the oxygen just wasn't getting to his lungs fast enough.

He saw me looking and gave me a faint nod.

"How far?" I asked.

"It should be the next turning," Samuel replied.

The path up ahead took a sharp right. Seeing our goal within sight, we redoubled our efforts until we came to a small clearing that gave us a good view of anything approaching from the jungle.

Skidding to a halt we got back to back in a small circle so we covered all areas.

The howling and snarling had stopped. The silence

raised the hairs on the back of my hand as I held my breath and scanned my surroundings. They were out there, waiting, prowling. A rustle to our left pulled our guns in that direction, but nothing appeared.

I tried to take a deep breath to steady my shaking hands. They were cramping from either lack of food or water. I saw Willis shaking his shoulders out too as he too must be feeling the effects.

The silence stretched for a minute. Then two. Then three.

A single bead of sweat ran down the side of my face. I was tempted to lick it off.

Willis and Tuari looked in my direction, their eyes saying what their mouths couldn't. Another rustle in the leaves ahead, then another to my left, then my right. They were playing mind games with us. A bark straight in front of me made me redouble the grip on my gun. I narrowed my eyes and waited.

A body burst from the undergrowth to my left; low towards the ground it came speeding towards me, I fired off one shot but missed as it changed direction; it didn't make it far as Tuari placed a bullet between its eyes.

Another came out of the brush, and another, and another. We opened fire as wolves appeared out of the undergrowth at rapid speed. Our circle tightened as we each took a couple of steps back from the oncoming onslaught. The surrounding jungle was alive with barks and growls. I fired left and right but no matter how quickly we cleared the surrounding area, more bodies kept on appearing like a zombie onslaught.

We had to do something and do it quick otherwise they would overrun us in a matter of minutes. I grabbed for some explosives shells but found I had run out. Gritting my teeth I checked how much ammo I had and wished I hadn't; I was running low and if the onslaught didn't let up, it wouldn't be long till I was completely out.

"I'm running low on ammo, how's everyone else doing?" I asked.

"I only have what's in my gun!" Tuari yelled.

"I have a few extra rounds, but that won't last two minutes if these wolves don't stop coming!"

We kept on firing, but nothing appeared to deter the creatures; they came towards us with an insatiable hunger that spoke of how crazed they were from whatever contaminated water source they had drunk from.

"On your six!" Tuari said to me.

I turned to face that direction and saw a black-haired beast sprint towards me; I squeezed my trigger, but nothing happened. Eyes wide in surprise I just had time to lift the barrel of my shotgun sideways towards my face as teeth that led into a black hole came towards me, The wolf's jaws clamped onto the barrel and I held on tight as the weight and momentum from its body forced me over.

We landed in a heap and the only thing that raced through my mind was to keep hold of my gun.

The wolf shook its head back and forth while I did my best to try and get up, but it was easier said than done. The thing weighed a ton. Saliva and drool speckled my face as it shook its head, trying to tear the gun from my grip. Getting my legs out from underneath it, I kicked it in the chest as hard as I could but it was like hitting a wall made of muscle and bone.

The muscles in my arms were being to tire. I tried to call for help, but the words caught in my throat. As it released its grip I got a respite as it tried to go in for the kill once more, but I was ready for it and brought the shotgun back and smashed the gunstock in its muzzle. It retreated a few feet and once again I smashed the gun into its black demon-like face as I finally got to my feet.

It was injured but it wasn't defeated as it took a few steps back and circled me.

Another wolf trotted next to it eyeing me just as hungrily.

I had stopped hearing gunshots. A quick glance over my shoulder told me the story as everyone had taken up similar stances to me; weapons now used as clubs everyone faced off against more than one wolf.

The action had slowed to a standstill as if the wolves knew we were done for and were just savouring the moment until it became unbearable. No one moved.

"I can't believe that some bitch-ass wolf is going to kill me. By all the ways I could have gone out, this is how you do me, Lord?"

"I would say, Ginger Nuts, that being shat out by said wolf is far worse," Tuari said.

"Our journey won't end here," I said through gritted teeth.

"Who you trying to convince—"

They moved as one. Teeth came towards us in a display of savagery that put us on the back foot. I grimaced as I swung my shotgun as a club, hitting the first wolf who came towards me in the jaw; it fell sideways but another had already taken its place and I just had time to use my gun as a block as it tackled me to the ground. Its head moved back and forth trying to get a firm bite and I did my best to evade its jaws, but I wasn't fast enough and felt teeth sink into my forearm.

I screamed in pain as my arm felt like it was on fire. The

beast shook its head and I felt the bones in my arms snap, causing another chorus of pain to escape my lips.

Shit! Where was my gun?

I had lost it in the scramble and had now resorted to using my free hand as a club to beat against the beast's face, but it ignored my feeble attempts at escape and redoubled its grip.

Biting back the pain that surfaced in the forefront of my brain, I fought and fought, but with each strike I landed against the animal the voice of doom was growing too strong to ignore. The voice that told me that this was it. I had reached the end of the road and no matter how bravely I fought, sooner or later I would end up just another meal for this animal to digest.

I saw nothing but black fur as a face made out of nightmares came for me.

10

I brought up my free arm to shield me and waited for the inevitable, but it never came.

A flood of light surrounded us and gunshots could be heard as cries of pain came from the wolves. The beast attacking me momentarily looked up and its life ended as a blade swept through its neck and sent its head spinning into the darkness. Blood gushed from its neck spraying me from head to toe. I tried to wipe my face but all I succeeded in doing was smearing the blood into my eyes.

It burnt.

I posted on my arm to try and get up to my feet but the arm gave away in a shower of agony, which caused me to land face first in the dirt. Right. Arm broken. I clutched it to my chest and rose to my feet but a firm hand pushed me back down.

"Stay put."

I recognised that voice. But it couldn't be—the person it belonged to should still be back in the city, safe and sound. Not amongst this chaos that could end anyone's life at a moment's notice.

I hurriedly used the sleeve of my shirt to wipe my eyes and looked up to see a slender back with brunette locks cascading down it. Two black knives that appeared to eat the very light were held tightly while the figure took a fighting stance. A wolf sprinted forward and leapt up but the knives found their marks and the wolf collapsed in a heap on the ground.

"Poppy! What the hell are you doing?" I asked.

"What does it look like? Saving your ass. Again."

"I thought I told you to stay back in the city?"

Another wolf leapt towards us but she darted forward with a speed my eyes couldn't follow, killing it before it hit the ground.

"You say a lot of things, darling, how am I meant to keep track of all of them?" she said, giving me a smile over her shoulder.

My lips pulled back in a fine line as the annoyance I felt in the pit of my stomach tried to surface. I finally made my way to my feet as men flooded the area with machine guns, shooting anything that moved. They moved with a precision that spoke of a military background. The wolves that had been attacking us turned their attention to them, but it was an ill-advised move, as they met their demise with a quick blast of rifle fire. The group parted like the Red Sea around us, protecting us from all sides as their rifles sprayed the vegetation.

As the last of the gunshots died away I finally saw who was leading them.

Scarface.

He had survived the cave-in and had made it back to the city alive to bring back reinforcements. For that I owed him a debt I could never repay as he saved us all from certain death.

A Dog Is Born

The chaos died down to a decrescendo as the last of the wolves were put out of their misery. Looking around, Scarface nodded his head in approval before walking up to Samuel and embracing the crying leader in a bear hug.

Samuel patted him on the back before they parted, then he surveyed the damage that had been done. "I want all the carcasses burnt, and a ceremonial goodbye shall be given in respects to these poor animals who threw away their lives because they were driven mad by humans' intervention."

"Shouldn't we get back to the city?" I asked, fearful of another attack.

"No," Samuel replied, "we stay here until the job is done, then we camp here for the night. My men have brought food and water. We have nothing to fear, not until we get back to the city at least. Now we must hurry; there is plenty to do before the night is over."

The ceremony for the wolves we had killed had been weird to say the least.

All the bodies had been collected and piled on top of a funeral pyre. The base of the pyre was then decorated with flowers and any items the men had that could be used as gifts. Once done the men washed with water scented with a fragrance I couldn't quite place; it reminded me of wildflowers after a heavy rainfall.

After they did this, the men gathered around the pyre and prayed on their knees. I couldn't quite make out the words said, but many had tears in their eyes and a few were openly wailing.

"What a bunch of nut jobs," Willis muttered before he sulked off into the shadows.

This went on for some time until Samuel stepped forward with a flaming torch in his hand. At his signal everyone got to their feet and stepped back while he made his way towards the pyre.

"We are gathered here today, to pray for forgiveness to the Almighty Mother so she doesn't judge us too harshly on what we have done. These wolves were once her sacred creatures, but because of man's greed and involvement in what doesn't concern him, they were poisoned and driven mad. I know many of you," Samuel said, eyes darting to Scarface, "have rallied for harsher punishments to befall these men who have trespassed on our lands. There have been whispers of violence. Of war. But that is not the path we should take.

"I want us all to remember that we have never been a violent people—"

"Maybe it's about time that changed," someone muttered in the darkness.

Samuel continued on as if the person hadn't spoken: "I repeat! We are not a violent people! These trials and tribulations are just the Mother's way of testing us. Of showing us the more we suffer the stronger we become. The more we endure the greater our knowledge and wisdom of all things will be. I know this last year has been a trying time. Enemies are pushing on our borders and testing their limits every day. But that doesn't mean we must stoop to their level.

"We must remember we created this place, this sanctuary, as a means to live a life free of violence. Free of the pain that conflict can bring. If we divert off that path then I only foresee a borough, a land, a place, like all the other boroughs that exist on this planet. Many of you have visited those places, but if you have forgotten I shall remind you that they are places of hurt, of pain, of addiction, of suffering brought on by greed and desire.

"They are not places I want to live!"

The flames of the torch in Samuel's hand flickered as if nature itself around him were giving him power. It threw his face in light—eyes reflecting the glow of the flames—before shadow overtook his features once again.

"We as a people value all life! Be it animal, human or plant. I will not stand by and allow us to become hypocrites, just because times are hard."

The muttering that had surfaced was slowly dying down as Samuel cast his gaze over the crowd. Many bowed their heads lower and avoided his gaze but I could still sense the tension under the surface.

The waters may have looked calm but raging torrents were whirling underneath.

"You have trusted me so far to lead you, to guide you, and I have not done so through violence or aggression but with kindness. With understanding. With trying to pave the way to a better life for the generations that are to come. Trust me now to lead you through this time as I have done before."

He said nothing as he kept his gaze over his men until the silence stretched to the breaking point, then he turned around and threw the torch onto the pyre where it exploded into flames.

11

Later at night, I found myself propped up against a tree some distance away from the funeral pyre that filled the air with the scent of burning hair. The fire flickered and leapt as the fat from the bodies added to the flames.

I rested on a bed of leaves and moss and was naked from the waist up. Poppy knelt next to me and held my broken arm in her lap. She ran her gaze up and down it slowly, inspecting every inch of it.

"I've got good news and I've got bad news," she said, finally looking up at me.

"Let's hear it then..."

"The good news is that the only thing broken is your forearm."

"You call that good news?"

"A jungle wolf's jaw has the crushing power to shatter bone; yours merely has a clean break."

"That is wonderful news," I said with an eye roll. "I must remember to keep my excitement in check, and thank my lucky stars at how favoured I've been by Lady Luck currently."

She looked at me but said nothing.

"Are you sure that's the only damage done? It sure hurts like hell and my skin feels like it's on fire."

"Eyes that can do everything from X-ray to see infrared, remember," she said, tapping the side of her head.

"Okay. Fine. What's the bad news?"

She scratched her neck while she looked off into the distance before looking back at me. "Your blood appears to be infected with whatever the wolves were carrying. Which would explain the burning sensation you are feeling."

"What? How is that possible?"

"The wolf that attacked you broke the skin, no different from being bitten by an animal that has rabies. The virus is spreading fast. Much faster than anything I have seen. It shouldn't kill you—"

"It shouldn't?"

"No," she said, looking me in the eye, "not before we reach the city, but I'm afraid you are going to suffer from whatever side effects the virus places on your body."

"Which are?" I asked in a soft voice.

"Sweating, fever, joint pain, vomiting, hallucinations, headaches... but that's only a guess. It could be all of them, or it could be none of them."

"How confident are you they can treat this once we get to the city?"

"I've scanned the virus's DNA strand from the wolf's blood and saliva and have already constructed a formula of antibodies to fight it. I have spoken to Samuel and he has assured me his labs have everything I need, as he is also interested in a cure for this virus. Now, it's just a case of getting you there."

"I see you have everything already figured out."

"What is your problem?" Poppy snapped.

"You being here," I spat, regretting the words before they even left my mouth.

She leaned back away from me, hurt in her eyes, and I gritted my teeth as I tried to think of the right words to say.

"Look, I thought we agreed it would be better if you stayed in the city—"

"No! You agreed. I merely went along with it to keep you happy."

"The reason why *we* agreed was because it would be safer. We can't only think of ourselves anymore. There are three of us now in this picture," I said, touching her stomach. "We need to be more cautious in the way we do things. In the way the crew operates. Things have to change—"

She pushed my hand off her and got up to her feet.

"You need to stop treating me like I'm made of glass. I can punch through a reinforced brick wall with ease. I've seen you, on the other hand, get injured by merely slipping on grass! If anyone should be protected, should be playing it safe, it's you."

"The grass was covered in ice! That's why I slipped and twisted my ankle. It could happen to anyone!" I said.

"Yet," she continued, "you constantly throw yourself in these situations because of what?

"Male pride?

"Ego?"

"What are you talking about?" I asked.

"Don't deny you feel threatened because of what I am. You feel you need to prove yourself. You feel if you don't, then the others won't see you as a worthy captain. But I don't care about any of that, I just care about you getting back to me safe and sound."

I shook my head, lost for words. Was there any truth in what she said? Did I feel threatened by her? Had I been acting more reckless now that I had become the captain of the Junk Yard Dogs?

Reckless was never a word anyone had used to describe me but things had changed.

"You have nothing to worry—" I began, but she cut me off with a look.

"Don't you dare. Don't you dare sit there with a broken arm and some virus crawling through your body and tell me I have nothing to worry about. It may not have occurred to you, but the chances of me surviving all of this, compared to you, stacks nicely in my favour. I can even do the math for you if you like."

"Poppy—"

"I'm scared, Quinton. I'm scared because I'm going through something I've never experienced before and I need you there with me. But if you keep on doing this, then...."

"Poppy, he's still out there. Alvis won't stop until he has you or he destroys you."

"We can run."

"Not forever. Not without always looking over our backs. Not without always living with this thing that hangs over our family, always wondering, always thinking—will today be the day, will today be the day that, that monster has finally found us? If we don't bring the fight to him, to all of them, then they will crush everything we have before it even begins and I won't have that. I refuse to be a doormat. I refuse to allow someone else to dictate how I live. Not anymore. Those days are over."

She looked at me with sadness that radiated from her very soul. Walking forward she grabbed me on either side of the face and kissed me softly on the lips before pulling away and looking into my eyes.

"None of that should matter as long as we have each other. People can't hurt what we have unless we allow them to."

"But they can hurt you, they can hurt our child. That's all they need to do to win."

"And what if they decide to hurt you?"

"I—"

"If I weren't here today then that wolf would have killed you. What would have I done then? You need to stop thinking only about yourself. I may not be human but my heart beats just the same. It works both ways, Quinton. It works both ways," she said as she walked away and left me to my thoughts.

12

We were walking through the jungle, my feet dragging behind me. This was after a fitful sleep that had me trying to get as comfortable as possible, while my broken arm woke me every ten minutes as I rested on it by mistake and my body's temperature slowly rose as the night went on.

Sweats had turned to shivers and shivers had turned to sweats, as I tossed and turned.

It was a night I wouldn't forget in a hurry.

Now I shielded my face with one hand as the blazing sun felt like it was melting my skin off my bones.

I took the water bottle attached to my belt and brought it up to my mouth and stopped. The snake on it was moving. But how... I closed my eyes and shook my head and looked again, but the logo was now still. Bringing it up to my mouth, I caught a flicker of movement and stopped, jerking the bottle towards my face.

I had sworn—

"Quinton!"

"Huh?"

I looked around to see Tuari and Willis looking my way. They said nothing but just stared.

"What?"

"What the fuck do you mean what? We've been calling you for the last five minutes and all you've been doing is looking at that bottle," Willis said.

"Oh."

I returned my focus to the bottle until a hand pushed it towards my face. Taking a long drink until I was full I let my gaze follow the hand towards a face, which belonged to Samuel.

"It's just the virus running through your system," he said. "The sooner we get you to—"

Whatever else was said I didn't hear as his mouth stretched into a cartoonish grin, forcing me to pull away from him sharply until I bumped into something. I turned and saw Tuari standing before me, hands placed out in front of him like he had encountered a wild animal and didn't what to scare it away.

"What are you doing?" I asked.

"Breathe," he said. "I just want you to breathe."

Why was he telling me to breathe? I looked at him in confusion but followed his advice nevertheless. The pounding in my head ceased momentarily and I sighed as I felt a cool sensation running down the back of my neck. Looking up I saw Samuel holding an empty bottle of water.

"The water won't do much, but it's the best we can do in the circumstances," he said.

"Poppy?"

"She's... she said she would be back, but first she needed to head back to the city and prepare the medical care that would combat whatever is running throughout your body.

She assured me once she was done there, then she would be back for you."

"She's left?"

He replied but I failed to hear his response. My thoughts raced back to the last conversation we had. It had been one of anger, of hurt, of feelings of hopelessness.

No wonder she left. She had been trying to tell me that everything was alright, trying to console me, but I had thrown it back in her face and now she had left me. Who was I to blame her?

"Come on," someone said, but I couldn't tell who, "the quicker we get moving the quicker we can get you help."

I took a step forward—and I was somewhere different.

I looked around and didn't notice anything familiar. Sweat coated my face and I used the back of my hand to wipe it from my brow as I looked around. Where... were we?

How far had we travelled?

I looked up and the sun was higher in the sky than it had been previously. Tree branches moved like arms twisting and lurching towards me as I did my best to avoid them. They tried to grope my body but I battered them away and sidestepped out of their reach. Frustrated at not getting their prey, they grew, forcing me to shuffle back until I turned tail and ran.

Leaves slapped me in the face and vines with thorns pulled and tore at my clothing but I didn't care. I needed to get away. I needed to escape. I needed to tell Poppy I was sorry. That I loved her.

I emerged into a clearing like a startled animal and looked around. The overheard sun felt heavy on my shoulders as I took in the scene before me. There were huts dotted about me. They looked familiar. Had I been here before?

Walking forward I heard voices before the smell hit me. It was the metallic scent of blood that hit the back of the throat. I dry heaved until bile rose from my stomach and poured from my mouth; the acrid stench burnt the hairs of my nostrils. I wiped the drool from the corners of my mouth and continued on. The party I was with had gotten there before me.

Samuel and Scarface were arguing but voices were not being raised. They both spoke to each other using hand signals but each gesture was sharp and to the point. The rest of their men were either shaking their heads or doing their best not to cry. I still didn't understand what the problem was until I saw the first row of blanketed bodies that rested on the ground.

Each hut had a similar scene in front of it.

Bodies large and small rested under sheets soaked in blood.

"What happened here?" I asked Tuari, who had just emerged from one of the huts.

"Nothing short of a blood bath. These people didn't even have anything to defend themselves with. It seems whoever rolled through here wanted to make sure no witnesses stayed alive to identify the culprits."

"This place looks familiar."

"It should," Willis said, walking up to us, "it's one of the villages we passed on our way to the cave. Whoever did this used weaponry from a small ship, then cleared up afterwards with an assault rifle."

"How do you know that?" I asked.

"Look around you."

I slowly swivelled my head around and took in the scene around me. Holes the size of fists had punched through the mud walls of the huts and had passed all the way through to the other side; the vegetation around the camp had been torn to bits, with branches snapped and leaves chewed to shreds. Walking in the centre of the camp I knelt on the ground and touched the burn marks that a small aircraft had made as it landed. The dry mud was caked in boot marks, which lead to each hut. I looked back at the bodies and noticed the feet poking out from under the sheet were barefoot.

This wasn't someone trying to cover up their deeds. This was someone who was looking for payback and I could only think of one person who had escaped in a small craft in the last twenty-four hours who would want any.

"The asshole who escaped from the cave did this," Willis said, teeth bared like a dog.

"We don't know that for sure!" came Samuel's voice from across the camp.

"Who else would do this but those Diamond District fuckers?" said one of his men.

"There is no point in casting judgement when we haven't got all the facts!" Samuel said.

"What facts do you need!" another man yelled. "Our people are dying before our very eyes, and you chose to do nothing but sit on your ass and think. There is a time for action and there is a time for thinking and this is a time for action, before our enemies gather more forces and make a push into our lands we aren't prepared for. If we wait any longer it will be too late. Now is the time to strike! While they think us weak and wounded."

"Do you know what you are saying?" Samuel asked, "our people have never been to war; our people have always kept in harmony with the other boroughs. That is how we have survived and flourished for so long."

"Maybe it's about time that changes."

"Not as long as I am in charge."

"Maybe it's about time that changes too."

Silence greeted the last sentence as neither party spoke. I looked out over the crowd and saw eyes cast down or afield, while others looked straight through Samuel like he wasn't even there. A few, like the last man who had spoken, stared at him, anger radiating from their very souls.

"Oi," Willis said, walking forward, "what's your name?"

The last man who had spoken pointed to himself and Willis nodded. "Jon."

"Have you ever been in a real fight, Jon?"

"Yeah. Of course."

"I mean," Willis said, slowly circling him, "a real fight. One where your life is on the line."

"There was—"

"And I'm not talking about a bunch of pussy-ass wolves who are half brain dead either."

"If you let me finish, then I was going to say that there had been a bunch of smugglers looking to take some of our marijuana stock a few years back, and some of the boys and I had to get into a fight with them; some gunfire was exchanged and we scared them off. It was all second nature anyway; some of the men in the borough go through weapons training, hand-to-hand combat, that sort of thing —I've done it myself a few times. There's nothing to it, really."

Willis continued to walk around Jon while he nodded his head. He looked to Tuari and gave him a slight shrug. "There's nothing to it. Hear that, big boy? Jon here says there is nothing to it. Silly me. Here I was thinking *taking a man's life* was something to be nervous about. Something to fear—"

"I didn't say I enjoyed it!"

"No. No, you didn't. But there are some men who do. There are some men that long to feel their enemy's warm blood drip down their forearms while the knife they hold plunges into their enemy's guts. There are some men who will look into your eyes until the light slowly fades, savouring each and every moment of it. There are some men who will break your limbs and leave you lying in the dirt with a front-row seat, while they rape your loved ones and pillage your home as you scream and beg them to stop, but you know deep down in your heart of hearts you can't do anything to stop them. Until you beg for mercy for them to kill you, but they don't give it to you, but instead leave you to forever live out your days with those haunted memories until you do the job for them and take your own life.

"Then...!" Willis said, moving in front of Jon so quickly, he failed to take a step back even as a knife was placed under his chin.

"Then... Oh, then, there are some bastards who just love chaos. They look around the universe and realise that none of it matters; no matter what they do, their actions are pointless and fruitless, so they may as well cause as much damage and destruction as they can in the name of fun and leaving a legacy. Those men are the ones who are most dangerous because they begin to believe, to convince themselves, what they do does matter, and that they were born to be rulers, conquerors, leaders.

"When you find those men... you put them down. Swift and hard. Because society can only take so many Alexanders, Genghises, Adolfs."

Jon said nothing as he tried to focus on the point of the knife under his chin as well as Willis's face.

"So, Jon, tell me. Which one of those men are you?"

Nobody spoke as Jon tried his best not to swallow. His

eyes darted to the men on either side of him but there was no help forthcoming there. Everyone had taken a step back from the madman with a ginger beard.

Samuel stepped forward but Willis's hand shot out and pointed his way, stopping him dead in his tracks.

"You see, Jonny boy, the people who are the first to call for war, first to pick up arms, are normally the people last to bleed on the battlefield or never see it at all. Until you smell the stench of another man's shit after he's been killed and soiled himself then your opinion really doesn't matter."

Jon audibly gulped as the tip of the blade inched closer to his Adam's apple, while the manic grin on Willis's face only broadened.

Jon's hands inched for the weapon at his side. If he reached it—

"Willis, that's enough," Samuel said, resting a hand on his shoulder and deflating the ball of tension in the air. "That's enough. Everyone pack up; we leave in five. Time is of the essence and the others must be made aware of this."

No one moved.

"I said we leave in five!"

They sent scornful looks his and Willis's way as the crowd broke apart and everyone went their own way. We had avoided bloodshed but I wasn't too sure if we would be so lucky next time.

13

We continued the journey with the sun still beating a rhythm on my upper back; I had stopped sweating, which I knew was a bad sign ,and the shivers and chills which accompanied it shortly after left no doubt in my mind.

Time felt like it slowed down and then sped up.

One minute someone was looking at me, the next nothing but trees surrounded me, I saw shapes and animals that had no business being in the jungle out of the corner of my eye. Every time I tried to focus on them, they would vanish and disappear amidst a rustle of undergrowth or burrow into the ground.

I stumbled into a clearing and standing in front of me was a white nine-tailed fox with piercing green eyes. I looked around and found I was otherwise alone. When I took a step forward the creature didn't move but sat upright facing me with an intelligence that stopped me in my tracks, I looked around me once again but still found I was alone.

"I do not bite," it said.

I was going crazy.

I took two steps hurriedly back thinking only of escape but yet again it spoke to me.

"What are you afraid of, young man?"

"Animals do not talk. Need I say any more?"

A chuckle that sounded like an autumn breeze escaped its mouth while it regarded me. Its voice sounded as old as time itself, yet it comforted me. It sounded familiar.

"There is nothing to be afraid of. You know me well."

"Err, can't say that I do. I would remember a white nine-tailed talking fox. That sort of thing tends to come up in conversation; it would be the most interesting point of my life. Someone would ask how my day was and I would be like, hey, do you know I have a talking fox as a friend, I mean—" I was rambling.

"Wait," I said taking a step closer, "I have seen you before."

I thought long and hard where I had seen the image and slapped myself on the forehead. It was the tattoo Poppy had; all members of the Junk Yard Dogs had a canine-related tattoo. Mine was the constellation of the Greek mythological dog called Laelaps.

"Ah! I get it," I said, finally relieved I had figured it out. "I'm just hallucinating right now, but you're actually Poppy. Damn, this virus must have me more messed up than I thought. As you're here I take it the medical care to get rid of this thing is ready?"

The fox looked at me but said nothing.

I rubbed my hands up and down my arms as a stiff breeze tore through the treetops.

"Poppy, it's alright. I've been seeing weird stuff all day. Once we get back to the city and I get the medical attention I need everything shall be alright."

Still, the fox didn't move but remained where it sat.

"Pop?"

"I have many names but Poppy or Pop isn't one of them. The Chinese know me as Húli Jīng, the Japanese know me as Kitsune, the Koreans call me Kumiho. I am the shapeshifter. The trickster. The creature who seduces men for her own deeds until she gets what she wants," said the fox, shapeshifting into a naked form of Poppy, who gave me a smile before turning back.

"So what do you want of me?"

"The question you should be asking, dear boy, is what have I already gotten?"

I took another step toward it as I felt the frustration from my chest rise up into my face.

"I don't know what you're trying to get at, but Poppy would never do anything to hurt me, would never do anything to betray my trust."

"It's interesting that's the first thought which occurred to you, when no such thought was spoken by me."

"If you're just going to talk in riddles, then I have better things to do than to listen to you."

"Such as?" the fox asked, head tilted to the side.

"Staying alive. Now if you would excuse me…"

"What I offer could very well save your life, maybe not now, but sometime in the future."

I folded my arms over my chest and just stared.

"Doesn't it seem strange to you, that the only AI humanoid woman in the whole universe has fallen for you? She's been alive for hundreds of years, has met countless people and yet you, dear Quinton, have somehow tickled her fancy. Has it never crossed your mind why?"

I would be lying if I said it hadn't. But as the time passed between us I had given it less and less thought. More important things had cropped up. Like killer robot spiders and gang lords who wanted nothing more than to separate my head from my body.

"I did at first, but then, stuff like that just didn't matter anymore. I'm pretty sure I love her and she loves me."

"Are you sure?"

"She says she does, what more is there to need?"

"How easily a pretty face can sway the emotions of the heart."

"Ha! If that were true then I would have cheated on my ex-wife a long time ago. Tracy from Accounts couldn't keep her hands off me at the Christmas party and she had a figure to die for. No, I'm with Poppy because she's smart, strong, can sometimes be pig-headed until she gets her own way but I like that quality about her, she's saved my life more times than I can count and will save my life that much more in the future. But the main reason why I fell for her was because she treated me like a human.

"She stood up for me. Had faith in me. Believed in me. I've never had that. Not from my parents. Not from my friends. Not from my wife.

"So yes, talking nine-tailed fox with more names than I can pronounce, she has my heart. I don't see why that should concern you."

"Because, my dear boy, there shall come a time when you may have to make the hardest choice any person has to make. One that may break you to your core."

"Which is?'

"To choose between the life of your child and that of the woman you love."

I stared at the fox and felt my teeth grind as I walked towards it, hands clenched at my sides. The wind picked up and stirred the leaves underfoot as the fox waited for me to complete my journey, and then I was in front of it.

"What did you say?"

"I am only the messenger. Do not be angry with me for delivering what needed to be heard."

"I think it's about time you leave."

The fox sat where it was.

"I said...! Leave!"

I grabbed a stick from the ground and by the time I looked up, the fox had taken off. I was still mad. I still wanted it to pay for telling me such lies. Stick in hand I gave chase as I lumbered after it through the jungle while it ran as if surfing on water. Nothing impeded its path, while branches, vines and roots got in my way, but I didn't care.

My only goal was to destroy the white streak ahead of me. My only mission was to make it pay.

I ran and ran until my legs burnt and my chest felt like it was going to explode. It was always one step ahead of me, always just out of reach—until it stopped and I had it where I wanted it. Stick held overhead I screamed from the top of my lungs as I charged forward but I never made it, as something tackled me from the side.

Face skidding along the forest floor and buried under a pile of leaves, I tried my hardest to break free from whatever held me down but I couldn't.

"Let me go! Let me go!"

"Quinton! It's me. It's okay. Quinton, you need to calm down. Please. Calm down."

The voice sounded familiar.

"Pop?"

The pressure on the base of my back relaxed allowing me to turn to my back and see Poppy above me; concern graced her features but a smile broke out on my lips.

"I see," she said, wiping dirt off the side of my face, "that

I can't leave you alone for five minutes without you trying to injure yourself."

"What do you mean?"

She nodded to the area in front of us and I turned my attention to see we were less than ten feet away from a sheer cliff. A few seconds more of me running in that direction and I would have been no more.

"What were you doing?" she asked me.

"A fox... a fox insulted you. I was trying to hit it with a stick."

"I love you," she said, leaning in and kissing me, "but we need to get you treated. You're more delirious than I thought."

14

I woke up with a snort.

Looking around me I saw the first signs of dawn breaking through wisps of clouds through the canopy of the treetops. A yawn that threatened to tear my face in half escaped me as I stretched my arms over my head and got up into a sitting position.

I looked at my broken forearm and noticed a new cast on it, silver in colour. I tapped it and was rewarded with a faint ping. It was made out of metal with a coloured graph-like indicator running alongside its length. I placed my hand on it and felt a slight hum.

The faint embers of a fire were slowly cooling off as I surveyed my environment.

We were still in the Jungle.

I saw Willis and Tuari some distance away, curled up in their sleeping bags, but apart from that there was no one else around. Where was everyone?—a hand on my shoulder jolted me a foot in the air. Turning around I saw Poppy trying her best not to allow the laughter she was holding to escape. I had let out a small girly squeal when she had touched me and although my face was going red, I refused to give her the satisfaction of letting her know she had gotten to me.

"Aww, whenever I am sad I shall always replay back that little squeal," she said.

Ignoring her, I got to my feet and gave the campground another look. "Where is everyone?"

"You were in a worse shape than I thought you would be; lucky I already prepared a vial to combat the virus, which I brought with me, and I administered it while you were passed out. I also placed the nanocast around your forearm. It should completely heal the bones in a day or two.

"I told Samuel we needed to wait for the antibodies to take effect before we continued on and he agreed, but his men wanted to go back to the city."

"Did he go with them?"

Poppy looked behind her, eyes cast in worry. "He opted to stay."

She didn't have to say anything more. The tone of her voice told me everything I needed to know. I got up, dusted myself off and walked the way she had looked. It didn't take me long to find what I was looking for.

Samuel sat on a large boulder positioned in the middle of a stream; water flowed gently around it while he looked into its depths and every so often flicked pieces of bread into it, to be eaten by the small shoal of fish that swam around his feet. I made my way through the water, its cool sensation a welcome release against the heat and humidity.

When I finally reached the boulder, Samuel scooted over so there was room for me to sit.

He handed me a slice of bread, which I ate.

"That was meant to be for the fish," he said.

"Tough luck. I'm starving and they're luckier than me; they have fish to eat, while I have dried bread."

He said nothing but continued to throw pieces of bread into the water. I watched the multicoloured fish at my feet and marvelled. Every hue and colour imaginable flashed underneath the surface of the water. They moved in a rhythmic motion that brought peace to the mind.

"You know they're not native to this planet. Fifty percent of all wildlife and plants you see around you were brought here by settlers from different planets. It's just the human way, I guess, to bring with you what you know, be that ideology or wildlife.

"I sometimes think about the species who lived here before us: what were they like, what were their dreams, their fears. Did they fight amongst themselves as we do? Was there war, famine, hate, greed? What wiped their existence off the surface of this planet? Was it them or something external like a meteor?"

He looked to me for an answer but I didn't know what to say.

"It's alright," he said, "it's just the ramblings of a man that's at his wits' end. A man who doesn't see a future for his people without blood having to be spilt."

"You think it will come to that?"

"War?"

I nodded.

He sighed as he kicked his feet slowly back and forth. "I would love to reassure myself and say there is a way around it, but... things have been stirring under the surface for a long time. I am the second-longest-running leader of a borough, the first being Mr Diamond of the Diamond District, and in that time I've seen many faces and leaders come and go who have tried to control both The Floating City and Paradise Lost, and none have maintained it.

"But that all changed when The Lady aka Lady Isabella Ivanov took control of Paradise. You felt the change immediately. The way she ran things was like a military operation. Control and order, the two things you never wanted to have in an opposing leader, she had it in spades. There were assassination attempts on her life to start with, but people quickly stopped trying after she started killing the attackers' families, lovers, business partners, friends and pets, all just to prove a point.

"It was after that that Mr Lee appeared, backed by Mr Diamond in an attempt to control her influence."

"I thought Mr Lee was in Xcorp's pocket?" I asked.

"Mr Lee plays whatever side he can; the only person he can't is The Lady, which makes him fearful of her. But he will always be Mr Diamond's dog, no matter how long his leash is."

A fish leapt out of the water and landed back down with a splash, soaking us from the hips down.

"I'm sorry about your people. I feel if you weren't sheltering us none of this would have happened."

"These events would have taken place without your existence on Safe Haven. Mr Diamond has been trying to push for my corporation for years, and he was happy enough to let my borough be because it was no threat to him. Now we're loosely allied with The Lady, things have taken a more hostile feel."

"Why did you ever decide to do business with her?"

Samuel lifted his arms in the air and gave a defeatist shrug. "I've been asking myself that same question every day since we got in bed with her and you know, I don't have an answer. It started simply enough; she wanted some products from us that only we produced and we were more than happy to deal with her, and the orders got larger and larger and we were only too glad to help because we were earning good money from it and then, one day, one of her men caught some intruders on our land and killed them before I got a chance to intervene."

"And let me guess, these men she killed worked for Mr Diamond?"

Samuel gave me a nod and chuckled. "I should have seen what she was up to, but everything moved so fast and before I knew it Diamond refused to take my calls and battle lines had been drawn and I had no weapons or soldiers and just, and just everything moved so fast. I couldn't keep track of it all. Within weeks, we had somehow joined a working relationship which was more us working for her than anything else, and here we are.

"Stupid really. All it took was her killing some of Diamond's men on our land but I guess the old man was really looking for any excuse to wipe us out. She just handed it to him."

"What will you do now?" I asked.

"The same thing I've always done, try to calm tempers down and see if there is a way out of this before more of my people are killed. No doubt news of what has happened has spread throughout the city and my people will want some sort of retaliation. But they are not fighters, only passionate dreamers who will get themselves hurt. What shall you do?"

"I do not know. The Lady and our crew have unfinished business since she put a bullet in José, I don't trust Mr Lee and I trust this Diamond character even less. But I need help defeating a foe that I can't take on alone."

"This Alvis Boman you told me about?"

"Yes. I've had Willis and Tuari pay off any contacts they

have across the galaxy to see if they have heard anything, but so far it's like looking for a needle in a haystack. I know he's just waiting to make his move, and when he does I want to be ready. But to do so, I need more support."

"Hmm," said Samuel, stroking his chin, "I think you have all the support you need, my friend. I think the issue lies in you not wanting to face a being who can take everything away from you, after you've just found it."

"Do you blame me?" I demanded, facing him. "I am older than most, but I only started living once I met this crew, once I met her. I was merely existing, just getting by. Now I have to jeopardise all that because stopping him is the right thing to do? That's not fair! I have just found what love is! I have just found what it means to be part of a family who would die for me, I've just found out what it means to live.

"I can't, I can't give all that up now. That's not fair."

"Who said the universe was? Men like you and I were born rightly or wrongly to take on the burdens of others and do what's right. It's why Poppy loves you, but if you allow it to, that burden can twist and turn you into the very thing you are fighting against.

"It's up to you what path you wish to take."

The journey back was uneventful.

I still wasn't a hundred percent, but with each step I took and each meal I had, I felt my strength slowly returning. We should have got to the city faster than we did, but I knew everyone was walking a step or two slower because of me. My ego should have raged at the childlike treatment, but I didn't care; still battered and bruised, with a broken forearm on the mend, I enjoyed the leisurely pace.

Poppy had assured me, if the nanocast hadn't completely healed my forearm then the labs back in the city would take care of the rest.

The jungle grew less and less restrictive as the hours passed by till our feet touched on a well-worn path; we passed the odd hut here and there but no one came out to greet us or ask how we were, unlike when we were passing through the first time. The occasional inhabitant we saw glared at us from doorways, face set in stone, arms crossed over chests.

Children we came across playing in the grass were quickly called inside, and men huddled in groups muttering amongst themselves but growing quiet the moment we appeared in view.

The closer we got to the city the more we saw small groups gathered. They all stopped and stared as we passed, no one offering a greeting or coming to ask how we had got on.

"Nothing good comes from men forming in small groups," Tuari said. "You either get a revolution or someone looking to kick the heads in of the opposing sports team. Either way, you can be sure of two things, violence and blood."

Samuel said nothing but hastened his footsteps as we entered the city proper.

The general mood of the city had changed.

Gone were the happy-go-lucky faces I had become accustomed to; instead women pulled their children's hand forcefully as they hurried down the street. The usual food stalls and shops that sold hand-woven clothes and goods had shut for business, or were in the process of closing. The streets we crossed were deserted and the electric cable car system normally always running was dormant.

"Don't tell me today's a holiday and no one told us?" Tuari said, as we crossed another empty street. "I mean I would have dressed to impress if that was the case; you all know how I love a good shindig."

"More like stuff your fat face with everything in sight," Willis grumbled, while he kept his hands on his pistols.

We continued on walking till we saw the enormous statue of the naked woman with vines wrapped around her and animals gathered at her feet, whose hands were lifted towards the sky.

"I always meant to ask," I said to Samuel, "who is that meant to be?"

Samuel looked up at the statue with a smile as we drew near. "Mother Nature in all her glory. She protects us from the evils—"

We all stopped as Lady Isabella Ivanov emerged from behind the statue; piercing blue eyes scanned us as she folded her arms in front of her. "You were saying, Samuel?" she said with a shark-like smile.

15

The tension in the air was like soup as neither party said anything or moved.

The last time I saw her was the last time José was alive. The man who inadvertently changed my life and gave me the tools to really live. I owed that man a debt I still hadn't repaid. A debt I had sworn I would, no matter the cost.

My eyes darted to Samuel and I could see his mind working as he tried to piece the puzzle together. Out of my peripheral vision I could see Poppy lowering her weight getting ready for what was about to come. We were out in the open, where The Lady no doubt had men all around us. But why were there no signs of battle? Where were Samuel's men?

I began to move but Samuel beat me to the punch as his elbow dug deep into Willis's solar plexus knocking the wind out of his lungs. An uppercut followed, catching Willis on the bridge of the nose and forcing him to stagger backward. Samuel didn't let up and swept the legs out from underneath him causing him to collapse in a heap on his back.

In one swift movement, Samuel grabbed hold of Willis's pistols and placed them in the folds of his tunic.

"I'll fucking kill you! Right after I kill that double-crossing Russian cunt of—"

"Lady Ivanov," Samuel said, cutting Willis off and walking forward arms outstretched, "how good of you to visit us. I always look forward to your visits but this one is most unexpected. If you had called ahead of time, I would have had the necessary arrangements made so we could have greeted you properly."

"Oh, no need for that, Samuel. No need for that at all. It was one of your men, the silent one with the scar on his face, who informed me of your predicament at the cave. Once I heard the news, I had to come here right away, to make sure one of my main *allies and friends* was okay."

At the mention of his name, Scarface rounded a corner and stood slightly away from us all, arms crossed over his chest.

"Psh, no need for all the concern. You can see I am alive and well," Samuel said, looking Scarface's way. "My man tends to get himself concerned in matters that are best left to his superiors. It was nothing but a slight mishap, a misunderstanding if you will."

"Really? I was informed there had been attacks against your people..."

"I... well—"

"I was also told there had been multiple reports over the last few months of rival factions trespassing on your land, taking vulnerable items that are only produced in this region."

"Overexaggerations; it was nothing more than a couple of bandits trying their luck. You know how it is. Plus, who are we to say what can and can't be taken? The Mother provides for all. We are all her child—"

"Not when I have invested large amounts of capital into your land. No, she doesn't provide for all. She provides for the people who have invested first, then whatever is left you have. If you want to give that to the homeless or downtrodden or even the wood fairies you can, Mr Moor, but not before I have my cut."

"Have I not always fulfilled our agreement?"

"It is not the past I am worried about, Mr Moor, it is the future."

"There will not be a—"

"There are always problems. You should know better than anyone that as soon as our foot touches the floor in the morning, we have to put out some fire that needs our attention. Some grievance that needs to be resolved. It is thankless, tireless work, but it is work that needs to be done nevertheless. Your people are not fighters, Mr Moor. This in itself concerns me—"

"It shouldn't."

"But it does. That is why I shall be placing my own men amongst your ranks just to make sure everyone stays safe and that these *bandits* do not continue to try their luck."

"That wasn't part of our original agreement."

"I believe I told you for a relationship to work both parties must be flexible; there must be a give and take, sometimes one party takes more and vice versa. I have allowed you and your people great freedom, to express this..." she looked around at the flowers, the statues of couples intertwined in loving embraces before returning her gaze back to Samuel, "...this free love, and I have not intervened. Our relationship worked well during the past as

I did so, but things have changed. Forces out of your control have started to make their move, and it will only be a matter of time before they run through this place and take what is yours, but more importantly what is mine.

"And I shall *not* allow that to happen."

Cheeks flushed, Samuel took a step forward, but I grabbed him by the back of his tunic before he could go any further. He looked back sharply at me, but I held his gaze before darting my eyes to the surrounding areas. I was certain those spots contained her men. Although ruthless and fearless, she was too smart to come here alone.

Samuel grabbed the hand with which I was holding him and gave it a squeeze before turning back around. "I take it you are here not only because of that?"

"No," she said, "there is much to discuss. Things are moving much faster than I first thought, but I see it was wise for me to come here as what I have to say also involves the Junk Yard Dogs."

Willis, now on his feet, growled under his breath as he moved forward but I blocked his path and placed a hand on his chest. He looked at me in disbelief, face turning the colour of his beard.

"Are you just going to stand here and do nothing?"

"Now is not the time," I replied.

"Not the time!" Willis screamed, spittle flying from his mouth. "Right there stands José's killer. The bitch who we worked for, who we sweated and bled for, who shot him like some common thug and didn't bat a god damn eyelid! And you tell me now isn't the time to put a bullet between her eyes."

"Yes."

Willis's head snapped towards Tuari, whose gaze was locked on The Lady, but he made no attempt to move. Willis then looked to Poppy, who walked forward and placed a palm on his shoulder.

"I understand how you feel. Tuari, you, and I knew José the longest; he was the person who showed me how to live. But Quinton is right, now is not the time for rash actions. I have detected multiple men dotted around us, weapons all trained on us. I doubt you will be able to get within six feet of her before a sniper puts a bullet in your head."

Willis's chest rose and fell but as he scanned the high grass around us, he settled down. Gripping my hand till I thought he would break the bones in it he said, "This debt will be paid."

"It would be a dishonour to his life if it wasn't," I whispered back.

He gave me a final nod and took a step back as I turned around and took in the sight that was Lady Isabella Ivanov. Wearing a red and white dress accompanied by a red cape with a hood, she smiled at me as I walked towards her; I stopped where I thought it was safe and didn't appear threatening. Her smile hadn't wavered during Willis's outrage but instead only grew.

"It's good to see you again, Isabella."

Her head crooked to the side with a slight frown, "I didn't realise we were on a first name basis, Mr Blake."

"What's names between friends"

"Indeed."

The wind rustled the leaves between us as I matched her stare for stare.

"I like your outfit."

"Oh, this old thing. I thought it suited the occasion as I am entering the woods and I was hoping to come across some big bad wolves."

"There are only dogs here I'm afraid."

"I guess that will have to do."
"Shall we?" I said, gesturing towards the buildings.
"It would be my pleasure."

16

Samuel, Isabella and I were all in a room gathered around a table in one of the underground bunkers beneath one of the mammoth trees that supported the life of the city. Brown dirt walls surrounded us on all sides. Roots like veins on flesh worked their way through the walls, their faint outlines just visible.

The table we were sat in front of was carved out of one of the roots of the tree, in a beautiful design that allowed the root to still grow freely, but it was still useable as a functioning table. I ran my right hand over it and pulled it back as what felt like a faint heartbeat pulsed under my palm.

"Everything is alive," Samuel said after seeing my reaction.

I placed my hand slowly back over the table's rough surface and closed my eyes as the slow rhythmic pulse gently put me at ease.

"What happened to your arm?"

I opened my eyes to see Isabella looking at my healing forearm with the metal cast over it. "Rival dogs."

"I can sympathise," she said, pulling away the neckline of the dress and revealing a fresh pink jagged scar that ran down her neck.

I looked upon it but felt nothing.

"My crew and I haven't been to Paradise for some time. I didn't realise it had become so dangerous."

"Paradise has always been dangerous; it was just my fault for thinking I had grown above it. Do you know why I stay in that hell hole, Mr Blake?"

I shook my head.

"It's because it keeps me honest, keeps me on my toes. It doesn't allow me to be weak, to not be as vigilant as my other colleagues that are in a position similar to mine. Because of that, and only that, I will triumph in this upcoming war."

"War?"

"War, Mr Blake."

"I think Miss Ivanov is being overdramatic," Samuel said, receiving a pot of tea from one of his people, which he poured in wooden mugs for us.

"When have you ever known me to be such a thing?" she said, taking a mug from him. "I only speak in truths, no matter how painful or hurtful. I find it allows people to know where they stand."

I took one of the wooden mugs from Samuel and took a sip of the tea; hints of honey and peppermint danced on my tongue as the warmth from the drink slowly warmed my body.

"Be that as it may, I have had no indication from any of my sources that such a thing is even on the horizon," Samuel said.

Isabella laughed and waved a dismissive hand his way. "Please, Samuel, I would hardly call those men of yours sources. They may be able to tell you when the next full moon harvest is but taking advice from them on matters such as this is ill-advised. My *sources* who are dotted all over Safe Haven tell me war is on the way and when they speak I listen. Why do you think Diamond's men were digging in that cave of yours?"

"How did you—"

"Sources," she said with a smile.

"Yes, Diamond's men have been mining our caves for a certain metal alloy we have not come across. We don't know what need he has for it but we can only guess it's more valuable to him than all the treasures that those cave tunnels hold. Why else would he risk war?"

"One of the few reasons a leader risks war for an item is because he thinks the item will give him an advantage over his opposition. I shall be very interested in finding out what your labs find concerning the properties of that metal ore."

Samuel gave her a nod as he sipped from his mug.

"Now, the real reason I am here," she said, turning her attention on me, "is that I need the help of your crew in completing a mission for me."

"Why use us when we have failed to meet your expectations in all these months?" I said, trying to keep my emotions in check.

A sigh escaped her lips as she placed her mug down on the table. Fingers laced together she studied me for a minute before speaking. "I had hoped we had overcome this, but I guess we need to discuss the elephant in the room. Firstly, yes, I killed your former captain. It was not personal. I liked José, I respected him as a captain and leader, but in the last couple of years his judgement had worsened and mistakes were being made.

"Mistakes such as allowing you to live. Mistakes such as

allowing my cargo to be destroyed by the Floating City leader Mr Lee. Mistakes such as antagonising Xcorp. Mistakes I couldn't allow to continue. In your former line of work, Mr Blake, if an employee was not performing then that employee would be fired. What I did was no different, it was only more final."

"All these things you have issues with—the root cause has been me," I said.

"But the responsibility always falls with the leader."

I sunk my nails into the table, wood digging underneath them. Who was this bitch to decide who lived or who died? She spoke about my friend as if he was nothing more than a business transaction that had gone wrong, as if the decision she had made was as simple as wiring money to a business account. She showed no remorse for the things she had done. It was just another business decision to her at the end of the day.

"You may not like what I have said," she continued, "but I see the way your men respond to you. They trust you. They have accepted you as their captain. It has been interesting watching your growth and development. Very interesting indeed."

"I take it this wasn't just a social call to praise me on my new promotion?"

"No, since your little *hiatus* from active duty—"

"Hold up," I said. raising my hand her way; "we are not in your employ, we are contractors that can choose when and who we work for. I know you and José had somewhat of an *understanding*, but look how well that worked out for him. The Junk Yard Dogs aren't yours to command as and when you please, nor are we your personal errand boys."

"I see."

"I only speak the truth, just so we know where we all stand," I said, burying the smirk on my face before it arose fully.

"Very well. As I was saying, since your vacation from Paradise Lost, there have been many attacks on my life and the lives of my crews. Normally this isn't something I would concern you with, but these attacks have been more... organised than I have normally dealt with in the past. I have hunted out all and every source of who and what they are, but they either allow themselves to be killed or take their own lives instead of getting captured.

"I have dug into my resources to find out who they are and the only thing I have been able to find is that they are some sort of group which call themselves the Mercenary Bloc."

"Never heard of them. Have you?" I said, turning to Samuel.

"Only in hearsay and rumour. They are a large secret organisation that operates across the galaxy. There are many cells of the Bloc, some which work together, some of which work against each other, some that stay neutral. No one really knows what their goals are, or who really controls the head with so many splinter cells being active. The only thing they all have in common is wealth and power."

"Which still doesn't explain why they are operating in Safe Haven. I do my best to keep tabs on my enemies or potential enemies," she said, giving me a prolonged stare, "but I have never come across this group—much less had reason to deal with them."

"Isn't it obvious?" I said looking between the pair. "Someone has paid them to kill you. That someone is most likely Mr Diamond. He has the means and the motive."

"You do not pay the Mercenary Bloc. It isn't that simple," Samuel said. "If you own a company they want half. If you can't pay in that way then you will forever owe them a debt which they shall call upon when they deem it necessary—and debts can range from betraying your loved ones to your country. Although not much is known about them, one thing is positive. You only go to the Bloc when you have no other options. It isn't something a person like Diamond would do.

"That way stinks of desperation, and that, he is not."

"I wouldn't be so sure," Isabella said. "There are rumours the old boy is sick or dying and he has partnered with an outside party, someone who has more wealth and influence than him to help him in this coming fight. I know little about this new party, but a few of my birds have been chirping and they say this unknown party is in league with the Mercenary Bloc. That the Mercenary Bloc were brought here because of them."

I passed my hand over my face and breathed out the heavy breath I was holding, "There appears to be a lot of assumptions about who and what we are facing. Knowing you, Miss Ivanov, and how well prepared you are when it comes to knowing your enemy, it speaks volumes about who you are facing."

She laughed softly, like chime-bells dancing in the wind. "I'm afraid you need to change that to who *we* are facing."

Confusion crossed my face as I shook my head. "What do you mean 'we'?"

"As well as attacks on my establishments, the one thing this group has been asking about is the whereabouts of your crew. They have attacked all your known whereabouts in Paradise and interrogated any known acquaintances you may have."

"Why would this group be after us?" I asked.

"It appears, Mr Blake, you have upset the powers that be. So it seems that once again, our fates are tied together."

17

I looked out of my hospital room situated in one of the gigantic trees that graced the city. Like most dwellings in The Jungle it showed that the people worked with the materials around them instead of trying to impose their will upon them. Through a window cut out of the bark, I watched the leaves dance as the fingers of the wind plucked them to a tone that it could hear.

Revisiting the meeting I had with Samuel and Isabella, I gritted my teeth at the predicament I once again found myself in. I had no idea why this group, the Mercenary Bloc, wanted me dead. In my short travels I had never come across them or Mr Diamond, but it seemed fate had put opponents in my way that I didn't ask for.

Not as if I didn't already have enemies who wanted me dead?

Alvis Boman was out there somewhere, waiting, plotting, scheming. He knew Poppy was alive and he would do anything in his power to either destroy or control her and the more time I wasted here, hiding away, the stronger he would become.

I had had enough of this. Enough of wallowing in my self-pity, enough of waiting, wondering, hiding out while other people made decisions for me. It was time we moved. Getting up off my bed, I unhooked myself from the machines behind me as the door to my room slid open.

"What are you doing?" Poppy demanded. "You are nowhere near healed! The nanobots haven't finished patching your forearm together and I would still like to monitor you for any late signs of damage from the virus in your system."

"I feel better than ever. The sleep in a nice comfy bed has done wonders but now we need to get a move on. We can't just sit here and wait for what's about to come. If this Mercenary Bloc wants us dead, it's only a matter of time before they find us here. I have come to love this place, but it's terrible as a defence hold and the people around us aren't exactly fighters."

"I would say it's safer than going back to Paradise Lost. At least any newcomers will stand out like a sore thumb here."

I made my way to the window and looked out. Life below had returned to normal. Mothers walked hand in hand with their children, while they browsed the market stalls that lined the road; groups of men and women alike tended to fruit and vegetable patches dotted around the city. It all looked so calm. So idyllic.

"I would agree with you, but I can't force this place to bear my mistakes any longer," I said, the images of the bodies covered in stained sheets coming to mind. "Paradise is used to violence. It's used to the fighting. It almost welcomes it. But they built this place for people looking to escape from all that. It would be selfish of us to impose that on these people."

Poppy walked up behind me and wrapped her arms around me; resting her head on my shoulder she nibbled my ear as we looked out onto the scene below.

"You still haven't told them, have you?"

I closed my eyes and groaned silently as I thought of something to say.

"It's alright, with all that has been going on I totally understand why you haven't, but—"

"No, why does there have to be a 'but'—can't you just end the sentence there? It was a perfectly good sentence. One of your best even. You could have even shortened it and just said 'I totally understand.' I—"

She bit my ear harder forcing me to squirm in her arms as I tried to escape, but it was like trying to untangle myself from cobwebs made of steel.

"Okay, okay," I said, finally giving in, "you may continue."

"Oh, why thank you, my master, how generous of you to let little old me speak. I shall remember my place next time," she said with a laugh. "All I was going to say, before you so rudely interrupted me, was that eventually you will need to tell them before they start asking questions."

"Why would they start asking questions?"

"Don't tell me I have to have the bees and the birds talk with you? Well, when a mummy bear and daddy bear make love, darling, the daddy bear leaves something inside the mummy bear that grows and grows, making her belly bigger as the days and weeks continue until one day she is ready to give birth to a brand new baby girl or boy."

"I hate to upset you, Pop, but I don't really think that's how it works, I think—ow," I said as she bit my ear once again.

"If you say nothing to the others, it won't take a genius to work out what's happened as my stomach continues to swell."

"Oh."

"What?"

"I don't know, I know this may sound stupid, but I didn't think your pregnancy would work the same as a normal woman's."

"What do you mean—"

"Wait. Wait. Wait," I said hurriedly as I felt her tensed up behind me. "I hate to break this to you, baby, but you're not a normal woman—hell, you're not even human. You're an AI humanoid, and being an AI humanoid, we don't know what is going to happen during your pregnancy or after. Have you given much thought to what our child will be like after the birth?"

"What do you mean?" she whispered.

"I mean, will it be completely human? Will it be a machine? Or will it be a hybrid of both?"

The silence behind me gave me pause for caution. We hadn't spoken much about the future, about what it meant now she was pregnant. It seemed silly now, thinking back on the time we spent together with nothing to do but be in each other's company. We had walked through the trees that surrounded us hand in hand, saying nothing but simply just being.

I had wanted to bring it up and I could sense she did too, but I didn't want to spoil the present with the uncertainty of the future.

But with the arrival of The Lady, that future had been forced on us and there was nowhere to go, nowhere to hide. The only thing we could both do was face it. I smiled and pulled her arms tighter around me.

"You don't have to answer," I said, "it doesn't really

matter now, does it? The only thing I really care about is that my child is healthy and happy. Whatever comes after we can deal with."

"Are you sure?" she whispered.

"You may be a pain in the ass but you're not human and you turned out—ahh," I yelled as she sank her teeth into my flesh and pulled me to the floor where we embraced in a tangle of limbs and lips.

A few days had passed since our meeting with The Lady; it had gone past in a blink of an eye with Poppy and me doing nothing more than taking long walks during the day and having long nights between the sheets. It was nice to not think about anything, but just be with each other. I did my best to shut out the impending sense of doom I felt, but it gnawed at the edges of my thoughts always just out of reach.

I stood at the base of the open cargo doors of *The Kennel* and surveyed the place that had once been our home.

I could almost forgive it for the humidity, the insects, the odour of its population, the food, and the never-ending chaos and ruckus that was the jungle, because it had given me something back that was immeasurable. It had given me peace.

It had taken its pound of flesh for that peace, as I flexed and twisted my newly healed forearm, but I guess nothing worth having comes for free.

Our bags had been packed and we had taken whatever supplies we could onboard. I sipped from a fruit that reminded me of a coconut, its yellow husk-like shell holding a sweet refreshing juice only found in this region of Safe

Haven. The Jungle had so many hidden gems and treasures that I would have to revisit here one day... maybe even settle down with my family. Once I took care of my troubles.

"Will you hurry up! You giant turd," Willis yelled, emerging from the bowels of the ship, "the sooner we get away from this hellhole the better."

"Not all of us wear the same uniform day in and day out," Tuari said, dragging a suitcase that left indentations in the ground behind him. "Some of us care about our personal hygiene and like to wear something different when the mood takes us."

"What a tart," Willis said with an eye roll.

"Plus, I've learned of some great ingredients which will help—"

Willis yawned loudly, failing to cover his mouth. "Sorry, were you saying something?"

"Oh, don't worry, Ginger Nuts, I'll remember that next time you're hungry," he said, lifting his luggage onto the ramp and causing the suspension to bounce.

"Is that it? Is everyone on board?" said Willis.

"No, Poppy said she had to speak to Samuel."

"Oh, for fuck's sake—"

"What's the hurry, it's not like —" I began but stopped when "Poppy accompanied by Samuel and Scarface came into view." Both Samuel and Scarface had bags. That wasn't a good sign.

"Oh, oh, I smell trouble," Tuari said as a mischievous smile broke out on his lips.

The weight that grew in my stomach only grew heavier and heavier the closer they got to the ship. I looked to Poppy as she walked towards me but she only lifted her eyebrows to the sky and continued on walking past me into the ship. It seemed I would have to deal with this myself.

"Erm, did we forget something?" I asked, nodding towards their bags.

"No. You didn't," Samuel said. "We're coming with you."

"Like hell you are!" Willis said, stepping forward.

"We have business that needs taking care of," Samuel continued; "business in Paradise Lost."

"Then you can make your own way there. The ship is cramped as it is already, without having your B.O.-riddled bodies on board."

"I assure you, if there was another way we would take it, but we don't have any aircraft belonging to The Jungle and none of our people really know how to fly one."

"That's because you're a bunch of—"

"Alright, Willis, that's enough," I said stepping in between him and his brother. "I really don't think this is a good idea, Samuel. Once we land in Paradise, our journey continues further afield. We won't be coming back this way for quite some time. So you could find yourself stranded with no way to get back."

"I shall find my way back to the Mother, I always do."

Willis groaned under his breath while I pinched the bridge of my nose. "Look, I really don't think you've thought this thing all the way through," I said.

"Quinton. The Lady has already made the decision. There is nothing we can do."

I closed my eyes and sighed as the weight I felt in my stomach just about drove me through the ground and buried me alive.

"Well then, welcome aboard," I said, trying my best to smile.

18

Thankfully the journey from The Jungle to Paradise Lost didn't take that long, but the tension in the air was thick and uncomfortable, like a wet wool jumper. Willis had stomped off as soon as we took off and shut himself up in his room, not saying a word to anyone. Part of me thought he would have stayed around and looked for any cause to start a fight with Samuel, but I was thankful he didn't.

The dull grey lights of Paradise Lost slowly came into view, and I thought I would have missed it; I thought a small part of me would have welcomed it with open arms. But staring at the ship's viewing screen I felt nothing but regret. We hadn't been back since José was killed and that was my fault because I couldn't face going to a place where I knew I had a hand in getting my friend killed.

The closer and lower we got the more of the borough came into focus and the uglier it became. Compared to the vibrant colours of The Jungle, which was alive with life, Paradise was a grey wash of lifeless buildings that leaned on each other for support.

We finally landed at one of the borough's ship docking stations and I let out a sigh of frustration as Tuari killed the engines and the ship came to a standstill.

"Right, let's get this over and done with."

Bundled in a van with each of us fighting for space, we drove through the streets of Paradise and got reacquainted with the embodiment of an ex-lover who had burned our house to the ground.

"Fuck me! Has this place become more of a shithole since we left?" Willis asked. "How is that even possible?"

Although night, it was still too early for the streets to be as deserted as they were. The only signs of life came from the occasional crack addict or sex worker looking for their next target, their legs shuffling along as if they were zombie extras in a low-budget movie. We passed burned-out cars that were nothing but black metal, and storefronts that had iron bars and security men outside their property giving anything that passed a suspicious look. The stores that couldn't afford protection were closed down or vacant as nothing but bullet-holed walls and broken glass remained of their legacy.

The other vehicles we passed on the road drove in twos with blacked-out windows and slowed down whenever they passed us by, getting a good look at us before speeding off.

"Things... have sure gone downhill around here, and just as I was looking to get into the property market," Tuari said.

A loud crack filled the air forcing Samuel to duck down.

"Relax, pussy, it's just a car backfiring," Willis said.

Another crack filled the air but this time it sounded multiple times.

"Now that, if I'm not mistaken, is an AR-15 rifle. Old school," he said with a manic grin.

"Tuari, swing past The Office, will you. We haven't seen old Jerry in a while and it would be good to catch up," I said.

"But Lady Isabella—"

"Can wait," I said, cutting Samuel off.

"That's the best idea you've had all year, boss," Willis said, giving me a smile.

"Thanks, let's just hope he's open."

The Office was alive with the sound of music.

Gone was the run-down bar front with paint peeling off letters; in its place stood letters that shone with lights and glistered with gold. Potted palm trees lined the bar front as strobe lights shone against the night sky illuminating the darkness with O's that had ties attached to their bases. I could barely make out the entrance as the crowd that stood in front of it heaved with people coming and going, while others stood round tables with overhead heaters and sipped cocktails and smoked everything from cigars to joints.

"What... the...hell?" Willis asked, as we rolled to a stop near the bar.

"Looks like old Jerry has outdone himself this time. Seems some people have gone up in the world as we've been away," Tuari said.

"What has happened to my drinking hole?" Willis demanded, with each word increasing in volume. "This used to be somewhere we could go and have a drink, find out a little bit of gossip and not wait an hour for something to wet our lips—"

"I've got something you can wet your—" Tuari began, but Willis cut him off.

"Instead—instead, this abomination has taken its place. Wait till I see the weaselly assclown—I'm going to use his foreskin as a turtleneck!"

"Whoa, whoa, whoa," Tuari said, holding his hands up, "too much information. Whatever you do in your sexual life is your business, but you don't have to make it common knowledge."

"Why don't you just—" began Willis, but he found himself at a loss for words and instead forced his way out the van slamming his door behind him.

"Why is he so angry? Well, more angry than usual," I asked.

"The Office," said Poppy, "was the only place I have seen Willis happy. I don't know if it's the drink or if it was just the environment, but I actually saw him smirk there once—it was close to a smile but in the end, I think his facial muscles gave up on him."

"The reason this place makes him happy," said Samuel, "was because it's a place like this that Mum was killed at. I remember coming to see him here before I made the journey to The Jungle. Its likeness was so eerie it gave me the creeps. I don't know if he does it to punish himself or just to remember. Either way, I think that is partly the reason why."

Silence filled the van as we all ingested what had just been said.

"Well, I guess we'd better go see what's up and try to stop Willis from killing anyone," I said.

We made our way out of the van and through the crowd,

pushing and shoving people when a polite "excuse me" failed to work. I felt eyes on us the moment we entered the fray. Normally at The Office, there was always a great deal of posturing and mean-mugging between the various crews who frequented the bar, but this felt different.

We were being cased as if we were targets on a job. Targets that had to be taken out.

I caught Tuari's and Poppy's gaze and they each gave me a small nod. They felt it too. If we turned back now, and entered the van, it would cause more of an issue than if we just pretended we hadn't noticed them. Plus Willis was too far ahead for us to escape without leaving him behind.

Ahh, the days when I had nothing to worry about but the font across my spreadsheets.

I would sometimes miss them, but as the adrenaline coursed through my veins making the world around me burst into colour and sound I pushed those thoughts away and smiled. Life was meant to be for the living and there was no better living than trying to outwit a bunch of murderous thugs who wanted you dead.

I smiled as we got near the entrance. Maybe this crew was having a negative influence on me after all.

Four bodyguards that looked as if their suits were spray-painted on blocked out the overhead lights as they towered over the crowd. Willis was in an animated conversation with one that didn't look impressed at how the conversation was going. I say conversation but the guard was being more spoken at than allowed to get any words out.

"What do you mean, not on the list?" Willis said.

"It means what it means, mate, I don't know how many times or ways I can spell it out for ya," said the guard, whose friends had now become interested in the conversation.

"When did this dump become a place with a list?"

The guard gave Willis a shrug.

"Well, it shouldn't matter anyway, we've been coming here regularly since before Jerry was sleeping with that one-legged woman, Sweaty Betty. I've been with this establishment through the thick and thin, and I'm not going to let some juiced-up monkey who can't scratch his ass tell me what I can't and can't do. Now get out of the way before someone gets hurt."

"Listen, mate, the only one who's going to get hurt is you if you don't piss off!" said the guard, advancing towards him.

Willis took a step forward.

"I would do as he says, fire-crotch," said another one of the guards.

"What... did you... say?" Willis asked slowly.

"I said—"

The guard never got to finish his sentence as Willis's bladed hand struck the man's throat causing him to choke on his words. Willis followed up with a stomp to the guard's kneecap popping it out of place before he finished him off with a headbutt.

Shocked silence filled the air as all the guards looked down at their fallen comrade. They should have been paying attention to Willis. They returned their gaze to him to find his hands now filled with his pistols.

"Now, fuck-boys, you have a choice," he said, manic grin plastered on his face. "You can either go inside and get Jerry and let him know we're here, or I can start shooting bits off you until either A, he comes out wondering what the noise is, or B, I clear out all his clientele and he wonders why no one is coming in. So, what's it going to be?"

The guards looked at each other, scowls on their faces, but no one moved.

A gunshot filled the air as the guard Willis had knocked

down screamed in pain. Other cries of alarm joined his scream around us as people pushed and shoved, trying to create some distance away from us.

"Willis!" I said, giving him a look.

"What? He was going for a weapon in his pocket."

"No, I wasn't, you ginger prick, I was going for my radio!" said the guard as he held his bloody wounded hand to his chest and pulled out a small radio with his other.

"Oh... my bad. But you shouldn't really be making sudden movements in a situation like—"

"What the bloody hell is going on!" came a voice from behind the guards. "What's all this noise about?"

Dressed in a pinstriped suit with his bald head shined and moustache waxed to fine points, Jerry looked at each of us in turn with disbelief and a slow-building rage that started from the base of his neck and made its way to the top of his dome.

"Jerry!" Tuari said. "Had a makeover, I see; can't say I approve of it myself, but I always like to see an old boy put his best foot forward."

"What have you gone and done with yourself?" Willis asked "You know that no matter how much you polish a turd, it'll still be a turd."

"What, what... what are you halfwits doing outside my place of business?"

"Place of business?" I snorted, which earned me a stare.

"Yes, place of business. Since you assholes have been gone I updated my lifestyle and my business. This establishment is no longer called The Office, but The Office," he said, saying the last word in a weird accent.

"Sounds pretty much the same," Tuari said, "apart from when you said it the second time you sounded constipated."

"Constipate—listen, this here is the only jam-swinging,

hip-shaking, ass-bumping bar slash club slash restaurant slash gentleman's club there is around. I've paid a pretty penny to get this place how you see it and I will not, I repeat, not, have the likes of you fuckers destroying it."

"When have we ever—" I began, but shut my mouth as Poppy elbowed me in the ribs, as Jerry turned a brighter shade of red. "Fair point. Fair point. Look, Jerry, we just want to have a few drinks, maybe find out what's been happening in town and we'll be out of your hair—" I looked at his bald head, "we'll be gone before you know it."

He looked between us eyes narrowed, lips pressed in a thin line.

"One drink?" he said, single digit quivering in the air.

"One drink," I said, giving him my best smile.

"Fine. You can come in, but he leaves that duffel bag in the cloakroom," he said, pointing at Willis.

I looked in Willis's direction and noticed the bag in question for the first time; about to ask what was inside I thought it best if I didn't. No doubt whatever was in it would only further halt our progress getting inside.

"He will," I said, sending a suspicious glare Willis's way. "Now about that drink."

19

We entered The Office despite the guard's best attempts to argue with Jerry that we shouldn't be allowed in. I offered to pay for the medical bills of the guard Willis had injured but I got a stone-cold stare before Poppy maneuvered me away.

The first thing I noticed when I walked through the doors of The Office was my feet; stopping in my tracks I bounced up and down before slowly lifting one foot then another. I repeated the process a few times before Poppy gave me a confused look.

"My feet aren't sticking to the floor," I said in bewilderment.

She shook her head at me and continued on while I took in my surroundings: velvet drapes hung in front of booths, which gave customers their privacy, while golden ropes partitioned booths off further making them no-go areas for people who weren't meant to be there. Guards stood near the ropes to illustrate the point further to you in case you didn't get the message. A dance floor dominated the centre of the bar with hanging round cages that had women, men, and couples trapped inside, who danced, kissed, and in a couple of cages were doing much more.

"Getting a good look are we?" said Poppy, who made me jump as she appeared at my elbow.

"I was—it wasn't like... Ah, never mind," I said, pushing in between a couple trying to suck each other's faces off.

We continued to follow Jerry through rooms that were nothing but strobe lights, loud music and smoke, while other rooms played soft music and had women who wore nothing but lacy underwear serve men who smoked cigars and drank glasses of whiskey. Finally we entered a small dimly lit corridor that brought us to Jerry's cramped back office.

It was a tight fit but we all managed to get in.

"Jerry, this office is a shithole," Willis said, looking around. "You could have at least gotten yourself something nicer."

Jerry moved a stack of papers, dirty plastic cups and paper plates off his desk to make it tidier, but all he succeeded in doing was clearing one space but cluttering another.

"You've got to make do with what you have in this business," he said, brushing crumbs off his suit jacket. There ain't much space left after all the renovations were done."

"How did you get all this space?" I asked. "Last time we were here, this place was barely big enough to swing a cat."

"Expansion is the name of the game, my old mucker. Now that most of the business owners in this borough are closing up shop, or running for the hills, it leaves discerning gentlemen like myself to buy up as much property as I can for next to nothing. I own everything on this strip, from the restaurants at the start of the block all the way to this bar. Beautiful, really. It almost brings a tear to my eye, to think old Jerry Jones finally has gotten what he's always deserved in this world."

I stopped myself from rolling my eyes. Jerry was as crooked as they came; he would sell his own mother, grandmother, and great-grandmother, after he dug her up of course, to the highest bidder if it meant he could make a profit.

"That's what we wanted to talk to you about," I said. "Why is everyone closing up shop? It's not like Paradise Lost hasn't always been dangerous. Gunfights and shootouts on the street are as common as your watered-down drinks. What's got everyone so spooked?"

"First off, that's a slanderous accusation. My drinks have always been the best in this area—"

"That doesn't say much," said Tuari.

"Anyway," Jerry continued, "people are running because there is a war coming. Hell, I'm looking to get out of town in a few months' time after I've sucked this town dry. Lucky for me the one thing the inhabitants of Paradise love more than a fight is a drink; that's the only reason I'm still in business. You can guarantee three business ventures that will do well in this borough no matter what—sex, drugs, drink.

"You supply one of the three to the pond-scum rabble out there, then you're in profit."

"I thought the upcoming war was meant to be hush-hush," I said.

"Hush-hush!" Jerry said with a laugh, slapping the table. "Who can keep a secret in this borough? Nah, mate, blood has been spilled too regularly on the streets for people not to start taking notice. To be fair, I can't blame The Diamond District for playing their hand. That bitch, The Lady, never knew where the line was. She kept on pushing and pushing. You and I both knew she had sights set on more than just

Paradise, but I think this time she's bitten off more than she can chew.

"With Mr Diamond and Mr Lee joining forces I don't see how she can win. It will only be a matter of time before a bullet finds its mark. If I were you lot, I would part ways with her sharpish, otherwise you may find yourself suffering the same fate."

This was not the news I wanted to hear, especially as we had already made ourselves a target by attacking Diamond's men.

"Alright, thanks for the advice, but before we go is there anything you can tell us about some people who may have been asking around about us?" I asked.

"What... whatever... do you mean?" Jerry stuttered.

"He means," said Willis, "have any nosy fuckers been asking way too many questions?"

Jerry licked his lips as his eyes darted back and forth between our faces.

"Come on, Jerry, how long has this crew supported you through thick and thin? We're not asking you to rat out anyone—just drop a few hints here and there, that's all, for old time's sake," Tuari said, slipping a wad of bills under one of the dirty plates cluttering the desk.

Jerry sucked his teeth as his eyes rested on the bills. "Right, you didn't hear this from me, but there have been a few fellas asking around about the Junk Yard Dog crew. Not your typical men who frequent my establishment either."

"What's that supposed to mean?" I said.

"It means they didn't look like coked-up pimps or drug dealers; they were too clean cut. If I would have to hazard a guess I would say military. Or former military. They were also flashing around way too much cash than was safe. I went to tell them that but before I could they had already smashed the head in of a thief trying his luck with one of their back pockets. Poor asshole didn't know what hit him.

"Shame. Not really his fault; you can't just go round flashing that sort of money and not expected to be robbed."

"Anything else you can tell us?" I asked. "Anything at all?"

Jerry stroked his chin while he looked to the ceiling. "There was something else I found odd—one of the geezers with them had been here before, a wiry bastard with a permanent unshaved five-o'clock shadow on his face and bags under his eyes that you could use for a boxing workout. Ring any bells?"

I shook my head as I looked to the others, but their expressions mirrored mine.

"Anything else about him that may help us?"

"Erm—ah, yes! He was friends with that posh bastard who came here to offer you a job some time ago."

"Mr Grey."

The bottom fell out of my stomach. I had thought he was dead. But if he was alive and looking for me, it could only mean trouble. What kind of trouble would remain to be seen.

20

hundred thoughts leapt for my attention as we made the walk back through the club.

Mr Grey.

The last time I had seen that asshole, I had nearly beaten him to death with a dildo. He had survived according to Edward Thomas, but what had become of him after Edward's death was not something I had given any thought to. Yet now it seemed like old enemies were helping new enemies settle old debts.

We passed through the lounge, where men were being served drinks by women in underwear. I could feel Poppy's eyes on me the whole time as I averted my eyes as best as I could.

Mind elsewhere, it came as a surprise when I saw the quivering handle of a knife embedded into a wooden pole only a few feet away from me. I looked around to see who my attacker was and was graced by the sight of one of the hostesses taking out another knife from one of her bra's cups.

"Where does she find space to keep those—" began

Willis, but had to duck a knife thrown by a different assailant wearing nothing but nipple cups and a g-string.

"Thank you to all the gods and goddesses that have ever existed," Tuari said, clasping his hands in prayer. "I didn't know this was my dream of how I wanted to die, but I now know you have shown me the error of my ways."

None of the customers gathered around the room moved; they instead looked at our attackers as if they were performing some art piece. Another woman reached under a table and pulled out a machete that had been strapped to the underside. Pulling it free she held it above her head. Screaming at the top of her lungs, she came towards me eyes filled with nothing but anger, but she didn't get far as Poppy grabbed her wrist that held the weapon and used her momentum to hip toss her across two tables.

Drinks and bottles flew into the air as she crash-landed in a heap.

The customers' expressions began to slowly change as they looked at each other in confusion. Isn't... this a performance? their expressions said. Shouldn't that girl who was thrown be moving? Should she be bleeding?

Another woman attacked Samuel, who backed away bumping into Willis, who had his hands in this pocket.

"Willis, what are you doing?" I demanded.

"Sorry, I don't fight women—nothing against them, you understand, just it's against my religious views," he said.

"Finally, something we agree on," said Samuel.

They both were backed up in the corner moving left to right as their female attacker did her best to put as many holes as she could in their bodies. As she went for another stab her hand was grabbed by Scarface, who backhanded her across the face, forcing her to spin on her heels before she collapsed on the floor.

Customers looked at each other in increasing panic as more and more of the hostesses produced weapons.

One took off her heels and held them like throwing axes. She slashed left and right trying to embed the steel tips into my flesh. I backed up until my back hit a table and there was nowhere to go; my hand searched the table behind me while I kept my eyes on my attacker. Seeing I had nowhere to go she leapt in for the kill as my hand closed in around a bottle; grabbing it I swung it towards her, catching her on the top of the head.

A dong-like sound echoed throughout the room and she collapsed to the floor in a heap.

She surprised me and got back to her feet, swaying before me, blood dripping down the side of her face. She screamed at me and rushed towards me once again, but my boot connected with her chest and sent her flying backwards, where she crashed into a table.

I stood opened-mouthed as she got slowly back to her feet once again. Eyes glazed over, she took a step forward but stumbled.

"For the City Girls!" she shouted as she threw the stiletto my way.

I dodged out of the way and looked behind me as an anguished cry tore through the air. A man dressed in a fine business suit brought his hands slowly up to his face but didn't want to touch the stiletto sticking out of his right eye. Blood gushed from the wound, and the men who were sitting around him, and everyone else in the room, slowly came to the realisation at the same time that this wasn't some act being played out by the women around them.

"Oh, my god! This shit is for real!" said someone in the room.

"Fuck me! I ain't into no sadomasochism shit," said another.

"Screw this—I'm out!"

That was the last thing I heard as all hell broke loose. Men leapt from chairs and pushed each other out of the way as everyone scrambled for the exits. Pushing turned to shoving and shoving turned to fists being thrown. A man dressed in a fur coat swung a bottle of champagne my way, but he was met with a straight right from Willis that blindsided him.

I looked for Poppy but I couldn't see her amongst the mass of bodies that were fighting for freedom.

I buckled forward as someone landed on my back; slender arms and legs wrapped themselves around me as my near-naked attacker tried her best to choke me. I sunk my chin down and brought my hands up to pry her hands off my neck but teeth sunk into my neck forcing me to scream.

Blood trickled down the side of my neck and onto my shirt as I spun in a circle to try and get her off me.

I threw my head back and managed to hit her face with the back of my head but that only infuriated her further. "Your bounty is mine, bitch!"

"What are you talking about?" I asked.

"Yeah, like you don't know. I'm tired of shaking my ass for these suits."

I stopped spinning in a circle as I felt myself go dizzy. She used that moment of calm to climb like a monkey onto my front. All I saw was fake tan, fake eyelashes, and fake boobs that had come out of their bra as she wrapped her hands around my neck and brought me in close.

I tried to breathe but I couldn't. The harder I pulled

away the more she suffocated me with her breasts. They were everywhere.

What a way to go. This might be every man's dream. To be suffocated to death by a beautiful woman whose name you didn't even know. Tuari would be kicking himself right now if he could see me.

My vision starting to fade, I was finding it harder and harder to keep my legs underneath me as she latched onto me with everything she had.

"Hey! Get off my man!"

That was all I heard before daylight returned to my senses.

It took a minute or two for the stars to clear from my vision but when they returned, I saw Poppy in front of me holding my attacker by her hair. Fire radiated from her eyes and the look of anger and disdain she cast upon the woman made me worried for her.

"Poppy, don't do—" I began, but it was too late as the woman was spun around in a circle and launched by her hair, to spin like a whirling top in the air taking out anyone she came into contact with.

She crashed in a heap of broken limbs amongst her friends, where she twitched once and remained still.

The girls looked to Poppy then towards their friend, then back at Poppy. Poppy didn't wait for them to come towards her. Instead, she ripped a metal pole from the wall and struck the closest hostess like she was a major league baseball player.

Metal hit flesh and bone and metal won.

She ducked an attack and smashed the pole into the woman's leg forcing the bone to jut out of the skin at a wicked angle; the woman didn't even have time to scream as the pole smashed against the side of her head flipping her off her feet.

An attacker leapt from the shadows and jumped on Poppy's back but she ignored her like a parent having a child crawl on their back asking for sweets.

She jabbed the pole into a woman's neck in front of her and I half-closed my eyes and turned away squeamishly as the woman made a gurgling sound from the blood choking her to death.

Poppy swung the pole with force and accuracy hitting anything that came into her path. I watched, half-stunned at the ferocity she was unleashing. It was terrifying to behold.

She dodged everything thrown at her. She moved with just enough speed to get out of the way of anything harmful. She made sure anyone who got in her way stayed down and didn't get back up. It was ruthless. It was efficient. It was not human.

That thought scared me more than anything. But I loved her. I was going to have a child with her. They had attacked us, so who was I to judge how they got dealt with? This wasn't the corporate halls of Xcorp anymore, where I could report someone to HR for a minor grievance. This was life and death and I would have to do whatever I needed to do to stay alive.

Otherwise, I would end up like José.

I saw one of the suited men in the crowd dig into his jacket, where the glimmer of steel appeared; I moved forward but I wasn't fast enough as he raised his gun towards Poppy and fired.

She moved with speed bringing the pole up to protect her. The bullet pinged off the metal.

The man looked at her in shock but it was short-lived. She threw the pole she was holding like a javelin, impaling him to the wall he stood in front of. Blood dribbled from the corner of his mouth as he looked up at her in disbelief. Death came quickly.

Most of the crowd from the room had scattered but by the sounds of it, reinforcements were coming.

"Everyone, let's move out!" I shouted. "Poppy, you've got something on your back."

She looked at me in surprise and remembered the woman who had leapt on her back. She was still attacking Poppy, raining down hammer blows across her neck and back but they did little. Poppy reached around and grabbed a handful of hair before launching the woman into a table across the room.

I held the exit door open as everyone from our crew piled out. Poppy was last to follow and there was an anger in her eyes I couldn't quite place. Jealousy?

"Hey, you okay?" I asked, grabbing her by the arm.

"You've got something on your face."

"What?" I asked, passing my hand across my face and looking at it. Sequins and glitter danced in the light.

"Look—I—there was nothing that I could—"

But my excuses fell on deaf ears as she walked past me out the door.

21

We entered the main part of the building where the dance floor and the DJ's booth were. I had hoped our fight would have gone unnoticed, but the chaos of what we had just left behind had sprinted ahead of us and had broken out amongst the crowd.

Bottles were being thrown, chairs were being swung, and people were launched through the air as everyone fought tooth and nail to escape the madness around them.

Poppy was just ahead of me but I had lost sight of everyone else. There were too many people for the area of space we were in; in typical Jerry fashion he had tried to shortcut on safety and had only thought about profits. I ducked as a bottle sailed over my head and smashed into someone's face behind me.

People had climbed up onto the cages suspended from the ceiling, but they were only meant for a limited number of dancers. The metal chain link ropes that secured the cages to the ceiling were intended more for decoration than function, and I watched in horror as they groaned and bucked under the weight of the customers that latched onto the cages in a vain attempt to escape the stampede. With an attention-grabbing snap, the chains broke free from more than one cage, which came crashing down onto the people below.

Shrill screams and cries of pain filled the air as metal twisted with bone and left many people trapped underneath the structure disfigured or dead.

I grabbed Poppy by the hand and pulled her in close as another cage fell inches in front of us. "Where are the others!"

She scanned the crowd but shook her head as she looked back at me.

Shit!

If we didn't get out of here fast then we would become two of the many casualties happening right in front of us. Most of the crowd were rushing forward and I finally saw the exit in a gap between a set of shoulders. There was our target.

I grabbed Poppy by the hand and moved forward towards it, but screams and a rush of people pushing their way back inside the building stopped me in my tracks.

I heard gunfire and Poppy pulled me down just as bullets tore into the wall above my head.

People tried to leap to safety but bullets tore into their bodies leaving them lifeless on the floor, their vacant eyes resting on nothing but the afterlife.

"What is going on?" I said, fear trapped in my chest.

More gunshots filled the bar, shattering glass and turning it into fine dust. Bullets tore into the leather upholstery of the chairs and sofas that surrounded us, turning them into white piles of cotton candy.

The gunfire continued on, then halted.

Silence swept over the bar as nobody moved. Faces lifted

from overturned tables and peered around corners as everyone held their breath. I inched forward but Poppy latched onto my hand securing it to her. It was like trying to escape from underneath a building. I looked to her and she gave me a single shake of the head.

"I think they're gone," said a man getting up to his feet. He looked to his friends, who looked apprehensive but he ushered them up. "Come on, everyone, I think they're gone. Now is the time to escape."

Others followed his lead and get to their feet. They made a mad rush towards the door but they didn't get far.

Another round of assault fire tore through the windows and the walls. It lifted people off their feet. It made people dance. It splattered blood across walls. I tucked my head under my arms as I waited for the onslaught to pass. The screams weren't as many as the last time and any begun were quickly cut off. This time the firers kept their fingers on the trigger until their guns were empty.

With silence once again returned, I lifted my head up and looked around me at the carnage that had taken place. Bodies smoked and bled out while whimpers and soft moans escaped the people still barely alive.

I looked to Poppy to see if she was OK; she gave me a thumbs up and nodded my way. Where were the others?

I heard a faint tapping and looked to my right to see Willis and Scarface huddled in a corner, backs pressed up against a wall.

"Where's Tuari and Samuel?" I mouthed.

"Outside. Made it. Before firing started," Willis mouthed back at me.

"You... think... they're... okay?"

He gave me a nod and pointed to the computer attached to his wrist. "Fatboy. messaged me. In van."

I let out a sigh of relief. At least they were safe and the only thing we had to worry about was us. Willis waved to me once again and unzipped his duffle bag. He pulled out my shotgun, The Peacemaker, and gave me a wink as he threw it to me. I caught it in both hands and thanked my lucky stars he had been thinking one step ahead and had retrieved our weapons from Jerry's cloakroom.

I looked to Poppy and saw she had unsheathed her blades. She weighed each one in her hand before flipping them back and forth between her hands. It was her signal to show she was ready.

I looked to Willis and Scarface and saw they were both armed. Pistols at the ready, they awaited their fates.

Multiple footsteps echoed on the hardwood outside.

Poppy and I pulled ourselves further into the darkness while shadows danced in front of the exit. They were just outside but were taking their time coming in. I heard a whirring noise that sounded like mini helicopter blades. Willis tapped for my attention and mouthed, "Play dead," before a miniature drone made its way through the entrance.

I pulled Poppy towards me and dipped my hand in a pool of blood on the floor beside me before wiping it along her neck and forehead; I did the same and prayed I didn't catch any diseases. Lying in a prone position with my eyes open and my head pointed towards the entrance, I watched the drone, as still as possible.

It hovered in one spot for a minute or two, cameras on its body rotating while it took in the scene before it.

I took small shallow breaths while I watched it. It came towards me slowly, all its cameras focused in my direction. It moved with a dogged purpose while I tried my best not to move, not to give anything away. I wanted to close my eyes but I knew that would be a mistake; it would be better to see my enemy than be blind and just wait for a chance.

It inched closer and closer towards me and I felt my mouth grow dry as I rested my hand heavily on my shotgun. Miniguns underneath its body began to slowly rotate. If it came any closer, I would be forced to shoot it down before it attacked me. My heart beat faster and faster as I had stopped breathing altogether.

Its guns rotated faster and faster as my hand slowly closed around the handle of my—

A cough to my far right tore its attention in that direction. It moved swiftly across the room as someone got up to their feet amongst a cloud of dust and grime. They coughed and heaved, slapping themselves in the chest. Seeing the drone before them they held their shaking hands up. "Please, I don't know what this is about but I just came here for a night—"

The drone opened fire.

Bullets ripped through the speaker's body, pushing it against the wall where it was held up until the drone finished firing. The body slowly slid down the wall leaving a trail of blood along it. The guns from the drone slowly spun until they came to a stop. It hovered in front of its victim and just watched, then another sound got its attention as a man in a suit drew a pistol and fired its way.

The drone turned to face its new target as bullets pinged off its metal frame. A bullet exploded one of its camera lenses leaving a smoking crater where the lens used to be. The drone staggered back under the assault and the man kept on firing as another bullet punctured another one of its lenses. Black smoke poured from the wounds it suffered until it spun wildly out of control. It smashed into a wall and pieces of metal flew off its body as its attacker walked forward and emptied his gun.

He reloaded as the drone tried to lazily regain attitude and emptied his gun once again into the drone's body until it gave a final whine and lay dead on its side. Nothing moved as the man walked forward and stood over his fallen prey. He brought up phlegm from the pit of his stomach and spat on the drone, giving it a kick in disgust.

"Now, time to get out of here," he said, turning his back on the drone and walking away. He didn't get more than five paces as an explosion tore through his torso lifting him off his feet and throwing him face-first to the ground. A smoking gunshot hole the size of a fist bled out, forming a pool of blood that expanded away from his body.

"If I done told you once, I done told you a hundred times, Grey, when you want a job done right you better off doing it yourself. That's your trouble—always *relying* on machines to do your god damn dirty work for ya, boy, instead of getting up inside the son of a bitch yourself. There's nothing like getting up inside of sumthin', if you know what I mean. Grey," said a booming voice. "Speaking of such, when was the last time you got that licklie old prick of yours wet, Grey?"

"Can we please focus on the task at hand?" said a voice I recognised

"If you ask me, if you got a little something, something, then it would bring some colour to those grey cheeks of yours. That ain't why you're named Grey, was it?"

"Do you think there's anyone left alive inside?"

"Shouldn't be, my boys and that drone done cleared out most of the building."

Footsteps approached the entrance.

I moved deeper in the shadows with Poppy; I looked

towards Willis and Scarface and they were also doing the same. Willis held a flashbang in his hand ready to throw it but I motioned for him to wait; I would give him the signal when I was ready.

"Look, if—and that's a big if—anyone is alive in there me and my boys will take care of them; don't you worry your pretty little head about that."

Men finally entered the bar and fanned out, rifles at the ready. They all wore combat fatigues with a patch saying MB stuck on their right shoulder; a miniature picture of Death dragging someone kicking and screaming was underneath the MB.

Two more men entered last.

One I had seen before, although it felt like a lifetime ago.

Mr Grey had been Edward Thomas's right-hand man. He was still unshaven, still looked as if he had gotten three hours of sleep, and still gave me the impression of a private eye from the 1950s. The other was a hulking brute of a man with a dyed red mohawk and a tattoo on the side of his head of the same image of Death dragging someone away that was on his patch.

"Tex, you sure we have the right building?" Grey asked.

The brute cracked his knuckles as he shifted his bull-like neck from side to side. "Yeah... sure enough."

"What do you mean, *sure enough*?"

"It means what it means."

"Well, I hope for your sake it is because the last two times were complete failures. I thought your outfit was meant to be the best of the best? I thought you were meant to be the people we hired when someone wanted a government toppling, or an assassination made to look like an accident, or a bounty being taken care of. Yet all I've seen is your asses being kicked left and right by this little planet," Grey said.

"Look here, how were we to know this planet was home to nothing but scum? I ain't never seen anything like it. An old lady shot Tuner in the left nut last week. The fucking left nut! All he was trying to do was help the poor bitch across the street, but she shot him and robbed him of everything he had. If we didn't get to him in time she would have finished removing his gold tooth with the pliers she had in her handbag.

"I hate this godawful place. It's unsanitary," he said, taking out a miniature bottle of alcohol disinfectant and rubbing his hands with it.

"Be that as it may," said Grey, "you were paid to do a job by my employer and he doesn't like to be disappointed. It would behoove you to complete this mission, so all of us can get on with our lives."

"It would *behoove* you to lick my balls but that ain't going to happen, so you and your *employer* shall have to wait. No two jobs are ever the same and seeing as you want us to take out two targets—"

"The number of targets shouldn't matter!" Grey snapped. "You are the Mercenary Bloc; I don't see why some Russian bitch and her lackeys should give your organisation such problems."

"Because the woman is trained. Military. Special forces, if I were to guess. She knows how to control a battlefield. She knows how to position and operate men. If I had known her full background then I would have asked for triple the price. There's a reason that little girl runs this here old city with an iron fist. People fear her and for good reason. My only regret is that I didn't meet her sooner; she would have made a great addition to the team and would have made a great mother to our future kids."

Grey pinched his nose as he breathed out heavily. "Getting back to the point at hand. We have paid your fee on top of all your expenses while this job lasts but we have yet to see any results. If what you say about the Russian is true, then I shall give you some leeway for that, but this Junk Yard Dog crew is nothing but a bunch of pirates led by a man who used to be the head of the Commercial department at Xcorp. It really shouldn't be so hard to find them and terminate them."

Tex passed his hand through his mohawk.

"Didn't this so-called office nerd bring Xcorp to its financial knees?"

Grey opened and closed his mouth but said nothing.

"My scouts saw them enter this here building not too long ago; it is why we choose to attack. As you can clearly see everyone is dead, or as near dead as can be. If they somehow managed to escape, or are hiding in this fancy dandy building, then we have a solution for that also. Jason!" Tex shouted over his shoulder.

A short, balding man with glasses came forward. He had a gas tank strapped to his back and he held a long tube that had a nozzle attached to it.

I had a bad feeling about this.

"You know what to do," Tex said, slapping Jason on the shoulder.

I looked to Willis and gave him a quick nod as I lifted my shotgun to my shoulder. Two flashbangs skidded along the floor and came to a rest at the base of Jason's feet.

The group of men turned and run even as someone yelled, "Flashbangs!"

I kept my aim steady and sighted along the barrel. Like

the rest of them, Jason had turned and was trying to make an escape.

Too bad for him he was central to my plans. Squeezing the trigger, I felt the gun buck against my shoulder as the slug fired penetrated the gas tank on his back. There was a whoosh, then an explosion knocked me backwards as Jason was engulfed in an inferno.

22

The blaze was more intense than I had expected.

Fire coated the walls and floor as Jason ran screaming, trying to put himself out but only succeed in spreading the fire further. He bumped into his other teammates, setting them alight as they pushed him away. Screams drenched in fear filled the air as everyone did their best to try and stay away from the human torch.

The flames grew as they touched the alcohol-soaked floor, sending up plumes of smoke that caught in the back of my throat.

I covered my mouth with one of my sleeves as someone pulled me backwards. I couldn't keep my eyes off the carnage I had created. Finally gaining some distance away from the flames, Poppy pushed me into the opening of a doorway that Willis and Scarface were keeping open. I took one last look at the scene behind me and wished I hadn't.

Tex strode through the fire eyes locked on mine as he came to a stop amongst the flames. His eyes glowed with hunger as he licked his lips and gave me a smile that was all predatory.

Flames danced along his arms but he didn't seem to care.

Jason came into view once again still screaming as he rushed towards Tex from his left. Eyes still on me Tex pulled out the biggest revolver I had ever seen and fired a single shot.

It turned Jason's head into mush.

The corpse continued on running until it collapsed some feet away from Tex.

"Whoa, boys! Looks like we done have ourselves a chase! Giddyup. Let's get after them sons of bitches."

I slammed the door behind me as the first men began running towards us.

"We've got company," I shouted as I followed the others. I ran through a corridor until Willis's face came into view, wire in his mouth. He beckoned for me to hurry as he held a door open with his foot.

He closed the door as I went through it and I looked back to see a web of grenades strapped to the back of the door, with a wire going through all their pins. He tied the end of the wire to the door handle and pushed me forward.

We took one turn after the next, my breath catching in my chest as I struggled to clear the smoke I had breathed from my lungs. They rattled whenever I took a lungful of air.

Poppy was stationed at the foot of another door.

"What's the plan?" I asked.

"You're the captain," Willis said. "Shouldn't we be asking you that?"

"Where does this door lead to?" I asked.

"To the roof," said Poppy.

"Well, I guess we're going to be making a rooftop escape."

A Dog Is Born

"Is that the best you can do?"

"Given the circumstances, Willis—"

An explosion rocked the foundations of the building, raining down dust upon my shoulders. No one said anything as we all looked at each other. About to open his mouth, Willis was cut off as another explosion rattled my bones and caused me to lean against the wall for support.

"The roof it is then," Willis said, leading the way.

23

Willis opened the door that led onto the roof slowly and peered out. Our journey to the roof had not been interrupted. No one had followed us and we had heard no signs of pursuit, which put us all on edge.

"Do you see anything?" I asked.

"If you stop yapping and give me a chance to look, then I'll tell you."

I took a few deep breaths as I could still feel the smoke in my chest. Poppy placed a hand on my shoulder and gave me a look of concern, but I smiled and gave her a nod as Willis popped his head back inside.

"It seems all clear, but even if it isn't, this is our only means of escape."

"Which means this is where they'll most likely be looking for us," I said with a sigh.

"There isn't much we can do. We either take our chances or sit here and wait for them to come up those stairs."

"Alright. Message Tuari and tell him to meet us at the end of the strip. We're going to run along the rooftops until we get to the very end of the strip and then make our escape in the van. Simple. Nice and easy."

"When has anything we have done ever been simple or easy?" Willis said with a snort.

"Alright. On three. We run and keep on running until we get to the end. On my count."

Everyone looked at me as I closed my eyes and took in a deep breath.

"One. Two. Three!"

We burst out from the doors and started running along the roof of The Office; I expected gunshots fired our way, but none came as we made it halfway across the roof.

The large gas giant that Safe Haven orbited shone like a marble surrounded by white flakes as it stood out against the black canvas of space. It was breathtaking to behold.

It almost took my mind off the burning taking place inside my chest. Almost.

I must have inhaled more smoke than I first thought as I struggled to take in enough air, legs growing weak by the second. The others were pulling away from me and it was all I could do to bite down on my lip and push myself onward.

Poppy slowed down so we were level. "What's wrong?"

"Nothing," I lied. Even talking was hard.

Eyes narrowed she fixed me with a gaze and looked over my body. "Don't you dare," I hissed at her.

"You're having trouble breathing," she said.

"Do... you know... how... intrusive that is," I gasped.

"Well, if you had told me the truth in the first place I wouldn't have had to scan you, now would I? If it gets worse I can always carry—"

"Do not touch me."

"Don't be so prideful. There is nothing to be—"

"Poppy."

She looked my way.

"No."

She continued to look at me and I could see she wanted to argue, but I wouldn't give in. Call me a fool. Call me a chauvinist pig. Call me a dickhead. I didn't care. I was the captain of this crew and as long as I was still breathing I would see this fight out on my two feet.

"Fine," she said, in the way that all women do, when you know it isn't.

She picked up the pace and left me behind; I looked up and saw Willis and Scarface had already jumped onto the next building along. Poppy quickly followed, which left just me remaining. I shifted gears and dug deep just as the building under my feet shuddered and shook; missing my footstep I fell forward just as the chimney to my right exploded in a shower of brick dust.

I looked up at the section of the chimney that had exploded and saw the marks left by a sniper's bullet.

They had found us.

Getting to my feet, I sprinted forward as the roof erupted with the ricochet of bullets missing their mark; I zigged left and right trying to make myself as small a target as possible. Willis and Scarface waited on the other side for me as they both pointed their weapons off into the darkness but didn't fire.

What were they waiting for!

I forward rolled under some scaffolding as sparks lit up the night sky and got back to my feet as I continued on. They still hadn't fired. The jump to the other building was fast approaching.

"Fire! Fucking fire," I screamed as I waved my arms their way, but they paid me no attention.

I pushed forward with the last bit of effort I had and

leapt off the building and on to the next, just as Willis and Scarface opened fire. I tucked and rolled and got up to my feet. They kept on firing, aiming for targets I couldn't see, but it didn't matter, as the sniper fire had stopped.

"Come on," Poppy said, tugging at my arm.

"Shouldn't we wait?"

"They'll catch up."

We began running as the firing from Willis and Scarface stopped; soon after the sound of their running feet joined us as they drew level with us, then slowly passed us by. A glint of light shone in the building to our far left. I switched to my pistol, which although not great at long-range shooting was better suited than my shotgun. Taking aim I opened fire on the window I saw the light from and was rewarded with the sight of men ducking for cover.

Another round of gunfire opened up around us but we had already crossed over onto the other building.

I saw movement out of the corner of my eye and did a double-take—a group of drones like the one that had first entered into the building were gaining altitude as they made their way towards us.

"We've got company!" I shouted as I switched from my pistol to my shotgun.

"Fuck a duck!" Willis said as he began shooting behind us. "We need to destroy them if we want to escape."

"I count four," Poppy said, bringing her knife up, which deflected a bullet.

The whirring from the drones' blades grew louder as they kept on advancing. I checked the amount of ammo I had in my shotgun and the answer didn't please me.

Two explosive shells. Three slugs.

Damn, I would have to make these count.

"How's everyone doing for ammo?"

"Shit," replied Willis.

Scarface gave me a shake of the head.

"Didn't you pack extra ammo?" I asked Willis.

"Well, *excuse me* for not having the foresight in thinking we would be in a prolonged firefight. I'm sorry, master, next time I'll bring some toilet roll in case you need to take a shit!"

"I didn't—"

The drones opened fire forcing us to leap to the side as their bullets scorched a line down the centre of us. I spun on my heels and took aim and fired an explosive shell that blew apart two drones close together. Glowing red-hot metal collapsed to the ground as the other two drones distanced themselves away from the wreckage.

Willis and Scarface opened fire on the other two but they ducked and dodged, getting hit with the occasional bullet but never taking enough damage to do any lasting harm.

I took aim and went to fire another explosive shell, but Poppy sprinted towards the drones, using her blades as shields as she deflected everything they shot at her. Leaping into the air she somersaulted and brought the heel of her boot down on top of one, driving it to the floor where it crash-landed and broke into pieces.

The other tried to get away from her but she was too quick.

Plunging her blade upwards she stabbed through its body, which resulted in a shower of sparks as it fell to the roof.

She landed lightly back on the roof and caught up.

The end of the strip was nearly coming to an end; we just had to push on and we would make it, we would be home free.

A Dog Is Born

We would—

A thunderous roar of wind and blades drowned out all thought as something that sounded like a beast emerging from hell rose from the road behind us. I turned my head and saw what looked like a red and black mini hovercraft the size of a car gain the level of the roof and begin to pursue us.

Tex leaned out of its open door, one hand grabbing onto the inside of the carriage while his other slapped the top of the vehicle in glee urging it forward. His wide-eyed stare locked onto me and he blew me a kiss and a wink as the craft opened fire.

Assault rifle rounds sounded like thunder as we did our best to escape.

Even if we escaped we couldn't allow that thing to follow us; it would only take a few rounds from its guns and our van would be toast. We had to stop it in its tracks.

"All of you, make your way to the van! I've got this."

"Quinton, no!"

"Poppy, now isn't the time. I'll meet you at the van."

She looked at me eyes full of fear, but I gave her a smile full of confidence that I wished I felt.

"Trust me. Willis, you got any weapons left on you?"

He patted down his pockets and pulled out a lonely flashbang. He gave me an apologetic shrug as he threw it my way.

"Get going," I said as I rechecked my ammo.

One explosive shell. Three slugs. I would have to make it work.

They sprinted ahead of me as I spun on my heel once more and sighted down my barrel. The craft bore down on me determined to finish what its drone kin couldn't. Finger on the trigger I waited. Tex's grin grew by the second. I waited. The bullets flew from its gun, one nicking me in the side. I waited. Tex's head leant back as he roared with laughter.

Then I fired.

The first three shots were the slugs. I aimed one at the cockpit's windscreen, which cracked the screen making seeing out of it impossible. The driver yanked on the controls causing the craft to buck wildly left and right. The next two slugs took out the rear rotors. Black smoke bellowed out of them as the vehicle spun wildly out of control.

The last shot I held and waited until I saw the target I was looking for.

Tex's wild grin still hadn't disappeared but I would give him something to change that. Gripping my gun in place, I locked onto him and fired.

He saw me at the last moment and pushed off from the vehicle as the explosive shell missed him and exploded inside the hovercraft.

The craft went up in flames in a whoosh as I watched Tex's body fly through the air towards the roof with the craft following him all the way down.

I sprinted forward as I tried to put as much distance as possible between myself and the flaming wreckage. I could see the last rooftop that would grant me my freedom up ahead.

The heat from the wreckage singed the hairs on the back of my neck as it crashed through the roof of the building I was on. The blast threw me off the roof and onto the next, where I barely made it.

I tucked and rolled and finally came to a stop. Laying flat on my back I stared up at the sky and thanked my lucky stars.

I got up to my feet slowly; my limbs protested, my bones ached and my joints popped but I was alive. I turned to look at the devastation I had caused and swallowed.

The entire street was up in flames. Every single one of Jerry's purchased buildings was being destroyed by fire.

There would be hell to pay when we next saw him. He would demand we reimburse him. It was a problem for another day; right now, I had to get to the van before anyone else from the Mercenary Bloc turned up.

Walking away I stopped as I heard something that sounded like a growl. I turned and looked behind me but couldn't see anything through the thick smoke. Safety was less than twenty feet away. This was no time to be distracted.

I was trotting towards the edge of the roof when I heard it again. I turned just in time to see a body sprint towards me. It rugby tackled me in the solar plexus, lifting me off my feet and throwing me through the air. The wind was forced from my lungs as I slammed on my back. I forced myself to roll to my feet, avoiding a kick aimed for my head.

Shotgun in my hands I fired at my attacker but forgot I was out of ammo; a swift kick knocked the gun from my hands, where it flew behind me off the roof.

I leapt back to create some distance and took in who was attacking me, surprised to see it was Tex.

"Surprise, motherfucker!"

He lunged towards me, not giving me time to think or recover. Punches came in bunches and I ducked, covered up and rolled with them as best as I could, but the man had hands the size of dinner plates and made of granite.

A blow sunk into my ribs and I bit back a cry of pain as I returned with a head-butt that staggered him backwards. I kept on the attack, kicking him in the inside of the leg then throwing an uppercut that connected with his chin.

It felt like I was hitting stone.

I shook my hands out and leapt back as he swung for me.

"Whoa! Whoa! God damn, boy! They said you were some sort of pen pusher. Where did you learn moves like that?"

I didn't respond as we slowly circled each other. The material of the shirt he wore was charred and frayed revealing burns along his arms and shoulders. His lip was split open where I had head-butted him but despite all that he appeared as happy as could be.

"Not a big talker during combat? A man can respect that. Best to keep the mind focused. Sharp. On point. Best not to get—distracted," he said, kicking brick dust from the roof up into my face.

I closed my eyes temporarily but that was all he needed; diving at my hips he locked his arms around me and picked me up over his shoulder. I saw glimpses of the roof—then the sky—then the roof, as I was slammed back down with him landing on top of me.

I felt something crack in my chest but I didn't have time to worry about it.

His fist descended towards my face and I hip-bumped him off me with all my strength. Rolling back to our feet, I got up and grimaced as a sharp pain stabbed me in the chest.

Damn. I had broken a rib... again.

"Is this really worth the money they're paying you?" I asked.

"Fuck no!" Tex laughed, "but I do it for the love. The love and joy. What's a man without purpose? Nothing, that's what. A man without purpose slowly dies on the inside while he plays golf on the weekend and does gardening. If he feels feisty he may sleep with the secretary or buy a sports car to make him feel something down there.

"Other than that, most men are just waiting to die in this day and age. There's nothing for them to do. Nothing for them to fight for now with war outlawed. So that's why I do this—to feel something between my legs. Feel something big and hard!"

He came for me and I danced and dodged all the while making my way closer and closer to the edge of the roof.

"Are you going to run all day or are we going to do this?"

I stopped and stood still, smile on my face. "Come and get me then, big boy."

Hunger in his eyes he rushed towards me, thoughts only on his prize.

Less than four feet away from me I pulled something from my back pocket and threw it towards him. "Catch!"

Like all humans since the day they were born, whenever something is thrown their way they instinctively catch it without thinking. Tex caught it with both hands and looked down at me as I give him a smile and a salute, then allowed myself to fall backwards off the roof.

The flashbang I gave him exploded in a dazzling display as my back hit the roof of the van and I slid off onto the ground. Hands grabbed me around the waist and yanked me inside as the doors closed and we took off, wheels spinning.

24

I rolled off the bed and placed my hands where my newly broken ribs had been healed by a nanobot chamber that we had taken from The Jungle. Although the technology wasn't something new and had been used on Earth for the last hundred years, the nanobot chamber from The Jungle worked ten times faster than those you would find on any hospital on Earth.

Big enough for a person to enter naked, it contained a gel filled with nanobots that invaded the cells, muscle structure and bones of the body and repaired any issues it found.

I had questioned Samuel as to how The Jungle had improved the invention, and he had spoken about a special team of warriors and scientists who had improved upon the original idea, and were now using the invention to help other struggling planets, who the World Government had left to fend for themselves.

Whoever they were I was thankful to them. Without the aid of their machine I would be most likely out for the count while I recovered, something that I couldn't have.

I stretched my arms over my head and let out a jaw-split-

A Dog Is Born

ting yawn. There was a high likelihood that the flashbang I used on Tex hadn't been lethal. I could always hope that it had been, but seeing how much damage the crazy son of a bitch had taken, I doubted it would even put a hitch in his step. I looked towards the bed and could see Poppy's sleeping form; how much she slept or how awake she was, was something I had tried to work out during our time together.

Did she sleep deeply? Or was she always alert, scanning her environment for any threats?

I walked towards the window and parted the curtains as I looked out onto Paradise Lost.

Even asleep, the borough looked like it had your worst intentions in mind. A thick fog had rolled onto the streets making the image I saw hazy; the lights from the cars and street lights dazzled and glowed as if they were out of focus. Resting my hands on the windowsill I thought, for the hundredth time, about what I had gotten myself into.

Rooftop fights with mercenaries who were trying to collect the bounty on my head.

Getting involved in a war between a man I had never met and an egomaniac madwoman who wanted complete control of a planet.

Fighting a mad genius who had turned himself into a cyborg who wanted the being he created, who I was madly in love with and was carrying my child.

Shit.

I didn't see how this could get any worse. I didn't see how this could be resolved without a lot of dead bodies. I didn't see how this could be resolved without someone I cared about being killed.

I had wanted this. I had asked for this.

When José had offered me a place on the team, I had

taken it with open arms. A chance to visit places I had only dreamed of, a chance to have adventures like I used to read about in books when I was a boy. The chance to really live life.

Yet, here, now, I wondered if I had done the best thing.

If I had given the details that Xcorp had wanted, none of the events which had preceded all this would have happened. But yet... I knew that was a lie. Edward Thomas would have gotten his hands on the details and location of Alvis Boman's prison, he would have freed him, Alvis would have either killed Edward and escaped or they would have formed a pact to work together; either way, Alvis would have escaped.

And by now... he would have already found Poppy, she would be back under his control, a mindless slave only kept around to do his bidding. Plus the war between Isabella Ivanov and Mr Diamond was bound to happen no matter what. Their egos couldn't cope with being on the same planet, no matter how big that planet might be.

Whether or not I liked it, I was placed in this position to do what I could do, to make sure the right people survived. To make sure my child had somewhere to grow up, without the fear of having someone always out to get them—my mission now was to create an environment that allowed them to grow up as normal as possible; what that looked like I didn't know.

All I knew was, it wouldn't be around this mess.

Arms encircled me and pulled me in tight.

"Have I told you how creepy it is that you can move without making a sound?"

"Once or twice," Poppy said, kissing the back of my neck, "but it wouldn't be any fun if I didn't get to see you jump in the air."

"Ha, jump in the air... you must be confusing me, madam, with a man with less courage than I. I stand firm in the face of—hahaha, no tickling," I said, trying to squirm out of her vice-like grip. "OK, OK, OK! Behave, will you?"

She nibbled my ear as she pulled me in close again. "What's on your mind?"

"I was wondering if you dream?"

"I—" She didn't continue as we stared out the window, watching the fog like two lighthouse keepers.

"I didn't mean to—"

"No, you didn't. It's just that I never gave it much thought. Sometimes when I close my eyes I think of things, things which haven't happened yet, or could never happen, things I wished happened, things that scare me, things I wished I didn't see. Is that... dreaming?"

I brought her hands up to my lips and kissed them repeatedly. "God, I love you."

"What?"

"I would class what you are seeing as dreaming my dear," I said. "It means you're alive and kicking, more alive I dare say than most human beings who are existing today."

"Hmm, that's nice to know. Doesn't make me feel any different."

"I don't think it should."

Silence enveloped us once more as we held each other and just were. I don't know how long we stayed like that but I didn't want to break it. I didn't want to leave this room. I didn't want another day to pass. Right now was just perfect.

"So, what are you going to do?"

I closed my eyes as I groaned inwardly.

"Well, as it stands, we have multiple enemies who are looking to take us out. Alvis. Mr Diamond. Tex. And possibly Mr Lee," I said, counting them off on my fingers.

"Don't forget The Lady," said Poppy.

How could I? The crack of the gun that killed José haunted my dreams every night.

"We will have to deal with her at a later date but right now I think it's in our best interest to work with her. With Diamond and Co all working together, we need support. We were lucky back there at Jerry's place but going forward, we can't just rely on luck. Although I hate to admit it, if we want to come out of this alive, we have to rely on her.

"She's got combat skill and knowledge of how to manoeuvre men in times of war. Even Tex respected her. Which shows me right now, I would rather she be on our side than have her against us. To be honest, even with her help, there is a chance we may not win this or come out of this unscathed."

"No one said having the life you wanted would be easy."

I said nothing as I tried to think of a way to bring up the topic that had been preying on my mind since we first departed The Jungle.

"There's something I want to talk to you about," she said, interrupting my thoughts.

I turned around and gave her a smile as I looked at her.

"It's about—it's about, well, it's about your reckless nature."

"My reckless what?"

"Nature."

"Since I have been alive that's one thing no one else apart from you has ever called me. I don't think I'm being reckless. I think I'm doing what needs to be done, so I can get my crew home safe and sound, and in one piece."

"Look how well that worked out for José."

I looked away from her and walked back to the windowsill to lean my forehead against the cold glass.

"I'm not saying this to disrespect his memory, and it's not a slight on the man, but José walked into The Lady's office knowing full well he might not come back out—I think he counted on it. He counted on the fact that he would take the blame and punishment upon himself so we didn't have to. He was fully willing to die for—"

"But that is the job of a captain. To die so others don't have to."

"It isn't and shouldn't be when that person has a child on the way. You are only thinking about yourself—"

"How can you say that? I'm trying everything in my power to make sure you come out of this alive. If I do this right, after this is all said and done, nobody shall be chasing us again. That is why I'm doing this.

"Before it was just for the crew, but now it's for our child as well. They trust me. They may not say it but they do. I can feel it. José gave me this task and I shall complete it to the best of my ability."

"What if... your best isn't good enough?"

I turned to face her with fire in my eyes.

"Then, I can meet my maker with my head held high knowing I gave everything I had. No one can ask any more of me than that. Before meeting this team, meeting this crew, I didn't have responsibilities to test me. I didn't know what sacrifice meant.

"But as a captain, that is all you do— sacrifice so others don't have to. You may not want to hear this, you may hate me for it, but my one and only goal is to make sure you and what's growing inside you stay safe. To make sure my crew is safe. My well-being comes after. That is the cross a captain has to bear and I shall bear it as long as I have to."

She opened her mouth to say something but I walked towards her and kissed her on the lips. "Do not let them break us apart. We are stronger together as long as you trust me."

She looked at me and I could tell there were things she wanted to say, arguments she wanted to have, but none of that mattered because each of us had a part to play, and whether we played it well or not, we still had to play it.

25

I walked down the stairs of our safe house, thoughts of my discussion with Poppy still fresh in my mind. She had gone back to bed and wanted me to join her, but I told her I would be along shortly despite her protests. I had said I just needed to grab a snack to eat and I would be right back, but that was only part of the truth. I hadn't brought up what I had wanted to talk to her about.

I knew what her answer would be even before I approached the subject… yet I couldn't live with myself until I spoke to her about it, until I brought her round to my way of thinking.

Was that selfish of me? Sure, but what other choice did I have?

I was in my own thoughts so completely I didn't realise anyone was in the kitchen until Willis and Tuari came into my view; spoons halfway to their mouths they both stopped and looked my way.

"Did I interrupt something?"

"Nah, lad, just trying to solve life's problems. Why don't you take a seat?" Tuari said.

I took a seat at the kitchen table while Tuari placed a bowl in front of me that had a brown sticky-type cake with what appeared to be custard drizzled over it.

"Sticky pudding," I said, scooping up a piece and placing it in my mouth. "I didn't know anyone apart from my mum knew how to make it. It's an old traditional British dessert that has fallen by the wayside."

"That it is. That it is," Tuari said. "In my travels, I tend to come across old cookbooks and I like to make forgotten dishes. Some come out great while others are destined for the bin. Anyway, how come you're up? Thought you would be enjoying the fine comforts of your woman."

I smiled as I scooped another piece of pudding into my mouth but said nothing.

"Don't tell me there's trouble in paradise? No pun intended," Willis asked. "Although you two are living in sin, not being married and whatnot, I would hate to see the happy couple break up."

I looked between the two, opening my mouth, but a rush of emotions surfaced that I couldn't quite put any words to. Shaking my head I spooned another piece of dessert into my mouth. Seeing my reaction Tuari nodded his head and walked over to a cupboard underneath the sink and rummaged in it before pulling out a bottle of rum.

"I think this shall be needed," he said, placing the bottle between us. I picked up the bottle and read the label, Beckford's Rum & Caramel.

Willis looked at the bottle in shock before turning his attention back to Tuari. "Where the hell were you keeping this?"

"I've got bottles hidden around multiple safe houses and around our ship *The Kennel*."

"Why?" asked Willis in disbelief.

"So your drunk ass doesn't drink them all, that's why. They are special reserves meant for special moments. Now," said Tuari, placing three glasses with ice in front of us and uncorking the bottle, then pouring generous amounts in all our glasses, "let's toast to better times, let's drink to the ones we have lost and let's drown our worries until the sun has come up."

He lifted his glass in the air and we all followed, clinking them together before we took a long sip.

Hints of honey and spice danced on my tongue as I licked my lips and took another stomach-warming sip. Placing the glass down on the table I looked at my hands as everyone kept on drinking and talking.

"Poppy's pregnant."

Silence greeted the statement as they both stopped talking and turned their attention on me. Neither said anything.

"We've known for some time... we've—shit, it's complicated but when Alvis created her he gave her all the necessary parts to reproduce, I guess. Don't ask me for the details, don't ask me how it works, but I'm guessing it's a similar procedure to in-vitro fertilisation," I said with a shrug. "But that's just a wild guess, all I know is she's pregnant with my child."

They both looked at me, mouths agape, before they turned to each other. Neither said anything as they locked eyes; in unison they shook their heads and took a swig from their glasses then turned to me.

"We plan to keep it, I mean, I think we do, we haven't really spoken about it all that much with everything that's going on, but I guess yeah, we should keep it, I mean we are going to keep it, it's a miracle in itself and I couldn't be happier but—will you two fuckers say something!" I said looking between the pair, tired of rambling, "instead of just sitting there and looking at me."

Tuari passed his hands over his head and uttered a sigh. "It's not that we're not happy for you, lad, don't take our silence as that, but you realise what this means, don't you? Everything changes. Not just for the two of you but for the galaxy. Your child will be the first of their kind, a hybrid between man and machine, not created like Poppy, or designed like Alvis, but born.

"Born just like you and me. They shall be the first of their kind, and when they grow up and have children of their own, they shall be creating something that is both exciting and scary. Another species. Similar to human beings, but different enough that they are separate.

"I don't know how humanity will react, but if history teaches anything about how humanity reacts to something it doesn't understand, then I fear for your child.

"If they're lucky, they shall live their lives unnoticed and unharmed, but when, not if, they get discovered, then they shall forever be persecuted, hunted, experimented upon; their lives won't be easy. Just like every minority that has been enslaved and won their freedom—they soon found out although not in chains any longer, being truly free takes generations.

"It may take longer than that for what you're bringing into the world to be accepted by humanity, if ever."

I sipped at my drink and took his words in. I hadn't thought about the future—with so much going on I was only focused on the present—but what he said was correct. If my child or even children hid and didn't reveal themselves to the public, then maybe they could have a normal life, whatever that meant, but what would happen to future generations, what about their children's children? People always said it wasn't the big acts that changed the future but the simple things, a word spoken here, a turning taken instead of going straight, but once my child was born I was dropping a nuclear bomb into the rippling waters of reality and hoping for the best.

This act, this decision to have this child would be felt for hundreds of years to come.

Yet what was I to do?

I had made my mind up to have my family no matter the cost.

Even if it means war or the end of humanity as you know it? said a little voice I refused to listen to.

"You've been quiet," I said, looking to Willis. "Nothing to say?"

"I want to be this child's godfather."

"What?" Tuari and I said in unison.

"You dickheads heard me, I want to be this child's godfather. Nay, I will be this child's godfather. What you have done, I admit unknowingly, is create a miracle. A miracle that hasn't been seen since the time of Jesus Christ himself. You have created a being that is not of this world. That is more special than any black hole or dying star.

"You have created a new life never seen before. You shall bring a being into this world that may truly be seen as a god to some people, and because of that, this child will need guidance—"

"From you?" I said with raised eyebrows.

"Who better?"

"The old hobo down the street," said Tuari, "or better yet —you could leave the child in The Jungle to be raised by a pack of wolves, and it would have a better chance of being brought up to be a balanced human being."

"Joke all you want, but I have made my mind up on this.

This child needs to be taught the lessons not only from religion, but from philosophers, writers, musicians, and any great teachers and thinkers from down the ages. Whether or not you like it, this child is important; they will shape the universe around them for better or for worse and for that outcome to be something other than a tragedy, you must prepare them as best as you can. To be the best they can.

"You need to create a leader, a thinker, a visionary, a carer, a fighter, otherwise the universe will impose its will on their young mind, creating something you never envisioned.

"It's your job as a human. But more importantly, it's your duty as a parent."

I stared at Willis opened-mouthed, not knowing what to say, but knowing he was right. Why didn't I think of that? Why didn't I see the bigger picture?

Tuari poured us all another drink and slapped Willis on the back. "My word, Ginger Nuts, if I was a woman I would be all over you. To think something as brilliant as that came out of that foul hole you call a mouth."

"You're right," I said, giving him a nod. "I've been too short-sighted in not thinking about the future."

I took another swig and looked at them both. I had been expecting anger, confusion and maybe even disgust, but I got none of that. All those fears I had about telling them were unwarranted. I just had to trust my crew and have faith in them not to judge me.

"I want to thank you all. I want to thank you all for accepting me as one of your own, I want to thank you all for not judging me, not judging us. I know things didn't get off to a great start, you dickheads were trying to—hell, you did kidnap me, but I'm happy how it turned out. I'm sorry how things ended with José. If I had the power to change the outcome, I would have. That man gave me this life, he brought Poppy into my life and for that, I am forever grateful, " I said, looking each of them in the face before I continued: "I knew nothing when I first started—"

"Still don't," said Willis.

"But I was determined to learn—still am. I never wanted to let José's hope of what he saw in me go to waste, I never wanted to just coast on by, I don't want what happened to him to happen to anyone in this crew. I know that may be out of my control, but I swear on my unborn child I shall lay down my life before anyone on this crew. But because of that, I need both of you to make me a promise, I need you to swear to me, you shall look after my child if anything happens to me, and I need you to swear to me, you two will try and keep Poppy out of danger."

They both looked at each other before speaking. "The first promise goes without saying," said Tuari; "your child is our child. But the second promise... that woman has a mind of her own. I know you want to keep her out of harm's way to protect her, but she's the greatest weapon we have. It would be foolish not to use her."

"I do not want to rely on her to get us out of trouble, nor do I want to place her in danger just because she's powerful. There's two of them now I have to think about, not one. And something tells me that's what everyone wants, to use her for their own means. Alvis is waiting in the wings till he has her back under his control or till he destroys her; and The Lady, well, she hasn't brought it up yet, but I believe she'll want to use Poppy so she can win this war."

"Speaking of madam," said Tuari, "do you have any idea what you're going to do in regard to her?"

There was that question again. The question everyone wanted me to answer. The question I didn't even have an answer to myself.

"Like I told Poppy, we have enough enemies looking to take us down and not enough alliances to back us up—"

"If you're thinking of working with that cunt—"

"What other choice do we have?" I asked Willis. "If you've forgotten who we're up against then I'll remind you. Alvis Boman, a crazed genius who's turned himself into a cyborg, and we don't know where he is, Mr Diamond, the richest and most powerful person on Safe Haven. Mr Lee, the second richest and second most powerful person on Safe Haven. The Mercenary Bloc, led by Tex, who has a fuckload of guns and a fuckload of men.

"If we add Lady Isabella Ivanov, then we might as well give up now."

"In any alliance, there must be a level of trust for it to work," said Tuari.

"I agree, but this is what we have. So tomorrow evening Samuel and I will visit her and hash out the details on the next plan of attack. A plan that doesn't get us all killed."

They both looked at me and shook their heads but I held firm. This was the best course of action we had. This was the only way to survive. I just hoped I lived long enough to be proved right.

26

Samuel and I drove in the Ford Mustang Mach 1 through the streets of Paradise. An argument had broken out when I had informed the crew that The Lady only wanted to see me and Samuel, and that the rest of them would have to stay behind. This had been met with silent stares and a nod from Tuari and Willis, but Poppy hadn't been so easily won over. The arguing continued all the way to the front door, until I silenced her with a kiss and promised her I would return.

A look that said this conversation was far from over was plastered on her face as I closed the door behind me.

The rumble from the engine brought me back to the present as we crossed a bridge that gave us a view of the setting sun. It was pretty enough to make even the grim streets of Paradise bearable.

After an hour of twists and turns and travelling back on ourselves and triple-checking we weren't being followed, we parked in an alleyway near our destination and got out.

Turning off the ignition I looked to Samuel. "You ready?"

"This is just another type of jungle. The only difference is the animals here are more unpredictable."

"I abide by a simple rule when in Paradise Lost: if it smiles, it kills," I said.

We got out of the car and Samuel looked back at it, concern lacing his features' "Isn't it going to get stolen?"

"They can try," I said with a laugh as I made my way out of the alleyway. I looked in the distance and could see the glowing lights of The Lady's residence. With a deep breath I looked to Samuel then gave him a head nod as I stepped out of the alleyway.

The short walk took no time at all and before long we were approaching the grand-looking Art Deco building with the words Hotel Moscow above it.

They shone like stars in the night as we made our way towards the entrance.

A small army of guards was gathered around the front; sunglasses on their faces acted like Xray machines that scanned for everything from concealed weapons to detecting whether a person's resting heartbeat was abnormally high, indicating they were likely about to act out violently, were fearful or hiding something.

I stopped a hundred feet from the entrance and just stared.

This was the first time I had been back to this spot. This was where it happened.

This was where José Battle had been killed.

I stared at the area in front of the hotel, which hadn't been marked or laid out differently, which hadn't been given any plaque to commemorate the event. His blood had just been washed away and allowed to spill down the drains and gutter as if it meant nothing. It wasn't right. To have the event erased like it was just another day—a hand tapped me on the shoulder and I turned to see Samuel looking at me, concerned.

I looked down at my hands and realised I had been clenching them so hard that my nails had bitten into my palms.

The guards around me all had their hands on their weapons as they regarded me with interest. Taking a deep breath, I calmed my racing heart and gave Samuel a smile and a nod and continued on.

I had counted up to ten guards before they stopped me at the door, but there were easily double that number plus snipers on rooftops and men hidden in plain clothing lounging on the streets around the hotel. It appeared Lady Isabella Ivanov was taking the threat to her life seriously.

The guard who had stopped us looked us up and down slowly before speaking. "Have you got a room or appointment reserved here?"

"That's a first," I said.

"A lot of changes have taken place in and around Hotel Moscow, all for the benefit of the customers, you understand."

"You must have some important customers staying here," I said, waving at the guards.

"That is not your concern. Now, I must ask again, do you have a reservation—"

"It is okay," said a voice, cutting him off.

Vlad walked through the entrance of the hotel in a grey suit, lifeless dead eyes scanning my face as he walked towards us. His hard face showed little as he stopped a few feet away from us.

"He is expected," he said, before turning on his heel and walking back the way he came.

"Into the lair we go," I said to Samuel with a flick of the hands. "After you."

We followed Vlad through the entrance and onto marble floors that stretched out before us in all directions. No matter how many times I visited this place it still awed me. Chandeliers hung from the ceiling and reflected light dancing along a ceiling that was a sculptor's dream; polished oak was used for the staircases and bannisters gleamed, and in the centre of it all stood a cherry blossom tree that always appeared to be in full bloom no matter the season.

It gave the visitor a feeling of inferiority—that they didn't belong here and were only passing by.

Our feet echoed along the floor as I took in the empty sofas and bar stools that had been filled with customers on my last visit.

"Sure is quiet around here," I said. "Been having a rough few months?"

"Some seasons are busier than others," said Vlad.

"Hmm, interesting. Very interesting," I said, drawing out my words.

Vlad stopped dead, staring straight ahead. We stopped a few feet behind him.

"I have promised Lady Isabella Ivanov I shall not harm you. She has repeatedly told me of your value to our organisation and how greatly you can further her dreams, but I fail to see it. I fail to see anything more than a man who hasn't suffered like we have. Who unlike us hasn't fought and bled for everything that wasn't given to him.

"You, Mr Blake," said Vlad, turning on the spot and looking me dead in the eye, "are a man who should be dead.

You have no useful skills. You are a burden upon the people who follow you, but because of them you have somehow managed to gain some measure of—"

"Hey, fuckface!" I said, taking a step forward. "If I remember correctly it was I who got the drop on you and your master before you could take that hammer and sickle out of your ass and do anything about it. Little old me, who showed your big bad boss mercy. Now, if I recall rightly, your master gave you a job to do, to escort men who are *your betters* to meet her.

"So, *why don't you do as you have been tasked* and lead the way," I said with a shooing motion of my hand.

Samuel's gaze flicked nervously between the two of us as we held each other's gaze. If this asshole thought I would be spoken to by him like that, then he had another thing coming. I was the captain of my own crew. A crew that deserved to be showed respect.

"Eventually, I shall do the same to you as I did to your former captain," Vlad said before he turned away and resumed walking.

I stood rooted to the spot watching his back grow smaller and smaller. Of course there had to be a shooter. There had to be someone who pulled the trigger. Who better than The Lady's right-hand man?

Why hadn't it occurred to me until now?

A hand touched my shoulder and jerked me out of my thoughts. Looking sideways, I met Samuel's concerned gaze.

"Shall we?" I said.

He gave me a nod but still looked at me as if I was about to explode any minute. With a smile and a nod I led the way.

We continued walking until we reached a set of ornate

gold doors carved in the shape of flowing water. Bullet holes graced both doors. Vlad stood to attention holding one door while we approached.

I allowed Samuel to go in first while I stopped and looked Vlad in the eye. "It is good to put a face to my friend's killer. It is something I shall use in the future."

"As you should," he replied.

I walked on through and entered a room whose high ceiling had stained glass embedded in it that depicted a scrawny old king sitting on a throne while Death knelt before him. Behind the king, an oak tree stood tall and proud—skulls decorated its branches like hanging fruit.

Lady Isabella Ivanov stood in front of a table that took centre stage in her office. The red leather chairs and drinking cabinets had been pushed to the furthest reaches of the room. Holding a pointer she moved miniature pieces across the table. As I made my way closer I saw the table was actually a map of Safe Haven. It displayed all four boroughs across the table, with miniature soldiers and ships positioned at certain points along the map.

The Diamond District was the most heavily manned. Its glass miniature soldiers covered all entry points into the borough. The closest borough that bordered its lands was The Floating City, but on closer inspection, I noticed the waterways of The Floating City also snaked through some parts of The Jungle. Its waters stopped just on the outskirts of Paradise Lost, but it was still close enough to give any leader sleepless nights. A few miniature soldiers were placed strategically along the river, giving Paradise some protection.

The blue miniature forces of The Floating City were scattered across the board, unlike The Diamond District's concentrated force. The Floating City's forces were spread thinly all across the planet. Their numbers were fewer than Paradise City's and The Diamond District's, but they were a large enough force to cause worry.

My eyes travelled to The Jungle on the map and I saw it was missing all its own forces. Samuel stood next to me and his face greyed as he saw that there were forces in his borough, but they belonged to The Lady. Red miniature pieces of The Lady's littered his borough, as well as a few pieces belonging to Diamond that were just outside The Jungle's borders.

Eyes travelling across the board, I noticed that here and there, a stray red piece dotted far-flung locations across Safe Haven or deep within enemy territory. It appeared The Lady had some spies well placed.

"What do you think?" she asked.

I took a step back and really looked at the board from an outside perspective. "In all honesty? You're fucked."

She looked up at me sharply but waited for me to continue.

"You are fighting two opponents with a limited number of resources. The first rule in winning a war is to have the bigger army. The second rule is to have the home advantage. The third, be on a superior terrain to your opponent. If you attacked Diamond head-on, he has the luxury of keeping his forces in one place while he endures a bloody siege, which becomes a waiting game of whose resources can outlast whose. By all counts, he wins that battle.

"But even before you get to him, you have to deal with all these little scattered forces of Mr Lee, who will no doubt be instructed to pick you off while you make your way across Safe Haven.

"If you decide to stay put, then Diamond will instruct Lee to use the waterways to first take The Jungle then slowly push his forces all the way until he gets to your borders," I said, moving all the blue pieces until they surrounded Paradise.

"While Lee's forces keep you in place, it won't take long for Diamond to join the party, effectively doubling the forces you are now facing. With two opponents battering down the door, I don't rate your chances of survival high. So like I said earlier—you... are... fucked."

"I think you mean *we* are fucked, Mr Blake," she said with a smile.

I chuckled, "I guess you're right, Miss Ivanov, I guess you're right."

"We are all in this together, I know blood has been spilt between us but this is not the time to hold such grudges. I'll come right out and say it, Mr Blake, I need your help. Just as much as you need me."

I was taken aback by her level of honesty, but then again I had never known the woman not to be upfront and honest about her intentions. If there was one thing I could say about her, you knew where you stood with her, even if it was the deep blue sea and she was a shark swimming below.

"So what do you propose we do?" I asked.

She tapped her finger against her lips before pressing the screen of the table, which brought up holographic images of me and Tex fighting against a smoky backdrop on the roof of a building. The image looked like something out of a movie. Determination was chiselled in my jaw, while a wolf-like smile graced Tex's face. Blood red flames licked the night sky behind us.

"First, I must congratulate you on smoking out our home intruders. I had been unable to get any surveillance on this individual for some time, but less than a handful of hours on Paradise soil and you have done a job my men couldn't complete in months. You see, Vlad," Lady Isabella said, pointing his way, "you must have more faith in our friend here."

The penny dropped.

"You—argh!" I said, biting my fist as I paced up and down. "You used me. You used me as bait. That's why it was so urgent to have this meeting here, when you could have just as easily told me what needed to be said back in The Jungle."

"I admit, that was part of the reason but I didn't have as much information then as I do now, so I couldn't make an informed decision on the best course of—"

"My men could have died!"

"But they didn't."

"That isn't the point!" I said, slapping the table.

Silence descended upon the room as Vlad moved closer in my direction, hand under his jacket.

Lady Isabella said nothing as she walked towards the drinks cabinets and picked up a bottle of vodka. "Would you like a drink?" she asked.

Samuel and I remained silent.

"I highly recommend it. This isn't the cheap knockoff stuff they serve at The Office, I imported this from Russia; cost me a pretty penny but it was worth it. No? Very well," she said, pouring herself a half a glass full. Taking a sip she made her way back to us.

"It seems that you think, Mr Blake, this is some sort of partnership—some alliance. But you are mistaken. The simple truth is you work for me. Much like Samuel here. Although he runs The Jungle, it's only that way because I allow him to. Much as I allow you to still set foot in my borough. So in the future, I would suggest you watch your tone—"

I chuckled; I couldn't help myself. Despite the situation, despite being unarmed in hostile territory, despite having a trained killer less than ten feet away from me with his hand on his weapon, I shook my head and just laughed.

"Do tell us what is so funny, Mr Blake." she asked.

"You..." I said, pointing her way, "you don't get it, do you? You have no power over me or my crew. José may have bowed down to you but I am not him. My days of laughing at the boss's jokes are long gone. If you need my help, then this has to work as an *equal* partnership, otherwise I wish you the best of luck with this upcoming war of yours," I said, making a move to leave.

"You believe I would allow you just to walk out of here?"

"Of course," I said, turning back to look at her.

"A potential enemy?"

"I am only an enemy if you make me one."

"In that case, I should kill you here and now and be done with it."

"But you won't," I said, walking back to her, "not with what you know, not with what would come after you if you ever harmed me."

"Ah yes," she said with a sly smile, "the female AI. I wondered when you would play that card."

"We must do what we can, to survive in this cruel galaxy. By whatever means we have."

She took another sip from her glass before turning her attention to Samuel. "What say you?"

Samuel looked between the two of us with a look that said he would rather be anywhere but here right now. He pulled at the sleeves of his tunic. "I say you need all the allies you can recruit. You have enemies within your walls and far superior ones gathering on the outside. To ostracise or antagonise anyone now over pride may very well be your downfall."

"And your thoughts on the situation here," she said, gesturing to the board.

"I would rather we do our best to avoid war at all costs. Violence should be man's last resort, but seeing as man is ignorant of the harm his ways cause others, I know whatever I say will fall on deaf ears.

"So the only option I say to take is one that leaves the fewer casualties. You have a lack of numbers, firepower and resources. When a state is in your situation, the only choice they have is guerrilla warfare and assassination. Cut off the head and the body will follow."

"Hmm, interesting that I would agree with a man such as yourself, Mr Moor. But you are right on all counts. The only way we can win this thing is by guerrilla warfare and assassination. That is why Diamond is using this Mercenary Bloc; they are a separate entity to his forces so he can claim ignorance. No one has declared open warfare yet and I am still in talks with the man, but he denies any knowledge of this Mercenary Bloc, stating it must be one of the other crews in Paradise that has hired them.

"If they fail, he loses no face and can still keep up the front he wasn't involved. If they are successful in taking me out, then he can swoop in here unopposed. I will not let that happen.

"Mr Blake," she said, turning towards me, "I apologise for using you as bait, but if you had known of my plans, then you wouldn't have acted natural and our mercenary friends would have known something was up. I can't say I will not try something like this again in the future, but what I can say is that you will always be highly reimbursed for your time and effort."

The computer on my wrist vibrated, notifying me of a deposit that had been made into my bank. Clicking on the message, I saw a large sum that had been paid to our company account. It was a generous gesture to smooth relations, but I wouldn't allow it to blind me to the fact that once again I had been used.

"Apology accepted and thank you for the payment. Now, if you don't mind me asking, why are we here?"

"Simple. I want you to kill Mr Diamond and Mr Lee."

27

I looked at her, brows knotted in confusion.

"Excuse me?"

"You heard me clearly enough, Mr Blake, I want you and your crew to assassinate Mr Diamond and Mr Lee. I don't care how you do it, as long as you do it. The rewards for completing the task shall be unlike anything you have ever—"

"The Floating City," I said, crossing my arms over my chest.

"The Floating City?" she asked, this time confused.

"If you want this job done, then I want The Floating City."

"Don't be absurd!" said Vlad. "You should be grateful—"

Soft laughter, hidden behind a manicured hand, came from Lady Isabella as she looked at me with mischief behind her eyes. They were the eyes of a cat who had released its prey and was now being entertained.

"Oh my, oh my, Mr Blake. I am so glad you took over the role as captain from José. Although I never had any complaints towards the man—well, just the one that proved fatal—he never had your ambition. He never wanted more. He was a man who was okay with his lot in life, he was a working dog who enjoyed the work more than the reward.

"But you," she said, shaking her finger, "you keep on surprising me. From the outside you appear nothing more than a simple man, but that is only a mask. No wonder the female AI become intrigued by you. Oh my, oh my, what games we play."

She downed the contents of her glass as if it was water and she went to the cabinet to pour herself another. This time she sliced a lemon and dropped it into the glass. "Tell me," she said, sucking on her fingers, "why I should even consider this request."

"Because I'm doing all the work. With Lee and Diamond out of the way, there's nothing standing in your way from claiming their boroughs as your own. You already have Paradise Lost, and I expect a woman such as yourself would want to call The Diamond District home, and let's face it, this borough doesn't exactly scream comfort and luxury. Which leaves The Floating City. For you to control that much land would leave you defenceless against the vast amount of crews who call this planet home. The one thing you can guarantee when the head of a state gets toppled is a power vacuum for the scraps that remain.

"Now, you already have an alliance with The Jungle; wouldn't it benefit you to have one with The Floating City as well?"

"Having it all to myself sounds better."

"Managing all that space, all those people...don't lose what you have taken before you have had time to make it yours."

She regarded me with a narrow gaze before looking to Vlad, then Samuel.

"What are your thoughts on this, Mr Moor?" she asked.

I looked to him and held my breath; I was pretty confident he wouldn't object to my idea but you never knew. I had come to see Samuel as something of a friend; not a close one, but enough of one I knew he wouldn't stab me in the back.

"I think it's a bad idea."

I stared at him open-mouthed in disbelief. The little shit was going to sell me down the river.

"Ohhh," said Lady Isabella, "I knew it was a great idea to invite you two along. Please explain yourself to the room, Mr Moor. We are all waiting on tenterhooks."

Samuel looked at me before looking down at the floor. I could tell he was trying to gather his thoughts but all I could do was try and suppress my rage as I waited for him to talk.

"I know you think I am betraying you, Quinton, but you have no experience in ruling a borough. Especially a borough as complex and diverse as The Floating City.

"Mr Lee has been in control of that borough for decades, decades of contracts, spies, and underlings who all report to him. To think you can just take over that is both ignorant and unwise. Ruling a borough is being everyone's first call when something is wrong and last call to share any good news or get any thanks. People will depend on you for—"

"Thank you for your vote of confidence, but my mind is already made up. Those are the terms," I said, facing Lady Isabella. "You can either take it or leave it."

"I shall have to think—"

"There isn't time for that. The enemy is at your door as we speak; if you want our help it's now or never."

She tapped her finger against her lips, eyes looking through me as she thought of what to do. I knew my demands had been unreasonable, but it was a game I was willing to play to ruffle some feathers and get some much-needed revenge on the man who was responsible for José's death.

Plus, we would need a new home that we could easily get lost in after this was all said and done.

"Alright, Mr Blake, I'll agree to your terms. But you won't get our reward unless the job is completed," she said, holding out her hand.

"I would need a signed contract stating that fact before the day is over," I said, walking over to her and shaking her hand; "also as much information relating to Mr Lee and Mr Diamond's movements, personnel, alliances, etc., etc."

She smiled at me. "You may be wrong about him, Mr Moor. He seems to have a firm grasp on what a leader should ask for relating to whatever deal he's about to agree to."

"Is our business done here?" I asked.

"With you, yes. But I need to discuss something with Mr Moor in private. You can wait in the hotel foyer."

The colour drained from Samuel's face as he opened his mouth to say something but thought better of it. I gave both of them a firm nod and left the way I came.

I nursed a drink while I waited for Samuel.

I had the hotel bar all to myself; no one had come in or left since I had arrived. A single bartender had been cleaning the same glass for the last twenty minutes, while he did his best not to look at me. I toyed with my drink and swivelled back and forth in my chair while I allowed my thoughts to dwell on the conversation I just had.

My goal wasn't to rule The Floating City. The thought had never crossed my mind.

But seeing the prominent smirk on the face of The Lady had brought up everyone that had been involved in José's death. It wasn't just her; it had been Edward Thomas and Mr Lee. I had dealt with Edward but Lee was still running around, forcing people into debt by cheating them at his casinos and then turning that debt into slavery. He was a man who had cheated and double-crossed us, while he profited off our ruin. But he would soon pay for that error in judgement.

The doors behind me opened and Samuel stepped out.

He walked towards me on unsteady legs as if he had just been told someone close to him had died. I watched him over the rim of my glass as he passed a hand over his pale face. He leaned his hand against a stone pillar and shook his head. Head lifting up he caught sight of me and made his way towards me.

"Bad news?"

"Huh?" he said, looking up at me sharply as he drew near.

"I said, bad news?"

"Oh, oh. No, no. Nothing of the sort, just a bit of bad indigestion, that's all. When I get nervous my bowels act up."

"Didn't know there was anything to be nervous about?"

"If you've worked as long as I have for The Lady, then you know every meeting you have with her could very well be your last."

"Yet you still work with her," I said, getting up to my feet.

"It is not a choice—" he started to say, but looked over to the bartender, who was staring at us. "I think it's time we got going. But before we do this is for you," he said, handing over a jet black data stick.

I pocketed it as I followed him through the lobby and out the doors, stopping when I got to where Vlad had killed José. I knelt down on one knee and touched the ground where his blood had splattered. It appeared no different but to me, it would always signify one of the most important events that had changed my life forever.

I closed my eyes and allowed the moment to wash over me. I knew what I had to do. I knew the risks I had to take. One slip and it would be over, but it was a risk I was willing to take if it meant everyone I loved could be safe.

Back in the car, neither of us said anything as I kept my foot on the gas and allowed the Ford Mustang Mach 1 to roar like a lion on the plains. I took each corner tighter than the next, smiling as the squeal of tires filled the air. I stomped on the gas again and was pushed back in my seat as the upgraded engine delivered as much of its power as it could through the tires.

I dipped in and out between cars too slow to get out of my way, and was long gone from their flashing lights as I kept on pushing the car through its paces.

I looked to my side and could see Samuel's fingers digging into his leather seat as he jumped and winced whenever I came too close to another car.

"Sorry," I said, easing off the gas and allowing the car to amble along comfortably. "Ever since I was a kid, I would watch the classic action movies and see the high-speed car chases and would always marvel and wonder what they would be like to be in, back before all Earth's traffic was controlled and monitored. You know one country had something called the autobahn which allowed you to travel as fast as you wanted?

"I would always look at the rich kids growing up who had classic cars as toys and feel envious, even a little ashamed, that my family couldn't' afford what they had, but I guess that's what most kids think about when growing up."

"In the way," said Samuel, "you were envious of nice toys, I was envious of nice clothes. I just wanted some that didn't have any holes. It's amazing how human greed can never be satisfied."

"Ha, you think me greedy?"

"I think vengeance is clouding your mind."

"Who said this had anything to do with vengeance?" I said, tapping the steering wheel.

"Please, don't treat me like some fool. I know it was because of Mr Lee that you were captured. I know he destroyed The Lady's cargo, which she blamed your crew for. This has everything to do with vengeance and nothing to do with justice."

I barked in laughter as I slapped the steering wheel. "Justice! Who said anything about justice?"

"Justice and truth are—"

"Don't you get high and mighty with me because it suits you. Did you forget the cargo Mr Lee destroyed were chemical weapons we picked up from you? Chemical weapons that were going to be used against the mass population of The Diamond District. We all have played a role in this mess we find ourselves in.

"Some have played greater roles than others but roles have been played."

"But there must be a better way than this. There must be something you can do?"

"Like what? Please, oh great and mighty leader from The Jungle, instruct me what you would do differently if you were in my shoes?"

He said nothing as he stared out the window, while I drove through the streets making sure we were not being tailed.

"I am tired of being pushed around, tired of it," I spat. "Ever since I can remember everyone has always taken from me and never given anything back, but now it's my time to take. My time to provide for my family. My time to make sure they are okay, and the only way I can do that is by taking out my opposition. I never asked for this, any of this, but now that it's thrust upon me I'm going to make sure I do what needs to be done, so I can come out on top."

"You sound like him."

"Who?"

"My brother," said Samuel.

"Maybe he's not as crazy as I first thought."

"Or maybe, you're just as crazy as he."

"Wouldn't that be something," I said, cutting off a car as I took a hard right down a side street. "So, what did Lady Isabella want to speak to you about?"

"What we always talk about. Death."

28

We were all onboard *The Kennel* in a small asteroid field not too far from Safe Haven. We had decided the best way to stay off the radar was not to be on the planet in the first place. It gave us the peace of mind we needed to plan our next course of action.

Seated around the ship's conference table we stared at the information Lady Isabella had provided for us.

"So let me get this straight," said Willis, pointing a hand that held a glass of whisky in it at me, "you agreed we would take out not one, but two of the most powerful people on Safe Haven. Two people who have a vast number of guards, assassins and staff at their disposal. One in the form of Mr Diamond who has just as much money as that posh ring-piece-licking asshole Edward Thomas—"

"Yeah, but look what happened to him," interjected Tuari.

"You say that as if we defeated him," Willis continued, "don't forget if it wasn't for that cyborg creep, Alvis, then we would all probably be dead right now. Edward had our number to start with; he had enough money and influence to control every move we made. He played us like puppets and if he could do that to us, how do you think it will go if we go up against Diamond?"

"We are already up against Diamond," I said; "we attacked his men back at The Jungle. He is the backer behind the Mercenary Bloc. Whether you like it or not, he sees us as an enemy who needs to be destroyed."

"Fuck's sake," Willis said, downing the contents of his glass and pouring himself another.

"Don't you think you've had—" began Samuel, but I placed a hand on his forearm as Willis sat up straight and glared his way.

"We're in this for the long haul so we might as well try and do something about it," said Poppy, magnifying the images that floated above our table. "This is a basic overview of all of Lee's domain. As you can see, although he controls The Floating City, his rule isn't as dominant as The Lady's or Diamond's. The main reason for this is that the people who live on the waterways of Safe Haven are somewhat free spirits. They are immigrants and travellers from different worlds, just looking to live their lives as peacefully as they can. Much like the people of The Jungle.

"The only difference is that they love to be in motion."

"Fucking water gypsies," Willis spat. "Thieving bunch, the lot of them."

"How did you ever get so narrow-minded?" said Samuel, with a shake of the head.

"Yes... they are quick-fingered and aren't always on the right side of the law, but who on Safe Haven isn't some criminal or outlaw?" asked Poppy.

"Speak for yourself, dear lady," said Samuel, pulling on the sleeves of his tunic.

"Oh, I'm sorry, I didn't know selling weapons of mass

destruction was legal under the World Government," said Willis.

"Safe Haven doesn't come under the World Governments jurisdiction. They've tried to conquer it many times but being bribed helps many people to look the other way. When that doesn't work drugs or sex are pushed the right people's way; and when that fails, then an old-fashioned bullet in the back of the head always takes care of any issues."

"Bah! Semantics," Willis said with a wave of his hand.

"Be that as it may," Poppy said, "if we are going to attack either of the two of them, then Lee would be the easier target and it would severely weaken Diamond's hold on the waterways, allowing us easier access to The Diamond District when the time comes to attack it. Plus, it would allow The Lady to move men and weapons across Safe Haven much easier, giving her and us the best chance of winning this."

Tuari scratched his chin, which sounded like sandpaper over coarse wood. "If The Lady is in charge of two territories instead of one then we may not even have to fight Diamond. They may come to some sort of peaceful agreement or better still they may put their differences behind them and fall madly in love."

We all stared at each other before we broke out into laughter.

"That's the funniest thing you've said yet," said Willis.

Tuari looked around the room, hurt. "I was being serious," he muttered under his breath.

"Lady Isabella will not be in charge of The Floating City," I said, looking at my crew, "we will."

They looked at me as if I had grown two heads. "Come... again?" said Tuari.

"The deal for doing this job was that we get to keep The Floating City, once Lee and Diamond are taken care of."

"What do you mean *keep it*?" said Willis. "It ain't a toy! We can't just store it away in the ship's cargo bay. This is a borough we're talking about. A borough with people and customs and… and… and gypsies and shit. We are a crew for hire. That's what we've always done. That's what we know. We don't know shit about running a borough."

"For once my brother and I are in agreement," said Samuel.

I gave him a look but addressed Willis: "Then it's about time we learnt. I'm tired of being at someone's beck and call because their pockets are fat and full of coin and we haven't eaten for days. I'm tired of people deciding our fates. I'm tired of these fuckers getting away with harming one of our own and nothing coming of it. We are pawns in this game, ladies and gentlemen.

"Fucking pawns! And I don't know about you, but I'm sick of being pushed around the board. It's about time we claimed a piece of the board for ourselves. It's about time we rose to power. That's the only way things will be different for us, that's the only way we will be safe."

Samuel shook his head while he gave me a look of pity. "Violence only begets more violence. What happens when you defeat Lee, then Diamond? Do you think she will give up a piece of what she's fought for all these years because she said so, or because she signed some contract? The Lady wants all of Safe Haven. She already has The Jungle and I've come to terms with that. I know my role in this game; maybe it's about time you come to terms with yours as well."

I looked at him in disgust. "There are no beaten dogs here."

No one spoke as Samuel slowly got up from his chair

and made his way out the door. We watched him go, none of us saying anything to stop him.

"Quinton," said Tuari, "I love the enthusiasm. Trust me, I do. But it's all just a pretty speech if we have no way to get to Lee."

"That's already taken care of," I said, switching between the images that floated above us. "Lee is holding some fancy invite-only poker night, between the strongest crews who reside in The Floating City. Lady Isabella thinks he is holding this as a way to secure allegiance and favour amongst the crews for the upcoming war.

"No doubt he will promise them spoils from the coming conflict. If we are going to hit him this is our best option."

"Have you hit your head or something? You want to attack the leader of The Floating City, when he's surrounded by the strongest men The Floating City has to offer," Willis said in disbelief. "Do you know how high security will be? Everyone will be packing. Everyone will be on edge. This is a terrible idea."

"How do you strike fear into the hearts of the people you want to conquer? By defeating them when they think they're untouchable. By attacking their leader when he is surrounded by his strongest forces. If we want the crews of The Floating City to take us seriously, to not oppose us when the time comes, then we have to send a message they shall never forget."

"Boy," Tuari said, "are you sure about this? We aren't or mercenaries. We are cargo runners, delivery boys—we collect things and sell them to the highest bidder. What you're thinking of doing here is a whole different ball game to anything we've done before."

"You're right. It is. But this is only the first stage to a

bigger plan I have in mind. For now, our goal is to defeat Lee and Diamond."

"That still leaves us with the first problem that Fatboy raised," said Willis. "How are we meant to get to Lee?"

I flicked through some more hologram images until I brought up a picture of an old southern American paddle-wheel steamboat. It glistened white in the setting sun.

Willis whistled as I made the image rotate. "Well, ain't she a pretty girl. I didn't even know those things still existed."

"They do," I said, "but only in museums back on Earth. Lee had one constructed from scratch just for this event. Although it looks like a steamboat, I believe the paddles are powered by electricity. This is where he'll be in a month. All we have to do is find our way onboard and take care of business."

Willis pinched the bridge of his nose as a frustrated sigh escaped him. He looked to Tuari before stabbing his fingers my way.

"What?" I asked.

To Tuari he said, "If you don't tell him I'm going to explode. The dickhead isn't listening."

"Quinton, you still don't understand us," said Tuari. "Knowing where Lee will be is only half the solution. That isn't a plan. How are we going to approach the boat? How are we going to navigate through the boat without being detected? How are we going to escape when we have despatched Lee? That's only the questions that are coming to the top of my head, but you haven't given us an answer to any of them. This is a great idea, but if there's one thing you should have taken from José it's that execution is everything."

I opened my mouth to argue but closed it again.

He was right. I wasn't thinking like a captain. I was only looking at the overall picture without taking into account all of the details. I brought up a layout of the riverboat and walked around it, tapping my lips. The biggest hurdle we would face was getting on the boat and keeping hidden until we needed to strike. "You're right," I said, looking to Willis and Tuari, "both of you. I was too caught up in the mission. The first thing we need is to somehow find a way on the boat; once that is taken care of, I think the rest shall fall into place."

"I think I may know someone who can help," Poppy said. I turned to her with a smile, my hopes suddenly rising.

"But," she said, smile matching my own, "if you want his help then I want to be on the ground for this mission. No being left behind or being kept in the shadows. I want to be where the action is."

"But I don't think we need that many bodies on the ground."

She said nothing but crossed her arms.

"I mean you coming isn't an issue, but as this will be a mainly male event you'll stand out like a sore thumb."

She stood like an expressionless statue.

I looked to the other two, who avoided my gaze as if they had suddenly taken a keen interest in the table's design in front of them.

I tried to think of anything, anything at all that would deter her from coming.

"Err—"

"Either I come—or I keep my contact a secret," she said, before stomping out of the room.

"Sooo," said Tuari, "I see everything is going well in paradise—"

"Where were you two when I needed you? You're both

the first ones to shit all over my idea, but the last ones to come to my aid when I need backup."

"Us?" Willis said in shock, "We know better than to involve ourselves in marital matters, although you heathens ain't married and continue to do the beast with two backs in front of the eyes of the Lord. We're afraid this one is on you. You're the captain, the lover, her partner—this is your mess to sort out. Come on, bigboy, I'm hungry and I know I've seen you preparing a batch of chilli with my name on it."

They both left, leaving me with a stone in my stomach at the conversation I knew I was going to have with Poppy.

It was one that was going to end in tears.

It was one I didn't think I was going to win.

29

I could hear nothing but the gentle lapping waves of the water as we waited in a boat on one of the many rivers of The Floating City. The boat in question was a rickety riverboat that had just enough space inside for a grown man to stand up at a slouch. One bedroom, one bathroom, one living space come kitchen. It had once belonged to a family but now was owned somehow by Poppy.

How she had come by it she wouldn't say.

We had left Samuel and Scarface in a safe-house back in Paradise, while the rest of us had continued on with the mission. It wasn't that I didn't trust them, just that I wanted this mission to be quick and efficient, and you couldn't have that with a large group of people. There was still one too many on this boat to begin with but that was a problem I couldn't resolve, not without putting a stop to the whole thing.

I leaned against the railings at the... bow? Starboard? Stern? I was at the back of the boat trying my best not to throw up. I rested my head against the cool metal of the railings and took in deep breaths as I stood back up and tried to concentrate on the stars. They were as always breathtaking. It was the one thing I loved about this planet.

The stars.

Not obstructed by the smog of Paradise Lost or the trees in The Jungle—out here on the water you felt like you were part of them. With nothing but darkness all around they felt close enough to touch. As if you were trapped in a painting and all you needed to do was step out onto the water and make your way towards them. They were—I groaned once more as I held my stomach and leaned across the railings.

"I did tell you not to have that milkshake before we left," said Poppy behind me.

I opened my mouth to respond but quickly decided against the idea.

"Your eyes are always bigger than your stomach."

"The waves weren't this bad the last time we were on them. How was I to know—" I clamped my hand over my mouth and leaned over the railings for good measure.

"Is our fearless leader still feeling poorly?" said Willis from my left. "Does he want his belly rubbed?"

I said nothing as the waves once again slapped against the boat.

"If I were you, fearless leader, I wouldn't think of anything green, or lumpy, or lumpy and green. Or ugh—" He gagged and pretended to be sick, making me turn away from him. He repeated the process until Poppy slapped him across the back of the head.

"It's not my fault he had a burger," he said, walking away rubbing his head.

I closed my eyes and tried to drown out everything but it just wasn't happening. The battle that raged inside my stomach felt like WW3.

"I'm glad you decided to have me on this mission," Poppy said, stroking the back of my head.

"I didn't exactly have a choice, now did I?"

"No, I guess you didn't."

"Just be careful, especially now," I said, looking at her stomach. It had grown rapidly in the last month and although she did her best to cover it up, it was still prominent. Every cell in my body wanted to stop her coming on this mission, wanted to sit her down and tell her how absurd it was for someone who was pregnant to be going into a mission where fighting would take place. But anytime I brought it up she either walked away or chose not to discuss the matter.

How I envied José; he never had these problems to deal with.

"You don't need to worry about—"

"Poppy," I said, taking her hands in mine, "whatever happens I want you at the rear. I don't want you to take needless risks. I don't want you in the thick of it. This isn't a request. This is an order from your captain. If you can't abide by those rules then I'm calling this thing off right now."

She started to speak and I could see by the tension along her brow it was an argument waiting to happen.

"No. I don't want to hear it. You either agree to this or I'm calling this off."

She bit back her original reply and gave me a curt nod. It was the best I could hope for but I would keep her to her word no matter the cost.

"My contact shall be here in an hour or so; try your best not to be sick," she said walking away, as Willis came towards me.

"Look at this," he said, shoving a bowl in my face. "It

must be fish guts the former family who lived here forgot to throw out. Look at the size of the maggots, they're as long—"

I pushed him out of the way and emptied my stomach overboard.

"Ha! You owe me, shitface," Willis shouted over his shoulder, "I told you I could make him spill his guts."

I closed my eyes as I tried to think of anything apart from the waves and prayed for this mission to be over already.

"I thought this contact was meant to be here by now?" Willis said.

I looked to Poppy, who gave us a shrug.

"Don't be so impatient. What have you got to do better than this?" Tuari asked.

"My daily prayers for one."

"You mean sip wine and chant some nonsense?"

"How... fucking... dare you? You insensitive, knuckle-dragging prick. I also bless the crew in my prayers, and don't I always say a little prayer before our missions?"

"Well, I wouldn't call them prayers as such, more like—"

"I see something," I said, taking a step forward. Nothing happened for another second or two, then a flash of light that blinked three times in rapid succession came across the water.

Torch in hand Poppy answered the message, then we waited.

Nobody said anything as the soft slaps of oars cut through the air. Clouds had covered the night sky extinguishing the light from the stars and making everything pitch black to the point I couldn't see my hand in front of my face, but I knew the boat was getting closer as the sound of the oars grew louder. Poppy would be tracking the boat's process and using her advanced senses and scanners to make sure we were in fact meeting who she said we were and not being ambushed.

"We all good?" I asked her.

"All good."

The boat continued to make its way towards us until I could just make out a vague shape in the distance, then something bumped into the side of us signalling its arrival. A faint light emerged from a hooded figure with his face shrouded in shadow. He gripped onto our railings and made his way onto the boat. He flashed a gold disc to Poppy I had seen before, but I couldn't place where.

"Were you followed?" Poppy asked.

"You would all be dead if I had," replied the stranger.

"Thanks for coming. I suggest we take this inside," she said, leading the way into the riverboat. We all followed inside the cramped space the boat provided. Tuari poured us all hot drinks while I watched the stranger's movements. He still hadn't taken his hood off but the voice sounded familiar... had I met this person before?

"So, are you sure you're up for this?" Poppy asked.

The stranger looked her in the face for a moment or two then slowly took his hood off. "I wouldn't be here if I wasn't," said Zhang Wei.

"What is he doing here?" Willis said, reaching for one of his pistols.

"I asked him to be here; he's how we are going to get close to Lee."

"By using one of his most trusted aides?" said Willis, "I don't like this. I don't like this one bit."

Zhang Wei had been the first person to greet me when I

had arrived at Lee's casino the Dragon's Lair, but he was also one of the last faces I had seen after Lee betrayed us to Edward Thomas. To say that seeing him now didn't fill me with joy was an understatement.

"Are you okay with this?" Willis asked, staring at me.

"If Poppy trusts him, then so do I. Let's hear their plan first before we abandon all hope."

"Thank you," Wei said, looking my way. He had lost a significant amount of body mass since I had last seen him; cheekbones protruding only highlighted the scar across his lip even more. Where once he had a moustache waxed to perfection, now only half the hair on his upper lip remained.

"This," he said, pointing to the scar, "I got this because Lee found out what Poppy had done for my family."

I looked to her.

"During my travels along the rivers of The Floating City, I helped a few families pay off their debt to Lee. I couldn't stand to watch families broken up and sold into slavery because one relative had a gambling addiction. Wei's was one such family." To Wei: "When did he find out?"

"At first he grew suspicious after he betrayed you to Edward. It must have been something in our interaction he noticed, but somehow, some way, he dug and dug till he found all the evidence he needed. Then one day he called me up to his office and there, sitting in a chair next to him, was my mother and father. I knew in that instant they would die in that room.

"And I was right.

"His guards held me and forced me to watch while his men strangled them with wire, their limbs kicking and struggling while they fought for air. I would love to say their struggle was quick and painless but that would be a lie. It took too long. After he killed them I knew I would be next but I didn't give them a chance, I fought off his men and jumped through a window into the river. I lived off nothing but the fish I caught while I moved from one location to the next. It's been tough living off nothing but scraps and hate, but I've been waiting, waiting for the day I could strike back.

"And now that day has arrived."

"I'm sorry to hear about your parents," I said.

"They—thank you."

"So what's the plan?" Tuari asked.

"Simple really; the paddleboat Lee is on cruises along this stretch of river in the next three hours or so," Wei said, getting out a map and laying it on the table. "Because the rainy season only finished last month many of the footpaths and trails that snake through the trees are flooded, creating miniature waterways. Unless you are a native to this area, then you would get lost, but lucky for you, I used to play around here when I was a kid.

"I suggest we take my boat, I have a silent onboard engine that should get us where we need to be. We shall have to navigate some stretches by oar as there is a risk of the roots snagging the propeller blades but there will be enough manpower on the boat that this shouldn't be a problem. Once we get to this point," Wei pointed to a section of the map where the river narrowed with greenery on either side, "we should have enough cover to make our way onboard. From there I leave the rest up to you."

"There are a lot of shoulds in this plan," said Willis.

"How many men are on board?" I asked.

"There will be a couple dozen staff just dealing with catering and making sure the guests' needs are all looked after, then there are five of Lee's men who will act as bodyguards. He has invited four other crews along, each with five of their top-ranked men. This meeting is not a show of force so firepower should—"

"There's that word again," said Willis.

"—be light."

"I was expecting something like this to be crawling with goons," said Tuari.

"As I said, posing and showing force is not the goal here. The information my contact has given me says this is more of a party, a poker night sort of get-together. So if we are looking to attack Lee then there is no better time than now. The people attending won't be heavily armed and by the time we strike, the party will be well underway, meaning that most of the attendees will be intoxicated."

"Can you trust your inside man?" I asked.

"Yes," Wei said looking me in the eye. "If they hadn't helped me escape when I did, then I wouldn't be here today. They're already in a lot of danger just still being employed by Lee; if he ever finds out about their involvement in my escape, well…"

I rechecked the map; judging by our location it would take some time to get to our desired location. We didn't have much time.

"Alright, I want everyone to get ready in five minutes and be on Wei's boat. Pack the essentials. Only what you need. And I mean only what you need. Willis, I don't want you to be rattling as you walk; this mission is one of speed and stealth."

"Awww, but I've got this lovely pair of—"

I gave him a look that silenced him. Everyone departed, leaving only me and Wei alone. He looked around the boat, a feeling of loss crossing his face. Walking to a large beanbag that acted as a sofa he ran his hands along it.

"My mother used to read me ancient stories from Earth,

about boys climbing giant beanstalks and boys visiting factories made out of nothing but chocolate, on this sofa. The hours used to sail past until I collapsed in her arms, then those nights grew less and less frequent, as she visited Lee's casinos more and more. This was before Lee was who he was. He was just some upstart, who owned a few local bars and casinos, but his methods of punishment for payment have always been the same.

"My mother thought she saw a way out of poverty through his casino... but all that happened was I was bonded into slavery before I saw my twelve birthday.

"Funny, after Lee took me she quit trying to win big."

I tried to think of something to say as he touched the large worn beanbag sofa. "Sorry," I mumbled, but even to my ears it sounded weak.

"You are not to blame, I should have warned you what Lee was up to back then. I didn't. As long as he pays for his crimes, that shall be enough for me," Lee said, walking past me and leaving me surrounded by his memories.

30

The air was filled with one part moisture, two parts insects.

I couldn't see them in front of my face but the buzzing sound they emitted was constant. I slapped the back of my neck as I was bitten for the hundredth time. Everything snagged on the mangrove type trees around us, their branches even pulling on hair if they got the chance. The going had been slow, too slow for my liking, and the effort required to cover any distance burned the muscles in my shoulders and back.

"At the rate we were going, my body will either be too tired to fight, or we will never see the light of day and die amongst these trees," Tuari said.

"Suck it up, buttercup. A little hard labour will do your lazy ass a world of good. Sins are absolved in the harsh light of sweat and pain."

"Can't they just as easily be absolved with a large donation and some song and dance?" Tuari asked.

"If we ever get out of here, I'm going to wipe my dick on everything you own."

"I. Prepare. Your. Meals. What makes you think I've not done worse?" Tuari said, merriment in his voice.

Silence greeted the question, before a frenzied unfolding of limbs as Willis tried to stand up and make his way towards Tuari.

"We're here," Wei said.

Everyone looked forward as we came to a gentle stop. Through the trees, we could just about make out a large river that flowed steadily past us. Wei tied the boat to a large tree trunk and looked at the computer fixed to his wrist. He did his best to cover the glow from the screen but I could still see the frown on his face. He twisted his head left and right trying to get a better look of the river.

"What's wrong?" I asked.

He didn't answer me as he typed a message, then went back to scanning the river. Repeatedly checking his computer he said nothing as we all sat tight and waited.

I checked my own watch. Five minutes had passed.

"What's wrong?" I asked again.

"I was expecting a message from my contact but I have received nothing," he said.

"Should we be worried?"

"I... don't know."

"Maybe the boat has passed," said Poppy.

"I wouldn't think so; we are well ahead of schedule. I obtained a copy of the ship's logbook. The captain has plotted a very specific course for this trip."

"I have a bad feeling about this," said Willis.

"It's probably the gin," said Tuari.

"What do you want to do, Quinton?" said Poppy.

I bit the inside of my cheek as I ran through our options. We had come a long way just to turn back now. It might have been the thought of making the muscle-burning journey back the way we came, but I wanted to see this through. I didn't think we would get a better opportunity than this anytime soon.

"We wait. If nothing happens then the worst-case scenario is we get eaten alive by these insects."

Willis grumbled under his breath but everyone else nodded as we turned our attention back towards the river. Wei checked his messages again and again as the time slowly slipped by, but whatever signal or message he was hoping to get never materialised. He tried to hide his frustrations but his breath grew frantic the longer and longer we waited.

"Don't tell me we're going to sit here all—"

"I see something," Poppy said, cutting Willis off. She pointed into the distance and the faintest of lights could be seen making their way down the river. I pulled out a pair of high-tech binoculars and looked where she was pointing. Tapping the zoom function on the device's side brought the boat into clear focus. It was an old American steam paddleboat just as the info The Lady provided said it would be. Fake smoke poured out of chimneys mounted on its decks and ferry lights draped over its body gave it a fairytale look.

"See anything we should be worried about?" Wei asked.

I double-clicked on the zoom button again and scanned the decks of the boat. All appeared quiet apart from the odd pair of men conversing in pockets here and there. I looked for anything out of the ordinary but I really didn't know what I was looking for. The scene presented to me looked like a party, but how would I know if something was off?

We weren't close enough to gauge the feel of it, and once the boat came along we would have to move straightaway and use the cover that we had or just allow it to pass.

"Everything looks okay, but without getting on board we wouldn't really know," I said.

No one spoke as everyone waited for my decision. I turned to Poppy, who gave me a smile and a gentle squeeze of the hand. Turning back my attention to the ship, I scanned it again but nothing screamed at me.

"What time does the poker game start?" I asked Wei.

"They should well be into the swing of things."

"I guess that explains the lack of a crowd on the deck, but there weren't many people invited to this event in the first place. But then—" I was second-guessing myself. This wasn't the time to do that. I needed to make a decision and stick to it. That was easier said than done when I had people's lives in the palm of my hand, yet what had José always told me? Everyone on the crew knew what they were getting into. They knew the risks. They knew the rewards.

It was up to the captain not to betray that.

We had come this far to the gates of hell; there was no point turning back now.

"Everyone suit up," was all I had to say. The crew knew what it meant. It was time to break down the doors of hell and announce ourselves properly.

31

The crew were all dressed in matching combat suits we had used many times before. Covering from head to toe, they protected us against the pressure and cold of space; they also allowed us to breathe underwater, and protected us from heat up to a certain point.

Wei wasn't so well equipped. Face covered in a balaclava, the rest of him only had on black clothes that had seen better days.

I lifted my helmet and looked his way. "We're going to be approaching the boat from under the water; these suits shall aid our breathing. You don't have to accompany us—"

"I shall be fine," he said, sliding in a square metal device which fitted in his mouth and clipped over his nose.

As the boat came closer towards our location, I double-checked everyone was ready. Finding everything in order I returned my gaze to the boat. It was finally upon us.

"Oh, one more thing," I said to Wei, lifting my helmet, "the crew and I can communicate through our helmets, but you don't have that luxury. All I want you to do is stay in the back with Poppy and follow her lead. Hold onto her hand while we're under the surface of the water and everything will be okay. She'll make sure nothing happens to you. My aim is to get everyone out of this in one piece. Understand?"

He gave me a hesitant nod.

"It's still not too late to back out."

"I'm fine," he said, nodding at me more firmly.

I returned the gesture and lowered my helmet. The boat was upon us and it was now or never. Taking a deep breath I slid over the side of our boat and entered the water, diving deep. A small map in the corner of my vision pinged the location of the boat as I swam forward through the dark murky waters. I looked at the image the helmet's cameras were feeding me but I couldn't see anything.

The water was dark as charcoal.

The helmets did have lights, but I didn't want to turn them on in case anyone from the boat saw our lights under the water. We would have to navigate using the map.

The current of the river was stronger than it first seemed and I used every ounce of my strength to keep me on track. I saw a large dark shape in front of me and swam towards it with more purpose. Looking up I could just about make out the underside of the boat. Swimming towards it I pressed my palms against the underside of the boat and activated the suction cups positioned on the tips of my fingers in the gloves.

They locked me into place and I breathed a sigh of relief as I allowed my muscles to relax.

"I'm in position."

"Locked on," replied Willis and Tuari.

I waited for a few more moments and looked around me but didn't see any sight of Poppy or Wei. Had they gotten lost? The swim would have been no problem for Poppy; the problem lay in the passenger she was carrying. Wei didn't come across as a man that had been in many situations like this and all it took was for him to panic or flail about and that would course enough of a problem to either ruin the mission or cause enough commotion that they would be seen from the boat.

"Poppy do—"

"Locked on," came her voice, cutting me off.

I breathed a sigh of relief, which must have been picked up by the helmet's mic, as Willis and Tuari chuckled.

"Let's get a move on," I said, ignoring them as I climbed. The going was slow but steady as every time I pulled my hand away from the boat to re-suction it further up along its body the currents of the water would pull at me, determined to drag me away. Pull, stick, brace. Pull, stick, brace. Pull, stick, brace. I repeated this sequence until my head finally emerged from the water. Keeping my body close against the boat, I listened through my helmet to see if any alarm had been raised.

I heard nothing to give me concern.

The others had also emerged from the water. Wei hung onto Poppy's back like a baby monkey, arms wrapped tightly around her neck. They all waited on me. I took a few more seconds to steady my breathing and to make absolutely sure we hadn't been detected; satisfied we hadn't, I continued on. Not obstructed by the water, the pace we climbed up the side of the boat was much quicker. I saw the railings of the upper deck in sight and slowed my pace.

I held my hand out so the others would stop as I continued on up. A gap between the floor and the railing gave me a view of the deck.

I saw a few pairs of feet clustered about talking, but the small groups I had first seen through the binoculars were now gone; only these stragglers remained. Their words carried on the air as they spoke loudly in slurred tones that indicated they were either boozed up or were on some form of drugs. Either way, it mattered little to me, as their current state improved our chances of taking them out without much effort.

I lifted up my body another inch or two and saw only four people were left on the deck.

Four men with sun-baked skin drank themselves silly as their heads tilted back and they roared with laughter. Tattoos covered most of their torsos and gold rings graced more than one finger. They looked like a cross between pirates of old and a biker gang. They moved unsteadily on their feet and I had to duck hurriedly as one knocked a bottle at his feet my way.

I clung to the side of the boat and watched the bottle roll past my face and over the side of the boat, where it splashed in the waters below. I held my breath and listened for the sound of feet coming my way.

"Hey, you fucktard! That bottle wasn't empty," came a deep voice from the group.

"Who gives a shit! Lee's stocked this boat with so much pussy and booze I don't ever want to leave," said another.

"To Lee!" they all shouted

I waited another minute or two to see if anyone would come my way before speaking softly into my helmet mic: "I have four pirate-slash-biker-looking-type dudes in front of me. We have to take them out so we can proceed further."

"They're most likely part of one of the crews Lee invited to this event," said Poppy.

"How do you want to go about this?" Willis asked.

"I want to keep fatalities to a minimum. We have enough enemies as it is without creating any more. For now, we attack everyone with non-lethal means. That includes you, Willis."

"I heard you, you big pu—"

"If things get too out of hand and it's them or us, you know what to do. Willis, Tuari, get in position."

They both climbed up on either side of me and stayed suspended by one hand as they pulled out their pistols with the other. I followed suit and pulled out a small handgun, which fired miniature darts that released a powerful general anaesthesia-type drug into the victim's blood system, knocking them out in seconds. The only disadvantage was that the darts had to impact skin to work.

We all took aim and fired.

Three darts pierced necks causing their victims to fall to the floor; the fourth dart missed its target and sailed harmlessly into the ether.

"You can't shoot for shit," said Willis, as the lone survivor looked down at his buddies in confusion.

"That was your dart," Tuari snapped.

"Like hell it was."

The lone survivor kept looking at his buddies, confusion plainly highlighted on his face. "Hey, you bunch of lightweights! What's wrong with ya? Some fancy booze and you all lose your heads, it doesn't matter to me, more women to go around."

He turned and started to walk away but before he could take another step, I shot him in the back of the neck causing him to face plant on the floor.

I quickly vaulted the railings and checked we were all clear, before looking down at the bodies. I checked they were completely out before relieving them of any weapons they had on their person.

"They should be out for a good few hours," said Poppy,

sliding up beside me, "more than enough time for us to do what we have to do and get off this boat."

I threw the men's weapons over the side of the boat and glared Willis and Tuari's way.

"What?" they said.

"We have better things to worry about than who missed what shot."

"Yeah," said Willis, "like how are we going to get off this boat."

"That's easy, we will just—" My head snapped to Poppy, mouth agape. No one said anything as we all allowed the realisation of what Willis said to sink in.

"Fuck," I hissed, slapping myself in the helmet. How had I forgotten about that? Through all the planning I had forgotten about the most important piece, our safe escape. The boat would still be continuing down the river, miles away from where we had boarded it. We didn't have a backup boat trailing behind the paddleboat, nor did we have any idea where the closest piece of land was, if we decided to jump overboard.

I lifted my helmet and turned to Wei. "Does this boat have lifeboats?"

"I didn't see anything on the boat design blueprints, but I would say yes, it would have. Every large ship like this has lifeboats, plus Lee is too much of a coward not to have built a few for him and his cronies."

"Alright. Once Lee is taken care of our next goal is finding where the lifeboats are kept," I said looking at the crew.

Willis lifted his helmet and looked at me as if I was crazy. "You're basing our escape plan on that? Some hunch this idiot doesn't even know is correct or not?"

"That's all we can go on for now until something better

presents itself."

"Fuck me," Willis said, throwing his hands up in the air before slamming his helmet down with a snap.

Poppy looked my way and I knew what she was thinking. I had messed up. I would apologise to the crew later. Right now I didn't want our focus to waver; we had a job to do, and for it to be done right, we all had to be on our game.

"Listen," I hissed, "I want everyone's head in the game. I admit I messed up and I'll address that later, but for now, I want us to concentrate on the task at hand. Willis and I will lead point. Tuari, cover our backs. Poppy and Wei will bring up the rear. Anyone got any questions?"

I passed my gaze over my crew but all was silent.

"Alright, let's move out."

32

I walked towards the fallen men and lifted them up and placed them on the lounge chairs that dotted the deck. To anyone who came across them they would appear as if they were asleep; I just hoped no one tried to wake them up. Happy everything was in place, I followed Willis's lead and entered a corridor that had white doors on either side. Each door we passed we placed small circular devices on the locking mechanism called lock-jammers ensuring the doors didn't open from the inside.

It was just another safety precaution that stopped us getting surprised, attacked from anyone opening a door to our rear.

We continued on for some time until we came to a set of stairs that led downwards. Wei had told us Lee's poker party was being held below decks. I halted the party and listened for anyone making their way up; helmet not picking up anything I nodded to Willis as we took a step at a time, pistols pointed ahead of us. The stairs brought us onto a second landing that had even more white doors with frosted glass circles at the top of each one.

Soft moans could be heard coming from behind more than one door.

Willis went to place a lock-jammer on the closest door next to us, but I held him back and shook my head. "We don't have time," I whispered, "nor do we have enough lock-jammers to secure all these doors."

He looked at me then back at the doors. "I hate to admit it but you're right."

I gave him a nod and took the stairs down to the bottom floor. The dim lights of this level gave the floor an eerie feel that made my skin break out in goosebumps. There were no doors on this level, just a long metallic corridor that stretched out before us until it made its way to a single door opposite us. I took a hesitant step forward but stopped, looking over my shoulder; the crew waited on me to move.

"What's wrong?" Poppy asked.

I looked back to the bare-looking corridor that seemed so unfurnished and out of place compared to the rest of the boat. "I... can't put my finger on it but something doesn't add up."

"What's the hold-up?" Wei asked.

I turned to him and frowned. "I want everyone to switch to their main weapons," I said, placing the little pistol back in its holster and taking out my shotgun. Willis lifted his helmet and gave me a look as he took out his pistols. It spoke volumes. I sent a nod his way.

Weapons at the ready we continued on our way down the corridor. The dim lights cast long shadows that did nothing to put my nerves at ease.

Mouth dry, I licked my lips as my breath sounded in my ears. The door came into sharp focus quicker than I would have liked. Rough metal spoke of an unfinished project that the designer had fallen out of love with. I placed my hand against it expecting what, I didn't know.

I looked to the handle and prayed it was unlocked, otherwise we wouldn't be getting inside without causing some serious noise.

Willis leaned against the wall gun pointed towards the door and gave me a nod as my hand extended towards the handle. My fingers wrapped around it and I looked his way once more to see if he was ready before pushing the handle down and pushing the door open. It swung back and slammed against the far wall with a thud that echoed throughout the corridor.

There went our element of surprise.

Guns at the ready we all leapt into the room, but what we saw stopped us in our tracks.

We were expecting men drinking and smoking; we found none. We were expecting a poker game; we found none. We were expecting to catch Lee unaware; he was nowhere to be found.

Instead, we found a single naked female suspended in midair by her hands, rope stretched her limbs away from her body like a martyr being crucified. A rough canvas bag covered her head, which rested on her chest. A single bullet hole penetrated the canvas bag that had been shot through her forehead. Blood trickled out of the wound down her chest and onto the floor where it dripped creating a small pool beneath her feet.

The scene looked like a religious sacrifice from times of old.

Whoever this poor woman was, she hadn't died peacefully. Burn marks covered her body and cuts had torn sections of her skin to shreds. The scene was hard to take in; I wanted to look away but like passing a horrific car crash on the highway, it was all you could do but stare. Wei pushed past us and took a shaky step forward; he took another and fell to his knees as he tore the balaclava from his head and brought it up to cover his mouth as he screamed silently.

I looked to him and then to the victim, confused at what I was seeing.

Willis walked up to the woman and reached for the bag that covered her face but he stopped as a cry of anguish and pain ripped from Wei's throat. "Don't touch her!"

We all stared at him as he slowly got to his feet and pushed Willis out of the way. His hands shook as he reached for the heavens. Fingers encircling the bag he slowly lifted it off the woman's head as a sob caught in his throat.

Long black curls cascaded down a face made up of more bruises than flesh. Wei brought up a hand slowly to her face and stroked it while tears gushed out of his eyes.

His lips touched hers as he wrapped his arms around her waist.

I looked at the scene in front of me, confused. How did Wei know this person? A hand on my shoulder forced my head to the left as I looked to see Poppy staring my way. Helmet up, there was fear and panic behind her eyes.

"We need to leave now," she said.

"I don't—"

"Marta," Wei whispered, "look what they've done to you, my love."

With those simple words, it all fell into place. This was Wei's contact. This was his person on the inside. This was the only person who knew we were coming for Lee.

"We've got to leave—"

The tannoy of the ship crackled and popped into life, cutting me off. A voice I hadn't heard for some time came onto the air.

"Gentlemen of the *Dragon Continental*. I have just been informed that we have some unwanted *guests* on our fine ship, who have sneaked on board. They are here to crash the party. They are here to put an end to the fun. Because of this, I shall offer a million a head to anyone who can kill these intruders. If you all look in the bedside cabinet in your rooms you shall find all the tools you need to complete the job.

"Have fun, gentleman, and remember, you've got to be in it to win it."

33

All faces turned to me.

I lifted the face of my helmet and pinched the bridge of my nose as I closed my eyes and tried to digest the shit I had got us into. The overhead speakers were now silent. No sounds could be heard apart from the wailing sobs of Wei, I tried to shut him out but like a crying child, the noise still got through.

Taking a deep breath, I went through the steps that would somehow get us out of this alive.

"Wei, where is the nearest exit?" I asked.

He said nothing but held the woman he once knew close to his chest and rocked back and forth.

"Wei—"

"This is all my fault," he said, voice muffled against her chest. "She would have left months ago if it weren't for me. But I persuaded her to stay on, I persuaded her to keep working for him, keep sending me all the information she could about him, in the hopes that one day, I would get the opportunity I was looking for to take everything from him, but instead, instead... he took everything from—"

Another wail was torn from his throat as he buried his head against her chest.

Willis looked my way as the distant sound of voices could be heard. "We don't have time for this shit. We need to—"

I silenced him with a stare and walked towards Wei to place my hands on his shoulders.

"I won't lie and say I understand how you feel, I respect you too much for that, but what I will say is if you stop here then nothing changes. You won't get the revenge you deserve, nor will you get the justice for her. There will be plenty of time for mourning later, but now we must act."

He shook his head, once, twice, then took a step back as he took in a handful of deep breaths. His hand went to her face and he stroked her lips before kissing them softly.

The voices from the ship were only growing louder and were now accompanied by the sound of running feet.

"As I said earlier, I didn't see any escape routes on the ship's blueprints, but the only logical place an exit or escape vessel would be kept is near the bridge. If this boat was built and designed for Lee, then the first thing that he would do is make sure his safety is taken care of above the needs of everyone else," said Wei.

"And the bridge would be where a captain commands a ship, right?" Tuari asked.

"Where else would he do it from?" Willis snapped.

"Which means the bridge is normally located on the top of the boat... right on the top... where visibility would be excellent, not located at the very bottom like we are now."

The noise from the men was now like a monstrous roar.

"And to get to said bridge we would have to...." Tuari trailed off, eyes travelling up.

"Everyone, weapons at the ready!" I commanded as I

checked my ammo before leaning against the wall closest to the door, Willis leaned on the other side while Tuari stood further back in the room and unpacked a parcel that had been strapped to his back.

I looked over my shoulder and made eye contact with Poppy, who stood out of the way with Wei. She lifted her helmet and blew me a kiss before lowering it again.

I took in as many calming breaths as I could as the stampeding feet were now only moments away.

"Aim for the corridor lights," I said to Willis before lowering my helmet. I reached up to the light switch next to me and flicked off the only bulb delivering light to our room.

"Clever," he said before taking aim.

The first wild man appeared at the end of the corridor dressed in nothing but leather trousers, holding a revolver in each hand.

He yowled and howled while he fired them in the air. His friends weren't far behind him.

Ignoring the oncoming threat we took aim and fired. I started with the lights from the front, Willis shot out the lights from the back.

Section by section the corridor got darker and darker until the only light remaining was a small section in the middle. The men kept on coming but now their pace was slower. Their chorus of shouts was dimmed. Bullets pinged off the wall around me but I ignored it all and took aim and fired at the last bulb.

The corridor descended into darkness and the footsteps stopped. Heavy breathing was the only thing that could be heard.

As the darkness finally settled into place my helmet, like the rest of the crew's, switched to night vision, giving us clarity in what was going on around us. I looked ahead and saw the group of men were struggling to come to terms with their newfound darkness, and like children scared of the dark they refused to move or talk.

I looked back to Tuari and saw he had finally unpacked and assembled the item he was carrying in the box. Securing the harness of the item to his shoulder he pointed it down the corridor.

I gave him a nod and smiled as I returned my attention to the corridor.

"I'm ready whenever you boys are," said Tuari.

I kept my gaze locked onto the men in front of us and waited. They didn't rush forward; they didn't scream or shout; they were professionals. Drunk—coked-up—assholes, who were professionals, but professionals nevertheless. Hands outstretched, they shuffled forward, but there were still more men who were rushing from the rear who bumped into the crowd.

"What is going on?" said someone from the rear.

"Why are the fucking lights out?" said someone else.

"If we knew that, dickhead, then we wouldn't be in the dark as if we were trying to cop a feel from your momma!"

"Who said that about my mother? I'll have you know she's an upstanding woman who wouldn't—"

"Will you lot shut the hell up! These Junk Yard Dog assholes are hiding around here somewhere and the sooner we find them, the sooner that money will be—"

I had seen enough, "Tuari, open fire when you're ready."

I closed my eyes and pressed my back against the wall as I readied myself for what was about to come.

I heard Tuari get into position, then without warning, I felt the roar of his modified assault rifle as it spat out shells into the corridor. The sound from it slammed into my chest as he held the trigger down and filled the corridor with nothing but hot lead. I knew that men would be screaming, I knew that the sound of running feet would be filling the corridor and the hallways as men looked for any means of escape, but I heard none of it.

The roar from the gun was all-encompassing. It was a beast from prehistoric times.

As I closed my eyes and waited for the pounding in my chest to stop, I felt almost sorry for our foes, almost. But it was a dog-eat-dog galaxy and we would show them who had the bigger teeth.

In less than forty seconds it was all over and quiet once again reigned supreme.

I opened my eyes and risked a look into the corridor. What I saw was... carnage. Complete and utter carnage. Blood plastered the walls. Limbs lay littered on the floor torn clean from bodies, organs still moved although out of bodies.

The unlucky ones lay twitching on the floor, their bodies trying to cope with the immense amount of pain they were experiencing.

The smell of gunpowder seeped through the helmet's filters as smoke obstructed the view of Tuari.

"All clear?" he asked.

"For the most part," I said. "I have no doubt there are others who escaped or haven't made it down, so I suggest we get a move on."

"Well, that trick will only work once, plus I'm out of ammo," said Tuari, disassembling the rifle and placing it back in its box.

"Right, alright let's get a move on," I said.

"We can't just leave her here," said a voice in the darkness, "not like this. Please."

I flicked the room light back on and then raised my helmet as I walked to Wei. "We can't take her with us. There is no dignified way to carry a body while one's fighting for their lives. But I'll make you a promise, Marta shall have a burial after this is said and done. You have my word."

"The people of The Floating City don't bury their dead, they sail them on a funeral pyre that they set alight."

"Then that's how she will go into the next life," I said, resting my hand on his shoulder, "but for now we need to get a move on."

He gave me a nod that I returned, then I turned and faced my crew. "I have a feeling that was only the first wave. No doubt there shall be more placed around the boat, but no matter, our goal is the captain's bridge and we shall make it there no matter what. Alright, let's move out, we still have a job to finish."

34

We were back at the base of the stairs leading up to the upper deck. We hadn't seen or heard anyone else after we had traversed the corridor of death, but I expected that. It would be easier to pick us off from the multiple doorways that littered the second and first floor than to risk a shootout with us down here. I frowned as I looked up at the stairs, doubt prickling the corners of my mind.

"Wei, is there no other way to the bridge?" I asked.

He gave a small head shake. I let out a sigh as I looked to Willis. Pistols in hand in he gave me a firm nod of the head as we ascended the staircase first. The helmet scanned wherever I looked, trying to pick up any heat signatures it could. I kept my shotgun in front of me as I trod lightly on each step. The eerie silence that surrounded me did nothing to put me at ease.

It appeared those that had survived the corridor had learnt their lesson when it came to sound.

Now they would try and stalk us, as we tried to reach our destination.

A Dog Is Born

Halfway up the flight of stairs, I saw the flickering movement of a shadow but it was gone again in a blink of an eye. I held my hand out and nodded in the direction it came from. Willis nodded in understanding.

He unclipped a flashbang from the utility belt around his waist and tossed it against the far wall above us so it bounced around the corner. We turned our heads in the opposite direction as the sound of hurrying feet sounded above us.

As soon as the flashbang went off Willis and I shot up the stairs.

Someone jumped out from a doorway at me and I fired off a round that blew him back into the room.

Willis shot two in the head as they were still reeling from the effect of the flashbang. I blasted another who dived behind a door, blowing the door apart and leaving inch-long splinters in his face. He rolled around on the floor and Willis ended his suffering with a bullet to the chest.

These men didn't scream and shout like the men we had encountered below. They moved quietly and with purpose.

These were the men that Lee had paid to finish us off if the clowns below deck hadn't taken care of the job.

I stepped forward and Willis pulled me back as a hail of bullets blasted the wall I was in front of; I double-checked the area ahead of us but couldn't see any heat signatures from our attackers.

"I can't get a read on their position," I said.

"Cover me while I take a look," he said.

I pressed my back against the wall until he nodded he was ready and swung my shotgun around the corner emptying as many shells as I could, Willis pulled back and I made myself as small as possible as returning fire came my way.

"They are wearing reflective suits that mask their body temperature. It would be a bitch to flush them out as they've tucked themselves behind a barricade, but unlucky for those sons of bitches I have special items that flush rats out of holes," he said, pulling two small circular discs out of a pocket within his suit.

Pressing a red button in the centre of each, he grabbed each of them by their edges and threw them around the corner like frisbees, then turned and hunkered down against the wall. I followed his lead and seconds later was shaken to my core as an explosion rocked the boat from side to side.

The boat pitched one way and then another until it came to a rest at a slight angle.

"Nice going," Tuari said, looking past us. "Ginger Nuts here has only gone and blown a hole in the boat, a hole I may add that is now gushing water."

I took a look for myself and sighed in frustration as I saw the carnage Willis's little devices had done.

Not one, but two holes wide enough to fit a small child in had been blown out the side of the boat, which was now letting in water at an alarming rate.

"Did I, or did I not, get rid of the men who were attacking us?" Willis asked.

"Yes, but—" Tuari began.

"Did I, or did I not, get rid of the men attacking us?"

"Yes, Willis, you did an outstanding job," I said, sarcasm dripping off every word. "Now let's all *swim* to the floor above before you get rid of any more men."

We all pushed through the water until we came to the set of stairs that would lead us to the upper deck. Even without the helmet sensors picking anything up I knew that men were waiting for us up there.

I took a shotgun shell from my gun and threw it above us, where it bounced against the wall before falling to the floor. An eruption of sound greeted its arrival tearing chunks of wood out of the floor and showing us what our own fate would be if we decided to venture up there.

"I've got just the thing—"

"No," Tuari and I said together, cutting Willis off.

"What? You don't even know what I was going to say."

"It doesn't matter," I said, "the boat can't withstand any more of your *help*. If we place another hole in this boat then we're going under."

"Well, we can't stay here for long," Willis said, gesturing to the water around us already waist-deep.

A head from above poked around the corner and was met by a hail of bullets from us. The headless corpse slumped down to the floor, blood dripping down the stairs.

We were stuck. They couldn't move down without our blowing them to pieces and we couldn't go up without the same happening to us.

"We need to move," said Tuari, as an arm floated to the surface in front of him.

The water was now chest deep and rising at a rate that would engulf us in minutes.

I tried to think of a situation but none—

"Stand back, I'm going up," said a voice that made me close my eyes and grit my teeth.

"Wait," I said, holding out an arm, and trying to rack my brains for a better solution.

"Quinton, we don't have time. I am our best hope."

I felt a hand on my shoulder and turned to face Poppy. Visor up she gave me a smile that I couldn't quite match. Once again, she was placing herself in danger just to save us, not only her but the unborn child growing inside her.

I knew she was right, which made it all that much harder to swallow.

"I do not want you taking any more risks than you have to, understand?"

She gave me a nod and a smile before lowering the visor of her helmet back down.

"Okay, Willis, cover her entry with all the flashbangs you have."

He unclipped a handful from his unity belt and gave her a nod that he was ready. She gave him a thumbs up then readied herself like a sprinter waiting to take off at the starting blocks.

Flashbangs sailing over her head, she moved before the first one vanished behind the wall

The speed at which she took the stairs was like watching a cheetah going after its prey. As the flashbangs detonated she jumped onto a wall and leapt sideways into the corridor above.

The sound of gunfire bounced against the walls and before I knew it my feet were already moving, but a backwards pull stopped me getting far. Turning around I saw both Willis and Tuari's hands on me.

"You'll only get in her way," Tuari said.

I bit back my reply and turned my head back to the action.

Flashes of gunfire illuminated the dim corridor. Shouts of anger and screams of pain danced on the airways. I heard what could only be a body slam against the wall. Then another and another.

The sound of running feet was making its way towards us before a body sailed through the air and came crashing down the stairs. He bounced against the walls and steps until he came to a rest at my feet, his twisted head pointed in a direction it wasn't meant to face.

Gunfire filled the air but this time it was more sporadic.

The water was now closing in on my chin and Wei had taken to treading water. I'd had enough of waiting around. Gripping the handle of my gun I waded through the water and climbed the stairs upwards. A man appeared before me gun pointed my way but I blasted him against the wall, leaving a hole in his chest. I pressed my body against a corner and readied my weapon before I poked my head into the corridor.

Bodies lay strewn on the floor with slashes to their throats and abdomens.

Smoke filled the tight corridor and I could just about make out a body bouncing off the walls as its hands flickered left and right dealing death where they struck. Willis to my right, Tuari covering our rear we moved forward in a tight formation sweeping the corridor in front of us.

We answered any movement on the floor with death.

This wasn't the time for mercy, this wasn't the time for second chances. These men had chosen their side, they knew the risks involved and so did we. Now, all it came down to was who wanted to survive the most.

We came to a halt as we all watched Poppy move with the grace of a ballerina. She ducked and dived cutting the men down around her with little effort. The few who remained struggled to get a fixed lock on her and fired wildly. I lifted my weapon in the hopes of assisting her but my shotgun wasn't made for precision. Instead, I took a step back and watched in amazement as she dealt death to whoever got near.

Diving under a pair of legs her blades swept up and sliced

between her opponent's legs causing all of us to wince as blood gushed from the wound. The man screamed in pain but his agony didn't last long as she drove a knife into the base of his skull. Another lunged at her with his own knife, flicking it between his hands as he smiled at her. She regarded him in bemusement before she gestured him forward.

He darted in low stabbing at her legs but she danced out of the way and returned with a spinning back kick that caught her attacker in the chest. He rebounded off the wall, wind knocked out of his lungs but still, he came.

He attacked high, then low as he tried to get some sort of read on Poppy, but by the look on her face I knew she was playing with him.

She was having fun.

Frustration now visibly on her opponent's face, he gritted his teeth and rushed in hacking left to right but he was always a second or two too late; hands on his knees he breathed out exhausted as the realisation finally dawned on him he was going to die.

"Look—wait—I know where—" But whatever else he had to say was cut short as Poppy flicked her wrist and embedded her blade into his left eye socket.

She turned to me covered in blood and for the first time I saw what she truly was, a machine of death capable of killing a whole corridor of men without getting a scratch.

What was she truly capable of?

How much of her abilities had she been hiding from me?

What would our child be like?

How was I supposed to raise a child who would one day be a god amongst men?

"I told you to have a little faith in me," she said.

"You see, you overbearing pussy," Willis said, slapping

me on the back, "there wasn't anything to be worried about—"

A groaning sound that reminded me of an unfed stomach rumbled through the floor as the boat tilted a couple more degrees on its side, causing the overhead lights to flicker on and off before they completely went out.

"What were you saying?" I asked, but I was no longer interested in the answer as the sound of rushing water could be heard in the darkness. "Move! Move! Move!" I yelled as the first wave hit me in the chest.

35

The water spun me around as I fought against its current.

Down became up and up became down.

It was relentless in its pressure as I tried to get my bearings. It pushed me down the corridor, bouncing me from wall to wall as I tried my best to fight a losing battle. The back of my helmet banged against something hard, rattling my brain and making me see stars. As soon as it felt like my senses had grown accustomed to their surroundings, I would be tossed against another wall or object and become disoriented again.

My breath grew jagged and sharp as the icy grip of panic's fingers began making their way through my gut.

I had to think. I had to calm down. Calm down! Relax, Quinton. Fucking relax—What little wind I had was knocked out of my lungs as my back slammed into another unseen object.

I tried to look out through my helmet but all I saw was darkness. Complete and utter darkness.

The water kept on pushing me backwards no matter

how much I fought until I found myself pinned against a wall unable to move. I tried. I willed myself with everything I had but no matter what I did, I couldn't move.

I had enough oxygen. More than enough to survive. All I had to do was relax and something would come to me, some idea or moment of inspiration that would save the day. But the longer the water kept me under, the more I panicked, the more thoughts of my death plucked at the recesses of my mind.

I had already used some air when I swam to get to the boat.

That in itself had taken enough time. How much gas did I really have left? I couldn't wait here all day in the vain hope someone would find me. I had to move. I had to move now!

Hyperventilating, I tried to swim with everything I had, but all I succeeded in doing was turning my limbs to lead, and causing the darkness to encroach on the edges of my vision.

Come on, Quinton, move your ass. Come on! Move your ass. Move... your... ass.

But with each flailing of my limbs, the only thing I accomplished was causing the darkness to grow larger and larger over my vision until that was all I saw.

36

Something hit me hard.

Hard enough to wake me from my slumber and force the water in my lungs to come shooting out of my mouth. I leaned to my side and coughed as something else hit me hard on the back, forcing even more water out of me.

My throat burned as I hacked and coughed up everything inside of me.

"Please... no more!" I said as I was hit once again.

"We're just making sure you ain't going to die on us," said Willis, from somewhere above me.

"I wouldn't give you the satisfaction," I said, rolling to my back. "What happened?"

"Oh nothing much," said Poppy, "just had to save your ass for the—what would this be, the fifth time?—is it, now?"

"Don't be ridiculous," I said with a wave of my hand. "It's only four."

"The boat flooded because of Ginger Nuts' handiwork, but we managed to get to the top deck, which is still above water," Tuari said, from somewhere out of my vision.

"What happened to my helmet?" I asked, passing a hand over my face.

"You took it off when you panicked; it's a common occurrence amongst divers who panic," said Poppy.

"Yeah, only dumbass ones," Willis said with a snort. "If you ask me it's the Lord's way of thinning the herd."

"Lucky no one did ask you," I said, sitting up and looking around me. "Did Wei make it?" I couldn't see the little Asian man anywhere.

"I'm still alive for my sins," he said, walking out of the darkness, "but I am not the only one."

Now that my senses were coming back to me I could hear voices shouting in the distance—voices of men that were furious that their boat was going down. Men who had thought all their tricks and bribes would pay off. One in particular was worried more than most. He knew what his future entailed if he didn't find a way to escape the boat.

I rolled to my hands and knees and allowed what little water remained in my sinuses to pour out before getting up to my feet. I stretched out my back and was rewarded with a loud crack before I cast my eyes over my crew.

They all looked the worse for wear, but no one was sporting any injuries, so I counted my lucky stars we had made it this far. By the sounds in the distance, we didn't have far to go to complete the task The Lady assigned us. I was thankful; I didn't know how much more I had left in the gas tank.

I turned around and could see light pouring out of what looked like a glasshouse. It sat raised on top of the deck. I could see people inside.

They moved around frantically while one man with jet black hair, with streaks of silver, stood in the centre shouting orders I don't think anyone was paying any attention to.

"Does that asshole always wear a white tuxedo?" Willis asked.

"Lee is a man with many flaws but he is above all else consistent," Wei said, walking forward.

"I like it," Tuari said; "a man who always wears a tuxedo is always ready to party."

"If that is the case, then I guess we should gatecrash," I said as Poppy handed me my shotgun.

Lee still shouted and screamed but stopped when he turned and caught sight of us. Diamond teeth flashed as he bared them in a snarl.

I took a step forward but was nearly thrown off my feet as the boat shuddered once more. Trying to stay balanced like the rest of the crew I looked to Poppy, who remained unfazed. Like a wine cork bobbing on the water, she didn't even have to hold her hands out to steady herself for balance.

"Try and keep on your feet, twinkle toes," she smiled as she gave me a hand.

I looked back to Lee and couldn't see him. The rest of the men who were still on the bridge were all picking up weapons and making their way towards us, no doubt in an act to try and give their boss time to escape.

"Our mission still is Lee. Remember that. No matter what gets in your way, he is the prime target."

All heads nodded in my direction as the first wave of gunfire came our way. We all took cover and made our way forward. A spark from a bullet that pinged off a railing illuminated the night in front of me forcing me to duck lower. The continuous gunfire pinned us from going any further; their goal was to hold us down as long as possible. That I couldn't allow, not when Lee was so close.

I switched my shotgun to fire explosive shells and waited for my moment.

The sound of gunfire was never-ending as our enemy continued to rain lead upon us. I huddled lower and counted under my breath. I waited till they had to stop and reload, and like the calm before the storm all noise ceased to exist.

Now it was our time.

I leapt to my feet and fired the first shell directly in front of me; it blasted apart a section of the boat lifting bodies into the air. Cries of pain and anguish surrounded me but I heard none of it. The rest of the crew didn't wait for me to tell them to move as they popped up around me and did their own damage.

I re-chambered another shell and blasted apart a group of men who were hiding behind a stack of lounge chairs. The few who survived tried to make a quick getaway but Willis gunned them down.

Reflected light flashed in the corner of my eye and I turned just in time to see Lee's vanishing back as he hurried down the stairs of the bridge and turned a sharp corner.

I made a beeline in his direction but was stopped as I saw something leap at me from the left. Half turning I saw nothing but a face contorted in anger. Time slowed as I kept on turning but knew I wouldn't complete the turn fast enough. He was coming towards me too fast. The knife in his hand had nowhere to go but in my guts. I willed myself to move faster, but I knew the effort was a wasted one. I was caught in a time loop of either trying to evade the weapon in his hand or trying to bring my weapon in range so I could get off a shot.

I didn't need to be accurate. I just needed it pointed in

his direction, but even that I didn't think I could achieve in time.

As each millisecond passed by and the thought of attack or evade flipped in my mind like a coin tossed in the air, the knife inched ever closer towards me determined to do the job it was designed for.

Fight or evade.

Fight or evade.

Choose, damnit!

But it was a choice I didn't have to make, as fingers shot out from nowhere and encircled the hand making its way towards me. The knife stopped inches away from my gut and I knew without a shadow of a doubt that no matter what I had chosen to do, I would have been stabbed. My attacker's eyes swept past the fingers keeping his hand in place, up the arm that refused to budge, to a face that was emotionless.

"Let go, you stupid bitch!" he yelled, trying to yank his arm out of Poppy's grip.

"Ask nicely," she said.

"Suck my—" but he never got to finish his sentence as Poppy bent his arm backwards and stabbed him in the neck with his own knife.

She was about to ask me something but from the look on her face, she knew I didn't have time to respond. "Just go!" she said, pushing me in the direction Lee had gone.

I gave her a nod of thanks and hurried after him.

More men jumped in my way but I blasted them apart with another explosive shell. Their bodies dropped around me in chunks that turned my stomach, but I pushed those thoughts to the back of my mind and kept on going. I had one goal, one thing that needed to be done, to get the ball rolling in securing my future and the future of my family. I would do whatever it took to make that happen, even if it meant allowing the whole world around me to burn.

I ran and turned the same corner Lee had taken and leapt back as a blade swept for my neck. The blade kept coming and I was forced to defend against it by bringing my gun up to block it; sparks flew in the air as the blade was pushed towards me, with nothing but the barrel of my gun keeping it from sinking into my flesh. I looked into the eyes of my attacker and saw the smiling face of Lee.

"Oh, Mr Blake, how good of you to finally join me. I would have sent you an invitation but it appears that none was needed."

I grunted as he pushed his weight down on the knife slowly pushing me back' "How could I miss the event of the year, Mr Lee? I so loved your last casino event so much I thought I just had to make an appearance. Sorry about the boat, but I do love to crash a party."

He said nothing but kept on pushing me backwards, getting the knife closer and closer to my neck. His strength amazed me. For a man well into his middle years, he had more strength than most of the men I had fought.

"Surprised?" he asked. "I wasn't always this tailor-suited gentleman you see before you; I made my living as a ship hand, on these very waters. The hardest work I have ever done. Work that calloused the soul as well as the hands. But unlike those fools I left behind, I wanted something more for myself. More than stabbing my bunkmate in the back and whoring every chance I got."

He kept on pushing me until my back was pressed up against the railing and all I could see behind me was nothing but black open water.

"That's the thing about Safe Haven, Mr Blake, it's a rat race like no other. Everyone is aiming for the top and will do everything in their power to make sure they make it there, and my path to the top is only secured if you're lying dead at the bottom of this river!"

He tried to knee me in the balls but I saw the move coming a mile away and blocked it with the outside of my thigh, and returned a head-butt that smashed the bridge of his nose, staggering him backwards.

"I would say something corny like *too bad your climb stops here*, but I'll just go for the time tested *fuuck youuu*," I said, gun butting him in the face and turning his nose into a fine paste.

I spun the shotgun round to finish him off but he kicked it out of my hand and rugby tackled me to the floor.

The wind was knocked out of my lungs as he straddled my chest and brought the knife high above his head; he drove it towards me and I just had enough time to hip bump him forward, forcing the knife to sink in the wood of the deck millimetres from my head. He tried to retrieve it, but the knife was buried to the hilt. I pushed him off me and got back to my feet the same time he did.

Chests heaving we looked at each other like two beasts fighting for territory.

"I heard a rumour you used to be nothing more than an office drone—a pen pusher—a glorified middle management asshole. All this," he said gesturing around him, "must be very frightening for you."

"Not really. Like you said, Safe Haven is a rat race, no different to the backstabbing, fake-smiling, fire-you-a-week-before-Christmas corporate world I'm used to."

He said nothing but took a small step forward. My eyes swept the deck for my gun and I saw it some distance behind him; I would have to go through him to get it, but it would leave me to exposed. If I wanted to finish this fight, then I would have to do it with nothing but my bare hands.

Strange.

The thought of killing someone with my hands felt barbaric to me. Wrong. Criminal. It was as if the gun was an extra layer in stopping me thinking about the act I was going to complete. Where my hands would never get dirty.

He took another step forward.

"What's wrong, Mr Blake? Isn't so easy to do the deed when you have nothing but your hands, is—"

I punched him in the mouth, forcing his words back down his mouth, and followed up with a roundhouse kick that smashed into his ribs, lifting him up. He dropped to his knees allowing me to grab his head and drive my knee into his face.

He staggered backwards trying to get away but I didn't let him.

A left hook to the body and straight right to the face splattered blood on my chest.

His face was a mask of blood as he once again dropped to his knees. He lifted his hands up in a vain attempt to protect himself but I slapped them out of the way and grabbed him by his bloodstained tuxedo.

The first punch closed his left eye.

The second split his top lip in two.

The third broke his front teeth embedding them into my knuckle.

"You know," I said, holding up his swaying form, "I thought I would get some sort of satisfaction from this, for finally taking revenge on one more person who caused José's death. But with you here and now, as I look upon your ruined face, all I feel is... emptiness.

"Emptiness and sadness."

Lee spat broken teeth and snot at my feet as he looked up at me with a defiant eye. "You will wish for sadness and emptiness after this is all said and done. You have no idea what's coming, do you?"

I ignored his question and lifted my fist up in the air; it was time to end this once and for—

"Boss!"

I lifted my head as shouts up ahead drew my attention to three armed men who were coming my way. I looked down at Lee just in time to see a blade swing upwards; I jumped back out of the way and this gave him all the time and space he needed to regroup with his men. Any thoughts of pursuing them were out of the question as they turned their guns on me and opened fire.

I dived behind a wall and pressed my back up against it as bullets blew chunks out of it.

I could hear feet pounding away as the firing lessened in frequency.

He was going to get away.

Back still pressed against the wall, Willis and Wei made their way towards me. Willis's face was covered in blood but he showed no signs of any injury; his eyes blazed with the fire of blood lust as they darted back and forth looking for their next target. Wei, on the other hand, looked like a husk of a man who was just moving because that's what his body had always done. It was hard to meet his eyes and not feel pulled in by the pits of blackness that lay beneath.

"Where's Lee?" Willis asked.

I pointed over my shoulder.

"Escaped?" he asked.

"Escaping."

"What!" Wei roared, stepping away from me. "You can't let him escape. This is why you are here. This is why Marta died! So you could kill the evil fuck! You can't just give up now."

I got to my feet. He was right. I had come too far to give up now; we had lost too much to just turn back now.

With a nod their way I ran the direction Lee went, picking up my gun on the way. I could see the backs of his men pushing what appeared to be an escape raft over the edge of the railings. Willis opened fire, taking out two men, before the white-tuxedoed form of Lee detached himself from the group and leapt overboard. Willis kept on firing but the last remaining man jumped after him.

We sprinted towards the railings and saw the escape craft floating on the open water with Lee and his man sprawled out on its floor. I sighted my shotgun and fired but nothing happened.

"Shit! I'm out of explosive shells."

"Hey! What are you doing?" Willis asked, as Wei unclipped Willis's utility belt and snatched it away from him.

"What the—" began Willis, but stopped as Wei pulled out all the pins from the grenades attached to the belt and looked me squarely in the eye.

"Make sure you keep your promise. Make sure the people of this borough are treated better than those who came before them!" he shouted as he sprinted away from us.

I looked to him then back to the craft that was slowly pulling away and knew he wouldn't make it. He was throwing his life away for nothing. But I couldn't stop him now. To do so would mean getting in the path of a man who carried a bomb that was going to go off, no matter if it was on this boat or over the open water. To stop him would be to risk my crew. My life. The life of my unborn child.

I knew the decision I was going to make. The same decision I would make if I had to choose a million times.

And I think he did too.

Head bent down, arms and legs pumping for everything they were worth, Wei sprinted and turned his head our way giving us a final nod before he leapt over the railings towards Lee's life craft below.

Lee and his man saw Wei in mid-air and fired.

The first two shots pierced Wei's chest and blew holes out his back, but I knew he felt no pain. I could see it by the look on his face when he gave us a final nod goodbye.

It was a look of joy. A look that spoke of seeing a loved one sooner than expected.

The third shot blew out his brains but it was already too late. Wei had thrown the parcel he was holding and it sailed in the air in an arc till it landed dead centre on the life raft. There was a moment of silence, then a frantic cry as Lee rushed forwards but it was a wasted effort.

The explosion from the grenades engulfed the raft in a hundred-foot fireball.

I shielded my eyes from the blinding light and only looked back after the flames had died to see if I could see Wei's body, but knew it was already sinking to the bottom of a river that had birthed him, raised him, and killed him.

37

We all sat on the last remaining life craft we could find while the flames of Lee's paddleboat illuminated the night sky.

I looked upon the sight before me and felt nothing but emptiness. This war had only begun yet it had already taken such a toll on my psyche that I didn't know how long I could go on for before I cracked. I had witnessed the deaths of loved ones and people that had tried to help me in this cause I had taken on, but the more the bodies piled up the more I asked myself if this was worth it.

The plan had always been to keep Poppy safe.

Yet... everything I had planned, everything I did, placed her in more danger than anything else.

We could have just gotten on a ship and sped as far away as we could and settled on some distant planet, yet with the threat of Alvis Boman hanging above our necks like a guillotine, it was only a matter of time before the psycho found us or his deeds did. This was why I was doing this, to amass power, to have the strength to combat Alvis when the time came. I loved our crew more than anything, but I knew we didn't have the strength to defeat him.

Not as we were. We needed more resources and the only way I could get them was if I continued on with my deal with the devil and made good on my promise.

Lady Isabella Ivanov wasn't someone I trusted or cared for, and when the time came she would meet the same fate as Lee, but before then I would use her as much as she used me to get what she wanted.

The flames continued to dance on the water.

I had kept my promise to Wei and gave Marta the funeral ritual she deserved. Another innocent bystander of the conflict I was waging. How many more would there be before this was done?

"You okay?" Poppy whispered in my ear, hand stroking my hair.

I nodded as I took in a deep breath and slowly let it out. "Message Samuel and Scarface, tell them to come and pick us up. We're done here."

As I continued to watch the flames dance only one thought repeatedly crossed my mind.

Was this life better than the one you had before?

38

I was back on *The Kennel*, sitting in its canteen eating leftovers Tuari had made the night before. Slow-cooked charcoal lamb with jasmine flavoured rice and an assortment of vegetables littered my plate as I forced myself to eat so I could concentrate on something apart from the thoughts bouncing around in my head.

I had first gone to the shooting range to let off some steam and get my thoughts in order, but as I approached the entrance to it I saw the highlighted red gun sign above the door that meant the range was in use. Although the room was big enough to accommodate the whole crew if we all wanted to practice shooting our weapons, the warning was just a precaution to let anyone entering know live ammunition was being fired and that they should proceed with caution.

Although the only one who would be using it at this time was Willis, I wasn't really in a sociable mood, even if all we would do was nod to each other.

Which had brought me here to the only other place I knew would be deserted this time of night.

The canteen.

Or so I thought as the doors to them opened and Samuel stopped short; he rubbed his eyes and did a double-take. He went to say something but a yawn cut him off. "Sorry about that," he said as he made his way to one of the tabletops and began making himself a hot drink.

"Want one?" he asked.

I shook my head and continued on eating, staring off into the distance.

He hummed a tune I had heard before as he finished making himself a cup of tea. I couldn't place where I had heard it before, but it sounded oddly familiar. He sat opposite me and I held back my sigh of frustration. He said nothing for a long while, and the only sounds were the noise from my cutlery as I continued to eat my meal.

He downed the rest of his tea and got back up, but only walked back to the countertop and made himself another drink while he hummed again. Walking back to my table he sat down once again. He closed his eyes and allowed the melody he hummed to play through him.

"That song," I said pointing a fork his way. "I've heard it before, but I can't place where."

He slowly opened his eyes and gave me a smile. "No doubt from Willis; our mother used to sing it to us all the time. It's a song about an orphan who was destined to be killed by a great king, but instead was sent drifting down a river and found amongst the reeds by said great king's daughter. Where he grew up to become a prince, living in the very house of the man who wanted him dead. The orphan's life was one of luxury where he would never need or want for anything until the end of his days. But one day he saw a slave being beaten and no harm came to the attacker because he was rich, and from there, the orphan's life took on a whole new meaning and he left all his wealth and riches behind and fought for the people who needed him the most."

"Hmm," I said before placing more food in my mouth.

"What?"

"I wonder why there are so many stories of men who are never happy with who they are or what they've become."

Samuel chuckled but I didn't see what was so funny. "It's amazing that out of that story, that's what you took from it."

"The orphan didn't help the slave out of some higher purpose or duty. The orphan helped the slave because he saw himself in the man that was being beaten. The orphan, no matter what gifts or love were bestowed upon him, would always be that, an orphan. He would always feel like an outsider in the royal courts, and he would always feel like he was nothing more than a royal pet being kept by the king's daughter.

"Men—women—people, are inherently selfish. We do what best serves us, even if that is being charitable or honourable, because it makes us feel good about ourselves. Kindness is as much of a selfish act as hate."

Samuel leaned back in his chair, a frown creasing the sides of his mouth, while he regarded me. "That is a short-sighted way to view the universe. Men such as myself have done things for people, because it was the right thing to do. Not seeking any thanks or reward for the act in and of itself. Yes, people are selfish, but if everyone selfishly gave their love away then think of what we could overcome as a race."

"But... would you do what you did if your background wasn't what it was?"

He looked at me in confusion before I continued.

"Some may say, you're only doing what you're doing because you feel guilt for your mother, because you feel you need to pay some debt to society, and if that wasn't the case then you would be just another thug trying to make a quick buck, however you can."

His jaw stiffened as he gripped the mug of his cup and sat bolt upright.

"Look, I don't mean any disrespect. All I'm saying is from where I'm standing, the only person who I have met so far who is honest about who they are is Willis. He is comfortable with who he is at his core. He knows himself inside and out and because of that, he knows his enemies even better. Many men like the orphan find themselves in places of power and reject it—shun it, and use some thin veil of an excuse such as helping the poor when they give away all their wealth and become prophets or gurus or spiritual leaders.

"But the way I see it, is if you want change, serious life-altering change for the people you care about or want to help, then you need power. Power that only kings and leaders have. Power only they can wield, and to get that, my dear friend, well, you need to either take it from the people who have it, or keep it."

He looked at me askance before taking a deep breath and stirring the remainder of the tea he had in his mug. He downed its contents in one then slowly rose from his chair. He made his way to the countertop and cleaned out his mug, then placed it on the rack to dry.

Everything was done with calm measured movements. Everything was done with care.

Done, he walked back towards me but didn't sit down. "These sleepless nights you are experiencing will only continue the longer you stay on this path. Take it from someone who has made the journey."

Before I could say anything he was already walking towards the door, leaving me with my thoughts once more.

39

"Congratulations, Mr Blake," said Lady Isabella Ivanov, raising her glass filled with neat vodka my way.

We were seated in one of the only two restaurants to be found in Hotel Moscow. Linen-covered tables accompanied with deep red fabric chairs that had elaborate golden stitching in the fabric were placed the right distance away from their neighbours so conversations couldn't be overheard. Art depicting classic Russian life could be found on the walls, all grim and doing nothing to lift the atmosphere of the place. The restaurant was a strange mix of garish over-the-top displays of wealth as well as trying to come across as a humble family-run restaurant, that had been in the family for generations.

"It was nothing really," I said, taking a sip from the glass of water in front of me.

"Come now, you're being far too humble," she said, nodding to the waiter who placed two dishes in front of us.

I looked down at my plate and did my best to hide my frown as pieces of meat in a brownish sauce that looked like cat-sick accompanied by pasta rested on my plate. Picking up a fork, I moved it around like a child being punished as I tried my best to think of how not to eat this without offending my dangerous host.

"It's called beef stroganoff," said Isabella, "whenever I eat it, it reminds me of my childhood and home."

"I'm sorry your childhood was so bleak," I muttered.

"Pardon?"

"Nothing," I said with a smile, taking another drink of water and looking at the empty restaurant around us. "Business still hasn't picked up?"

She followed my gaze around the empty restaurant and smiled. "This restaurant has never been popular. It only serves traditional Russian cuisine, which is not to everyone's taste," she said, looking at my plate, "but no matter what my accountants say about this place not making money, I refuse to change it. The other restaurant is always packed and more than makes up for this one's losses. Plus, I can always get a seat here."

"The decor..." I began but couldn't find the words I was looking for.

"When people who have nothing develop wealth, they... want to show off the wealth they have and keep something back to remind them of their roots. It's a flaw in most of us, it's something I have tried to rid myself of, but alas," she said, gesturing to the restaurant with a fork, "it's not something I have accomplished. But anyway, on to business. I hate to ask this but you are sure Mr Lee won't come back to haunt us?"

Visions of the flaming wreckage that had become Lee's craft surfaced. "Yes," I said with a grim shake of the head, "after what happened to him there won't be anything left to bury."

"Excellent, that is wonderful news. Most wonderful news indeed," she said, giving me a shark-like smile. "Now, when you were fighting Lee's men, you didn't happen to come across any members of the Mercenary Bloc, did you?"

I thought back to the mission in question and frowned. "Now that you mention it, no," I said in a thoughtful voice. In preparing for the fight against Lee, I had completely forgotten about Tex Jonson and his band of merry men. It seemed strange now that Diamond hadn't thought to enforce one of his major allies with members from the Mercenary Bloc, but if the accounts of them were true, then acting like bodyguards really wasn't their thing.

It appeared they only cared about the mission they were paid to do, which was taking out my crew and The Lady.

"Now you mention it, it is strange Mr Diamond didn't get them to protect one of his most valuable assets, but I guess his loss of foresight is our gain."

Lady Isabella frowned as she took another swig of vodka. "If there is one thing I can trust Mr Diamond to do, it is cover all his bases. It is unlike him. But, I guess we all make mistakes. Now on to the main reason I called you here. Vlad," she called to her right-hand man, who had been lurking unseen in the shadows. He made his way silently towards me and handed me a small leather-bound folder.

I looked to it then back to her confused.

"In there you shall find payment for a job well done, and a more formal contract relating to the ownership of The Floating City. Although the agreement was for you to take ownership of The Floating City after both Mr Lee and Mr Diamond were both dead, I trust in your ability to get the job done so I am handing over the ownership of The Floating City to you early."

I looked at her then slowly lowered my gaze to the folder

in my hand while I tried to digest everything she had just said. I smiled. That was the game she was trying to play. Clever.

"I don't think that I've earned this just yet. A deal was a deal and until I finish taking out Mr Diamond, then I won't feel right taking—"

"Nonsense, I *insist*."

I tapped the folder against my lips and took in Vlad's tense posture as he stared daggers my way. Giving her a single nod I placed the folder in the folds of my clothes.

"Wonderful! Now that's all sorted, shall we discuss how we are going to take out our biggest threat?" she asked, as she dabbed the corners of her mouth.

"If I'm honest I've not given it much thought; I'm still recovering from dealing with Lee. But when I think about it, I don't really see a way to tackle Diamond without a shitload of bloodshed and firearms. He is too well-fortified to be taken out as easily as Lee and he has more than enough men and resources to wait us out. From the way you speak about the man, it appears you respect him, which in turn tells me he isn't a person to be taken lightly."

She nodded her head and gave me a smile, as she held up her glass to be refilled by Vlad with more vodka.

"All perfect assumptions. As you may or may not know, Mr Diamond—ridiculous name, I know—has been the longest-running leader of any borough in the history of Safe Haven. He came to power when he was but a young man and has seen this planet grow from a dust ball to a cesspit to something now akin to gutter water—drinkable, but you may still die from dysentery.

"Unlike most of us, he was born on this planet; he grew up seeing the settlers, his parents struggle and toil over the land trying to make it liveable, trying to make it sustainable.

He knew hunger, real hunger. He knew pain, but more importantly, he knew what sort of hard work it would take to get him to where he is today.

"Unlike most of these new up-and-coming crews who want respect and power without actually putting the work in, he was born with nothing but a wooden stick to play with and now he is one of the most powerful men on this planet, who has far-reaching influence over other worlds too. Who can't respect a man like that? To not do so would be foolhardy on my part and yours.

"So yes, Mr Blake, I respect the man. I suggest you do the same."

"But that still," I said, "doesn't help us with our problem in how we are going to deal with him."

"I think I have a solution for that. Although my forces have tried their best to stop his men digging the caves in The Jungle, there are still reports of people taking out metal ore under the cover of darkness, or when I have had to pull my men away from the sites to deal with more pressing issues. I think the only way you'll be able to enter the Diamond District is if you somehow manage to smuggle your way on board a ship that is delivering ore to the Diamond District. Once in the district half the battle is already accomplished and the rest is, as they say, history."

"Half the battle is already accomplished?" I said in disbelief, "I think you mean the battle has only just begun. Once in the district, we won't know where Diamond is stationed, how to get to him or what forces he'll have around him. We'll be in the wolves' den with no way out."

"Tut, tut, Mr Blake, you have such little faith in your and your crew's abilities. I have the utmost faith you'll figure something out when the time comes. In regard to Mr Diamond's location and his forces, all the information you need shall be arriving on your ship's databanks as we speak. The information I am giving you is everything I collected on the man since I landed on this planet. Use it well."

I looked at her in disbelief not sure what to say.

"If I may give you one more piece of advice, it would be to wait a few days or even a few weeks before you attempt to smuggle yourself aboard a ship. I shall slowly pull men away from the caves, forcing increased activity and hopefully making the men involved in the operations lax enough in their surveillance that you shouldn't face that big of a problem getting yourself onboard. Now, before you finish, do you have any questions?"

A million thoughts raced through my mind but they failed to reach my mouth.

One way or another, I had agreed to do this job, and her plan was the only one presented to me at the moment so unless I came up with something better, this would have to be the one I went with. Even though it felt like we were being set up.

"Excellent. I'm glad we are on the same page. Now if that is all I believe our business is done here for the day," she said.

I sat rooted to the spot until a cough from Vlad brought me back to reality. As I was getting up from my seat and about to leave her voice called out to me once more: "Oh, and if you would be so kind as to wait outside the restaurant, Mr Blake, one of my waiters shall place your meal in a doggy bag. I do hate food going to waste."

40

I walked the grimy streets of Paradise Lost, with a doggie bag I didn't want and a mission I was regretting ever agreeing to. Trash crunched under my feet as I watched out for the occasional needle or steaming pile of human waste. A junkie with sore-covered lips lifted a hand with nails hidden under black grime. He looked up at me, hand searching in the air as if he was trying to recapture the last pieces of his soul before they escaped him forever.

I looked into his eyes and saw nothing but a pit of despair. I placed the parcel containing my leftover meal in the palm of his hand and closed his fingers around it before departing.

Everywhere I looked trash covered the streets or was piled up against building corners, while junkies scuttled down alleyways or vanished into boarded-up buildings that had no light apart from that created by burning trashcans.

A car screeched around a corner, back tires billowing smoke while two men hung out the window, pistols visible in their hands, I dived for cover behind a dumpster but their target wasn't me. The passengers opened fire upon a small group of men gathered at a corner. The men tried to get away but their paths of escape were cut short by the bullets fired. Gunshot after gunshot filled the air until the sound of screeching tires could be heard once again, then all was silent.

I had expected my heart to be pounding in my chest. I had expected my palms to be sweaty. But as I sat on the ground in a puddle of water that was slowly beginning to soak into my jeans, all I felt was numb.

Numb and angry.

This was nowhere to raise a child, not amongst this filth and chaos! What sort of upbringing could I ever hope to give my son or daughter if I kept them on this planet? What damage would I be causing to their psyche? To the way they viewed things. Even now, after being on this planet only a handful of years, the way I viewed violence and reacted to it wasn't normal. Instead of fearing guns being fired, my first thought was to take cover and return fire when the best opportunity presented itself.

I viewed death and suffering as part and parcel of living.

This place had twisted my way of thinking, because if you didn't harden yourself, if you didn't bite first and ask questions later, then you were the one that was going to be a victim. You were the one that would end up face down in the gutter while people stepped over you. Life was cheap on Paradise Lost, and freedom came at a cost that was greater than it had been back on Earth. Back home, all one needed to do was find some way to save enough money to cover all your basic needs for the long term and then you could do as you pleased.

Travel, paint, write, whatever your heart could imagine.

But out here, getting the money was only half the problem; keeping it was the other.

I got to my feet and poked my head around the dumpster. The only sight that greeted me was of a cluster of bodies lying face down in the dirt with a rapidly expanding pool of blood extending out from them. Nobody rushed to their aid. Nobody came to see what the commotion had been about.

Looking at the bodies I knew two things. One, my child would never grow up in a place like this. I didn't care what I had to do, I just knew that whatever it was, no cost would be too great to make sure it happened. And two, before this was over and done with I needed to show Poppy how much I loved her.

41

I fidgeted in my captain's chair while I piloted *The Kennel* towards the target I had in mind. It was just me and Poppy alone on the ship. I had given the rest of the crew the week off to blow off any steam they needed to before we tackled our next target, Mr Diamond. There had been complaints when I had said I was taking the ship for a little trip, but I ignored all of them and had told them that if they were so eager to come along, then the toilets we all used could do with some attention as both Willis or Tuari had been ignoring the cleaning rota for weeks.

This had shut down all and any complaints and allowed me to focus on the task at hand.

We had been travelling for two days and no matter how many times Poppy asked where we were going, I would just smile and kiss her softly on the lips before making sure everything was in order.

"It's a surprise," I would say, when she would badger me again and again, asking innocent questions that would reveal more than I wanted to let on if I answered.

I had caught her a few times lingering on the bridge

when she thought I wasn't around trying to see what destination I had programmed into the autopilot; it had gotten so bad I had banned her from coming anywhere near it, much to her annoyance.

It was cute in a way seeing her act normal again. Out here we didn't have to worry about mercenary hitmen or borough leaders wanting us dead. We could just be in each other's company and exist. Thinking about it now, it wasn't something we had done a lot of, apart from the months we had spent in The Jungle after the Alvis Boman affair. This was one of the only times where we could just be.

The console in front of me beeped. We had arrived at our destination.

I took a deep breath and passed a hand down the tuxedo I wore. Pressing a button in front of me I opened the viewing screen of the ship so it extended all around me. It gave a complete three hundred and sixty-degree view of the space we were in. Getting up from my chair I walked around the bridge and just took in the amazing sights that surrounded me. It felt like I was floating in space.

Different hues of reds that bled into pinks were dotted with the shine from distant stars. The whole thing looked like a silk scarf clustered with diamonds. The last time I had been to this spot had been years ago, and after much searching through the ship's records, I had finally found what I was looking for. I didn't know what I would find when I got there, hoping for some sort of light show, but knowing I would probably just get a black canvas.

Now, here, I was happy the universe had come through for me. I couldn't ask for a better light show.

My tongue felt like sandpaper. I looked around for a drink but couldn't find one. I tried to take a deep breath to calm the pounding of my heart, but all I succeeded in doing was being keenly aware of how fast my heart was beating.

"Relax, man. You've done this once before."

I paced back and forth, trying to build the courage I needed, but whenever I went to press the button that would broadcast my voice over the speakers, I hesitated, nerves getting the better of me.

I resumed pacing.

"You've fought against killer robot spiders and armed thugs, you've been tortured mercilessly, you've had your entire life ripped out from underneath your feet, plus a hundred other near-death experiences, but you can't do this one thing! Come on man, stop being such a pussy!"

I walked towards the button and pressed it. "Ugh, Poppy—" Why did my voice sound so small? "Poppy, do you mind coming to the bridge?"

I gripped onto a console next to me, to steady myself as my legs wouldn't stop shaking. Taking another deep breath I patted my jacket pocket for the hundredth time.

I had rehearsed what I was going to say over the two days we were travelling through space, but now the time actually came, my mind was a blank. What had I come up with? There was something about being happy and... and... being together....and... being happy—shit!

The doors to the bridge opened and Poppy walked through, looking around the bridge with some confusion that only increased when she took in the attire I was wearing.

"Hmm, hello," she said sheepishly.

"Hello," I replied back with a smile.

Hair draped over her shoulders, she wore a simple loose-fitting jumper that tried its best to cover her bump but it only enhanced her beauty, taking my breath away. Bare legs distracted me from what I was going to say next.

"Is everything alright?" she asked.

I shook my head, emerging from my daze, and as I took her all in I realised something. When I extended my hand she walked towards me and I just smiled.

"Looking at you here and now, I realised something. I realised no matter what I say it will never really matter, not because I don't mean it, not because it isn't true, but because whatever feeble words I manage to conjure up would never be good enough, would never truly express to you what you mean to me, how I feel about you, how my life has changed since I met you. How you allowed me to find courage and strength within myself that I didn't know I had, that I didn't believe was there.

"How I keep finding a way to survive and strive no matter what is placed in front of me, because I know if I don't, we as a family won't live to see another day. It's because of you, Pop, that I found the strength to lead this crew, it's because of you I have grown—evolved—changed into someone nobody from my past would recognise.

"It's because of you my life is what it is, good or bad. So, I must thank you for everything you've done for me, everything you continue to do for me, and everything you shall do for me in the future.

"So because of that, I have a question I need to ask you," I said, getting down on one knee and pulling a small velvet box from my pocket. "Will you marry me?"

I held my breath while I looked up at her and she looked down at me, face blank. She said nothing as the only thing that I could hear was the pounding of my heart against my chest. What felt like ten minutes passed and still she said nothing. I licked my lips and I stared up at her, open—vulnerable—true, but still, she said nothing.

Did I do the wrong thing?

"Err—" I began but she cut me off by placing her finger across my lips.

"I love you, but you didn't have to do this to show me you loved me. I already knew that, silly. I knew we would be together as long as you lived when I first laid eyes on you. Don't ask me how, but I just did. I can't see a future without you, but since you've asked of course the answer is yes!" she said, bending down and kissing me on the lips. "Yes! Yes! A thousand times, yes!"

I rose to my feet unsteadily and slipped the ring onto her finger, then kissed her again until my heart stopped pounding and my hands grew dry.

Some time had passed and now we both lay amongst a pile of discard clothes.

The stars still sprinkled around us making it feel like we were the only two people that existed, I hugged her close, and kissed her on the top of the head while I watched a comet travel in front of us.

"Do you know where this is?" I asked.

She shook her head.

"This," I said, gesturing before me, "is the location we first met."

She looked up at me sharply and I only smiled in response as I watched her turn her attention back to the viewing screen, where a smile grew on her face, mirroring my own.

"This is where it all began," I whispered in her ear, "this is where you kidnapped me against my will. This is where I learned how foul a mouth a human can really have when I met Willis, this is where I learnt how good food can taste because of Tuari, this is where José decided I was worth more to him alive than dead and he took me under his wing and showed me the life I was living wasn't really a life at all. My life changed forever that day and I have never looked back."

"Not once?" she asked. "When things were simpler? When things were safer?"

I opened my mouth to protest but closed it slowly and really thought about it. Had I ever prayed that certain things we had been through or done would have gone easier? Sure. Had I ever thought about my past?

I would be lying if I said no. But I had made my choice and life was now at warp speed and if I tried to look back, I would miss what was in front of me.

"Sometimes, I wished things had turned out different. José. But I have never once looked back at my life and missed it. My life was hell. Worse than hell. Looking back now, all I wanted was someone to love me for myself, and I have found that in the unlikeliest of places. Amongst the stars, with a person who isn't human but has more humanity in her little finger than most of the people I meet.

"Don't get me wrong, this war we are in, I would rather we were not in it, I would rather it had nothing to do with us, but sometimes life doesn't work out like that. The only thing keeping me going is knowing that one of the most traumatic experiences of my life was when you and the crew made your way on the ship and kidnapped me. That experience at the time felt like it was the end, but it grew and blossomed into this. So who knows what shall happen after this war?"

She grabbed my hand and brought it to her lips, then stopped suddenly as she placed her hand gently on her stomach.

"What is it?" I asked.

Saying nothing, she took my hand and placed it on the spot she had been touching and looked up at me. I felt nothing at first, then the tiniest movement against my hand that I would have missed if I wasn't paying close enough attention.

"The little guy sure can kick."

"Or girl," said Poppy, nudging me in the ribs.

"Have you decided what you're going to do about getting a scan to make sure everything is alright?"

She gave a chuckle and shook her head. "What would I tell the doctor?

"'Hello Doc, I know this may be hard to believe but I'm an AI humanoid built by a crazy genius hundreds of years ago who has made it so I can get pregnant?' What do you think they'll do to me?"

Nothing good, that was for sure. They would most likely hook her up to as many machines as they could find and then perform tests on her and also the baby. Her kind hadn't been seen for hundreds of years and was thought to have all been destroyed. If she turned up now, that would only be opening up a can of worms best left untouched. Plus, they would wait till my child was born and keep it locked in a cage, like some zoo animal, always testing, always experimenting.

I shuddered as the thought passed through my mind.

"What's wrong?" Poppy asked, looking up at me.

"I was just thinking, what would happen if the news got out about you, about us, about our child. I don't think I could survive if anything happened—"

"Shh now," she said, as she stroked my face. "None of that is going to happen. I trust you and you haven't failed us yet. In regard to getting a scan done to see if the baby is alright, I had checks done while I was in The Jungle by Samuel himself. He's a smart man, who has had to deliver a lot of babies by hand because of the nature of the people who live in The Jungle, and I'm fine. I would know if I wasn't, but the baby has a strong heartbeat and everything is coming along as normal."

"You trust him?"

"Samuel?" she asked. "He's a man... he's a man with a troubled past for sure, but he wouldn't cause harm to anyone. He's too busy paying for his past mistakes."

I was still concerned about Samuel's involvement with The Lady, but with him being the brother of Willis and how he had treated us when we needed help, I couldn't come out and accuse him of anything. Still, something just didn't feel right. It wasn't that I disliked the man, far from it, but I knew that above all else he would have his borough's best interest at heart and do whatever it took to make sure it wasn't negatively impacted in any way.

But that was a conversation I didn't want to bring up in the here and now.

"Did you..." I swallowed, "did you happen, did you happen to find out the sex?"

I could feel her smile even though I couldn't see her face. She pressed her back into me and buried the back of her head into my chest. "Who said I didn't know it from the start?"

"What!"

"You'll just have to wait and find out. I don't want to ruin the surprise."

"But—"

"But nothing. My decision is final."

I opened my mouth to argue but knew it wouldn't get me anywhere. When she made up her mind there wasn't much I could do to change it. I would have to try and pry the information out of her one way or another at a later date.

"How did you know?" she asked, lifting her hand in the air so the engagement ring caught the light. The band was made out of the same metal that Mr Diamond's men had been stealing from The Jungle caves, but I had used rubies from that same cave to create a petal of flowers that resembled a poppy with a diamond acting as a small centrepiece.

"I remembered the story you told me about walking a dangerous mountain path just for the hell of it, and it was the first time you had ever done something just on a whim, just to see the poppy flowers that grew on the mountainside. So I thought what better way to always remind you to trust your instincts, even though your programming or wiring, or whatever is inside you, may be telling you to do something different."

She turned and looked at me with an expression I couldn't read.

Had I said something to offend her in regard to her being an AI humanoid?

"I didn't mean to of—"

She kissed me full on the lips and rubbed her nose against mine before turning back around and collapsing in my arms. "How long do we have?" she asked.

"Not long. A handful of days. Then I've got to get back to dealing with Diamond."

"What!" she said, turning to me. "But we still haven't discussed wedding plans and where we're going to get married and who we're going to invite and—"

"We'll have plenty of time to discuss that and so much

more; we don't have to get married right away. We can do it after I've finished my business with Diamond. There shall be plenty of time—"

"What if there isn't?"

The question hung in the air. I closed my eyes and thought of what to say.

"I... I won't lie to you and tell you I know that I'll come back from this one, because it wouldn't be fair to you. You also can't come with us, not this time. It's too dangerous. Doing so would just jeopardise the baby and put needless stress and complications on the whole mission. I know you would like to be there and god knows we need all the help we can get, but it is what it is. All I can say is that, no matter what happens, you and our unborn child shall be fine. I've made arrangements that you'll be taken care of—"

"I don't need—"

"I have already made the arrangements. We're not only dealing with Diamond here, there's also Alvis lurking in the shadows god knows where waiting to make his move. Something is going on in Safe Haven, that just... the metal—something just doesn't feel right, and if, I'm not saying that we are, but if we are walking into a trap, I can do so more easily knowing both of you and our child are safe and sound."

Silence dominated the room as I felt something wet drop onto my forearm. I brought my hands up to her face and brushed away her tears as I kissed her on the side of the head.

"Funny, I always wondered why I was created with tear ducts. Now I know."

"Look, let's put all that aside for now and just be," I said, hugging her tight.

She said nothing back, but I knew her thoughts were

only on whether I would come back or not. To be honest, I wondered that myself. I had tried to ignore it but the closer I got to the upcoming mission, the more I felt like I was walking into a trap. It was a feeling I couldn't shake, but I had already made a deal with the devil to ensure my family's safety.

If I had to sacrifice my life so they could live on free, then it was a deal I would happily make.

42

"What the fuck do you mean we control The Floating City?" Willis demanded, fist slamming against the table.

"First of all," Tuari said, placing his hand over his heart, "I just want to say congratulations. I had a feeling you were going to propose but I didn't want to jinx it, so I kept quiet. But I knew deep down the time was right, and that's why you needed the ship. I must say red rubies on an engagement ring wouldn't be my personal choice; it's a bold statement and was in fashion some years ago, but not so much now. That's not to say I'm not happy with your ring choice, Quinton, just some things should stay traditional. Now, have you thought about what sort of wedding you'll be having? Will it be the classic church wedding? Although religion was outlawed after WW3 churches are still used—even if in secret—for such occasions. Or you could go the rustic route and maybe have it in a barn or in a field. Or there is always the more outlandish—"

"Will you shut your meat-hole! In the name of Christ, man! You sound like an ovulating woman," said Willis.

"Sorry, some of us have other interests apart from drinking and cussing," Tuari replied, hurt lacing his voice.

"Oh, don't give me that bollocks—"

I pinched the bridge of my nose as I listened to them go back and forth. The entire crew plus Samuel and Scarface were seated in the conference room on *The Kennel*.

Poppy and I had gotten back two days ago and although I would've liked to have this meeting sooner, it took longer than I thought just finding Willis, let alone the others.

"Enough!" I said looking between the pair as the noise quietened down. "First of all, I thank you, Tuari, for all your wonderful comments and the gift basket you got us. It shall be put to good use."

"You got them a gift basket?" Willis mouthed silently to Tuari, whose face was plastered with a smug grin.

"To answer your questions, the ring is designed after the poppy flower, that's why I went with the red stones—"

"Ahh," he said.

"And secondly, we aren't too sure what we're going to do in regard to the wedding. We haven't given it much thought because the only thing I can—well, both of us—can think of, is this upcoming mission. That's why I called all of you here today. If we could have found everyone sooner," I said, looking at Willis, "then we would have told you the news as soon as we landed."

Willis threw his hands in the air in mock innocence as he looked at me. "Hey, you told us we had shore leave and we could do as we pleased and that you would be back in a week or so. If you had been more *specific* with when you were going to be back then I would have been ready and waiting. It's not my fault I had important things to take care of."

"Yeah, all of them to be found at the bottom of the bottle no doubt," said Samuel.

"You got something to say, tree-hugger?" Willis said, rising to his feet.

Ignoring Willis Samuel looked to me. "I am happy for you and Poppy. It always brings a smile to my face when love blossoms despite this planet's best efforts at stopping it. I wish your love a thousand blessings and I am sure the Earth Mother shall grant you much joy."

"Thank you, Samuel," I said as Willis sat back down and rolled his eyes.

"Now like I was saying at the start, yes, I own or I'm the current leader or ruler or whatever you want to call it of The Floating City. I never thought Lady Isabella would hold up her end of the bargain when I placed that deal on the table. I asked for it in part because I wanted to get back at Mr Lee, but more so, to see what her true motives where. When she agreed to it but only after we got rid of Lee and Diamond I knew she would get rid of us once we had completed the mission."

"Lady Isabella has always been fair," said Samuel. "Ruthless, cold, calculating, yes. But she has always been fair. If she agreed to a deal with you then she wouldn't go back on her word."

Willis snorted and shook his head.

"I would love to agree with you, Samuel, but we are only alive because we're useful to her *now*. We know too much about her and her activities to be left alone. The more we accomplish for her, the bigger the threat we are to her and the more likely she is to get rid of us. You and she have a perfect relationship. You're a man of peace whose main fighters are all off-world. You are no threat to her, yet. Whereas she has seen what we have done to Xcorp.

"There's a reason she gave me The Floating City. There's a reason why we attacked Lee without being aided by her men. It's because if we fail she can hold up her hands and say we were acting on our own. That we attacked Lee to gain control of his territory. It's the perfect play. She gets what she wants if we succeed and if we don't then she gets to wash her hands of the whole thing and play the innocent victim. But there is nothing we can do about that now; all we can do is proceed with caution and plan for the worst."

"What is the plan?" Tuari asked.

"Simple, really," I said looking at the crew. "We head back to The Jungle, where Lady Isabella has pulled out all her forces near the caves and wait at one of the main digging sites. As soon as we see a digging crew, we hijack their ship and use it to enter The Diamond District under the disguise of being them. From there we locate Diamond, do what we have to do and go home."

They all looked at me as if I had gone crazy.

"What?" I asked. "That is the shittiest plan I have ever heard, and if you've done this as long as me you'll hear enough of them, but if that one doesn't rank at the top for the most harebrained, simple, half-assed excuse for a plan that has ever been brought up in the history of mankind."

"This is what we have," I said jabbing at the table. "Diamond knows we took out Lee. I've been hearing the rumours on the street and if they're on the street already, then you know he found out about it weeks ago. Because of that we can't wait any longer; the longer we wait the more reinforcements he'll have surrounding him, the harder it shall be to get close to him. This is our best shot and we have to act now! God knows how much longer they'll need the ore from the mines, but I'd rather take this path now than wait for another opportunity. Lady Isabella has already supplied us with a map of the borough and a map of the building Diamond will be in. Plus a bunch of details about escape routes once the job is done. She has men placed amongst the population of The Diamond District who will help us once we get there.

"We may not get an opportunity as good as this again anytime soon. I know this is risky as fuck, but when hasn't this crew taken a risk? Sometimes it pays off for us, sometimes it doesn't, but we keep on pushing, keep on going no matter what. That's the Junk Yard Dog way."

"Well, shit," said Willis, wiping a fake tear from his eye, "if that isn't the prettiest speech I've heard all year then I don't know what is. Count me in."

"How can your best man not accompany you on a dangerous mission like this?" Tuari said.

"Best... what?" I said.

"Why would he want your big ass as his best man?" Willis asked.

"Don't worry about it, we'll discuss the details later," Tuari mouthed to me.

I looked to Samuel and Scarface. "We could do with a couple of extra hands."

Samuel lifted his hands in mock defeat. "I am no fighter and would be more of a hindrance than a help."

"Pussy," Willis spat.

"Be that as it may," he continued, giving Willis a dirty look, "I know how important this mission is to The Lady and more importantly to The Jungle's way of life, so I will offer you our best fighter," and he gestured to Scarface. "Although I have tried to talk him out of going with you, it appears his mind is already made up and set on the act of getting revenge. He doesn't understand that that path will

A Dog Is Born

consume him from the inside and burn him alive, but one can only offer advice, even if it is falls upon deaf ears."

I looked between the pair and could see the tension that was still there after a conversation that had no doubt left words out in the open that should have been best kept unspoken. I wasn't a hundred percent happy taking along a man whose motivations I didn't know, but beggars couldn't be choosers and right now I needed all the men I could take with me along for this ride.

Scarface looked to me and gave me a single firm nod. I guess it was the best I was going to get.

"Well, that's pretty much the mission in a nutshell. We shall leave for The Jungle in a day or two, so collect all the supplies you need because I don't know when we'll get a chance to restock again."

As everyone got up, I held my hand out and said, "Samuel, you and your man can go; the rest of you, I need a few minutes of your time to hash out a few key details."

Samuel frowned as sadness crossed his eyes but it was gone in a second as he nodded my way and left the room with Scarface.

I waited for a minute before I spoke. "I won't lie to you lot," I said looking at their faces, "but this is probably going to be one of our most dangerous missions. I know I say that every time we decide to do something batshit crazy, but I think this one may be at the top of the list. I would love to reassure everyone that we are all going to make the journey back in one piece, but it's likely some of us may not. So, if anything happens out there, I just wanted all of you to know it was my pleasure in being your captain and having all of you under me. I couldn't ask for better people to be part of a crew, part of a family. So thank you."

More than one pair of eyes were wet as Willis stood up

quickly and looked about the room. "Blah! What's with all this lovey-dovey bullshit? We'll be fine. We always are. No need to get all emotional like some pregnant woman, for God's sake." He shook his head as he swiftly left the room.

I looked at his retreating back with a worried expression.

"He'll be fine," said Tuari. "Sometimes when the moment gets too much for him, he just needs some space to vent and be by himself. We each deal with stress in our own little way. Which reminds me, I've been dying to try a new steak and kidney pie recipe I picked up; I think I'll get started on that now."

He left the room leaving just me and Poppy together. I walked over to her and placed my hands in her palms.

"The last and most important person I wanted to speak to is you," I said, kissing her hands. "I want you to find a little boat and stay out amongst the rivers of The Floating City. I don't want to know where you will be, I don't want to know your destination. All I want you to do is stay safe and stay hidden. I'm going to give you a computer so I can contact you when I get back, but if you don't hear from me, I don't want you to come looking for me. Do you understand?"

"Quinton, I don't—"

"I don't want you to come looking for me, Poppy, I want you to travel somewhere safe, give birth to our child and leave this planet. Promise me that."

"Why don't you want me to come—"

"Because I'll probably be dead."

She stared at me, at a loss for words.

"I need you to promise me you won't come looking for me. Right now I shouldn't be your highest priority," I said, touching her stomach. "You're going to be a mother soon and you're going to be protecting someone who will need your help a lot more than me. So promise me you'll do as I say, find somewhere safe and once I come back then I'll message you and pick you up wherever you may be. But if that doesn't happen, you know what to do."

"Why can't I stay in The Jungle?"

"Because I don't trust Samuel and that's the first place they'll come looking for you. The rivers of The Floating City cover a wider range and it's easier to get lost amongst those waterways, plus you've spent some time on the City's waters so you know where you can go safely and where you can't."

She lowered her head, tears dripping down her cheeks, but I lifted her chin back up and looked her in the eye. "Everything shall be okay. This is just a protective measure in case the worst happens."

Even as the words left my mouth I knew how they sounded. Hallow. Empty. Worthless.

43

I grunted as the weight slammed into my chest, refusing to budge. It was the last set on the bench press after a gruelling workout that would leave me sore and achy tomorrow. I knew I had added too much weight as I lifted the bar off the rack with arms already shaky, but it had nowhere to go but down as it pinned my body to the bench.

I gritted my teeth and tried to raise it but to no avail.

Damn.

I was the only one in the ship's gym and at this late hour, no one else would be turning up. I was fucked with a capital F and would be trapped under the bar unless I thought of something to do to escape. I tried to tip the weight one way so it toppled off me, but I just didn't have the strength to move it. Panic now setting in as the weight crushed my chest with each inhalation of breath, I tried to wriggle my weight out from under the bar but this too proved ineffective. I could feel my energy getting sapped with each passing minute.

I gritted my teeth in anger at the thought of staying here

all night until Poppy decided to come and find out where I was.

"Come on, you bastard! Come on!" I said, as I tried shifting the bar again.

"Hello, is there someone in here?"

"Yes! I'm in the weights section!"

I heard the sound of footsteps running then Samuel's face appeared before mine. "Good heavens man, what are you doing?"

"Hosting a dinner party! What does it look like? I'm stuck under the bar—give me a hand to shift it before it crushes one of my ribs."

He went around the back and grabbed the bar with two hands. "After three. One. Two. Three!"

He lifted and I pushed until inch by inch the bar rose from my chest until we could safely re-rack the weight. I rose to a sitting position with my head between my legs taking in one big gulp of air after another. I felt a hand on my shoulder but I refused to look up. That had been close. What was I thinking? The last couple of days I couldn't sleep and there had been a growing void between Poppy and me as we spoke less and less, as each passing hour crawled until the time I had to depart. It had been stupid to load that much weight on the bar; what was I thinking?

"I'm okay," I said finally lifting my head up. "Lucky you came down, otherwise that could have really turned nasty."

"I normally take a long walk every day when I'm back home in nature, but since coming along on this trip I've not really had time to stretch my legs and I can just feel the pent-up energy flowing through me. I thought the best thing to do was to come down here and try and work out somehow, although I haven't been to a gym like this since I was a young man."

I picked up my towel on the floor and wiped myself down. "Well, I'll leave you to it. Try and not make the same mistake I did."

"Quinton, wait."

I turned back around while he bit the inside of his mouth trying to put into words what he wanted to say to me. "You don't trust me, do you?"

"No."

We looked at each other, trying to find something else to say but what was there?

"Why?"

I sighed as I passed a hand through my hair. "Look, now isn't really the time to get into this."

"As I see it, there's no better time than the present."

"Fine. I like you as a person, Samuel, really I do, but you're tied too closely to The Lady. You've been in her pocket for years, doing her bidding, and even if you're not out there putting guns to temples, you're still supplying her with weapons, weapons she doesn't care who she uses against. You can play the peaceful monk who lives in the woods all you want, but eventually you'll have to take some responsibility for your actions. You can't just bury yourself in the jungle and not take stock of what is happening around you, what your actions are causing around this planet. That's why your people are angry at you; unlike you, they are tired of burying their heads and ignoring the world around them. Their loved ones have been slaughtered and they're now living in constant fear of who will be next.

"As a leader, it's your responsibility to take that burden off their shoulders."

"You're giving me advice on leadership?" he said, anger creeping into his voice. "How long have you been in charge of this crew? Leadership is not as easy as it seems from the outside. Maybe once the years have passed you'll begin to realise that."

"I'm not saying it is, what I'm saying is that unless you decide to take some action then one of your own people will usurp your place and knock you off that high horse of yours. But I am not here to give advice—"

"You could have fooled me."

"You're right, I gave a response to a question you didn't ask me. So I'll lay my cards on the table and be blunt with you. I appreciate the help you have given us and I thank you for your hospitality in housing and clothing us; it gave me time to think, to recoup and to plan my next move. But it is unsafe to be around you, Samuel."

"What do you mean?" he asked.

"The most dangerous man in a time of war is not the man who carries a gun or looks to kill, but man who kneels down amongst the corpses and prays for things to be different than they actually are."

"I..." he began, but trailed off as he lowered his head.

"This war is at your door. Do you think once Diamond is taken care of The Lady will be satisfied? Her type never are. I saw it in the corporate world all the time. People making more money than they could spend but never being happy, always wanting more and more to fill some void they have; and she is no different. Once she has claimed this planet as hers it won't be long till she moves onto the next one and then the next."

"Don't be absurd. The last time someone existed like that WW3 hadn't happened yet. The World Government would never allow something like that to happen."

"That is where you're wrong, The World Government can barely control the twenty or so planets closest to Earth; it cares very little about the people way out here. The World

Government uses the chaos of the outer realm to ensure another power doesn't rise up to threaten it. If you have multiple pirates, thugs, warlords and gangsters all jostling for power on whatever piece of land they call home, then you never get one power that is strong enough to lift itself from the ashes, and if one such power does arise, well... you simply arm his enemies with better weapons and the circle continues all over again. The tactic is old as the day is long, but for whatever reason the World Government has been paid a lot of money to turn a blind eye where Safe Haven is concerned. That shall be their downfall."

I could see he wanted to argue with me. That he wanted to tell me I was overreacting. That I was wrong. But the time for such arguments had long since passed. Now the only thing any of us could do was survive the best way we knew how.

"Look, Samuel, I understand you're trying to make up for past mistakes, really I do, but I can't afford to let your guilt destroy me or my crew. I have enough enemies at my doors without being killed by your misguided kindness."

"Sometimes kindness and love is all the universe ever needs," he said softly.

I threw a weak smile his way and began to walk away.

"Quinton, no matter what you think or feel I am not your enemy. I owe you a lifetime of debt for just keeping my brother safe and sound. If he wasn't in this crew then he would have died from alcohol poisoning or worse. For that I thank you. If you ever need anything from me, then my borough is yours to use as you please. Just do one thing for me?"

I turned around and looked at him.

"Just... just... tell my brother I love him. If this mission doesn't go well—or just make him understand he's the last thing I pray for at night."

"When we get back you can tell him yourself. I think he'll prefer it coming from you," I said walking away and leaving him to his thoughts.

44

The cold cave walls did their best to try and steal the heat away from my body.

I had cursed the humidity and heat earlier in the day when we were making our way through the jungle but now, I wished for it back.

My combat suit was doing its best to try and keep me warm, but we had turned the heating function down in all our suits so as to not give away our position, in case the mining crews had guard patrols who were equipped with heat-seeking goggles.

I turned my head and took in my group of men huddled next to me, all wearing the same identical combat suit as me, the head-up display in my helmet designated each member with their own name tag so we could tell each other apart.

I shuffled my butt for the hundredth time trying to get a comfortable position on the hard rocky ground we sat on, but it was to no avail. Every movement I made somehow dug a sharp pebble or rock deeper into my ass. Sharp rocks I could just about handle; it was the various insects with more legs than I could count crawling along my legs that had me on edge. Insects that buzzed, insects that clicked when they walked, insects that followed other insects eating whatever came out of their rear end.

The section of the cave we were in was covered with hollowed-out carcasses, insect eggs, and animal droppings. The filters in the helmets did their best to combat the smell but it still made my eyes water.

"Why did leather-face bring us to this section of the caves?" Willis asked, pointing to Scarface. "If I remember rightly, we didn't have to deal with all this animal shit last time we came through these caves. It feels like my eyes are being boiled from the stench alone, and these suits are meant to cut off all smell."

"The real thing you need to worry about isn't the smell, but getting a disease from all this poo-poo," said Tuari. "Normally people don't think anything is wrong, but then they begin to suffer from flu-like symptoms, they get headaches, chest pains, then the real fun starts and they start to bleed from their anus. I'm not talking a little blood either. Ohhh nooo. I'm talking about it just gushing out, like a rusty tap spewing out mud. Then, when you finally pray and wish it's all over, that's when the hallucinations start. There have been reports of people eating their own hands, they become that enraged and crazy, but I'm sure that won't happen to you, my fine ginger-bearded friend."

"But... but... we've got the suits on," Willis said looking around in panic. "I mean, the suits will keep us safe from all sorts of contamination, won't they?"

"I wouldn't bet my life on it," Tuari said with a shrug. "All it can take is one micro tear for the spores to get in, then you're off to the races."

Willis started to stand up, but I placed a hand on his shoulder and pushed him back down.

"Tuari, stop being a dick. Willis, you'll be fine. These suits are brand new and were checked by our ship's computer for any anomalies before we took them. The reason why....."—shit, I still hadn't learned Scarface's name—"Samuel's friend here took us this route was because it's further afield from The Jungle's patrols and the ore they want is more plentiful in this region."

"Well, if it's so plentiful, how come we ain't seen a soul in twelve hours?" said Willis.

He had a point; I knew we would have to wait to catch our prey but I didn't expect to wait this long. We had brought enough supplies to last us two days, but that was only on a worst-case scenario basis. If we didn't see anyone past the twenty-four-hour mark, I would have to make a judgement call on whether we move location and try a different spot or abandon the mission completely, and regroup back at base and take another stab at it, at a later time.

I sighed as I flicked another undiscovered insect off my thigh. The truth of the matter was I had no intention of going back. Not without completing the mission first.

Poppy and me... I wished things had ended better before I left, but ever since we had arrived back at Safe Haven the mood between us had grown more and more tense, like the feeling of a man waiting out the remainder of his time before his execution date. We had spoken less and less as the hours counted down; I had tried to strike up a conversation on many occasions but they were all met with one-word answers until I gave up altogether. I could feel the anger and frustration radiate off her as the final day approached. I understood why. She wanted to be part of the mission, and had never been left out of one before, but because of her condition we all knew it wouldn't be possible.

So she secretly blamed herself. She secretly blamed me.

But I knew if I never came back, then that blame and hate would turn into something nasty, turn into something no one could control. I dreaded to think of the rampaging killing machine she would become, all because of me.

All in the name of love.

Another couple of hours passed by and still nothing.

"I would rather be fucked in the ass with a cucumber covered in razor blades than wait another minute in this godforsaken—shit infested—" I leapt sideways and tackled Willis to the ground as a noise down one of the tunnels froze all of us in position.

"Did you hear that?" asked a voice that sounded like tombstones collapsing.

"Hear what?" asked another voice, which was squeaky and high pitched.

"I don't know, sounded like a voice," said Tombstone, "maybe we should check it out."

I lay on top of Willis and glared at him as we all held our breath.

"Look, I'm not searching these tunnels again all because you think you heard something," said Squeaky, "fool me once, shame on you; fool me twice, shame on me; fool me again, and I'm just a dickhead you're taking advantage of."

"But I thought I heard something back there," said Tombstone.

"Yeah, and both times it was some damn creature that had more eyes than I could count and teeth that wanted to take a bite out of my sweet ass. If Bobby and Shane hadn't been taken by those things than it would have been us who got eaten instead. God, I can hear their screams. Anyway, come on, this is the last shipment of ore Diamond will be needing for some time and it's heavy as shit. So the sooner we unload it back on the ship the sooner we can say goodbye to this Aladdin's cave of horrors."

I held Willis down and waited for a few minutes until I was sure the miners wouldn't be coming our way, then I slowly got off him and motioned for everyone to rise to their feet.

"What creatures were they talking about?" I asked Scarface, but his helmeted head just looked my way and all I got was a disinterested shrug.

Great. Not only did I have to worry about miners looking to put a hole through my head, but I also had to worry about man-eating creatures that not even the inhabitants of The Jungle knew about. This mission just kept getting better and better.

"Alright," I whispered, "let's move out."

45

I was worried about not being able to follow the miners discreetly without being seen or heard, but it appeared luck was in my favour as one of their hovering wheelbarrows wasn't working properly, so they had to drag it along the cave floor leaving a nice deep groove in the dirt we could easily follow. The sound of it bounced from wall to wall making enough noise to wake the dead.

We moved as quickly as we dared, darting from shadow to shadow and using the cover of darkness to our advantage. On occasion, we had to risk being seen, as sections of the caves were well lit by the fluorescent bugs that lived in the cave's ceiling. Lucky those lit sections were few and far between and we made good time as we kept a steady pace hunting down our prey.

The grooves in the ground suddenly stopped because the ground before us stopped being soft sand and had turned into hard rock. The rocky outcrop continued for some time until it led to a large tunnel mouth opening. Sounds emerged from it.

"Will you give me a hand, you lazy bastard?" said Squeaky.

"Come on, son, you know my back's been playing up something chronic for the last couple of months. It's all I can do to stand up without feeling like I have knives repeatedly stabbing me in the lower back," said Tombstone.

"Give over! Your back wasn't hurting you last week when you were chasing that young thing around town like a dog with his dick out. If I remember correctly, you jumped two fences to get away from her brothers."

"But that's the thing, you see," said Tombstone. "It was all them hormones coursing through my system that gave me the strength. It's testosterone and adrenaline and whatnot."

"Well, how about this? If you don't help me load this cargo onto the ship, then I'm going to hit you in the back so hard that you wish it was broken."

"Come on, mate, why do you always have to resort to violence? Don't you know the way of love is a much more satisfying and easier path to follow?" said Tombstone.

"I know one thing, if Diamond doesn't get this shipment on time then it shall be our asses and no amount of smooth-talking by you shall get us out of the trouble we'll be in. Now, I won't tell you again, give me a fucking hand."

"Don't you think it's weird?"

Squeaky sighed. "Don't I think what's weird?"

"The Diamond District? The whole thing of not being allowed to land anyway, apart from the little strip of airfield a couple of miles outside its borders. I know we ain't citizens of that borough but I've never heard of anything like that before. Normally we would always deal with someone inside the borough, but the way they've been doing things lately, what with paying us as soon as we've landed and not having anyone come out to check the cargo, just seems all a bit weird. It's not only us who get treated that way either, I heard Ryan and his crew deliver their goods the same way. He said one time he delivered to the airstrip he waited a good half an hour to see if anyone would come and collect it, but no one came, but the next day he went to drop off his next shipment, the airstrip was completely empty.

"And he said he ain't seen Smithy—you know Smithy, the one with the wandering eye who runs poker nights at the King William's pub—well, he said he ain't seen him in months, he even messaged him that he had the money he owed him but Smithy never replied back, and you know how Smithy is with money. I just think—"

"That's your problem!" Squeaky snapped. "Always thinking about other people's business instead of your own. Now I could've sworn I told you to help me load this cargo."

"But don't you think it's all a bit—"

"Have you, or have you not, been paid for these jobs?"

"Yeah, but—"

"No buts!" Squeaky bellowed. "Just get to loading this cargo before I lose my temper. The sooner we get out of this hellhole, the sooner we can get paid and I can get to the Pink Pussycat Club."

"Oh! Why didn't you say that? You know I think Crystal is working tonight?"

I looked to the crew and motioned for Willis and Scarface to cover the right, while Tuari and I brought up the left. I took out my pistol and left my shotgun holstered across my back as we all crept forward, until we were at the foot of the entrance of the tunnel mouth.

A small tarnished cargo ship with more dents and rust spots over it than I could count sat perched on the lip of a sheer cliff face. The drop went into pure darkness and I had no way of knowing how far down the gorge went.

The ship in question had its cargo doors lowered and two men, one small, one large, had their backs turned to us as they loaded up the metal ore they had mined, from the hoverbarrow.

I looked to Willis and Scarface and gave them a nod as we moved silently forward.

Darkness surrounded us on all sides and I couldn't see where the cave walls began or ended.

I held my breath as we crept forward—weapons trained on their backs. We were almost halfway to them when the small one turned around and spotted us. He yelped in surprise and reached downwards but I fired at his feet halting his movements.

"No you don't!" I said, keeping my gun trained on him as I continued to walk towards them. "Hands in the air!"

They both raised their arms slowly.

"Big guy, do us a favour and turn around," I said.

He did so slowly until they were both facing us; he gave his partner a look that could have pinned his soul to the wall and then turned to face us fully.

"Do you know—" he began, but I stopped him in his tracks.

"Hold up, hold up. You are the one with the squeaky voice? A big guy like you? A guy who looks like he eats rocks for breakfast? Damn, I guess it's true what they say, you can't have it all."

"I bet he has a little dick too," said Willis.

"Your momma won't complaining when I last saw her," said Squeaky.

Willis fired a shot just above Squeaky's ear that pinged

and sparked against the metal of the ship. "Talk about my mother again. I dare you," he said, stepping forward.

Squeaky went to open his mouth but thought better of it.

"Now, I want everybody to relax and calm down and no one will get hurt," I said, looking between the pair. "If you two play your cards right, then this will all be over and done with, in no time at all, and you can be on your way."

"Do you know who you're stealing from?" Squeaky asked with a raised eyebrow.

"Technically we aren't stealing," I replied.

"Then what would you call this?"

"Apprehending."

They both looked at each other in confusion before they turned back to me.

"Let me explain," I said. "We do not want your cargo. Couldn't care less about it. What we do want is your help transporting us to The Diamond District."

"In case you haven't heard," said Tombstone, "The Diamond District is a no-go area. You can't get in, you can't get out. So I'm afraid you're flat out of luck. Now if you would kindly fuck off to whatever hole you crawled out from, we would appreciate it, as we have a rendezvous with a couple of special ladies at—"

Willis fired another shot. This time the bullet nicked the shoulder of Tombstone before it bounced off against the cave wall.

"We weren't asking," said Willis.

I sent a glare Willis's way. "Look, we can either do this the hard way or the harder way. I'm not particularly fussed either way, but I can tell you that one way does involve a lot more blood than the other."

"He shot me in the shoulder," Tombstone wailed, clutching the injured body part.

"Look, fella," said Squeaky, "there is no need for all this violence. If you wanted a ride then all you had to do was ask. But as my big mouthed friend here said, getting you inside The Diamond District is something we can't do. What we can do is put you—"

"Shoot them," I said to Willis. "If they can't take us where we want to go, then they're no use to us anyway."

Willis gave me a nod and raised his gun their way.

"Wait! Wait! Wait!" Tombstone said, backing up. "There may be a way in."

"We don't—"

"Just listen, will you?" he said cutting me off. "Just before you get to the walls of The Diamond District, there is a large abandoned service tunnel to the south of the city near the mountain range, which travels under the wall and puts you underneath the borough. I used to use it as a kid to smuggle things in and out because citizens not belonging to the district and found on its streets were punished harshly. I'm not too sure if it's still there, but if you want to get inside that's your best bet. You won't get inside there any other way. The borough is surrounded by a retractable metal wall and is located on a mountainside, making it an impenetrable fortress like something out of a fantasy novel. Add the anti-aircraft gun turrets on the wall, and flying any way close to that thing is suicide."

I chewed the side of my mouth while I thought of what to do. If what they were saying was true about seeing no one come out of the borough, then our best bet would be to use this service tunnel to somehow sneak inside. The wall was a surprise though and not something mentioned in The Lady's notes. I had a sinking feeling we would be learning

A Dog Is Born

on the job with this mission, because her royal highness aka Lady Isabella had forgotten to mention it.

"Alright," I said, placing my hand on Willis's arm and lowering his gun to the ground, "you show us the way, then we'll let you go and as a showing of good faith we'll also pay you. Half now. Half when we reach our destination."

"How do we know we can trust you? We can't even see your faces," Tombstone said.

We were in full black combat gear with matching black helmets, which gave nothing of our appearance away—just our voices, and even that was distorted from the helmet speakers. True, it would smooth over relations if they could see our faces, but if this whole mission went sideways and became a shit show, then I'd rather any information about us were kept to a minimum.

"You don't" I said, "but the way I see it you're not really in a position to—"

I did a double-take as a creature the size of a large pit bull, with the body of an ant, crawled up out of the gorge that the ship was parked in front of. Abdomen covered in jet black hair, its face was made up of a mix of far too many eyes and far too many teeth. Thick legs knotted with muscle ended in serrated claws. The thing swept its head back and forth as a flicking tongue jetted out of its mouth as it focused on its prey.

"What is that?" Willis pointed, as the two miners spun on their heels.

"Oh fuck! Oh fuck! They're back!" Tombstone shouted as all hell broke loose and the sound of numerous claws echoed around the cave.

46

The creature that came out of the gorge wasn't the only one.

Scores of the ugly things emerged from the darkness. Teeth clicking, they were a sight to behold as they focused their gaze on us.

None of us moved. We all stood stock still as they regarded us with those soulless eyes. The only thing that could be heard was the clicking. I licked my lips as I slowly lowered my pistol to my holster and retrieved the shotgun strapped to my back. Still, they didn't advance forward. All I could hear was the sound of my own breathing as I redoubled my grip on my shotgun.

Tombstone was the first to move as he fired off a shot into the crowd of creatures. When he took one down, it bled out onto the ground, thick blackish blood oozing from its wound. That was all they were waiting for. At the sight of their wounded pack member the rest of the creatures exploded into action.

Some leapt onto the wounded, ripping it apart and devouring it to the bone. The rest sprinted towards us looking to do the same to us as they were doing to their fallen colleague.

I didn't need to shout "fire," as the crew opened fire upon the creatures, stopping as many of them as they could in their tracks, but it still wasn't enough. Dozens of the things climbed over the bodies of the fallen and just kept on coming. We fired round after round, but it was like they didn't feel pain or know fear.

"More of the fuckers are descending from the walls!" someone shouted.

The helmet's night vision just about picked them up as I fired and blasted as many as I could off the walls. There were too many of them! If we stayed here they would overrun us.

"Into the ship!" I said, sprinting towards it as the rest of my crew followed my lead. Tombstone and Squeaky had stopped firing; the idiots were trying to load the rest of the metal ore they had left onto the ship.

"Leave it," I shouted, waving my arms their way, but they ignored me.

A set of teeth lunged at me from the shadows and I ducked just in time, allowing it to sail over my head. I didn't stop and see where the creature landed but just kept on running. Another creature leapt onto Willis's back tackling him to the ground, and he bucked left and right as it tried to get a firm hold while its jaws snapped at him.

I swung my shotgun round so I held the barrel in my hand and used the gun-butt as a club and swung at the thing's head with all my might. I hit it with a sickening crunch that sent shock waves up my arms and knocked it off Willis's back. It staggered back towards me but didn't get far as I flipped the gun the right way round and blasted its head clean off.

"Come on," I said, lifting Willis to his feet.

The creatures didn't make any noise.

They didn't growl, cry, yelp or hiss. The only thing that made a sound was their teeth clicking together as they came towards us. That in itself was terrifying enough. They swarmed towards us like a pack but there was no loyalty amongst their numbers; whenever one would fall injured the others would leap upon it, feasting to their heart's content. They were ruthless in their single-mindedness to devour whatever couldn't fight back—and if it could, it was only a matter of time until it couldn't.

Tuari and Scarface were the first to reach the ship, sprinting past the two idiots still loading their cargo onto it. Tuari didn't wait but continued onwards, no doubt making a beeline for the ship's controls. Scarface waited on the lowered metal ramp of the cargo doors and fired at anything that moved.

I pushed myself with everything I had, legs pumping. I could feel the creatures' presence only feet away from me.

"Leave the *fucking* ore!" I bellowed at the top of my lungs.

Tombstone and Squeaky both looked up at me, and I could see the panic finally dawn on them as they saw the number of creatures chasing me. Tombstone fumbled with the ore he was holding and dropped it on his partner's foot; Squeaky leapt into the air holding his now broken foot. He hopped back and forth while he tried to slap Tombstone over the head, but he lost his footing and fell backwards into the jaws of a creature who had been sneaking up behind him.

I tried to warn him but it was too late.

"Get this thing off me," he yelled, as the beast gripped one of his arms in its mouth and shook its head back and forth. Blood squirted out from the puncture wounds and covered his face as we tried to get a clean shot.

Upon seeing his friend's predicament Tombstone leapt onto the ship behind Scarface and ran inside.

"You spineless cunt! I allowed you to marry my sister! Helllp!" Squeaky tried to beat his attacker with his free hand but I could see that the limb was already tearing from the joint. If he survived this, there was no way he was keeping the arm.

Willis was the next one to make it onto the ship, leaping over the chaotic scene of Squeaky still fighting for his life. I tried to get a clear shot to save the miner, but I was in danger of hitting him and the beast, as they rolled back and forth across the ground. His cries were now shrill as the limb was finally ripped from his body. Blood poured from the injury as he stumbled to his feet and swayed side to side, but it was all for nothing as he was tackled to the floor by two more creatures.

I slowed my pace to see if I could help but before I could get to him a single shot rang out and his head exploded.

Willis held one of his pistols in Squeaky's direction, barrel still smoking.

Seeing as there was nothing I could do, I quickened my pace. "Get the engines started! Raise the ramp!"

"What do you think we've been trying to do!" Willis replied.

With a splutter and a shudder, the rust-bucket finally kicked into life and the ramp slowly rose. Slowly. Far too slowly. The ramp jerked and halted, then rose, then jerked and halted again, then rose. The thing moved like an old-age pensioner from a deep sleep. Finally, making it onto the ramp I turned and brought my gun up as a set of jaws was opened wide and making a beeline for my face. I could see all the way down the thing's throat. It felt like I was staring into the pits of hell.

I fired, removing its head from its body, and the body flew backwards into the pack coming our way.

More of the vicious creatures were pounding their way towards us. With each one we killed another three would take its place.

And still the ramp hadn't fully closed. Gunsmoke surrounded me as we fired with abandon, not caring what we hit as long as we hit something in front of us.

"Tuari!" I shouted via the helmets comms. "How we doing?"

"This thing is a bag of shit, but I'm nearly here. Just keep them busy for a little while longer!"

I suppressed a groan of frustration and kept on firing. Nearly at a close the ramp was having trouble fully shutting as the weight from the creatures was weighing it down. The mechanisms on either side of the ramp smoked as they worked overtime trying to close the ramp. With each inch of upward movement from the ramp, there were three inches of downward movement as the ramp lowered back down.

"Tuari, get this ship moving now!"

"But the ramp isn't—"

"Fuck the ramp. Just do it."

"But I don't know where the exit is."

"Just fly!"

I stumbled forward and Willis caught me as my face came inches within the range of a set of teeth as the ship moved. It jolted back and forth then moved forward as the ramp lowered even further. We redoubled our efforts firing, gun-butting and attacking the creatures with everything we had as the ship picked up speed. I leapt back as one made its way through the gap the ramp offered and landed in the cargo bay.

I brought up my gun but I didn't get off a shot as it launched itself toward me, knocking me off my feet. With my gun between it and me its crooked teeth snapped at my face, as its foul warm breath washed over me fogging up the glass on my helmet. I pushed it back but the thing was stronger than it looked; muscles in its neck bulged as it tried to get to me. Throwing my helmeted head forward, I smashed it in the face and sent up a prayer to the gods that the helmet wouldn't break as I went in for another head-butt.

Dazed, the creature shook its head and relaxed its forward energy and that was all I needed to flip it sideways off me so I could get back to my feet. It came at me again but I swung a kick at its head knocking it back to a safe distance. Gun raised I went in for a shot but missed as the ship jerked forward, throwing me off my feet and causing me to land on my back.

"Hold on, boys!" said Tuari. "We are going to need to freefall this bitch to get the engines working properly."

It felt like my stomach was being forced out of my ass by a ten-foot pole as my body slammed into the side of the ship. I wasn't the only one that had been taken by surprise as bodies flashed before my eyes, some human, some not. I tried to lift my head as the G-force from the freefall did its best to pin my body to the wall. The ramp had come to a stop halfway up and the creatures that had been trying to get in had all fallen by the wayside as the ship dived into the gorge.

But our problems were only half over as a few had made it inside the cargo bay.

I gritted my teeth with everything I had and pushed

myself off the wall and in midair tackled one of the monsters trying to attack Willis. We crashed against the wall, man and beast fighting for survival. It tried to bite me but I got my legs in front of me and kicked it away where it spun away from me and was sucked out of the hole the ramp had created.

Willis was wrestling with another beast, bleeding forearm in its jaw. It shook its head from side to side and I was amazed at Willis's resolve as he didn't utter a sound from the pain but instead brought his pistol up, and fired it under the creature's chin. The bullet blew through its jaw and came out the top of its head.

Scarface fought another that had him pinned against the wall. In his hand, he gripped a blade and thrust it into the side of the thing again and again, but it paid him no attention as it kept on trying to find a chunk of flesh to sink its teeth into. I pushed off against the wall and threw myself towards him but the effort was a wasted one as the ship jerked upwards with force.

I tumbled head over heels, seeing ceiling then ramp opening, ceiling then ramp opening. In my confused state, there was one thing I was sure of, that I was falling ever closer towards the still opened ramp exit and if I didn't do something quick then I was going to find out how long it took to get to the bottom of that gorge. I spun once more and a hand grabbed me by the arm, stopping me from going through.

I looked down and saw my feet dangling outside the ship with nothing but blackness below me. Looking up I saw another helmeted head inches from mine holding me by my arm, while the other held onto a strap that hung from the ceiling. The HUD showed my saviour was Scarface, but how long we could stay like this I didn't know.

A Dog Is Born

"Tu—Tuari! Level the ship. Level the ship!"

"Not until we clear this cliff face, otherwise we're fucked."

Metal ore—dead carcass—boxes—and other pieces of shit dropped past me as Scarface held onto me for dear life as I fought the urge to look down. The ship shuddered and shook as it continued to climb, the engines whining against the strain being forced on them.

Something flashed past my face and I grabbed it instinctively with my one free hand.

It was Tombstone. The piece of shit must have come loose from his hiding place and had nearly fallen out of the ship.

"Let him go!" Willis screamed through my speakers.

I held on, tight hand encircling Tombstone's.

"We need him."

"If you don't you'll take everyone with you. We can find the tunnel on our own."

But I wasn't so sure. This man was the one key to a mission I dreaded—that I fought against and hated. The knowledge this man had could keep my family safe. Could end this war before it even began. I redoubled my grip.

"Quinton. For the love of God. Let go!"

I felt movement above me and looked up to see Scarface's grip loosening. Millimetre by millimetre, his grip grew looser and looser. I looked down into the face of Tombstone and could see absolute fear as his eyes were closed and he shook his head from side to side. I looked back up. Any second now Scarface's grip would give out.

"Quinton!"

Scarface's grip gave out and I felt myself falling but not before the ship levelled itself sharply; still, it wasn't enough. With Tombstone's weight pulling me down I was dragged along the cargo floor while my free hand tried to find anything to stop myself from sliding out the ship. It finally did in the form of a deep groove in the ramp's lip.

I jerked to a halt and gritted my teeth as Tombstone's weight yanked on my shoulder. I was holding onto the ship by the tips of my fingers.

I kept holding on, body hanging from the ramp with another dangling from my hand, and I breathed a sigh of relief as Willis and Scarface leapt towards me and grabbed a hold of me. They pulled me back in and I pulled Tombstone aboard as we collapsed in a heap and the ramp finally closed.

47

The journey towards The Diamond District was a silent one.

Everyone sat in their own little corner while they replayed the traumatic events that had unfolded only hours previously. It had been a case of pure survival. I had never experienced anything like it. I had fought men plenty of times now, but you could reason with men, you could intimidate men, you could frighten men, and if all else failed and the odds were stacked against them, men would succumb to their own survival instincts and flee before being killed.

But those things... they were relentless in their pursuit for a meal.

They didn't seem to feel pain and they didn't cower when the odds were against them. They just purely attacked until they overcame whatever prey was before them.

I looked to my left and saw Scarface tending to Willis's injury. The bite from the animal had broken the suit material along his forearm leaving it a bloody mess. I got up and walked over to them. Willis's helmeted head looked my way,

I had instructed everyone to keep their gear on as we still had Tombstone on the ship and now wasn't the time to be lax.

"How is it?" I asked Willis.

"It's... fuck if I know. This idiot doesn't speak so even if there was something wrong how could he tell me? All I know is I don't think it's broken. I can move it around and I don't feel any pain like a broken limb, so I should be thankful for that, I guess. But without a proper scan, I won't know if the bite is infected or not. All I can do is take these strong antibiotics that have some basic nanobots in them and hope they stop the spread of any infections."

Without seeing his face I could hear the worry in his voice but there was nothing I could do for him. I patted him on the shoulder and gave Scarface a nod of thanks before I continued deeper into the ship; it was a lot smaller than I had first thought and I did not have to go very far to find Tombstone huddled in a corner rocking himself back and forth.

I stopped in front of him and kicked his feet forcing him to look up at me.

"Our deal still stands. You get us to this tunnel and I shall pay you double what I had first agreed, then you can be off on your way and enjoy the fruits of your labour."

"I thought that was it," he said, fixing me with an intense gaze. "I thought my life was over. Hanging onto your hand looking down into that gorge and seeing nothing but darkness, I thought that was it. I wondered how long it would take to hit the bottom. I wondered what I would think about on the fall down. I wondered if I would cry. I wondered if I would find peace, but worst of all you know what I came to realise as my life flashed before my eyes?"

I gave him a shake of the head.

"I came to realise my life is amazing!"

"Err—" I began, but he cut me off.

"I have no kids. I have no nagging wife. I have no sick mother or father to take care of, I have no family at all that needs any handouts or anyone to console. I have no responsibilities whatsoever. My life has been a constant state of partying and sleeping with less than respectable women, and I love it! God. Who knew I was so lucky? I tell ya, I would pay to be me. Drinking till all hours of the day and waking up on some planet you don't know the name of, next to some woman you vaguely recall. Damn, I'm living the good life. It's a life a lot of people wish they had and that near-death experience taught me that."

I opened and closed my mouth slowly while I looked at this half-pint of a man in complete confusion.

"Well," I said finally, "that's one way of looking at it."

I let him be and made the short walk to the cockpit where Tuari was seated nestled amongst an array of half-broken instruments, wires poking out from metal fixtures and consoles that occasionally sparked. His normal carefree demeanour was lined with worry as he gave me a swift nod and returned to the controls.

"Problems?" I asked.

He ran a hand through his hair and gestured at his surroundings before answering me: "Where do I start. I'm surprised this heap of junk is flying and I doubt we would have got it started if we didn't kick-start the engines like we did. Plus, there was the issue with the load capacity. I don't think those idiots knew how close they were to dying; they had gone over the load capacity of this ship by tenfold and as soon as they'd tried to take off with that much weight they would have crashed. So in a sense, the ramp not shutting properly was a lifesaver, as it allowed us to get rid of all the unnecessary weight."

Lifesaver.

I thought back to me hanging by my fingertips looking down into a pit of darkness, praying my grip wouldn't give out.

"Anything else?"

He hesitated, "I... something doesn't add up and I'm not sure what it is; the ship is showing that we are still carrying cargo but I've done a quick sweep of the cargo with my own eyes and it's empty. It just doesn't make sense."

"This is an old ship, maybe the readings are just faulty."

He gave me a look that said he wasn't so convinced, but where I was standing we had bigger problems to worry about. I patted him on the shoulder and walked away but his voice stopped me.

"What were those things?" he asked.

I took a deep breath as a face with more eyes and teeth than I had ever seen flashed before my eyes. "I wish I knew. It surprises me the people of The Jungle have never encountered them before, but judging by how vast those caves are, maybe it really shouldn't come as a surprise. Maybe all the mining that has taken place in the caves disturbed them or the water being contaminated has made them crazy and rabid like the wolves—who knows? I'll message Samuel later on and inform him about them. How long till we reach our destination?"

"I've reduced our speed to give us some time to regroup before we hit The Diamond District. I thought we needed it."

I gave him a nod of thanks. "You did the right thing. I'll tell the others we've got some time before we arrive."

48

"Ginger ladies and esteemed gentlemen, this is your handsome, daring, intelligent, sexiest-man-of-the-year captain speaking," came a voice over the ship's speakers that made Willis curse under his breath. "I would like to inform you we shall reach our destination shortly. I can see the walls of The Diamond District as we speak and it looks magnificent. It just goes to show you that wealth and power can really create anything it desires."

"Alright, you heard the man," I said over the helmet speakers as I got to my feet. "I want everyone ready so the moment we land we can move. Double-check all weapons because from here on out, there's no going back."

"Fuck me," said Willis, "I forgot the mission hasn't even started yet."

I chuckled. "Nah, it hasn't."

I walked through the ship and passed the snoring curled-up form of Tombstone and kicked him awake as I passed. Continuing on I walked into the cockpit and stopped and admired a view that was... that was terrifying.

A matte grey wall twice as high as the tallest skyscrapers

back on Earth surrounded a borough that had a mountain range at its back. Snow-covered peaks defended its rear as a waterfall that would put the Victoria Falls to shame swept over the walls at its front. Inside the walls, I could see nothing but skyscrapers and high-rise apartment buildings. The only thing missing was a glass dome covering the top, and the whole thing would look like a city trapped in a snow globe. Even from this distance, I could see gun nests on top of the wall containing large anti-aircraft weapons that looked more akin to a scaled-up mediaeval cannon. They gave the impression they could take out our ship with one shell.

"I don't get it," I said. "If you're so wealthy, why would you want to live in a place surrounded by a metal wall?"

"Because the wealthy like to keep apart from the rest of us. It keeps the common folk out, my good man," said Tuari.

I shook my head at the absurdity of it. No wonder The Lady wanted us to tackle this mission before she made her move. There was no way in hell she would have been able to breach those walls. Now, seeing the vast wealth this borough had with my own eyes, I didn't get why Mr Diamond just didn't deal with Lady Isabella once and for all. Judging by the borough in front of us, he had the resources and money to wipe her off the face of the planet without a second thought.

"The miners said something about the wall being retractable; does that mean it isn't always up?" I asked.

A sound like sandpaper echoed through the cockpit as Tuari scratched his chin. "This is the first time I've been to this borough. José always gave it a wide berth because he saw it as too much trouble to get involved with. There are certain rules and codes you have to adhere to in The Diamond District, and he wasn't willing to work by them.

But to answer your question, what I can remember is the walls were only ever raised up in times of war against another borough or when a storm or something of that nature passed through its lands. Originally the waterfall you see before you was actually a river that runs through the borough, but when the walls are raised it creates the spectacle you see before you.

"People who regularly do trade with this borough have said for the last year or so, the walls have remained up and contact with the district has been limited, to say the least.

"I don't know what's going on behind those walls, but I have a feeling it's nothing—"

The ship shuddered violently and I was thrown off my feet where I slammed into the wall to my left. My shoulder took most of the impact, but it was the same one that had been jarred when I had been keeping Tombstone from falling to an untimely death. Gritting my teeth, I tried to get back to my feet but was thrown right, where my side struck the sharp edge of a console.

"Sit down, man! Can't you see we're being attacked," Tuari said.

"By who?"

Tuari rapidly jabbed some buttons in front of him, then he secured himself in his seat using the seat harness that came with the chair. I quickly took a seat next to him and looked to do the same, but as I pulled my harness straps towards me they came apart from my chair and dangled in my hand. I looked at them in disbelief as the ship shook once more and threw them to the floor.

A startled cry came from the back, which I had no doubt came from Tombstone, as Tuari disabled the autopilot and took control.

"What is happening!" Willis screamed. "Don't tell me

that giant hairy axe wound has fallen asleep at the controls again."

"Ginger Bible floggers and other fine members of this trip, I regret to inform you we are being attacked by an unidentified ship. I don't know how the bastards crept up on us unaware but they somehow have—"

"If you had been doing your job then they—" began Willis, but Tuari cut him off.

"Let's not start playing the blame game on whose fault it was; that will get us nowhere. What everyone can do is strap themselves in because shit is about to get bumpy."

A red warning light flashed in front of me then stopped as the lightbulb exploded inside the console case, sending up acrid smoke straight into my face.

"Quinton," said Tuari, "grab the joystick in front of you. It controls the weapons we have—"

"This thing has weapons?"

"A single railgun, but it's better than nothing. Put on that helmet over there and it'll give you a view of our attackers."

I did as he said, jamming on the too-tight helmet, and grabbed the joystick tightly. I saw a camera view of the outside of the ship on the HUD but couldn't see our attackers anywhere.

"I don't see anything!"

"Turn your head around and as you move the camera feeding you the image will move also," said Tuari.

I did as he said and saw more of my surroundings. I got a view of the wall, sky, earth, but still no—shit, what was that? I twisted my head hard to the right and caught view of an all-black ship with red trimmings. Something told me I had seen those markings before, but I couldn't place where. As I moved the joystick a small faint green circle appeared on the HUD. I moved the stick left and right but however hard I

A Dog Is Born

tried I couldn't get the circle to land on the ship for longer than a second.

"Can you keep her steady?"

"Yeah, no problem, buddy, just ask them to stop shooting at us and I'll get right on it," Tuari replied.

"Doesn't this thing have shields?"

I got a harsh bark as a response.

The ship shook once more and this time I could smell smoke. It stung the back of my throat.

I concentrated once more and held my breath as the green circle blinked red briefly every time I managed to get it to lock on, but I couldn't keep it locked on for long enough.

"Tuari, you got to give me something."

I didn't get a response but the ship levelled off long enough for me to get a lock on the target; I squeezed the trigger and watched as a computer-generated line of red dots that represented bullets struck the near side of the enemy ship. I pumped my fist as I saw a small trail of black smoke rise from the impact.

"Nice going," said Tuari, "but they must not have expected this ship to have any weapons, because their shields were down. It won't be so easy next time."

And he was right, it wasn't. No matter if I got a lock on the ship or not, the railgun did little damage. I squeezed the trigger until my finger went numb, but our bullets bounced off their hull without doing any damage.

The ship shuddered once more, and this time a high-pitched siren that echoed through the cabin accompanied it. I kept on firing but knew it was a pointless exercise. All our enemy needed was one good shot and we would be done, and eventually they were likely to get it unless we did something.

"Tuari, if you have any suggestions now would be a fine time to bring them up. Don't be shy. Anything at all."

He looked at me and gave me a shrug before turning back to the controls.

"Well, ain't you as useful as a chocolate teapot. Remind me—"

"We have an incoming hail," he said.

"Put it through. Maybe I can try and convince these people that keeping us alive would benefit them more than killing us."

"Alright, but it's audio only as this ship is so old it doesn't have a screen for the visuals," he said, before pressing a button.

"Surprise, motherfucker!" said the last voice I wanted to hear. "I honestly don't know how an office nerd like yourself has survived on this planet so long. I tell you it's a goddamn mystery. I've lost half my men—half, ya hear me—to the scum who call this planet home. Robbers, ambushers, old ladies, even god damn children—children!—have taken chunks out of my forces, while you, Quinton Blake, still remain alive and kicking. Ya gotta tell me your secret. Ya gotta tell me how a son of a bitch like yourself didn't get killed in the first five minutes of setting foot on this planet."

"Well, Tex, I guess I'm a people person and it really comes down to how you talk to people."

Booming laughter echoed around the cockpit while I hurriedly thought of what to do. Talking him out of killing us was out of the question, but maybe I could keep him talking while I thought of something

"I find," I continued, "that if you're just polite and greet everyone with a smile then people will be polite back to you."

"What a crock of shit! If the Mercenary Bloc wasn't the

wandering entity it was, then I would have called this planet home. It rewards the strong and violent and punishes the weak. Most planets now are so pussified that anything resembling strength gets punished. Before long all men will be nothing but neutered puppies looking for approval from the powers that be. Men like you and me, Quinton, are a dying breed."

"I'm nothing like you."

"Ha! You think so? I heard what you did to Lee and his men. Nasty. Nothing I wouldn't have done myself, but you didn't have to burn the man's boat. That's like pissing on someone's grave."

"I did what I needed to do to survive."

"Exactly! You done did what you needed to do! That's what life is all about."

A thought had occurred to me but we needed to get closer to The Diamond District; I just hoped we had what we needed on board. I tapped Tuari on the shoulder and pointed towards the walls that surrounded the borough. He looked at me in disbelief but I nodded my head and gestured with force towards the wall.

"I'm surprised you're here if I'm honest, Tex," I said.

"Why?"

"Because I know you were hired by Mr Diamond to take both The Lady and me out, and as I lasted checked she was still alive and kicking."

"Shows what you know, don't it? Who said this Mr Diamond character hired me? Who says I'm working for The Diamond District? Who says I'm not on vacation looking for a bit of fun?"

Tuari looked at me, worry lining his face. If Diamond didn't hire the Mercenary Bloc then who were they working for? Was he just lying to mess with me?

"I would love to believe you, but I know the Mercenary Bloc doesn't work for free. Now, I know we've had our differences in the past, dear Tex, but what if we put that behind us and I made you an offer you couldn't refuse?"

"I'm listening."

"I've just become the proud owner of a rather large piece of land called The Floating City, and I would be willing to hand it over to you, plus a nice money bonus on top if you came and worked for me. All I would have you do is three jobs tops, not even that, and you would have a prime bit of real estate on this planet that you've fallen in love with so much. Not to mention it has the best waters on this planet to fish in. I know a fisherman when I see one, Tex, and you, sir, come across as a man who loves to be on the water, trying to catch the biggest fish that he can."

There was silence on the other line.

"What do you say, old chap?" I said, laying it on thick.

"My, my, you are a dirty old dog, ain't yea?"

I smiled. "I wouldn't be the captain of the Junk Yard Dogs if I wasn't."

A heavy sigh vibrated on the other end of the line. "I'm tempted. I would be lying if I said I weren't. Don't get me wrong, I like you, Quinton Blake, honestly, I do. You may disagree and think we're not alike but a mean son of a bitch recognises a mean son of a bitch and you are he. Now, on any other occasion, I would have taken the offer, and be on my merry way if it weren't for two things.

"One, my employer wouldn't take kindly to my betrayal and he's not someone I want on my back and two, I've never allowed a man to walk away free without some kind of payback who placed a scar on my body and you, Quinton, have left me scarred indeed."

I thought back to our last encounter. The flashbang I

had thrown for him to catch on the roof. I knew it wasn't going to be fatal, but there had to be some damage.

"I guess there is no point in saying let bygones be bygones then?" I asked.

"If only it was that simple, bub. If only it was that simple," he said, before the connection went dead.

49

Tuari looked at me but I was already getting out of my seat and making my way to the back. "Just keep heading for that wall," I shouted over my shoulder.

I leaned against a wall for support as the ship shook violently once more. Continuing on I looked for Tombstone but he was nowhere to be found amongst the seats in the back; looking high and low I couldn't find him. I made my way to the cargo bay but stopped when I heard movement to my left. Turning around I walked to a rusty row of lockers, I shook my head as I kicked the nearest one in front of me, buckling the door inward.

"Ow, that hurt," said a muffled voice, as the door to the locker creaked open and Tombstone fell forward holding his chest.

I looked at him.

"What?"

"Were you just going to hide in there till the bad men went away?" I asked.

"Nah, nah. I was just looking for something, that's all."

"With the door closed, in the dark?"

He looked at me at a loss for words. The ship shuddered once more.

"I don't have time for this. There's more metal ore cargo on this ship, isn't there?" I asked.

He gave me a bewildered look and shook his head. "I... don't know what—"

"Listen! You are a backstabbing, good-for-nothing mining thief, and you know what a backstabbing, good-for-nothing mining thief does?"

"Well, that's just hurtful," he said, ignoring the question.

"A backstabbing, good-for-nothing mining thief looks out for himself first above all else. So here's what I think happened between you and your deceased partner. I think you got curious about the metal ore you were mining and decided to test its properties out to see if it's valuable or not. Upon finding it was, you decided to still keep working for The Diamond District, but on every mining mission you did for them, you'd take a little cut off the top. Not too much. Just enough that nobody would notice, and you would store what you took in a secret compartment somewhere on this ship. Am I getting warm?"

Eyes round, he looked at me before they flicked to his feet.

"It's underneath the ship, isn't it?"

"Come on, mate. Leave it out, will you? I don't know what—"

A gun barrel was placed to the side of his head.

"I think the captain asked you a question and he would like it answered."

Tombstone didn't move his body but allowed his eyes to shift to his left where the helmeted head of Willis was looking at him. All Tombstone could see was his own reflection in the visor, but I knew from past experience that Willis had a shit-eating grin on his face.

"Look, mate, you can take it alright; the metal appraiser we took it to said it was like nothing he had ever seen before. Strong as diamonds and able to withstand extreme heat up to one thousand degrees and cold of minus two hundred. My guy said it would be worth a fortune on the open market if it ever got out. But it's all yours. Honestly, just—"

The ship lights flickered on and off.

"Quinton," came Tuari's voice over the speakers, "whatever you're planning to do needs to be done now!"

"Where is the ore kept?" I said, grabbing Tombstone by the shoulders.

"In a compartment that lines the bottom of the ship. There is a yellow button on the console dash in the cockpit that opens it. But be careful, mate. There's over ten tonnes of the stuff hidden in there."

Perfect, I thought as I made my way back to the cockpit.

I took my seat and looked to strap myself in but remembered the straps were on the floor; picking them up I tied myself to the chair and took a deep breath. The wall was fast approaching and I could now see the anti-aircraft cannons had come online. They moved lazily in our direction, confident in the destruction they could bring.

"Alright, here's the plan. I want you to continue flying towards the wall; get as close as you can to it then hug it and continue along its length making your way south. When I say so, I want you to shoot upwards and try to make it over the wall. Once we're high enough, I'll release the little treasure trove our little mining buddies have been keeping for themselves."

Tuari looked at me as if I was insane. "I don't think this is going to—"

"It's the best plan we have, now punch that shit!"

The ship picked up speed, bringing the view of the wall closer and closer until it was the only thing we could see. Shots from Tex's vessel flew past us and hit the wall as Tuari did his best to keep us alive. We ducked and dodged left and right and I aimlessly fired our railgun knowing it wouldn't do a lick of good, but firing it just to keep my nerves at bay.

"Everyone," I shouted through the ship's speakers, "strap yourself in. Things are about to get bumpy."

"Like they're not already!" called Willis from the back.

I gripped my chair as the now fully active cannons turned towards us and fired. I saw nothing but a cloud of smoke where the cannon had once been as the ship took a sharp left. An explosion somewhere behind us sounded. Thank fuck! We were still alive. But the cannons weren't done. Another one some half a mile away also fired our way. The ship did a barrel-roll and I saw the explosion kick up a mountain of dirt below us.

"You know," said Tuari, sweat pouring down the side of his face, "the whole point of this mission was to sneak in and out without anyone knowing we're actually here. We weren't meant to announce our presence for the whole fucking borough to know we're coming."

"What can I say, I like to make an entrance!"

Another cannon fired at us and the shell was so close to striking us that the aftershock of the explosion rocked the ship, causing the lights to flicker once more. Fast approaching the wall, we made a sharp bank turn and flew along it so close, we were scraping metal.

"It's your buddy again," said Tuari.

"Put him through. Tex, you calling me to say you've reconsidered my offer?"

"Woohoo! Boy, you a crazy motherfucker! I love it. Yes.

Yes. Yes. I knew from that last chase on the rooftop I would love doing this job. This is what I needed. A job to put some gumption back in my pencil. A job to get me hard in the morning. But I'm afraid every good job must have an end, so this is a big heartfelt thank you from me, because I can't remember the last time I felt this way. It's been emotional," he said, cutting off the connection.

"You know what?" Tuari said, looking over to me. "In a weird way, I'm gonna miss him."

We continued flying along the wall dodging Tex's fire. We didn't have far to go until the next stage of my plan came into action. We just had to stay on course and pray nothing went wrong.

"At least the cannons can't reach us—"

"Why would you say that?" Tuari said, cutting me off. "You never jinx a mission like that. Now we're definitely going to die."

"Oh, don't be so para—"

I watched in horror, mouth opened, as a hatch popped open in the wall and a small sleek laser-type weapon rose from it. I could feel Tuari's eyes on me, but I refused to turn around and face him. As I watched more and more lasers popped up like Jack-in-the-boxes.

"Just say it," I said.

He yanked the ship hard right as the lasers fired. The blinding light they emitted made it almost impossible to see. How Tuari was still able to fly was beyond me, but I wasn't going to say anything to disturb his focus.

"You know what?" he said. "Just once, just fucking once, I would like it if a mission just went according to plan, instead of us having to pull a rabbit out of our asses to seal the show."

I donned the gunner's helmet once more and fired in

front of us in a wide arc, destroying as many of the guns as I could. Thankfully, they weren't shielded or as heavily armed as Tex's ship, and many went down before my onslaught, but the more I destroyed the more that appeared to pop up. A laser gun popped up to my left and I turned and fired but didn't destroy it in time as it struck the side of the ship.

"Warning! Warning. Warning. Shields down to ten percent. Please find the nearest safe location to land," said a robotic voice from the ship's speakers.

"Well, that's a fine how do you do," Willis screamed from the back. "If you fucktards are done pissing around maybe you can—"

"Maybe we can what, Willis?!" Tuari snapped. "If you think you can do better then be my guest."

"I can do better with my eyes closed. It ain't rocket science—just avoid getting—"

"Why don't you come up here then and show us how it's done, Billy Big Bollocks?"

"I would love to," said Willis, as I heard a commotion from the back.

"Willis! Stay in your seat and shut your mouth. Tuari, on my order I want you to take this ship up."

No one said anything as I continued to fire in front of us, clearing a path so we could fly straight up and over the wall. I did a quick check behind us and saw Tex was still following close behind, although his ship was smoking just as badly as ours was.

"Err," said Tombstone in a small voice, "do you still want me to show you where the tunnel is? We should be approaching it any—"

"Change of plans; we're not going to make it. Tuari, now!"

I gripped my seat as the ship shot upwards with lasers

and Tex's ship in hot pursuit. We continued gunning for the top of the wall and I fired everything the ship had until we finally cleared the wall and were flying straight up above it. I used the gunner's camera to look back and could see that Tex was still coming after us.

The view below us was awe-inspiring.

A light show of lasers and smoke like a rock concert on steroids obstructed the view of the ground. We continued to gain altitude and I could just make out the monstrous metal shafts of the cannons as they all converged upwards taking aim.

Everything went silent. I had to time this right or we would be blown to kingdom come.

My hand hovered over the yellow button and I stared at the HUD in my helmet, watching everything play out frame by frame. Tex's ship exploded out of the smoke like a creature rising out of the sulphur mists of hell. The cannons reared back ready to release their load. Lasers could still be seen lighting up the smoke. And through it all, all I thought of was Poppy and our unborn child. They needed me to survive. I made that woman a promise. One I would keep no matter what it cost.

I slapped the button and felt a shudder roll through my chair as the ship released its payload.

Everything sped up.

I watched as Tex's ship, which had been within spitting distance of ours and ready to fire the killing blow, was engulfed by the metal ore debris that fell from our ship. It wasn't only metal ore that fell, but a plume of metal dust that blacked out the sky and no doubt made their job of seeing us impossible. As the ore and dust did its job the cannons went to work.

They fired a symphony of destruction that lit up the

smoke below us.

Tex's ship did their best to avoid being destroyed, but they stood little chance against the onslaught they found themselves in. Missiles came from below and metal from above. The missiles struck the ore and blasted it apart creating shrapnel that tore through Tex's ship, ripping it apart.

The resulting explosion shook our ship and threatened to engulf us.

"Tuari! Evasive movements," I screamed.

"Well, duh," he said before yanking on the controls.

I watched in horror as the explosion behind us grew larger and larger. We were putting distance between us and it, but the ship just wasn't going fast enough. I watched on my HUD as flames engulfed the camera causing it to short circuit, giving me a view of nothing but static. I ripped the helmet off my head as the ship shook violently.

"Warning! Warning. Warning," came the voice of the ship over the speaker. "Shields down to seven percent. Shields down to five percent."

"Someone do something!" cried a voice behind us.

"Shields down to three percent."

"Our father who art in heaven hallowed be—"

"Shields offli..."

Whining to a stop, the voice of the ship went offline as well as the lights.

We were in total darkness.

"I've lost all power to the engines. Brace yourself, we're going—"

But whatever else Tuari was going to say next was snatched out of his mouth as my stomach felt like it was going to come out of mine as we plummeted towards the ground.

50

There was nothing but screams and darkness.

Nothing but screams and darkness as the ship tossed and turned like it was on the fast cycle of a washing machine. I held onto my chair, my neck fighting against the G-force I was being subjected to as my body slammed against the restraints of my chair. As my body lifted from the seat, I was thankful that I had the foresight to tie myself to it.

Something hit me in the face causing my vision to become blurry and star-studded.

"Hold on," I thought I heard Tuari say, but I couldn't be sure.

My vision started to clear and as soon as it had, I hit my head again against the back of my chair causing stars once again to return to my vision. I could feel the veins in my neck straining to keep my head in one place; bile from my stomach rose up and I did everything I could to push it back down. Round and round we went as everything blurred into one.

I could smell smoke. I felt heat. I felt warmth run down my face.

"I'm gaining—control—descent—may."

Words were being shouted at me but I could only catch snippets from Tuari as I tried to do everything in my power to stay conscious. Although everything was black, I could still tell I was going to black out any minute. I needed to think of some way to help. But nothing came to mind as the ship did a barrel roll, lifting me once again off my seat. My hand touched the top of the ceiling before I came crashing back down with a thud.

"I've got it!" Tuari shouted.

The ship had indeed straightened out to some extent and I could see through the viewing screen that we were level, although we were still falling at some speed.

We passed buildings almost as tall as the wall we had just gone over. They rushed past us as Tuari fought with the controls to try and evade them as best as he could.

One building larger than the rest stood out like a giant amongst men.

Its rooftop was so large that it had the space for multiple spaceships. Windows in the shape of diamonds, it glistered blinding me temporarily before it vanished from my sight.

"Watch out," I said, as the narrow tip of a building appeared before us, but it was too late. We crashed through it sending glass and metal tumbling below as part of the wing of the ship snapped off from the impact. The collision spun us around in a tailspin, and everything once again became a blur. Round and round we went for what left like an eternity until Tuari straightened us out once again.

Bile rose from my throat again and this time I couldn't hold it in. Leaning my head to the side, I threw up as I saw another building out of my peripheral vision coming towards us. I wanted to shout "Watch out." I wanted to yank Tuari's controls to the side but with a mouth full of bile all I could do was watch in horror as the other wing of the ship sliced through the building, breaking off inside it.

I heard the sound and felt the rumble of an explosion but I didn't know where it came from.

Thankfully, we stayed level but now without any way to manoeuvre the ship we were just a barrel flying through the air. Another skyscraper came before us, and this time there was nothing we could do to avoid it. Grabbing the controls of the railgun I prayed it still worked as I pointed it towards the building and opened fire. Bullets tore through glass and metal and we quickly followed behind, making our way through the building. I got a flashing glimpse of office chairs —conference tables—and water-coolers before we shot out the other side of the building.

An almighty snap echoed through the ship and I felt a sudden rush of air pulling me backwards. I looked over my shoulder and was taken aback by the sight I saw. The bottom half of the ship had been sheared off leaving a huge gaping hole. Willis, Scarface and Tombstone all held onto their chairs as the suction from the hole threatened to pull them through. I turned my attention forward and saw we were going to go through another building.

Railgun at the ready, I blasted an entrance for the ship to pass through and was nearly thrown out of my seat as the bottom of the ship crashed against the floor of the building that we had entered; we bumped and skipped along the floor, the friction it created sending sparks into the air. The journey lasted longer than I thought possible and all too soon I saw the other end of the building came into view. We continued towards it but the closer we got to it, the slower we moved.

"Has this thing got any brakes?" I shouted at Tuari, but he looked at me as if I was an idiot.

The ship kept on its journey and the front crashed through the other side of the building until the ship came to a gradual stop. Half the ship hung out the side of the building, while what remained stayed inside.

I slowly let out the breath I was holding while I felt the ship tilt back and forth on its axis. I tried not to make any sudden movements as the sensation of being on a seesaw wouldn't go away. With every downward dip the ship made, it showed us how far we were off the ground. Let's just say the first floor may have well been a million miles away.

"Alright, everyone," I said, "if we handle this carefully then—"

"Let me off this ship!" Tombstone screamed at the back. I heard frantic movement and I whipped my head round to see him trying to unbuckle himself from his seat.

"Don't move. Do you want to kill us all?" I said, but he paid no attention to me, as he continued to unfasten himself.

Still seated Willis leaned over to him but he slapped Willis's hands away and continued to unfasten himself. Every movement that they made rocked the ship more and more, but he either didn't notice or didn't care. Scarface, seated next to him, slowly went for his gun and I tried to signal to him not to, but he took no notice of me and continued to reach for the weapon.

The more the ship rocked the more everyone's movements became more and more frenzied until all I could see was a tangle of limbs as Willis and Scarface tried to do their best to handle the situation. With a push off his seat Tombstone leapt forward off his chair and stood up.

The ship creaked, silencing all.

"Listen to me," I said through gritted teeth, lifting up the visor of my helmet and looking Tombstone dead in the eyes. "You take one more step and this ship is going down. You understand?"

He nodded.

"Good. Now all I want you to do is slowly, very, very slowly, back up step by step towards the back of the ship until I say stop. Then when I say stop, I want you to stay perfectly still at the point you're at, until someone else gets up and makes their way towards you. I don't want any sudden movements. I don't want this to be done with speed. If we all do as I say, with measured and controlled movements, then we'll all get out of this alive."

He nodded to me once more.

"Good, now take a step back."

He did so, but as his foot came to a stop, the sound of material ripping at the seam sounded throughout the ship. I watched in horror as his trouser pocket came apart and a small piece of metal ore tumbled towards the floor.

We all watched it in fascination as it made its steady descent downwards.

Tombstone leapt forward to catch it but I knew that was a mistake. He caught it with one hand but it slipped through his grip and as he tried to catch it with the other it bounced in his palm and flew forward, where it sailed between me and Tuari and landed on the dashboard of the cockpit.

We all watched it with bated breath. But nothing happened.

We all let out a small sigh.

"Well," said Tombstone, "that could have been a lot—"

A shriek of metal tore through the ship as it pitched forward and then fell.

51

We fell.

We fell fast.

Too fast to do anything but scream.

One minute there was nothing but solid surface underneath our ship. The next we were falling towards the ground. The straps bit into my shoulder and I heard Tombstone's anguished screams to my rear. I turned my head and could just make him out in my peripheral vision. He clung to the headrest of a chair trying his best to stay inside the ship but his efforts were for naught. With a wordless scream and face full of fear he was sucked out of the ship.

I turned my attention back to the matter at hand and saw we would not hit the ground as I first thought, but instead, we were going to crash through another building. I opened fire once more, praying I could somehow cushion our fall but knowing it was worthless.

The railgun kicked and splattered as it came to life, but before I knew what was going on we had already crashed through the roof of a building. My body slammed against the straps of my harness as the front of the ship punched through the floor of the building.

Each floor we punched through gave us some resistance but it wasn't enough to slow us down. Jerking drop after jerking drop shook my body as we crashed our way through the building one floor after the next. The noise of the destruction we were causing was the only thing I could hear as my body was yanked back and forth.

Until it just stopped.

Silence.

That's the only thing that greeted my ringing eardrums as I opened my eyes and looked around. The ship had come to a stop between floors and we were wedged—suspended in midair. Below us was nothing but destroyed office equipment.

I looked to Tuari, who was silent. "You all good?" I asked. He didn't respond, and not being able to see his face because of his helmet, I couldn't tell if he was conscious or not. I leaned over and was greeted by the creaking of the ship. Slowing my movements down I tapped him on the shoulder.

"Huh!" he said, startled.

"Hey, big fella, how you doing?"

He took a deep breath and looked around. Argh... Fuck. I take it I didn't die."

"You sound upset."

"Yes, because if I had died I would now be surrounded by experienced beauties on a sand-covered beach with nothing but cocktails and lots of adult fun."

"Experienced beauties? I thought people always wanted to end up in the afterlife with virgins?"

"Blah. Virgins, where's the fun in that? I only want to spend eternity with women who know their way around a cock like the back of their hand," he said with a wave of the hand, which caused the ship to rock once more.

"One of these days I hope you get a disease that eats your dick from the inside out," said Willis.

"And there's another sign I'm still alive," Tuari said. "The powers that be couldn't even grant me one small gift in taking the pain in my ass that is Willis Moor away. No, I have to listen to his foul mouthed nonsense for the rest of my days."

"You keep talking like that, asswipe, and I'll grant you the death you are seeking."

I moved my neck from side to side, which caused the ship to creak once more. "Alright, is everyone accounted for? No injuries?"

"I'm good," said Willis.

"Same here," said Tuari.

"The mute gave me a thumbs up," said Willis.

"I'll take that as he's okay," I replied. "Alright, this next part is going to suck. We've got to make our way out of this tube of death and up to the floor above. No sudden movements. Willis, make your way out first with our mute friend, then Tuari will follow, with me bringing up the rear. Got it?"

A round of yesses greeted me as everyone moved.

The going was slow. I held my breath with my eyes closed as every movement from Willis and Scarface rocked the ship, causing my stomach to do backflips. They moved as fast as they could, because we all knew the ship wouldn't stay in this position forever. Each creak or collapse of rubble caused a sharp intake of breath, until I heard the words I had been waiting for.

"We're out," Willis shouted.

Tuari exhaled loudly, causing me to smile. "And here I

was thinking I was the only one trying not to shit myself," I said.

"More fool you, I've already gone twice," Tuari said, unclipping himself. "I'll meet you up there."

He patted me on the shoulder as he manoeuvred his body through the ship, leaving me to my thoughts. Alone in a tube can that had once been a ship but was now nothing more than a shell of itself. I had envisioned some problems in getting here but nothing like what we had encountered. We hadn't even set foot in The Diamond District yet. The mission so far had been nothing short of a clusterfuck. I thought back to José and wondered if he ever had any of these problems to deal with. Bloodthirsty bounty hunters come mercenary men. Psychotic geniuses with God complexes. Gang-leaders you had never met but who wanted you dead.

And the list went on and on. I shook my head at the absurdity of it all.

"You're up, Cap," said Tuari.

I sighed, took a deep breath and extracted myself from my restraints. With each movement I made I could feel the ship shudder and move. I climbed out of the cockpit and into the main body of the ship, scanning it looking for anything we might need on this mission that we might have forgotten. Seeing an extra box of explosive shells for my shotgun, I picked them up and tucked them in my pocket. Happy there wasn't anything else, I continued to make the climb over chairs and bits of equipment, until I could see helmets looking down at me from the hole that had once been the rear of the ship.

"Give me your hand," Willis said, extending his towards me.

I reached up but a shudder tore through the ship.

"Hurry!" he said.

The ship began to move and I continued to climb up with everything I had as items fell around me. I could see his outstretched hand but it looked like it was a mile away; no matter how fast I moved it felt like I wasn't getting close enough. With a roar I leapt up as the hole's edge that was holding the ship up gave way. Grabbing onto Willis's hand I dangled above the destruction as the ship continued to make its way down through the building.

"Fuck me, son," Willis said, "you've put on a bit of weight."

"Just lift me up, you idiot. It won't be long before someone comes and investigates what all the noise is."

52

But no one came.

It had been over an hour since we had crash-landed in The Diamond District and so far we had seen nothing but ghosts. The streets shined with a gleam and tidiness that was almost unnatural. There was no litter on the streets. There were no cars. There were no dilapidated buildings with boarded-up windows. There were no beggars or hustlers on the street corners.

It had the orderly presentation of a middle manager's office.

We hunkered down at the back of an alleyway behind a dumpster so clean I could eat off it. We had escaped the building we had crash-landed in, not finding a single soul.

The streets were more of the same.

"This is weird," said Willis. "Where is everyone? What the hell is going on?"

"The angry ginger has a point. All that commotion, from the cannons to us crash-landing in that building, should have drawn enough attention to us that you would have thought we were royalty from England. Instead, everything seems dead and I don't mean dead quiet either."

I nodded my head at them. "How many inhabitants does this borough have?"

"It's always hard to say," said Tuari, opening his visor and scratching his nose, "but The Diamond District has the lowest population of all the boroughs. They have a high degree of hate for outsiders and refugees, basically anyone who isn't rich enough to afford their own private ship. I used to date a girl from this way—well, when I say date, I mean we banged like demons until I was drained of my life sources—she was married to some investment banker or board of director for some weapons company or something like that. Anyway, if you weren't born here or wealthy enough to buy your way in, and were found walking the streets of this borough without a worker's permit, then they would throw you over the wall... literally."

"What's a worker's permit?" I asked.

"The actual workers of The Diamond District far outnumber the residents. Every day without fail tens of thousands of people flood through those walls to serve maybe five to ten thousand who call this borough home. They make up the cleaners, cooks, service staff, retail staff—you get the picture. The only people who work here and live here permanently are the bodyguards that the rich use to protect themselves."

"Hold on," I said, shaking my head. "If all the workers go home at night, then what happens if someone wants a cheeseburger at one o'clock in the morning or open-heart surgery?"

"They get the service bots to do it," said Tuari.

I shook my head in confusion. Although man had created AI humanoids and robots that could do manual labour and everything in-between, the distrust humans held for them because of the actions of Poppy and AIs like her during WW3 had all but wiped them from every industry. Robots and basic AIs were now only used to do the most menial jobs. Jobs where they didn't have to think. Jobs where they weren't a threat to the public.

"I understand on Earth, AIs and robots ain't used for much, but in The Diamond District the residents use them in secret for most of their needs when the servants go home. The bots they have working in this borough are smart, but handicapped to a set level of intelligence. It's a dirty secret the residents of the borough have kept well guarded. If it wasn't for what's-her-face I was dating at the time I would have never found out about it."

"And you thought now would be a good time to inform us of this?" Willis asked; "You didn't think that we would need this information during the meeting or briefing?"

"Like I said, all the bots here are at such a low level of intelligence they would make even you look like Einstein. They won't give us any problems."

"Sometimes I just want to shoot you in the left nut," Willis said with disgust, turning away.

"I still don't understand," I said, jumping into the conversation before a fight started. "If they have the service bots, why have the human staff as well?"

"Come on, Quinton, don't be naïve. It's human nature," said Willis. "When you have as much money and power as these people do, you want to show your dominance not only over other humans but also over AIs that other people deem too dangerous to work with, even if they haven't got the intelligence of Poppy or her kind. It's ego. Pure and simple. Why does a man want two billion when he already has one? Ego! It's what drove the human race to conquer

Earth. It's what drove them to conquer space. And it's the fine line called ego, that they have to walk where on one side lies self-discovery and the other side lies self-destruction."

He had a point.

"But that still doesn't explain where everyone is," said Willis.

"No, no, it doesn't. And I have a sinking feeling we are not going to like the answer when we find out," I said.

We continued our journey through the deserted streets, darting from one corner to the next, guns always at the ready but never being needed. We had decided to wait in the alleyway behind the dumpster until it was dark and use the cover of darkness to move about more freely.

Walking along the streets of this borough brought up memories of home, memories I had not thought of for many years. This was the first borough that was so much like New-London in the simple things like clean buildings and working street lights that I smiled at what I would have been doing now if I was back there. With all that was going on, I didn't really get time to reflect on my past. Reflect on things like family or friends.

It was a shame my mother and father would never get to meet Poppy, would never get to meet their grandchild. But they wouldn't understand. I could already see the fear and hate in their eyes. The judgement. The scorn. Plus, with the amount of enemies I was collecting daily staying out of the picture, for their own sake, was safer.

I walked past a restaurant window and stopped. Getting closer I pressed my helmet against the window and looked inside to see a restaurant whose tables still had cutlery and glasses set on the table.

"Hey, look at this," I said, pointing towards the glass.

The others stopped and looked inside but said nothing. Tuari walked towards the entrance and pushed it open.

"What do you think you're doing? Can't you see food and not want to eat it?" Willis said.

Tuari gave him a shrug and walked inside. I stifled the groan that wanted to escape my lips and followed him, with a reluctant Willis and Scarface in tow.

Linen tablecloths covered glass tables with designer chairs sitting before them that looked pretty but weren't functional. Chandeliers hung from different points in the ceiling and a fish tank that covered one wall had fish of all different sizes and hues.

We swept our guns across the restaurant but there was no one there.

I walked up to a table that had something mouldy and unidentifiable resting on a plate; a wine glass with a smudge of lipstick on the rim sat next to it. "I'm guessing whatever is on this plate was once food, but God knows how long it's been here."

"All the tables are the same," said Tuari, picking up a menu. "Although anyone who comes to this pretentious, sorry excuse for a restaurant deserves to be served this mouldy slop. Look at what they're serving the baked potatoes with? And I don't care what anyone says but cheese doesn't go well with *everything*! And the prices these poor assholes will pay for this crap just beggars belief. And the house wines they have don't pair well with any of the meals. I mean—"

"I thought we were on a mission here?" Willis asked.

"Not a bunch of restaurant food critics trying to determine if this restaurant should get an award."

I continued to walk amongst the tables noticing all the cutlery was still on the tables; none had fallen to the floor or been swept off the tables, which would indicate a struggle had taken place here. "It's weird, it's like someone's removed the people but left everything else. The lights are still on. And the fish are still alive, which means someone must be feeding them."

I stopped in front of a robot stationed behind the drinks bar. It wore a white tuxedo with a red bowtie; its metal head shone under the spotlights of the restaurant as its circular eyes stared straight ahead. I looked to my left and saw an identical bot sat behind a black grand piano, skeletal fingers resting idle on the ivory keys.

I walked off but stopped as I saw a flicker of light behind the eyes of the bot behind the bar. Licking my lips I slowly waved my hand in front of its face and jumped out of my skin as it latched onto my wrist with its hand.

"Shit! Shit! Shit!"

I tried to pull my hand out of its grip but it was like trying to pry something out of a metal vice. The rest of the team advanced on my position, weapons at the ready. No matter how hard I tried there was no way I was getting my hand back.

"Well, that was a stupid thing to do," said Willis with a shake of the head.

"Very stupid indeed," said Tuari, inspecting the limb. "I think the only way we're going to get you out is if we cut off the hand at the wrist. Don't worry, it will only hurt for a second and they have amazing prosthetic replacements that are almost as good as the real thing."

"Stop messing about and try and get me out of—"

"Hello, sir," said a male voice that came from the robot, "and welcome to the finest restaurant in all of the borough, The Last Meal."

"Ugh, how pretentious," said Tuari.

"We at The Last Meal are tasked with making sure your experience here shall be one to remember. We will do everything in our power to make sure you pick the meal that best compliments your DNA code and taste buds to make sure that anything you choose will not send you into an allergic fit, but will instead put you in a coma of your own joyful bliss."

"Shoot me now," said Tuari.

"Now, do you have any questions?"

"Erm... yes, could you please release my hand?"

"It is customary to first take a blood sample so we can best match what foods—"

"No, that won't be needed. I already rang ahead and gave the person I spoke to all of my details," I said in a hurry.

"Well, if sir is sure?"

"Quite sure."

With a soft hissing sound, the robot's hand slowly unfolded enough to the point that I could pull my hand out. I massaged the feeling back in my hand as I inspected the robot closer. It didn't show any signs that it was on, but apart from its own hand coming up to grab mine, it hadn't moved since we entered.

"I was surprised that you were open. It's normally full this time of night, but the restaurant is empty," I said.

"The restaurant never closes, sir. Now, would you like to see the menu?" the bot asked.

"Not yet. I would like to book a table for the same time tomorrow night; can you tell me if there are any tables free?"

A Dog Is Born

"You are in luck, sir, we have no bookings for this time tomorrow."

I tapped my fingers against the drinks bar. "That sounds great, but before you book me in, I need your help with something. The last time I tried to book a table at this restaurant it was fully booked and I had an important meeting on that date, but for the life of me I can't remember the exact date it was—my dumb secretary lost all the details. Could you look back in your records and tell me the last time this restaurant was completely booked out?"

I waited, but the robot said nothing. I turned back to the others and gave them a shrug. It was worth a shot even if—

"The last time this restaurant was fully booked was four months ago today."

I looked back at the others but said nothing.

I turned back to the bot. "I'm from out of town, in this borough for business, and I wondered if you could tell me if anything eventful has happened in this borough of late. It doesn't appear to be as crowded as it once was."

Silence.

"Would sir like to see the menu?"

"No, not right now. I just wondered if you could tell me if you've noticed any changes around here. Lack of customers. Lack of orders being placed. That sort of thing."

Silence.

"Would sir like to see the menu?"

Willis sighed, "It's like the big idiot said, these robots are just machines. They follow a set script and will only respond with certain answers; if they encounter a question not on the script then they default back to the first or most important question."

I frowned. I was missing something. Something important. I— "I've not seen the owner in a while. He and I are best of friends and I wondered if you could tell me the last time he was around the restaurant? Maybe give me some contact details to reach him if he's not around at the present?"

"The last time Mr Franzio visited the restaurant was four months before this date. Regarding contact details, I'm afraid I'm not at liberty to give such information out. Now, would sir like to see the menu?"

"Thank you, but I've lost my appetite; maybe another time."

I nodded to the others and as we made our way towards the door, I stopped. The robot that had been sitting behind the grand piano had moved. It stared at me, fingers hovering above the keys.

"Shall I play our guest a tune, Sammy?" it asked.

"Sure, Frank," replied the bot behind the bar. "Play them one last tune."

We all looked at each other while the bot played a medley that sent chills up my spine. It was beautiful. It was sorrowful. It reminded me of the last song to be played at a funeral.

"This place is giving me creeps. "Let's get out of here," Willis said, making a quick exit for the door.

I followed the rest of the crew out but could feel eyes on me. I turned back to see both robots staring at me, unblinking. They watched me with an intensity that made me feel like prey.

A hand slapped me on the shoulder making me jump. "Come on, there is nothing else to be gained here," said Tuari.

I took one more look at the restaurant and wondered what had taken place in this borough four months ago. Whatever it was could only spell trouble for us.

53

Our journey through the borough hadn't given us any more clues than the restaurant we had first visited.

Every store we passed had clothes lying on the floor, every restaurant still had its tables ready for its customers to enjoy their meal. It was as if the whole population had been beamed out of existence without a struggle. Cars were parked in neat lines along the road and private ships sat on top of buildings ready to take off at a moment's notice. The one thing ever-present no matter where we went was the service robots that manned the shops, restaurants and hotel foyers. We passed another apartment building designed in gold and metal; I stopped and pivoted, looking at the robot who stood at the front of its doors. Dressed in a purple velvet bellboy's costume it regarded me silently.

"You've noticed it too, huh?" asked Tuari, coming to a stop at my shoulder.

"Yeah, wherever we go they are always watching. I've caught a few of them out of the corner of my eye but I don't know what it means."

"It means," said Willis, "once we find out who's controlling them then we find out who's done this."

"Don't be preposterous," said Tuari. "It's not that easy to control a robot; no matter how much money these poor fools had, it just doesn't work like that. The World Government has inbuilt protocols to ensure no one can easily hack these machines, and I mean no one. After the fiasco of WW3 steps were taken to ensure that would never happen again."

"You're forgetting something, my oafish friend. We're a long way from the World Government's umbrella of influence and where there is a will, there is a way."

"I don't think you—"

"It doesn't matter," I said, cutting Tuari off. "What matters is finding Diamond and getting this job done. If someone has killed him, then that's just one less job for us and we can go home early."

"When is it ever that simple?" Willis asked.

I chuckled as I brought up the details the Lady Isabella had given me. Searching through the files I looked up the address of her spy who lived in the borough and the residential location of Mr Diamond.

"Alright, until we find out more, all this guessing will get us nowhere. The next thing we need to do is find The Lady's spy and see what information they can give us about what the hell is going on around here."

"That's if he's alive," said Willis.

"Oh, you're such a ray of sunshine," said Tuari.

"They're not far from here, less than fifteen minutes away. Keep your eyes peeled and let's get moving."

～

A Dog Is Born

We arrived at another imposing building that was all twisted glass and metal, that appeared to have been conjured up out of an architect's mushroom trip. There were no robots stationed outside the building, which I was thankful for. Walking up to the building we swept our guns left and right until we got to where the front door of the building should be, but instead of a normal door we were greeted by a large round circular hole that tunnelled through the glass into the building.

The words "Every day should be one of play" was engraved above the tunnel.

"I hate this place a little bit more every second I'm here," Willis said.

We looked for another way to enter the building but couldn't find any; I went in first and crawled into the hole and through a tunnel that reminded me of a children's play area. Once out I stood up and surveyed the area I was in, a plush lobby with white marble floors and soft lighting. A reception desk made of dark oak stood against one wall, but there was no one behind the desk.

"On the way back, I'm going to blow a hole through that wall and walk out on my own two feet like a man," said Willis, looking back the way we came in disgust.

"Alright, our person of interest is located on the second floor, room 88. I suggest we take the stairs because I don't want to be trapped in the elevator," I said, leading the way.

We made our way up the stairs and entered the second floor, where dark wood doors graced walls on either side of us. I heard nothing apart from our footsteps as we made our way forward. Stopping in front of a random door I went to reach for the handle but noticed there wasn't any; instead a flash of red light emanated from a circular lens in the middle of the door and scanned my body, the lens flashed red, then went dead.

"I guess that means no entr—"

Two soft thuds cut Tuari off, as two small holes appeared where the locking mechanism was in the door. Smoking pistol with silencer in hand, Willis gestured for us to enter.

I pushed the door open and took in a small corridor that led to a kitchen. Taking a step forward I stopped and stared down at a bloody trail that started from the kitchen and made its way between my legs and out the door. I pointed it out to the others, and we all gripped our weapons a little bit tighter. Walking forward, I kept as quiet as I could and tried to detect any sounds. There was a living room to my left; two white sofas with scatter cushions occupied the room. A large grass coffee table with a layer of dust rested in front of them. Pictures lined the walls of the same middle-aged man but always with a different person. A quick scan of the rest of the apartment showed no one had been home for quite some time.

There were no other signs of blood or of a struggle anywhere else in the apartment. A large dried bloodstain occupied the tiles of the kitchen floor, but there was no broken cutlery or furniture anywhere to be found.

I came back to the living room to find Willis tapping on the coffee table, which was, in fact, a computer.

"Judging by what I can find on this, the last time one Mr Paul Costa logged into this computer was—"

"Four months prior to this date?" I said.

"How did you guess?" Willis said.

We entered a few other apartments and found the same thing. Dishes that had been left in sinks unwashed. Clothes that had been dropped on floors. Cups that had been left on coffee tables. A few apartments had bloodstains similar to

A Dog Is Born

the first apartment we entered, but we found no bodies or weapons to speak of. One thing common in all the apartments was the layer of dust and grime that had gathered on surfaces because of neglect.

We finally came to the door we wanted and entered it the same way we did the first. This apartment was different though.

There were no pictures of loved ones on the wall, no bloodstains to be found, instead only a detailed pyramid map of a bunch of faces I had never seen before. Sat at the top of the pyramid was a black elderly man with a bull neck who still looked like he could show the younger generation a thing or two. He was dressed in a tailor-fitted pinstripe suit; his piercing eyes stared ahead. He looked as if he hadn't smiled in generations. Beneath the picture was the name Mr Diamond written in sharpie.

Below him were two other gentlemen. One was a red-faced pudgy man whose neck nearly hid the tie he wore; small beady eyes stared out under a thick set of heavy eyebrows. The name Mr Ruby was written under his picture. The other man was named Mr Pearl, whose face was expressionless and grey; he looked like a watercolour painting done by a bad artist.

Below those two were a whole host of underlings and people who worked for them. The pyramid tree went on for some time.

"Well, looks like our boy's been busy," said Tuari.

I folded my arms as I took all the information in. Much like all the other apartments we had entered this one had a large coffee table that acted as a computer. I walked over, turned it on and saw lines like spiderwebs connecting documents on the computer to pictures on the wall. Each document appeared to be information containing to a certain individual.

I pressed on the document that connected to Mr Pearl. The folder opened and was projected above the table. An audio file started to play.

"Not much is known about the man named Mr Pearl; his appearance always changes as well as his daily schedule. Pearl acts as the head of the secret police force Mr Diamond uses to keep order in the borough. Through the use of fear, intimidation and brutal violence, he has allowed Diamond to keep a stronghold over this borough for decades. He is a man of few words and fewer actions, but make no mistake—this man is dangerous and must be taken out first before even thinking about going after Diamond."

The audio clip ended and we all looked at each other, lost in thought. I pressed another file.

"Mr Ruby. This man is a fool and Diamond's second in command. Quick to temper, doesn't trust anyone apart from himself; a liar, a thief, an egomaniac and all-round scum of the earth. When I first started this assignment, I was unsure why Diamond kept this man as his second in command but the longer I have watched the big man himself the clearer it has become.

"Diamond's biggest skill is reading people. Keeping people around him, he knows how they will act and react before they do. By keeping Ruby in the position that he is in, Diamond will never be surprised by any of his second in command's acts; he will never lose power to a man who outsmarts him or outthinks him. By always pressing the right buttons, he can forever keep Ruby running on the hamster wheel of his own design."

Eager to find out more, I pressed another file.

"Mr Diamond... real name unknown. Age unknown.

Birthplace... somewhere on Safe Haven, but exact location unknown. How he accumulated his wealth is unknown. Most likely through illegal means and by using fear and intimidation. Little is known about this man, but what I do know is that he is ruthless, smart and calculating. He is not a man to be taken lightly. His is a man to be feared."

The audio ended and we all looked at each other. "Well, that was a bunch of help," said Willis with a shake of the head.

"I'm not sure if he's being sarcastic or not because I can't see his face," said Tuari.

"When is he not?" I said, clicking through the files on the computer. "There must be something else on here that can give us some clue as to what has happened."

I continued to look while the rest of the crew roamed about the apartment trying to see if they could find anything else that could shine some clue on what was going on. They came back sometime later with Tuari holding up a brown box labelled toys.

"I found this under the bed," he said in a mischievous tone.

"Okaaay," I said, "is it something important? Can it shed some light on what's going on?"

"Well... not what's going on per se, but more of what sort of man our spy was."

"I'm not following you."

"Let's just say that our spy friend here had some exotic tastes."

I stared at him with my hands raised in a confused gesture.

"He liked the wilder side of life," said Tuari, lifting his visor and giving me a wink.

"What?"

"Oh, for fuck's sake," Willis said, grabbing the box and emptying it out on the floor where a whole host of sex toys bounced in all directions. A leather mask with a ball gag flopped on the computer screen in front of me. I picked it up with two pinched fingers and examined it silently.

"I see," I said before dropping it on the floor. "Well, as interesting as that may be—"

I drew closer to the computer screen and looked at a file I hadn't seen before; it was labelled with a question mark. Selecting it I looked to see which picture it was connected to but there wasn't one. There was white noise on the audio before the speaker came on; he sounded rushed, with the sound of his voice bouncing off the walls making the audio echoey.

"There is a new player in town. Someone with a lot of power and pull. He arrived a little over five months ago and has been disrupting the ecosystem of the borough. I can't find much about him, but he has brought a small army of mercenaries with him that Diamond is using to wipe out any opposition that he may have had in the borough. There have always been enemy gangs and crews in the underbelly of any borough, but now, there is none in The Diamond District. Diamond has completely wiped out the opposition.

"The Diamond District has never been more under his control. Lady Isabella was right, it appears he has plans on making a move on the rest of the boroughs before the year is over and he has enlisted the help of this mystery group to help him. If nothing is done, then all shall be lost." The audio stopped for a second or two then another clip played; screams in the background made it difficult to hear what the speaker was saying and the sound of his heavy breathing made his words unclear.

"I've never seen anything like it! If someone is listening

to this know that—he has set in motion a plan unlike—the whole of Safe Haven is in danger—he's looking to—wipe out—humanity—please stop him—they're coming!"

The audio cut out and we all stared at each other, lost for words as the sound of feet could be heard coming from the hallway outside.

54

We all stared at each other, guns at the ready as we each moved to a position that offered us a hiding place where we could fire from, but wouldn't be seen straight away when whoever was outside in the corridor came into the apartment.

The footsteps sounded heavy; they were feet in boots. I couldn't tell how many there were but the number was high enough to give us enough trouble.

"Are you sure they went into this building?" asked a gruff voice from the corridor.

"Well, Paul said he saw some people on the cameras make their way this way, but he wasn't specific on the exact details," said a voice that spoke through its nose.

"I didn't ask you what Paul saw, Ted, I asked *you*."

"Well, the thing is, Mark, I didn't see which way they went, what with Tex's ship getting blown up—which by the way wasn't my fault no matter what Miguel and Luis said; how was I supposed to know the cannons could be programmed so they didn't fire upon certain ships—"

"Because they're highly advanced weapons that you

were told to watch the video briefing on, but like everything in your sad sack of shit life, you fell asleep during the video so now Tex and our men are dead, and God knows if *he*'ll still honour the agreement now that Tex is dead. All because you couldn't sit through a twenty-minute video!" said Mark.

"That's not fair, Mark. I mean, it's not like there weren't other people involved in the running and operating of the cannons," said Ted.

"Yes, there were many people, but they all fell under you. Head of Weapons Control. That's the title we gave you. That's the title you asked for, so all decisions, actions, and faults rest on your shiny dome of a head. You fucked up. You should have double-checked shit was working properly. You killed Tex. Now *he* hasn't spoken to anyone since the Junk Yard Dog crew crash-landed on this borough, and we can't lie to him and tell him they're dead because he somehow knows they're still alive. So if I were you, I would think very hard and fast on how you're going to fix this, Ted, because what little remains of our crew, blame you for this fuckup, and if we are going to get fucked over for this, know that there will be a mile-long line of men waiting their turn to fuck you before they themselves get fucked!"

"You think he knows," said Ted, lowering his voice.

"I think he knows everything. He scares the living shit out of me—you've seen what he's done to the people from this borough. You've seen what they've become. We've all had a peek behind the curtain and wished we hadn't. If we mess this up... I would rather die than become what he turned them into and if he's done that to people he needs, then what do you think he'll do to people he doesn't? People who displease him?"

"Look," said Ted's voice shakily, "I was just following orders. I don't see—"

"Just following... If the World Government ever get wind of this you think that sorry-ass excuse will fly?" Mark asked.

"Well, if I go down, I'm taking you with me! I've seen you stealing tech from—"

There was a loud bang against the wall and what was said next I couldn't hear.

"Well, that's hardly—"

"Shut up and come on! I want to search every apartment of this building before we leave."

"I don't see why I have to—"

A man yelped as a heavy slap echoed in the corridor outside. They kicked doors down one by one and with each increasing thud of my heart, I knew they were getting closer by the minute. I looked around the apartment and took in everyone's position.

Tuari was in the kitchen on his stomach, heavy assault rifle lying on the floor pointed towards the entrance, Willis was to my far left behind a bookcase, his pistols tucked close to his chest with his head bowed down in prayer, Scarface was to my right behind one of the sofas while I was tucked behind the other.

The footsteps were getting closer.

The door creaked open and I steadied my breathing. A man's shadow appeared against the far wall. It stopped and I could feel the person's gaze looking around the room.

"Ron, see anything?" asked Mark.

"I don't—wait, there's—!"

A loud crack filled the air and blood splattered the wall as cries of alarm came from the corridor. Footsteps could be heard running our way, then the door to the apartment was kicked open and more men rushed inside. Tuari waited till he got a clear shot, then three more cracks filled the air and the sound of bodies falling to the floor quickly followed.

"What is going on?" screamed Mark.

"We're taking heavy fire. We're taking heavy fire! What should we do?"

"Then fire back!"

We all hunkered down as they blew the door apartment off its hinges and bits of wood scattered everywhere. Bullets ricocheted against metal and smashed glass and furniture into a million pieces. Feathers and foam stuffing inside the sofas floated into the air as bullets tore into them. I lay as flat as possible to the floor waiting for the onslaught to be over.

But it didn't stop.

The bullets kept on firing as round after round was placed into the apartment. Then as quickly as it started it stopped and silence dominated the environment.

"You think they're still alive?" shouted Ted.

"How am I supposed to know that?" replied Mark.

"Willis," I said into the helmet mic, "I want you to throw a flashbang into the corridor. After it's gone off I want everyone to fire against the wall that separates us from the corridor. Spread your fire high and low. Ready?"

Willis gave me a nod.

"I'm telling you, Mark, they must be dead otherwise they would have fired on us already. Boys, go and check it out so we can get paid, get our reward and get off this Godforsaken planet."

The sound of footsteps brought a smile to my face. I looked at Willis and nodded.

He threw two flashbangs overhead and I watched them as they flipped end over end until they disappeared into the hole that was once a doorway. Getting up to my feet I lifted my shotgun to my shoulder in one smooth motion.

"Flashbangs!" shouted someone on the other side as a stampede of feet tried to escape.

We didn't give them a chance. We opened fire upon the wall in front of us blasting chunks out of it as our bullets punched through the plaster and hit whatever was on the other side. Screams of pain and anguish greeted our ears as more than one of us found our mark. My shotgun slugs tore football-sized chunks out of the plaster. I saw a head appear before me but it vanished in a cloud of gore as it was blasted off its shoulders. Running legs were visible but we cut them down bringing our enemies to their knees before ending their lives.

"Pull back! Out through the window and along the ledge!" I screamed as we moved backwards, each covering the other's back as we made our escape. I covered everyone's escape as they climbed through the living room window. A grenade appeared over my shoulder and I took it, pulled the pin and threw it through one of the holes in the wall before making my way out the window.

The explosion that resulted from it blasted out hot air over my back and toppled me forward.

I tried to get my feet underneath me as my arms windmilled in the air, but with a sickening realisation, I knew I was going to fall forward and there was nothing I could do about it. Although only two floors up we were still a good hundred plus feet in the air and if I fell I might not kill myself but I sure as hell would have a broken limb or two.

The ground below appeared to rush towards me and I felt myself tip forward despite my best efforts, then my movement halted and I was jerked backwards where my back slammed against the wall and the breath was knocked from my lungs.

I looked to my side to see Scarface. He gave me a thumbs

up, which I returned weakly. Patting me on the shoulder he moved off following the rest of the crew.

I took a deep breath and forced myself not to look down. Shit, that had been close.

"Are you coming? Or are you going to stand there all day and enjoy the view?" Willis asked.

I bit back my reply and followed the others along the ledge, paying special attention to where I placed my feet. The others were some way ahead of me and were making good progress. I tried to increase my speed but nearly missed my step a few times and had to catch myself. Willis had come to a stop at a window and was prying it open, while the others waited.

I hurried forward but as I took another step the window ahead of me that separated me from the rest of the crew exploded outwards with the sound of gunfire. Glass flew in all directions. I pressed my body against the wall as the firing continued. Willis had finally opened the window he was trying to get into and allowed the others to go in before him while he held it open. He looked at me but I motioned for him to go inside; he was no use to me out here and would be better suited drawing the fire away from me from the inside.

He gave me a nod and disappeared inside while I waited.

Gunfire still held me down. I checked my ammo and waited for the firing to stop. Finally it came to a halt and I replaced my shotgun with my pistol and positioned it to the side of the window just out of sight. I steadied my breathing while I waited.

"You think you got them?" came a voice from inside the building.

"How am I supposed to know?"

"Well, go and look," said the first speaker.

A sigh was uttered, then I heard footsteps before a head popped out and faced the opposite direction to me. I waited till he faced me then fired two shots to his face, blowing the back of his brains out.

"Frank!" shouted the first speaker, before a hail of bullets once again spewed out of the open window.

The shooting kept on, then stopped as cries of alarm came from the apartment the shooters were in. "They're inside! They're inside."

I recognised the tone of my crew's weapons as they opened fire upon our enemies inside. Shouts and cries were cut short as bullets found their mark. Two men sought to escape the carnage happening inside by trying to escape from the same window they had been firing through only moments earlier, I stood back and watched in amusement as a bald man pushed his colleague out of the way, forcing the man to topple forward and fall screaming. Baldie stepped onto the ledge and shuffled his way towards me, not noticing I was there until the barrel of my gun touched the side of his head.

"Ted, I presume," I said, forcing him to freeze where he stood. He didn't turn his head to look at me but instead allowed his eyes to shift to the side.

"Who's asking?"

"That shouldn't be your biggest concern right now, Ted, what should be is whether or not you can answer my questions correctly."

"Look, I don't know nothing. I'm like a mushroom, kept in the dark and fed shit. They only give me responsibility so they can lay the blame on me when it all goes to shit. I told Tex he shouldn't come to this hellhole, but would he listen? Oh no! The rewards were too great. The chance to be stronger, faster, more evolved than any human—" He stopped himself and shook his head.

"Go on," I said, pressing the pistol hard against his head, "you were just getting to the juicy bit."

"I'm not saying nothing. That monster we decided to work for is unlike anything anyone from the Mercenary Bloc has ever seen. He's cold-blooded and knows things no man should know. It was a mistake getting involved with him. A mistake that cost our unit most of our men and will no doubt make us the laughing stock inside the Mercenary Bloc organisation. I would rather die than tell you anything about him because if he finds out I ratted him out... I've seen what he can do to people. They're not themselves anymore. They're inhuman. Stripped of their—" He shook his head.

"Come on, Ted, I'm not asking for much—just a bit of information then we can all go home. That's it. Just some information. Like, why were you hired to kill us? Why am I being hunted? And finally, where did everyone in this borough go? Three simple questions, that once you answer you can walk away from here and live to see another day."

He said nothing as he brought his hand up and scratched the back of his head. Dried flakes rained down upon his shoulders.

"Oh, you're him, are you? Quinton Blake. I finally get to meet the person behind all of this. If I'm honest, I thought you would be taller, broader too, but none of that matters now because he knows you're here and there's nothing you can do to change your fate. It's written in stone. I feel sorry for you. The pain and heartache coming your way destroys men from the inside. I hope you can withstand it."

"Who is this person?" I said, grabbing him by the lapel, "and what have I done for him to hate me so?"

"You'll have to ask him that when you see him, but word

is you took something very important from him," he said, pushing me off him. "Now, I think... I think I'll take my chances down there," he said, stepping off the ledge and plummeting to the ground below.

As I watched his body free fall head over feet then slam into a parked car, it finally clicked. I finally knew who was behind all of this and felt like a fool for not realising it sooner.

55

We had exited the apartment complex without facing any further obstacles.

True to his word Willis blasted the apartment complex's entrance out instead of opting to crawl back through the child-sized tunnel to get back out. Telling him off at the amount of noise and destruction he caused had crossed my mind, but if what Ted had said was true then *he* already knew we were here, and no amount of silence could ever mask that issue.

Huddled behind yet another dumpster, I bowed my head and thought of what to do.

This mission that first had appeared straightforward now was more complicated than I could ever imagine. Did Lady Isabella know what we were up against? Was she allied against us with this enemy? Did she plan this? Did she make a deal to save her own skin? Shit! Was Poppy safe? I had told her to head to The Floating City, but what if she had been captured? What if... what if... what if—

Argh!

I pulled off my helmet and drew back my arm to throw it

against the alleyway wall but stopped myself. My chest rose and fell as the anxiety and emotions I was feeling pounded my chest like a silverback gorilla. I pinched the bridge of my nose, then closed my eyes and took in deep breath after deep breath until my nerves and emotions finally got into check.

I could run. I could leave this place and never look back, but I knew if I did then I would be endangering my family. They would come looking for me no matter where I went, no matter what I did. I had to face this threat head on once and for all and hope against hope I somehow came out of this alive. But if I didn't, then at least I could take our enemy down so my family could live safe and sound.

"So what is the plan?" asked Willis. "And why are we always hiding behind a dumpster!"

The crew looked at me while I looked at each of them in turn. What exactly was the plan? It had been to kill Mr Diamond but now he might not even be behind all of this. Would the men follow me to combat this new foe?

"Alright," I said, taking a squatting position in front of the group, and placing a small palm-sized computer on the ground, I switched it on and it presented a holographic image of a glass tower with diamond-shaped windows. "This building here is where Mr Diamond lives, does his business deals, eats, shits, fucks, you name it. According to all the information we have, he hasn't left the tower in more than ten years. It's become a prison and a home for him. The tower has everything he would ever need. Gyms, swimming pools, tennis courts, shooting range, botanical gardens, a nature reserve, even a small man-made ocean—"

"You're kidding me?" Willis asked.

"Nah," I continued, "if I were to list the things in that tower it would take days, let's just say the tower is like a planet unto itself. If we want to get Diamond then that is where we need to go, but I've got to be honest with you and say I don't think he's alive, nor do I think he's the one behind all of this."

"Who do you think—" began Tuari, but I cut him off.

"Right now that doesn't matter. What does matter is that this isn't what you signed up for; the goal post has moved, and I want to be completely honest with all you before we move forward. Our enemy is now longer Diamond and I don't think it ever was, but like I said that's not what you signed up for, so if you want to leave now, then this is your chance to do so. I won't hold it against you. I won't judge you. There shall be no repercussions." I looked at each helmet in turn but nobody said anything or moved.

"Look," I continued, "this mission... we may not make it out alive. This new target is dangerous. Once you agree to this, there won't be another chance to leave."

Willis popped off his helmet and looked me in the eye. "We know what we signed up for. We're in this together."

Taking off his helmet also, Tuari gestured to Willis and said, "Yeah, what the ginger idiot said."

I looked to Scarface, helmet still on, who said nothing but gave me a thumbs-up and a shrug; I guess it was the best I was going to get from him. I donned my helmet again and inputted the coordinates to the tower so all our HUDs inside our helmets showed a green line of arrows we had to follow to get there. We all checked and rechecked our equipment one last time, before we headed out to our certain deaths.

56

Miraculously, we got to the tower without being attacked or coming across any goons. The streets were still silent, still dead.

The tower shone across the street from us like a shining religious artifact. Its diamond-shaped windows did their best to hide the lights that shone inside, but we could still see them at this time of night. Cameras covered every exit and entrance leading up to the tower. I ran my eyes up and up so I could see the top but my neck gave out long before my interest did.

The tower came complete with underground parking for private ships, tanks and cars alike. I had looked to see how many floors the monstrosity had but I couldn't get an exact number.

"I'm surprised this thing hasn't got mounted gun turrets," said Willis.

"I have to agree, but I guess it would be bad form and not in keeping with the decor," said Tuari.

"Normally there is a constant armed squadron of men patrolling the streets around the tower, with many plain-clothes guards roaming the streets at all times and another armed squadron of men stationed right outside the tower. But it looks like it's our lucky day and someone has taken care of all that for us. Don't feel too disappointed though," I said, slapping them both on the shoulders; "there's no doubt a whole host of untold goodies waiting for us inside."

I took the lead and moved across the street toward the tower, keeping an eye out for the opposition.

I would rather we entered the building more discreetly, but not having the inside information of Lady Isabella's spy, this was our only course of action—to lead a forward charge and hope for the best. No matter how stupid the idea seemed. We crossed the street without any trouble and I made my way towards the front entrance but was stopped by Willis.

"Really?" he asked, disbelief lacing his vocals.

"What?"

"We're just going to walk up to the front door and do what? Knock?"

"You got a better idea?"

He looked at the tower then back at me, then back at the tower.

"I know what you're thinking, but all the information on how to get into this place covertly is with the spy and he is probably dead, so our best bet is to take a course of action they don't expect."

"And that's walking through the front door?" Tuari asked.

"Yes," I said as I moved off once again. The closer I got to the entrance the more the absurdity of what I was doing kept banging against the doors of my confidence, but it was too late to turn back now. My pride wouldn't allow it. The entrance to the tower loomed before us and it was something to behold; glass doors in the shape of a diamond reflected the lights around the tower. The closer I got to the entrance the grander in scope it became.

"Are those diamonds embedded in the glass doors?" Willis asked.

"It appears so," I said, heart pounding in my chest as I walked towards them. I licked my dry lips and kept on walking forward and almost fell over in relief when the doors opened before me. I stopped and kept a firm grip on my shotgun as I swept the area in front of me.

A lobby with ceramic glass floors greeted us; sofa chairs clustered on one side of the lobby with coffee tables littered between them; on the other side a large open office workspace with reclaimed wood benches and chairs took up space against the far wall. In front of us was a large hotel-sized front desk made out of glass that surrounded a diamond the size of my fist, which was placed in its centre.

Willis moved toward the glass desk and tapped it.

"What are you doing?" I hissed.

"You think it's real?" he asked.

"Probably, but I'm guessing the reason it's still here is that it's impossible to get to unless you what to blow through a couple of tonnes of glass."

He tapped the helmet of his chin while he looked thoughtfully at his grenades then back at the desk in question. "You know—"

"No!"

"But it won't take—"

I stared his way and said nothing until he sighed in frustration and threw his hands up in the air. We continued to move through the lobby taking in the sights. Everywhere I looked I saw the finest materials used to design everything from the chairs to the floors. It spoke of attention to detail that had been used by only the greatest architects. Soft lighting pulsed around the edges of the jet black ceiling, reflecting off the diamond flakes that sparsely coated it.

"If this is what the entrance looks like, then I can't wait to see the rest of the floors," said Tuari.

"What better way to show visitors your power and wealth than to bamboozle them with all of this? The other floors may not be as nice as this but somehow I doubt it."

We came to a stop outside a set of golden elevator doors and I pressed the button to call it down.

"Right, the last ten floors of this tower Diamond uses as his own personal residence. If we are to find what we need then we are to make our way to the top. These elevators can only take us to the start of those floors; to make our way to his penthouse we'll have to use the stairs or find another way there. The details on how he travels between the ten floors are sketchy, but I doubt an old man like him climbs ten floors every day. If we can't find the elevator he uses then we use the stairs. Either way, we need to find a way to the top.

"Any questions?"

Everyone shook their head.

The chime of the elevator doors signalled their arrival and they opened before us. I took one final look behind me at freedom, then I took a deep breath, turned around and walked into a metal cage that offered no way out.

Forty buttons glowed on the wall of the elevator, which meant the top floor of this tower was the fiftieth. Fifty floors that our enemy could use to hide. Fifty floors that offered us nothing but death. Fifty floors where my body might lay and never be seen by my loved ones again. My heart began to beat rapidly and I tried to breathe but no matter how many breaths I took they all felt shallow and inadequate, I tried to force more air into my lungs but no matter how hard I tried it was never enough.

How did they expect me to do this? How did they expect me to make sure everyone came out of this safe and sound and in one piece? They didn't know who we were up against but I knew. I knew what he was capable of. I knew he was expecting me, that he knew every move I had made up until this point. Like a bug caught in a spider's web, no matter how hard I struggled and looked for a way out, all I saw was death, not only for me but for all those I loved.

I had to think of a way to defeat him but every scenario I came up with only ended in death.

I felt my vision blur and the corners of my sight darkened, forcing me to put a hand out against the wall as my legs felt like jelly.

"Quinton, you all right?" said someone in the background.

I tried to answer but my tongue felt too large for my mouth. I tried to speak but nothing came out. I felt like my words were choking me, forcing their way down my throat so they blocked the only bit of air I could get.

"Quinton?"

I wanted to respond, but the darkness had already closed in.

57

"How do you manage it?" I asked.

José looked at me in confusion and shrugged, not understanding the question. We sat outside a bar on a fuelling station in the middle of space between nowhere and back and beyond. We had just completed a mission, and while the others had gone to do whatever one does after a mission I had tagged along with our captain. He had promised me he would buy me one of the most mundane run-of-the-mill drinks I had ever had, but the view it came with would be second to none.

He wasn't wrong.

We sat outside a bar best described as a rusty shack; metal folding chairs were dotted outside it and in front of us was a glass wall that offered the bar's customers a view of the space outside. It was breathtaking.

Blues, reds, greens, purples, oranges and everything in-between swirled in a vortex, like a master painter's rendition of space. It was unlike anything I had ever seen. The image would swirl and change and never stay the same, and every so often the space in front of us would spit out a piece of space rock that would fly over our glass wall, coming so close to it you felt like you could almost reach up and touch it.

Now I knew why those first space voyagers had taken the leap and ventured where no man had travelled before.

"How do you manage it?" I repeated.

"How do I manage what, boyo?" he asked.

"The pressure. The insurmountable pressure of doing the right thing, of knowing the people who follow you are putting their lives in your hands. That if you fail or make one miscalculation, their shining light could be gone forever and there's no one to blame but yourself. How do you keep going when the fear surrounds you? When you're scared of making a decision. When all you see around you is death and despair."

He regarded me silently before he looked off into the distance, taking in the light display before us. He stared out to space for some time, not saying or doing anything till a crooked smile filled with sadness graced his face and he took a pull from his cigar. Blowing out a couple of smoke rings, he downed his whisky and poured himself another shot from the bottle that rested on our table and downed that as well.

"Before I was a captain of this crew, I was the captain of another. I was but a boy who thought he knew the galaxy better than any star, who was brave and had cojones the size of coconuts. I would prove how brave I was at the drop of a hat too. God forgive the man who insulted my manhood. Like the saying goes, the graves are full of young men who are brave and willing to prove it. I didn't care who insulted me, anyone could get it. I was willing to do the most dangerous and craziest missions because yet again, how did one prove they were the best in the business, if they didn't take the jobs that made others go grey with worry?

"With that mentality, I chose a crew also befitting my nature. They were all young. They were all brash. They all had something to prove. There wasn't a voice of reason among us. Each one of us pushed the other to bigger and higher heights. And at first, the risks paid off. Boyo, how they paid off! Growing up I never had two coins to rub together but now I had more money than I knew what to do with. So much money that I once burned a whole bag's worth just to keep warm because it was the closest thing to me. We lost the value of money. It became meaningless to me and the more I went after it the more empty it left me. Till the only thing which gave me any sort of joy was the thrill of the chase and the danger of the mission.

"I kept saying yes to jobs I had no experience in. Yes to jobs where time after time, our close calls became closer and closer until one day, it all came crashing down. My whole crew died with me the only survivor."

He downed another shot and took a pull from his cigar and continued.

"Nothing sobers a man more than having to bury five young kids barely out of their teens. Nothing changes a man more than having to look into the faces of those kids' parents and tell them you're sorry. Nothing haunts a man more than looking into the face of someone's parents that saved your life when you know you're the reason they're dead.

"That it should have been you, not them."

He looked at me and the pain behind his eyes made me lean away from him; I was looking through the window of a tortured soul. I opened my mouth to say something but I didn't know what. Anything I did say would only be paying lip service to whatever pain he had been through; it wouldn't be enough, it wouldn't be right.

"It's alright, you don't have to say anything. What is done is done. But that experience taught me a valuable lesson that day. It taught me no matter what happens you have to take ownership of the situation. I chose to be in this position, so there's no use complaining or whining about it. The pressure of the job, the stress, the heartache, the nightmares, drowning your sorrows in cheap liquor and drugs, the emotional burden, all of it, comes with being a captain and I chose to be a captain so I must take ownership of everything that comes with that role."

I shook my head, still not getting the answer I wanted. "But how do you cope?"

"Argh! Boyo!" he said, throwing his hands up in the air in frustration. "You can ask the question as many times as you want in as many different ways, but the answer will always be the same. You just do. There is no secret recipe to this shit, amigo. How do you manage? How do you cope? You just do!"

I looked at him but didn't believe him. It couldn't be that simple. I tried to find another way to express what I wanted to say but he placed his hand on my shoulder and squeezed.

"You... just... do. It's as simple as that, amigo. It's as simple as that, and it's as hard as that."

58

"Quinton!"

I felt my body shake as the darkness pulled back and I slowly got my breathing under control.

"Quinton." Tuari was in front of me shaking me back and forth. I placed my hands up indicating I was okay and he backed up and gave me some room.

"I'm alright," I said, taking off my helmet so they could see my face. "I didn't realise how stuffy these things got after you've been wearing them for so long. I just needed a quick breather, but I'm all good now and looks like we're about to reach our final stop any second now."

The doors to the elevator pinged as the marker above the doors showed that we had reached the fortieth floor. They parted before us and the floor greeted us with nothing but darkness. We all looked at each other and said nothing. Putting my helmet back on my head, I clicked my neck from side to side and stepped forward, José's words still ringing in my ears.

"Alright, we've got a job to do. Keep your eyes and ears open and don't take any unnecessary risks. Let's finish this shit!"

59

We stepped out of the elevator and onto the fortieth floor taking each step with caution. We hadn't taken more than ten steps when dim lights came to life around us. I raised my fist, halting the others' progress, and took in our new surroundings. A floor that stretched out before us showed nothing but greenery. Long grass rose to waist height, swayed back and forth with trees of different species dominating the horizon.

I spotted English oaks, maples and sycamores as well a whole host of different trees that varied in colour and size. A tree with bright purple fan-like leaves with red veins was to our right, with another to our left that bore bulbous lime green spiky fruits.

"What... the..." Willis said, head turning to take in the surrounding scenery.

"It appears to be some sort of nature reserve," Tuari said.

"If that's the case then why is it so quiet—"

An explosion of sound cut Willis off as different animal sounds grew in volume around us. Everything from birds to insects made their presence known. I thought I even heard the shrill cries of a monkey.

"Don't nature reserves hold animals?" Willis asked.

"What do you think you're hearing right now?" Tuari replied.

"I mean big... animals?"

We all looked at each other as what he was saying sank in. The rustle of leaves in the far distance made us all jump as we pointed our weapons in that direction.

"Look," I said, "I'm sure there is nothing to worry about. This place probably only holds birds and at most a few monkeys."

"Yeah, it's not like rich assholes keep dangerous animals as pets," said Willis.

"I can't see an exit anywhere so I'm guessing we have to venture through the reserve to get to one."

"You're guessing, huh?" said Willis.

"Hey, if you have a better idea I would love to hear it. But at the moment, all we can do is venture through and see where it takes us."

"I hate nature!" Willis muttered under his breath.

"I'm surprised. Shouldn't you love all of God's creations?" said Tuari.

"Listen, you fu—"

"Come on," I said, getting in between the pair, "time's a-wasting."

We had been walking for some time and in that time we had seen sights and sounds that were completely alien to me. Monkey-like creatures with forked tongues and scales covering their entire bodies, white foxes with four tails, butterflies as big as dinner plates with wings that varied in colour like the fingerprints of a nation.

I took it all in and tried not to get distracted by what I

saw but the beauty of it all was just breathtaking.

We continued to push forward through the tall grass, sometimes being able to see over the top, sometimes not. Whenever the grass went over our heads I got the feeling of being swallowed whole.

"If you had the money," said Tuari, "what would you buy?"

"A chapel," said Willis, "one of those old medieval English ones built in the 15th century. With coloured glass windows and a graveyard that had headstones so old the writing on the stone had vanished. I wouldn't want it anywhere busy, just somewhere positioned in a little English village where everyone knew each other and I could speak the word of God. Although I would have to do it in silence in case the filthy pigs got wind of it, but that's another matter."

"I would want my own private beach, where I would have a little hut on the sands I could experiment with different meals and serve them to the local girls. All meals would be free but to enter my exclusive beach restaurant customers would have to be two things: one, naked and two, female."

"That hardly seems fair," I said.

"Oh, I'll be naked too," said Tuari.

"You're such a pervert," Willis spat.

We continued through the grass for some time until the noise around us had completely stopped. I raised my fist in the air halting the group. I turned my head from left to right. Something didn't feel right. Back the way we came the lights had gone off as the sensors didn't detect our presence anymore.

"Why have we stopped?" Willis asked.

I didn't respond as I dug my shotgun deeper into my

armpit.

"Why have we stopped?"

"It's silent. Too silent," I said.

"Normally when a jungle becomes still..." said Tuari.

"It means a predator is—"

A roar that punched through my chest sounded to our rear, forcing all of us to spin around. As quickly as it sounded it went away leaving nothing but deafening silence.

We all held our breaths as we scanned the grass.

"Does anyone see anything?" I asked.

"Nothing," said Tuari.

"The camera's ain't picking up any heat signatures either. Whatever this thing is, it can mask its presence like a pro," said Willis.

He was right. No matter how many times I used the helmet's embedded cameras to scan in front of me, it wasn't giving me any readings. There still wasn't any movement in the grass but I had a distinct feeling we were being watched.

I strode forward, shotgun in the air, and fired off a warning shot.

Still nothing.

I fired off another shot and this time I was rewarded with a deep bass growl followed by a roar. The grass in front of me began to move.

"Pull back! Pull back!" I shouted as I tried to get my legs underneath me, then I spun around and sprinted.

"Why are we running!" said Willis, who was keeping pace with me to my left. "Why don't we just shoot it?"

"I didn't know you could see through long grass," I snapped.

"Why don't we just wait—"

"Because! Whatever it is is camouflaged and we are in its element. It will pick us off in this grass before we can even do any—oh, just fucking shut up and run!"

Another roar sounded at our backs and we sprinted like hot pokers had been placed on our asses. We burst into a clearing where a group of monkey-type creatures huddled around a large puddle taking turns to drink; they scattered upon our approach, whereupon they darted up the nearest trees howling and shrieking while they threw something brown and mudlike our way.

"What the fuck!" said Willis, as a brown mud bomb hit him on the side of the head. "They're throwing shit!"

"Best keep your mouth closed then," said Tuari.

We continued on as the monkey-type creatures' howls and shrieks became louder and more panicked as whatever was behind us snarled. I grabbed my pistol from its holster and fired blindly behind me. Another roar sounded in response but it was one of anger, not pain.

We continued sprinting until we all erupted out from the long grass and came to a halt in front of a vast lake.

A man with his back to us faced the lake. Dressed in trousers and a black polo top jumper covered by a white lab coat, he had in his hands a loaf of bread, which he broke pieces off and threw into the lake. Brown hair fell to his shoulders. I knew this man. I had dreamt about this man. I had thoughts of killing this man. Now here he stood in front of me, back turned, unarmed.

The world around me fell silent as I lifted my shotgun up and walked towards him. Finger on the trigger I sighted along the barrel till his head was in my sights. I would end this once and for all.

He turned to face me at the same moment I pulled the trigger.

60

Smoke obstructed my vision.

Had I killed him? Had I put an end to this madness?

"Come now, Mr Blake, you didn't think it would be that easy, did you?" came a voice from the smoke.

"You know what, Alvis," I said, "for a moment there, I was hoping it was."

As the smoke cleared, I could see he had ducked allowing my slug to sail over the top of him. Straightening himself back up he brushed a hand down the front of his lab coat as he turned around and continued to throw pieces of bread into the lake. As the bits of bread landed on the water, small ripples formed as fish sucked them off the top.

The rest of the crew looked at me, tension rippling along their ranks, but I was only focused on the target in front of me. Once I destroyed this man who had made himself into a machine, then everything would be okay. I could live my life in peace knowing that the mother of my child would be safe from his hands.

"You know," said Alvis, "I adore nature. It's the absolute

master builder, its creations are always made to function in the environment that they're placed in without any added extra features. Without any add-ons that are just there to stroke the builder's ego. A tiger is perfectly designed for its environment, as is a shark or goat. If a creature isn't then nature takes care of its failures, its runts, and continues on designing until it gets it right. Humans always speak about nature and say only the strong survive, but that is not the case; it is only the most well adapted for their environment that make it to the top.

"It is simplicity itself."

"Then by your logic what you are trying to do is flawed," I said.

"Oh," he said, tearing up the last of the bread and throwing it into the lake, "how so?"

"Your aim is to improve upon mankind, but from where I'm standing humankind is the most adaptive creature of them all. What other creature has conquered its environment even if that environment isn't its natural home? From the seas to the deserts to the stars. Wherever mankind has gazed upon their footsteps have soon followed. We are gods of this universe. Rightly or wrongly."

Alvis said nothing as he shook his head. Passing his hand through his hair he gave me a look as if I was an equation to be solved.

"Quinton? We've come here to do a job, and I'm guessing he's it, so let's finish it so we can get out of here," said Willis.

"I still don't get what 16-15-16-16-25 sees in you. You're so normal. So average. There is nothing extraordinary about you whatsoever—"

"Well, fuck you too, buddy."

"All I see before me is a fool who can't see the shortcomings of the human race. Who can't see what I offer.

Who can't see the possibilities. Who can't see I am pushing the human race into the next stage up the evolutionary chain. Our forbears gave birth to the technology we improved on and use today. Electricity, the internet, satellites, rockets, machines that build things, mobile phones, 5G—and the list goes on and on, until we ended here.

"Can't you see," he said, arms spread wide, "the logical next step is humanity interbred with AI. Like no human being before I am offering a solution to starvation, disease, poverty, suffering. The prophets, spiritual leaders and gurus, could only talk and offer dreams and illusions of what I am saying, but I offer reality. I have the solution! Yet men like you want to stand in my way! Would rather have us back in the good old days when only the rich were comfortable and everyone else suffered.

"I am offering a solution. Unless you have a better plan, I suggest you stay out of my way unless you want to get hurt."

I looked to my crew. "What do you think, guys? Should we just leave him be?"

Willis looked to Tuari who in turn looked to Scarface. They all turned back to me and although I couldn't see their facial expressions, I had a pretty good guess what they looked like.

"That was a nice speech. Really nice," said Willis. "A bit too heavy on the old saviour of mankind bullshit, but apart from that, he hits all the right points. If I wasn't married to the faith, I could see myself getting behind the cause as most of humanity are a bunch of fuckwits, and we could do with starting over again, but alas the good Lord frowns on that sort of thing and it's not my place to judge, so I think I'll pass."

"I agree, as much as it sounds like a good idea, I'm not a

fan of plastic if you know what I mean," said Tuari, as he cupped the air with his two hands and squeezed.

Lastly, I turned to Scarface, who gave Alvis the middle finger.

"Couldn't have said it better myself, boys. You see, Alvis, as much as I want to believe you, that you'll leave us be, your past actions say otherwise. If I'm not mistaken, you hired a band of mercenaries to hunt us down and kill us, you have been farming the mines of The Jungle for any metal you can get your greedy hands on, and let's not forget what you've done to the people of this borough. I can only imagine what horrors they had to endure before they died.

"So no, Alvis, I can't leave you be. This planet is lawless, but if you think for one minute you're not going to pay for your actions then you're sadly mistaken, my friend."

He said nothing as he stared at me, finger tapping on his lips. There was a rustle from the long grass to our left and from the grass emerged a creature that wasn't born, it was created.

It resembled a large cat but that's where the similarities stopped.

Glowing red eyes encased in a metal skull followed our every movement. Its long sleek body was composed of a flexible type of metal alloy that allowed it to move with a grace almost as good as the real thing. A long tail swished back and forth as it walked towards Alvis and rubbed its head against his leg.

"I admit to trying to kill you. You had taken something of mine I built, slaved over, poured my heart and soul into, and dreamed about since I was a little boy. I was angry, hurt, and wanted revenge. It is strange, no matter how far I try and advance myself those pesky things call emotions always seem to rear their ugly heads, but I digress. Yes, I wanted you dead, but after seeing how determined you are at living, you did something that surprised me, you gained my respect. I threw assassins and murderers your way, but yet here you are, alive and kicking. That in itself deserves a reward, so your reward is this. Turn around and leave here. No one shall harm you, no one shall get in your way.

"You have my word on this."

I lifted my visor up and looked into his eyes and could tell he was telling the truth. I turned my gaze back to the others, who said nothing. Could it be that simple? Could all the fighting, the looking over my shoulder, the fear and worry really end like this?

"And Poppy?" I asked.

It was only for a mini-second, but I saw the truth flash across his waxy features like a pike darting out of the reeds after its prey.

"That has yet to be decided—"

"The tricky thing about being human, Alvis, is that no matter how many upgrades you give yourself, no matter how many hours you spend redesigning the hardware, the software is still the same. Those pesky little emotions of yours will always play out, because you have been a human longer than anyone who has ever lived. It's ingrained in you. It's part of your makeup. It's what you are at your core. It's what you will always be. An egomaniac genius who thinks the world should bow down to him, that thinks he has a right to a living being with her own thoughts, dreams, desires.

"She isn't yours to own, Alvis. Nor is she mine. The sooner you realise that, the sooner we can come to terms."

"Come to terms," he said with a snort. "Come... to... terms. Come to fucking terms! I'll tell you what I shall come to terms with, with taking everything you hold dear. Stripping away from you piece by piece everything you love, you care about, you cherish. When I am done you shall be bowing down by my feet, then and only then *shall we come to terms.*

"In the meantime, why don't you play with some of my pets? They're in much need of the exercise," he said, walking off into the long grass without a backwards look.

61

The creature that had just been purring against Alvis's leg was now growling under its breath. It pawed the ground in front of it; claws extending outward reflected the light. I took a step back as it snarled. Mouth open its teeth grew as it flicked its head back and forth between us.

I moved in the direction Alvis had gone but it leapt in my path and swept a paw at me, forcing me to jump back. I brought my shotgun up, but it knocked the gun out of my hands with another strike from one of its paws. The gun bounced in the grass and came to a stop some ten feet away from me. My eyes darted to it then back to the machine in front of me.

I got low, ready to leap sideways toward the gun but an eardrum-shattering crack filled the air and the side of the creature's head exploded in a shower of metal and sparks. It tilted sideways one way then back the other before falling over on its side, where its tail twitched once, twice, then came to a rest as the reddish glow behind its eyes went out.

"Stop assing about, will you!" said Willis, smoking gun

still in his hand. "We don't have time for this bollocks. It's only one poorly designed machine meant to look like a cat. You're acting as if—"

Several snarls came from the grass.

"I'm acting as if what?" I said backing away until I could bend down and pick up my weapon. "That we are fighting more than one of those things?"

"You had to open your big furry hole of a mouth didn't you?" said Tuari.

Willis turned back and forth between the pair of us before he threw up his hands in defeat.

Another snarl came to my left and I fired a slug in that direction and was rewarded with a wounded howl. The others moved back and I with them. With our backs facing the open water, there wasn't anywhere for us to flee. Another round of growls sounded, and judging by the noises they had formed a semi-circle around us.

A silver dart of a beast shot forward and was met by a round of bullets that peppered its metal body. Sparks flew but it still kept coming forward until I fired blindly and hit it in the head.

It came to a skidding halt at my feet and much like the first, its tail twitched then the red glow faded behind its eye.

"Aim for the head!" I shouted as another darted out of the undergrowth.

This one met the same fate as the other with Scarface delivering the killing shot to the head. The grass became silent as we scanned the undergrowth for anything that moved. A flash of silver appeared before us causing us to fire but it disappeared back into the grass. I tried multiple lenses on my helmet, everything from infrared to thermal imaging to pick their movements up, but they gave off nothing.

Another flash of silver, much closer this time, but it disappeared without any of us scoring a hit.

"They're playing with us," said Willis, as another flash appearance was made.

A face burst from the grass and we fired, but it pivoted allowing the bullets to bounce off its side. I caught a flash out of the corner of my eye and saw another speeding towards us from my left; it was making use of the crew's blind spot, and closing the distance fast. I spun on my heels and pointed my gun its way; it leapt into the air as I fired but I missed the head and it tackled me to the ground.

Claws dug into my flesh causing me to scream as I placed the barrel of my shotgun under its chin, stopping its forward momentum. The vibration of its jaws snapping at me rattled my brain as I tried with all my strength to keep those razor-sharp teeth away from my face.

"A little help!"

"We've kind of got our hands full," Tuari said. "God, some people."

My arms shook from the effort it took to keep the thing at bay. With each passing second its jaws got lower and lower until they were less than an inch away from my face.

"Fucktards!"

"Alright, you big baby," said Tuari, as he blasted the top of the machine's head clean off, forcing red goo to flow out of the top of its head and splash onto my arms.

I threw its carcass to one side and thanked the heavens my suit had kept whatever the red goo was off my skin. Wiping it on the grass I watched in horror as the grass quickly withered and died.

"Don't let the liquid that's inside them make contact with your skin," I said as I got back up to my feet and surveyed my surroundings. A few metal bodies lay littered on the ground in front of us, but I could hear many more snarling and growling in the brush cover. I wanted to fire into the brush and destroy everything in there, but without a clear line of sight, we would only be wasting our much-needed ammunition.

Another cat burst from cover and sprinted towards me. I took a step back and fired but as I did, I tripped over a machine corpse behind me and fell backwards. My stomach lurched in horror as I knew the only thing behind me was water. I closed my eyes and waited for my body to splash into the water and sink below the surface, but it didn't happen. Instead, I hit something solid that jarred my back and stole the breath from my lungs.

I didn't have time to inspect what I was lying on top of before the machine was nearly upon me. It had leapt towards my throat and my sudden backwards fall had caused it to sail over my head and land some way past me. I got to my knees, swooping up my gun in one fluid motion, and blasted its head clean off.

Still on my knees, I looked down at what I was kneeling on and saw it was a fine blue mesh bridge that blended with the water; even this close to it I had trouble distinguishing it from the water around me. Getting up to my feet I faced the crew and saw they were still battling the cat-like machines, who had now adopted a peekaboo strategy.

They were making us waste ammo. They were smart. They were learning.

We couldn't stand and fight them because it would only be a matter of time until we ran out of bullets, then they would come en masse. We had to flee and try and find another way to the floors above.

"Everyone fall back! We'll use the bridge that runs through the lake to escape. I'll give supporting fire."

One by one they edged back with me firing at anything that moved until I was the only one facing the machines. Sensing we were retreating, more and more shapes appeared through the grass. I spun on my heel and sprinted as hard as I could after the others. My chest burned not only from the claw marks I'd sustained but from the energy output I had used so far.

If we didn't find a place to escape, then I didn't know how long we could last out here.

"Where does this thing lead?" said Willis over the helmet comms.

"Just keep running!" I replied.

"Oh, you don't say. Great advice that is. Thanks, Cap."

Despite the burning of my chest—despite the yowls and snarls behind me—despite the impending fear that creatures that didn't need to eat to survive would eat me, I couldn't help but marvel at the beauty of the lake.

Crystal clear waters stretched out in all directions with an occasional fish leaping from its waters to splash back down again. It was a place built for reflection. A place built for meditation. Not one where people ran for their lives as machines built only for death chased them.

A growl sounded behind me and this time it sounded way too close for comfort. Keeping a steady rhythm I kept on running until I could hear the footsteps of our attackers more clearly behind me. Waiting until I was sure it was only a few feet away, I spun on my heel till I faced behind me and fired a slug.

Slug met metal face and face was no more.

I spun back the right away and continued on. The whole thing had lasted seconds, but it was still enough time for me to get a clear picture of what lay behind us. More metal creatures than I could count were on our tail. The shine as the light reflected off their metal bodies blinded me to the exact number but the single line following us snaked some way back.

"There is some sort of boat thing up ahead," said Willis.

I shook my head. "Would you like to be more specific?"

"It's a fucking boat thing! How more specific do you want me to get? It's boat-shaped and it's floating on the water and is doing what all boats have done since the creation of them back when men hacked at men with blunt swords."

"Can you see an elevator?" I asked.

"Nah. It looks like our only way out of this is on that boat."

This place was getting weirder and weirder by the second. Why was I surprised, though? When you have more money than God, simple things like using elevators to get to the next floor up were simply too conventional and boring.

"Secure the boat and start her up. Everyone get on board. I'll be coming in hot."

I kept on running and could see Willis and Scarface up ahead jump into a small boat that would barely fit all of us in. Tuari knelt at the side, assault rifle secured in place pointed my way.

"What do you think you're doing?" I asked. "Get on the boat, there's no way you can make a shot, I'm blocking your field of vision."

"Nah, don't worry, I won't hit you... much," he said.

"Wait. Hold on. Wait! Wait—"

The first cracks of the assault rifle split the air, forcing me to close my eyes as I kept on running. I heard the sound of bullets impacting metal and although I was thankful I was still alive; I waited for the moment when a bullet would go astray and bring me down.

With each round Tuari let off, I said a silent prayer to anyone who might be listening.

Crack. Pray. Crack. Pray.

All I could do was keep running, all I could do was try and make myself as small a target as possible.

"Quinton! Stop. Stop. Stop!" said Tuari.

I opened my eyes and saw I was nearly upon him. Digging my heels into the bridge I skidded to a halt but it wasn't enough and I crashed into him in a tangle of limbs.

"Come on, you assclowns" Willis screamed.

Untangling myself from Tuari, I saw a pair of jaws open wide as a robot leapt forward. I grabbed my shotgun and fired one-handed, blowing the top of its jaw off.

I got to my feet and pulled Tuari up as more of the things were coming our way. The boat was already moving, forcing us to sprint alongside it. I pushed Tuari forward waiting for him to jump aboard as I fired a slug into one of the machines behind us. Once he was onboard I followed and had to be grabbed as I nearly toppled backwards into the water.

We were all inside the boat but looking back at the line of machines following us; it was only a matter of time before they caught up.

"Can't this thing go any faster?" I asked.

"If you've not noticed this isn't exactly a speedboat," Willis said.

"Speedboat or not, if we don't get this thing moving those things are going to start jumping on board," I said, as Tuari fired, picking off as many as he could.

Willis cursed under his breath as he fumbled with the controls in front of him. I reloaded my gun and took up a defensive position as the machines kicked up another gear and sprinted towards us in earnest. Scarface, Tuari and I opened fire at anything that came within range of us, but it was like stopping a flood with nothing but paper towels.

No matter how many we killed, there was always another to take its place.

A machine sprinted alongside us, this one in the shape of a wolf. I targeted it but didn't have time to fire as it leapt towards the boat. Luckily there wasn't enough space for it to land as half its body landed inside the boat while its back legs tried to get some traction on the wet wooden boards on the outside. Teeth were snapping left and right as Scarface kicked it in the jaw, sending it splashing back into the water.

"Got it," said Willis as the boat lurched forward at a faster speed.

The wolf that had been kicked overboard broke the surface of the water as it tried to swim towards safety with all its might, but no matter how hard it tried it kept dipping below the surface. The other machines chasing us stopped and looked at the wolf while it struggled to swim before it finally sunk below the surface for good.

They took one more look in our direction and as one they turned back the way they came and sprinted away.

"Who would have thought they would be scared of water?" said Tuari. "I'm guessing the new metal alloy Alvis made them from isn't all that buoyant."

"I hope that's what it was," I said, doubt creeping into my voice, "and not something else."

As the boat powered on and I watched the machines' retreating forms, I couldn't help get a sense we would be seeing them again soon.

62

The boat ambled along at a leisurely pace, now that we won't being chased by killer machines designed as animals. I had wanted to keep pushing the boat through its paces, but the engine powering the boat began to fire off warning readings along the dashboard, until it forced us to lower the speed of the boat. As we continued travelling along the lake I was amazed at the sheer size of the floor we were on, and the level of construction involved to create something like this.

The further we travelled the more the space wowed me.

Fish of varying sizes and colours leapt between lily pads the size of tables, water birds sat delicately on the surface bobbing every so often for their meals, while others flew in formation low to the water. I sat back and took it all in and almost forgot about my troubles. But no matter how hard I tried I couldn't forget about Alvis, I couldn't forget about the empty streets and the blood-stained apartments, I couldn't forget the look he gave me when I mentioned Poppy.

I needed to take this man out once and for all. I needed to destroy everything he had built, before he completely took over the rest of Safe Haven like he had taken over this borough.

"Do you think Diamond is still alive?" Tuari asked.

"Does it matter?" I replied. "I'm guessing whatever happened in this borough wasn't done with his blessing. How could it be? Alvis has destroyed everything he has built. People in power only have power when they have someone to control. As soon as you take away their subjects, followers, whatever, then they're just another delusional nut screaming at the side of the street corner. No, whatever happened here wasn't done with Diamond's blessing; he's probably dead, as is everyone in this building."

"But how is that possible?" Tuari said. "Alvis, although a genius and part machine, wouldn't have the power to just take over a borough as strong as The Diamond District."

I drummed my fingers along the side of the boat as I thought it through. "No, you're right, he wouldn't. But he did have the backing of Tex Jonson and his band of merry men. Something one of Tex's men said back at the apartment building has been playing on my mind; it was about the man they were working for, i.e. Alvis, promising Tex and his men power.

"I've been racking my brains to trying to think what it could be, and the only thing I've been able to come up with is that Alvis had promised to build Tex AIs that only Tex and his men could control. With advance weapons like that Tex would be unstoppable. He would rule whatever planet he landed on with an iron fist. I'm not even sure the World Government could stop him, if Alvis made him enough AI soldiers."

"You sure?" Willis asked.

But I wasn't paying attention. "What else would Alvis have to offer? I mean, after he fled his prison he was alone with no friends, no allies and no money," I said, speaking out loud.

"You're forgetting something," Tuari said, interrupting my flow of thoughts. "When Alvis escaped the station he escaped on Edward Thomas's ship. A ship that belonged to one of the richest men in the known universe. A ship that still had Edward's lackey Mr Grey on it, a lackey who no doubt knew more about Edward's business dealings than anyone alive. Alvis may have been wounded when he got on the ship, but I'm betting he was powerful enough to make Mr Grey come round to his way of thinking."

"But why didn't Grey just go for Edward's riches himself?" I asked.

"Because," said Willis, "Grey is an obedient dog. Men like him would rather work under someone than take the risk and strike out on their own. Men like him need someone to give them direction, someone to tell them what to do. Men like him will always be number two in the organisation. It's a choice and decision that comes from fear."

"Okay, okay," I said trying to find space to pace about in the small boat but failing. "So Alvis steals Edward's ship, makes a partnership with Mr Grey, takes Edward's money and finances this borough takeover just because I live on this planet? It all seems a little—"

"Far fetched?" Tuari said.

"Yeah, I mean, why not set up shop on the hundred other worlds out there that are like Safe Haven? I doubt this metal ore he is mining couldn't be easily found on some asteroid or another planet. Why risk it all just to come after me?"

"Quinton," Willis said as he slowed the boat to a snail's pace and looked my way, "you still don't understand what you're dealing with, do you?"

I looked at him at a loss for words; the only response I could muster was a shrug of the shoulders.

"You stole a man's dream. Not only did you steal it, but you fucked it six ways to Christmas and got it pregnant. Alvis dreamt about Poppy when he was a little child; he built her when everyone thought it was impossible; she is the first of her kind and your child will be the first of their kind. I pray to everything that is holy he doesn't find out about your child, because it will be an even bigger slap in his face."

"That shouldn't—" I began as heat rose from my neck making my face flush, forcing me to pull off my helmet.

"What? That shouldn't matter?" Willis asked as he pulled off his helmet also and stared my way.

"Don't you get it?" he continued. "Poppy was created so he could impregnate her, as sick as it sounds. *He*, not you, was meant to create this machine-human hybrid. He envisioned a grand history-changing moment when he created Poppy. He didn't envision her getting married to the likes of someone like you, so the two of you could play the happy little suburban family life. This vision of changing the history of mankind, of having his name placed above people like Nikola Tesla, Isaac Newton, Leonardo da Vinci and Elon Musk has kept him going through all those years of him being caged on that station. This is all about ego. Brilliant minds like his want to be recognised for their work, but if you ask anyone who Alvis Boman is, all you'll get is a blank stare.

"That's what this is about. Recognition and dreams. People stole that from him once, and you're stealing that from him again. This won't end until one of you is dead."

"People can't help who they fall in love with, Willis," I whispered.

"No, but a man's dreams are more valuable than all the precious metals in the universe."

I opened my mouth to say something, to say anything, but couldn't find the right words. I was saved as the section of the lake in front of us narrowed into a river less than ten feet wide. Giant palm trees grew on either side of us, their overhead leaves creating a canopy that shaded us from the lights. As the boat entered the shaded river, we all gripped our weapons tighter as gloom surrounded us, but it didn't last for long as the river below us exploded into colour, pulsing a light blue.

I looked over the side and saw the light was being given off by patches of floating algae, as well as jellyfish that swam lazily past the boat.

The whole event was magical to behold. The movement of the boat not only stirred what was below us but also the flowers and insects on the banks of the river, which blossomed to life in colour. Fireflies flew around us and flowers opened slowly, excreting a pleasant fragrance that would put any boudoir to shame.

The river finally came to a stop and on the bank to our right was a golden elevator door. We got out and made our way towards it. All of us held our breath as I pushed the button to call it down; nothing happened for a second or two then the doors to the elevator opened and we all let out a collective sigh as we found it empty and free of danger.

63

The journey in the elevator didn't last long.

It only travelled up one floor. Floor Forty-One.

After everything we had experienced, fought against, struggled against, it was a kick in the balls that left us all breathless and angry.

The doors pinged open and we were greeted by a snowstorm that had us rubbing our hands down our bodies to get some heat into our limbs. A white endless expanse stared us in the face. It appeared to go on forever. The floor we got delivered to had been converted into a rugged mountain-like terrain that you would find on any mountain pass. Jagged stones and whirling pockets of snow dotted it here and there, but apart from that, there was nothing else to see.

"Well, this blows a fat one. doesn't it?" Willis asked, as he took a step forward.

I shook my head as I placed my helmet back on my head. A trail that had been walked many times stretched out in front of us; carved out of the landscape, it crawled up the mountain pass before vanishing in the distance.

"I don't know about you but my suit isn't heating up—

guess it's taken too much damage—so the only thing we can do is move as fast as we can and try to warm up. I don't see how this can be that difficult, as Diamond was an old man and wouldn't build something in this building if he couldn't complete it himself."

Oh, how wrong I was.

An hour later we were still traversing the snowy trail fighting against the bone-biting wind, battling against the snow that didn't allow us to see more than a few feet in front of our faces, and trying to do anything we could to keep warm as we struggled on. There had been a few close calls, as one of us would misplace a foot and have to be grabbed by someone else as we suddenly found ourselves staring into a hundred-foot plus drop to the bottom.

"I know no one wants to hear this," said Tuari, "but this is amazing. I mean to create something like this when you're as rich as Diamond just to test yourself, just to make sure you don't get too fat and comfortable, so the thing that got you to the top always stays sharp... if that doesn't earn your respect then I don't know what will."

"How often did you think he came through these floors?" I asked.

"He was the longest-reigning borough leader in recorded history on Safe Haven."

"So every day?"

"Every day," replied Tuari with a nod.

"Great, I can't wait to see what the other floors have in store for us."

Floor Forty-Two gave us nothing but heat.

Our helmets did their best to cool our heads, as we

dragged our feet through the desert sand, but the oppressive heat slapping us across our shoulders made every step we took harder than the last as our calves cramped when we moved our feet through the sand.

I wiped my hand across the back of my neck and stared up at the artificial sun hovering above our heads.

It was hard to breathe; it was hard to think; it was hard to move.

Everything in my body was telling me to turn back, that salvation was only a short walk back to the elevator where I would find something to drink and have enough time to think of some other way to reach Alvis. But I knew the longer I waited and the more I allowed this environment to beat me, the longer I would give Alvis to plan his next move. The only thing I could do was push on and hope he forgot about us. Hope his ego was so large he didn't see us as a threat.

"I fucking—" began Willis, but he gave up halfway through and just waved hopelessly at me.

"I... know," I said, voice cracking, "but we have to keep moving. Not long to go now."

We reached floor Forty-Three and Willis was none too pleased about what he saw—a mini-jungle that didn't offer us any respite from the heat, but had in fact added humidity to the mix for good measure.

"Fuck this building! Fuck Diamond for building such a stupid thing. Fuck this jungle, just—fuck—fuck—fuck!" he said as he picked up a stone and threw it into the brush.

"At least we got to have a drink back at that waterfall," I said, trying to lighten his mood, but this was met with a stare that pinned my soul to the tree I was standing in front of.

"It could be worse."

"How, Quinton, how could this be worse?"

"Well, for one, those machine-like animals could still be chasing us—"

A roar cut through the trees that made me close my eyes and shake my head. I let out a heavy sigh as all eyes turned on me. "Say it," I said with a shake of the head; "just say it."

"You know what, for once I can't be bothered," said Willis, as he wiped his brow and placed his helmet back on his head. "I—just—can't—be—bothered."

More roars and howls followed the first as the jungle became alive with the sound of music. I double-checked my gun, held my breath as long as I could as I placed my sweaty helmet back on and looked at my crew, who had gone through so much and come so far, yet had to travel so much further that the distance might as well be light-years away.

"Come on, the longer we stay in one position, the easier it will be for them to pick us off."

The next half an hour involved running, shooting and hiding.

A cat made out of nightmares leapt out at me and I blasted it in the face before moving off. I was clawed in more than one place and although my suit had stood up to its fair share of abuse, it was now looking reminiscent of something one of the junkies would wear back at Paradise Lost. Parts of my back were now exposed and the material on both my arms was hanging like ribbons on the handlebars of a bike.

I ducked as something silver leapt for my head and kept low as Scarface emptied his gun into it. I could only see my reflection in his helmet as I gave him a nod of thanks, which he returned.

The artificial light had dimmed, turning day into dusk, and still we pushed on, shooting anything that moved and trying our best not to get tangled up in the vines that hung down and covered the jungle like a spider's web. We continued pushing on—tired, sore, angry. I had a feeling Alvis was watching this, laughing at our discomfort, and it gave my muscles fuel. Pushed me onwards like nothing else would.

I saw our sanctuary less than fifty feet in front of us. The golden doors of the elevator looked like heaven's gates beckoning us onward. Multiple roars erupted behind us; none of us looked back as we pushed on. Scarface got to the call button first and pushed it waving us on. The closer we got the more likely the doors looked like they wouldn't open.

Thirty feet. Still closed.

A big cat leapt from Willis's left and was met with a single bullet through the eye.

Twenty feet. Still closed.

Come on. Open. Open. Open!

Ten feet. Still closed.

Willis and Tuari had made it. Backs against the doors they opened fire.

Five feet. The doors began to part.

I pushed forward with everything I had, but in my haste I tripped over my own feet. Arms windmilling in front of my face while I tried to keep my balance, I started to go down. Ahead of me the doors had now fully opened and the crew were inside waiting.

I knew I was going to hit the deck. There was nothing I could do. But I was only five feet away from the doors and I would rather burn in hell than gave Alvis the satisfaction of seeing me die here. Pushing off with my feet, I used the forward momentum and tucked myself into a ball and forward-rolled towards the waiting doors of the elevator, while the rest of the crew laid down suppressing fire.

The landing wasn't graceful but as I crash-landed inside the elevator it was all I needed as the doors closed behind me and we climbed one more floor up.

64

We rested our backs against the elevator walls, exhausted.

I still hadn't got up from where I lay. Everything hurt; I hardly dared move because even breathing was becoming painful.

"Like hell Diamond does this every day," Willis spat.

"There was a rumour he used to, but going through those floors…" Tuari said with a shrug.

"All rumours have some semblance of truth in them; maybe the old boy used to, but I highly doubt he does them anymore," I said rolling onto my hands and knees. "Myth and legends protect kingdoms far better than guns ever could."

I got to my feet and winced as my knees popped. Although we were only going up one floor it was taking us longer to get there than any other floor before it.

With a shudder we finally came to a stop. We all looked at each other but said nothing as the doors finally opened onto floor Forty-four.

We were met by rain and wind.

We were met by a vast rolling beach with waves that stretched twenty feet into the air.

A single boat, paint peeling, rested on the pebble beach. Oars lay inside of it half-submerged by rainwater. With a heavy heart, I knew we would have to cross the storm-lashed ocean if we wanted to get to the elevator on this floor.

"Look," said Tuari, "do we really need to kill Alvis today? I mean, wouldn't it be better if we—"

"Stop being such a pussy," said Willis.

"I don't doubt there is another way to the top floor," I said. "There has to be, but we don't have time to try and find it. The easiest thing to do is also the hardest, that's the way they design these floors. We all just have to suck it up and cross this man-made ocean, as fast as we can."

The going was rough.

I had to pull off my helmet more than once as I threw up over the side, while Willis snickered.

We were thrown left to right, up and down while we took turns rowing against the elements. Sometimes it felt like we were just rowing to stay in the same spot. Sometimes we rowed twice as hard to cover the ground we had lost from being pushed backwards. And sometimes we just rowed because our brains were dead tired and the only thing we could think of doing was wrestling those oars back and forth. Back and forth.

At certain points, all I could see were walls of water as the water blocked out the horizon on all sides.

It battered us as only water could. It sucked our life forces from our very souls and demanded more.

The ocean was a cruel mistress that day. We each had to pay her something to cross those waters.

The elevator door was presented to us on an isolated rock that had a little jetty attached to it for the boat. It shone like a beam of light coming down from the heavens amongst the thunderous black clouds.

No one had spoken for the entire trip. No one spoke when we disembarked from the boat. No one spoke when we bundled into the elevator and pressed the button to take us up.

~

The doors opened onto floor Forty-Five, and the smell of flowers and the sound of gentle running water greeted us.

An area best described as a natural spa stretched out before us. Hot springs large and small with water crystal blue nestled amongst flowers and alcoves that dotted the scenery before us. Waterfalls cascaded down moss-covered rocks and came to a gentle ebb in river basins that looked right out of something from a fairy tale book about wood pixies and dancing elves.

Small wood cabins with fishing rods resting on the walls outside them were the only buildings in sight.

A wooden signpost stretched across the entrance with the words "Remember what it took to get here" written in black ink.

I looked at the signpost once more and couldn't agree with the message more.

The whole thing put one at ease. It was the reward for a journey well-travelled.

"Alright," I said taking off my helmet, "you have fifteen minutes to find something to eat and drink, and to treat any wounds that any of you may have sustained."

Tuari looked at the hot springs. "Only fifteen?"

"We can't take our feet off the gas and rest here; we don't know if we're being watched or where Alvis is. So yes, it's only fifteen. But look on the bright side—once we defeat Alvis we can spend as long as we want here."

This was met with rumblings as everyone sloped off. I gazed at the hot spring closest to me, with its steam curling off the top just inviting me in, offering to cure me of all my aches and pains.

I let out a sigh and shook my head. The reward hadn't been earned. Not by a long shot. I may have made the quest through the elements but I had yet to slay the dragon.

We were once again on the move and this time we found the elevator with ease, with the added bonus of its going all the way to the fiftieth floor. My finger hovered over the button that would take us all the way there and this time, I hesitated.

"What are you doing?" said Willis. "Press the button already so we can get this shit over with."

My finger inched towards it but I stopped.

"This doesn't feel right," I said.

"Argh! For the love of God, what doesn't feel right about it? We've just crossed enough environmental barriers to test even Moses's patience and he lived into his hundreds Just push the button so we can—"

I pushed the button for the forty-eighth floor.

"For—" Willis began but threw his hands up in the air before shaking his head violently. "I just hope you know what you're doing."

So did I.

65

Flickering lights and wires torn from walls greeted us. The cold air raised goosebumps on my forearms as I pointed my gun one way then another trying to cover as much ground as possible. Light wood flooring gave under my feet as I moved forward with the others fanning out behind me.

A large stain, gone dark from age, stopped me in my tracks. I looked down at it and back at the others as the elevator door behind me closed.

Nobody said anything but we all grabbed our guns that much tighter. Continuing on, we walked down a frosted-glass-lined corridor with doors on either side of us. I stopped in front of a glass door that had a bloody handprint in the middle of it. Moving off to the side I pushed the door open and was greeted by a room that had once been an office.

Files and paper littered the floor and what had once been a wooden desk was carved in two. I nodded to Willis to cover me and entered, to see the wires from the computer banks had been stripped bare.

A sofa pushed up against the back wall had bloody stab holes in its cushions. I surveyed the room for any further clues but found none.

We checked office after office but they were all similar to the first until we got to a large set of glass double doors twelve feet in height and just as wide across. A diamond symbol formed of lights was etched into the glass doors. They looked pretty and out-of-place considering the bloody mess we had just seen.

I pointed to Willis and Scarface to cover our left, while Tuari and I would cover the right.

We approached the doors and they slid silently outwards, giving us a view of the largest single office I had ever seen. To call it that was disrespectful to the name "office".

The room was twice the size of a football field.

Desks had been arranged haphazardly across the space with many being cluttered with instruments and tools, belonging in a workshop rather than on a plush office floor. I noticed scratches and scraps across the wooden floor indicating someone had dragged the desks into the space and they weren't there originally. The original layout of the room must have been beautiful once, with enough open space to think, but now it reminded me of the laboratory of an insane genius, which it was.

I signalled for everyone to be on guard before we moved forward.

The desk and workbenches we passed had everything from diagrams to charts with complicated math equations. A metal limb made of the same alloy of the creatures that had been chasing us rested on a bench we passed.

It looked like Alvis had been busy.

The further we walked the more evidence of his

A Dog Is Born

tinkering unfolded. We passed clear tanks of red liquid stacked high on top of one another; computer components and circuit boards were everywhere as well as bundles of wires. We kept going until I came across a metal male torso; it was hollow inside but light enough to lift. Further along from it was another male torso, but this one had been coated in what looked like skin. I lifted it up and inspected it closer, running my hands along it and nearly dropped it when I realised *the metal had been covered with human skin.*

Fine hairs covered the pectorals and the stomach.

The skin was loose in certain areas but nevertheless, it was skin that covered metal. A sick sensation grew in the pit of my stomach, as the further we walked the more limbs and human torso prototypes covered in human skin we saw.

A question was slamming its fist against my consciousness but I refused to give it any heed. I knew the answer. But coming to terms with it now would only cloud my vision with rage.

We continued on until we came to a workbench that was the largest we had seen so far. It faced a large floor-to-ceiling window that gave a magnificent view of the borough below. Body parts in different stages of completion were scattered over its surface. A holographic image of a human body floated high above the table; it was broken into sections.

All of this was interesting but the only thing I had eyes for was the man whose back was towards us. His hands danced in the air on a holographic keyboard while he hummed to himself while he worked. The once spotless lab overcoat he had worn when I had first seen him now had specks of blood at the base of the hem. I motioned for everyone to be as still as they could as I raised my shotgun to my shoulder and took careful aim.

He hadn't seen us. He hadn't heard us. We wouldn't get an opportunity like this again.

I stilled my breath as I placed my finger on the trigger. It was now or never.

I squeezed the trigger again and again, and watched as slug after slug tore through his body, slamming it against the edge of the desk. He fell forward, collapsing on the workbench, and I moved towards him while the others covered me. Large red stains spread across his back as his arms twitched. One arm rose but I blasted a hole through the centre of his back large enough to fit both my fists in.

I stopped and waited. But nothing moved.

"It can't be that easy?" said Willis.

I said nothing as I checked my surroundings and moved towards the corpse; I poked the back of his head with my gun but there was no reaction. He was dead. I let out a sigh of relief as I grabbed his shoulder and turned him around.

The sigh caught in my throat as I saw it wasn't Alvis. It was someone who looked like him, but up close I could tell the bad forgery for what it was. The eye colour was correct, but the shade was wrong. The teeth were a little too straight, the hair a little too thin. I checked the wounds I had inflected and could see wires and components masked behind a tissue-like flesh substance.

"You nearly had me there," said a voice from the shadows. "I thought you would have gone straight to the top. I was not even going to use that dummy and would have continued working at that exact bench, if it hadn't been for how tenacious you were going through the lower floors. Bravo, a man after my own heart. Well, if I still had such a thing. You have surprised me once again, Mr Blake. Who knew a man as ordinary as you could possess such... gumption."

"I do aim to please," I said, searching the shadows, as I gestured to the others to do the same.

"How do you like it?" Alvis asked.

"The workmanship is a bit shoddy," I said, dropping the AI body to the floor. "If it was meant to be a look-alike, I think you've failed. But I'll give you a C for effort."

"You do not realise the significance—" A light chuckle filled the air. "Ah, well done. My mother always said I shouldn't take the other kids' teasing to heart. Emotions, how they rule us. Anyway, the dummy wasn't meant to be a look-alike; I chose it from random out of my stock and was pleasantly surprised that it looked like me. For all I know, he could be some long-lost relative but I didn't have the time to do a background check. Too many plates being juggled in the air. I normally like to take my time with my work but you didn't afford me the luxury.

"After I heard what happened at one of the mining caves, I knew it would only be a matter of time before you made your way here. I had to rush, you see. I couldn't allow you to impede my work."

"And what work is that?" I asked.

"The greatest work humankind has ever known, the work of pushing simple apes up the next stage of the evolutionary ladder. I was wrong, you see; I thought machines had to take over from humans and that humans would fall extinct like so many creatures before them, but then the more I thought about it, the more it came to me, why couldn't humans and machine be one being? Inseparable down to their very core. So I created 16-15-16-16-25 with the capability to give birth to something half human, half machine. But before I could complete the act, so to speak, I was stopped and imprisoned. Bah! Me. For just trying to make us better than we were yesterday.

"People are always afraid of change, even if it's for their own good. So like a mother, I have ushered in the change that needed to happen."

The question that had been slamming its fist against my consciousness was now silent as the words left my mouth that I had been too scared to ask since I had first arrived in this borough: "Alvis... where are the residents of this borough?"

"Alive... well, some of them. It has been messy work getting the designs I had envisioned for all those years while I was caged to come to fruition, but I believe I have finally cracked it. I have finally done what I had been trying to do since I was but a young man. I have moulded machine and human as one."

"Alvis," I repeated slowly, "where are the residents of this borough?"

"Were you not listening?" he said just as slowly. "I have made them into something better than they were before. Behold!"

Out of the shadows came five people who walked with a strange gait. It was as if they were unused to the function, as if they had just been born. Two women. Three men. They stopped some way from us, and all wore the same fitted silver uniform that reminded me of a revolutionary party who suppressed art. They made no move to come any further; they didn't have any weapons on their person, which was more worrying than anything else.

"I must admit. Machines are more durable, faster, and easier to replace than humans, but like all great artists know there will always be a flaw in their masterpiece and it is something I have to come to terms with. It is something I will change over time. What you're seeing here is just version one."

My mind boggled as I tried to take in the information he was telling me. These were not machines he had made come alive like Poppy, these were people he had used like some sick Frankenstein experiment.

"I don't understand... why use people in this way and not just create AI machines like before?"

"Because people are easier to control than any self-thinking machine. The human mind, although miraculous in almost every way, can be easily brainwashed, manipulated, and conditioned to do your bidding, when it believes it's doing it for its own sake. The problem with creating another thinking AI, like the one you call Poppy, is that they begin to think for themselves, they begin to learn, adapt, and keep learning. Whereas most human beings are comfortable with just being. Comfortable with their lot in life. They love to complain but never to fix the complaint. Never take action when action is needed.

"Oh, you get the odd few that rise to the top like myself, don't get me wrong, but I have taken measures to weed out troublemakers like that."

I felt a knot in my stomach that almost doubled me over. "What do you mean, taken measures?"

"I believe a demonstration is in order. Walk forward," said Alvis.

Nothing happened for a moment or two, then the men and women in front of us walked toward us.

"Stop."

They stopped.

"Turn about slowly."

They did so. But as they did, I noticed a small blinking blue light that flashed just under the temple of each person. The group completed their turn and faced us once again.

"You see, what I lacked before was control. I was foolish

to think when I created new life it would abide by my rules, be happy it was just alive and faithfully serve its creator, I thought a machine would understand the need for discipline, understand its place in the world and not ask questions. Certainly not question me. But it seems intelligence is too risky a thing to allow to run wild. I learnt from that mistake once; I won't make it again."

"You've not created new life!" I shouted in disgust' "You've just created slaves! Slaves to do your bidding and that's all."

"Ahh, my poor uneducated fool. But I *have* created new life. Once these people breed their offspring shall be part machine, part organism. Much like your child."

The room fell silent as I took a step forward but Willis grabbed me by the arm. My heart pounded against my chest as my vision narrowed. How could he know? How was that possible? Only a handful of people at the most knew about my child and most of them were in this very room with me.

The Lady?

No, if she knew then I would have already known about it. She would have used the information to her advantage a long time ago.

But if not her, then who....

Samuel. shit! He had the most to gain out of this; he had a borough to protect. Wasn't he tired of The Lady's rule over him? Didn't he say he would do anything for his people, anything to keep them safe? What would guarantee their safety more than siding with the very man who held all the cards, the very man who had conquered The Diamond District and had the help of the Mercenary Bloc? It was the most logical thing to do, especially if Alvis showed Samuel what he could do.

"What did you—"

"You heard me. Let's not play this game. We're well past that stage now. That child of yours was meant to be mine. It was meant to signal a new era of mankind but you stole that from me, Quinton, you stole the only dream I ever had as a child."

"You're one sick freak if your dream was to create a sex robot who could give birth to a child," said Willis.

"You're a monster.... a complete monster," I said slowly, shaking my head.

"From where I'm standing," said Alvis, "that is you. You stole my dreams, stole the only thing I loved, and are stopping me from putting an end to conflict, poverty, and suffering. I...."

I didn't hear him, not anymore. I had stopped listening as I thought of the woman I loved and the child I hadn't yet met, who depended on me, who needed me to keep them safe—yet here I stood in front of a mountain that I could never possibly climb. Who knew how many of the borough's population he had turned into these mindless slaves? I didn't see a way of getting to him without first going through them.

Yet I had to. Somehow.

I had to think of a way to defeat him before he took away everything I loved.

"Nothing to say?" asked Alvis, bringing me back to the present.

"You destroyed a whole borough just for this? You turned everyone who called this place home into slaves for what? For some narcissistic dream of you saving the human race?"

"I didn't change everyone. There were a lot of failures, like all noble experiments. But I believe I have finally gotten the procedure right. But what do you care? These people that called this place home were the worst of the worst. Men filled with nothing but greed, women filled with nothing but envy, who went about their meaningless lives, contributing only to their bank accounts.

"No, you should thank—"

My shotgun rang out in quick succession, blasting the five people in front of me off their feet. I left holes in them that kept them down. I felt a sense of guilt and pain at killing people who had done me no harm, but I knew if I had a choice and I become what they had, then I would want someone to put an end to my misery. I was showing them mercy, but in the harsh light of day, it was hard to even convince myself of that.

The smoke rose and curled from the end of my barrel and with it came silence.

"You think that will make a dent?" Alvis asked. "Let me show you the army at my disposal."

Beams of light from the floor began popping up everywhere projecting holographic screens in the air. They showed nothing but darkness at first, but in time my eyes slowly adjusted until I saw that the rooms the screens were showing us were just dim. As if on cue, lighting emerged from around the rooms showing me what I hadn't been able to see.

I wish it hadn't.

Rows upon row, of human-size capsules stood upright and in them, floating in murky liquid, were the population of The Diamond District. Humanoid machines worked on the capsules, monitoring them like newborn babies before they moved on to the next. Large cables as thick as my waist intertwined on the ground between the capsules, giving them power. I noticed some capsules were empty, doors open, goo-like liquid dripping from them onto the floor. The camera angle panned out and up and I could see how many rows there actually were.

Thousands upon thousands of rows stretched out into the distance.

"So you see, there's nothing you can do that will affect the outcome of this—"

"On me!" I said, sprinting back the way we came.

The others didn't move at first, confused at my sudden outburst, but they quickly followed me as I pushed with all my might for the doors that led out of this room.

"Why do you persist in this! Don't you know when you are defeated?" said Alvis with a heavy sigh. "Very well, if this is how it must end, this is how it must end. This was fun while it lasted."

We made the doors in record time, and I pushed out into the corridor looking left and right for some sign of the elevator that would take us up.

I heard noises to my left so I went right.

"Where are we going?" Willis asked over the helmet comms.

"Up!"

"What the fuck is up?"

"Freedom," I said, as the noises behind us grew louder.

66

We turned corner after corner, head down, running at full speed. Luckily I had seen a wall map to the nearest elevator that would take us to our destination. I was surprised at the discovery, but I guessed unlike the last floors that were just for Mr Diamond's personal use, these were for his staff and the people who worked for him. So, a map like the one we passed would come in useful for the newbies.

"They're gaining on us," Tuari said.

"We ain't deaf, we can all hear!" Willis said, pointing his gun behind him and opening fire.

We turned another corner and before I completely went round, I unloaded a few shots in the mass of faceless humanoid AIs chasing us. I blasted a few back but didn't make enough of a difference to keep us safe.

I was happy we weren't being chased by the people of this borough. The time would come when I would take care of their suffering but it wasn't yet. We still had two floors to go before we got to the top of this tower.

The elevator came into view quicker than I expected and I pressed the call button up.

Willis and I took one side, while Scarface and Tuari took the other with the elevator doors to our backs. We fired at any target that came into range, making our shots count. Soulless red eyes kept on staring at us, as the wounded AIs refused to give up and dragged themselves along the floor.

"These elevators are the slowest doors in the history of mankind to open! It's like some grand event," Willis yelled as a robot latched itself to his back. He tried to shake it off but it clawed at his face scoring deep marks along his helmet. He turned left to right trying to dislodge it but it wouldn't move. The elevator doors opened in front of him and he sprinted backwards ramming the robot's head into the wall until it collapsed onto the floor.

We followed in after him shooting and pushing anything that got to close until the doors closed. Two buttons faced me, one for floor Forty-Nine, the other for floor Fifty. I pressed the button for the forty-ninth floor.

"What's with you!" Willis yelled. "It's like you want to drag this mission out as long as you can. We ain't getting paid by the hour."

"He'll be waiting for us up top. We go to the forty-ninth floor and take the stairs up. That way we at least get a fighting chance," I said.

"And once we get to the fiftieth floor?" Willis asked. "What's your plan then? Abseiling down the tower?"

"Close but no. When we were coming over the wall there was a ship parked on top of this tower. We just need to board it, then the second part of my plan will kick into motion."

"Oh great leader," said Tuari, "how many parts are there to this great and almighty plan?"

"Three," I said, taking a deep breath as the elevator climbed up one floor and the doors pinged open.

I poked my head out of the door and looked left and right. The coast was clear. I looked back at the crew, who appeared to have knocked on death's door and was just waiting for it to be answered. They had gone above and beyond in their line of duty, and I couldn't ask for a better crew. Now it was up to me to get everyone home and make sure my family could live a safe and peaceful life.

"Alright, this is the home stretch. Stay sharp, fire at anything that moves and—"

"For the love of God, people, let's have some fun. It's not every day we get to run wild through a billionaire's tower shooting robots," said Tuari, lifting his helmet and giving us all a wink and a smile before bringing it back down.

"I couldn't have said it better myself. Alright, let's finish this shit!"

We journeyed through the forty-ninth floor and found nothing but sofas and antique furniture; art of different environments from the sea to the savanna graced many a wall, as well as tribal masks and ancient weapons. Although this was Mr Diamond's living space, it felt more like a museum. Everything was placed on a stand at the perfect angle. Everything had just the right lighting to highlight the features of the art piece being displayed.

You wanted to touch nothing lest you broke something that was priceless.

I passed an axe as long as my arm with coloured feathers tied to its broad head. I picked it up and tested its weight in my hands, It felt good; I strapped it to my back.

"Well, if you're getting a trophy," said Willis, "I'm taking this mace." He picked up a weapon that looked like it was made from the forges of hell. Jet black with spikes, it wasn't a thing of beauty.

"Hey, no fair, I want to play," Tuari said, grabbing a broadsword.

We all looked at him.

"What?" he asked.

"Don't you think that thing's a little ungainly?" I asked.

"No, why would you think that?"

"Because, you ring-piece," Willis said, "it's five feet in length! How are you going to swing it without injuring one of us?"

"I'll figure it out."

Willis and I shared a look as we followed Tuari at a safe distance.

We passed through the living space with no trouble and found the stairs that led up to the floor above. We took them two at a time, but after five minutes with no end in sight, we had to slow down our pace.

"Still think it was a good idea to take the stairs?" Willis asked from behind me, but I refused to answer.

Ten minutes later and slightly out of breath we made it. I pushed the door in front of me ajar and checked the to see if the coast was clear. I signalled the others to follow me as we crept out into another living space that Diamond must have used as a home. Whereas the floor below us was filled with antiques and art, this floor had none of that.

It was the embodiment of minimalism at its finest.

Bamboo-covered floors gave way to a floor-to-ceiling window, which wrapped around the entire top floor. A made-up mattress that would impress any drill sergeant lay in the centre of the room. Next to the bed were a few grainy pictures of a family. The family had dressed in their best outfits for the picture, but on closer inspection, I could see the tell-tale signs of a family that was poor.

The father's suit was a touch too shiny. The mother clutched her handbag as if she feared its flying away. The eldest son wore a suit two sizes too big, no doubt his father's, the daughter wore shoes that gripped her feet like vices and the youngest son, who looked like the father the most, who was a spitting image of Mr Diamond, wore trousers frayed at the ends showing his ankles.

I looked at the young boy who would become the leader of this borough and saw nothing but steel and determination behind his eyes.

Placing the photo back I read the words above the mattress: "Remember what it took to get here".

Allowing the message to sink in I thought of the heat, the cold, the monsters, the creations, and knew I still had so far to go.

We continued on, passing nothing but open empty space, until we came to a single high-backed chair that sat in front of a window showing the borough for miles in all directions. The view it gave was awe-inspiring. I made my way toward the chair and sat in it and just looked out. I felt like a king of everything I surveyed. I understood what drove him now—what pushed a man at his age to keep going through those floors that held everything from freezing rain to scalding heat.

It was a desire to not get soft. It was a desire to not forget where you came from. It was a desire to still prove he had it.

It was a shame I hadn't met the man. I would have liked to. Although on all accounts he was no better than The Lady, he was still a remarkable man.

"We need to get going," said Willis. "I've not heard a noise so far and that worries me."

"You're right," I said giving the view one last look; with a sigh I got to my feet and took a deep breath. "Come on, sightseeing is over."

We continued walking but the space held nothing of interest. It was just a large open-plan floor with nothing to view but the borough below. Noises up ahead halted us in our tracks. It was faint, just above a whisper, but we heard it nevertheless. Guns at the ready we continued to move forward. The space in front of us was empty, there was nowhere to hide, yet we had all heard something.

I looked to the others to confirm I wasn't going crazy and each gave me a nod in agreement.

We were not alone.

We came to a spiral stairway that led to the roof above; all we needed to do was ascend it and we could gain access to the ship stationed there. Whether or not it still worked was another matter, but I refused to focus on that. We had to make it there first.

We proceeded with caution, sweeping our guns in front of us. There was nowhere for anyone to hide, yet the hairs at the back of my neck still stood on end. I placed one foot on the staircase and looked around me at the vast space, yet nothing stood out.

Taking a deep breath, I climbed and hadn't got more than six steps up when the walls around us burst forth releasing the robots that had been hiding between the walls. A mixture of humanoid and animal robots stormed toward us. Some were the same ones that had been chasing us from the start, so many floors below, but the others were new. They were half-finished things that looked grotesque in the light of day.

Some walked on legs little more than stumps, some had arms that ended at the wrist, others were missing an eye or a limb completely.

Although Alvis had been expecting us, we had crashed the party a little too early. His robotic troops were half-finished and the people whom he'd captured from this borough were still being worked on, and were not ready to join the party.

"Move! Move! Move," I yelled, sprinting up the stairs while the others brought up the rear behind me. I fired at anything that got too close, but there were too many of them. Tuari replaced his rifle with his sword and swung at everything within reach.

Heads flew in the air as his sword sliced through necks.

"Why are you not using your gun?" Willis asked, putting two bullets through a wolf's eye.

"Because when else am I going to have a chance to use this?" said Tuari.

"Guns were created because they were more—" Willis battered away an arm that lunged for him and shot the offender under the chin, causing sparks to fly out the top of its head.

"Guns were created—" Willis ducked as another robot flew over the top of him. "Just use your fucking gun!"

But Tuari paid no notice to him as he swung left and right like a barbarian of old.

The robotic animals who had been chasing us for what felt like eternity ran up the outside of the stairs using whatever foothold they could find to reach us. I continued to fire blasting as many of them as I could off the side, until my trigger finger kept on squeezing and nothing came out. Swapping the shotgun for the axe on my back, I renewed my attack.

A demonic head that looked like a saber-tooth tiger snapped its jaw my way. forcing me to lean back against the far side rail. I felt the sickening twist of my stomach as I fell backwards and swung my axe downwards into the top of the saber-tooth's head before me. I kept hold of the handle with both hands and pulled my weight forward, saving myself from the fall.

Shoving the now lifeless corpse to one side, I swung at anything that popped its head over the side of the handrails.

Tuari cried out in pain as his helmet was knocked clean off his head. Blood poured out of a broken nose as he collapsed backwards, stunned.

Willis picked him up and Scarface took up the rear, laying down fire to cover their retreat.

I bit off a cry as a metal paw knocked me backwards, the metal railings digging into my sides. I sideswiped the offender with my axe, taking off the lower half of its jaw.

And still we continued.

We were getting desperate but our sanctuary was less than five feet away.

I reached it first and kicked open the fire escape that led to the roof of the tower. Wind tore at my clothes as I scanned the deserted rooftop for any signs of life but didn't find any. Two ships rested on the tarmac of the roof.

One was a small flyer used for short distances to travel overland that could only support one person, and the other a luxury small ship just about big enough for our crew.

Sleek in design, it was used to ferry its important passengers in comfort and style. It would have to do.

I held the door open as Tuari and Willis bundled through.

"Tuari!" I said, grabbing him by the shoulder. "Get those engines started, I want us off this tower now."

He gave me a nod but before he left I took his sword from his hands. "I'll be needing this."

"Make sure you bring it back."

"With what I've got in store for it, I doubt you'll be able to use it again," I said, causing him to grimace before he took off.

Scarface shot everything that came into range as he slowly brought up the rear. The robots were closing in fast but he was holding his own. He continued walking backwards and was only a few feet away from us when a metal arm without a hand punched him across the jaw like a jackhammer, causing sparks to fly from his helmet. It ripped the helmet off his head sending it and his blood flying into the air.

He staggered back and landed in our arms and I looked down at his face in shock. Blood came down a face that should have been Scarface but instead, it was Samuel.

67

Samuel, who should have been back in The Jungle. Samuel, who was a pacifist and didn't dare use guns. Samuel, who loved his borough more than anything and would do anything to protect it. Samuel, who I thought had betrayed me to Alvis.

Yet here he lay in our arms.

I looked at Willis, who also had lost his helmet in the ongoing struggle, and could see the conflicting emotions cross his face. I went to say something, but the oncoming horde coming up the stairs stopped me. The time for conversation would come later, now was time for action.

I grabbed the sword in my hand as Willis dragged Samuel out of the way and slammed the door shut, wedging the sword in between the handles. I helped Willis pick Samuel up from the floor, and we hurried towards the ship as the banging on the door drowned out my thoughts.

Willis looked at me then back at the door. "That was your brilliant plan?"

"It'll hold, ye of little faith."

He gave me a look of disbelief as the foundations around

the door shook and wobbled, causing us to increase our speed. The ship's engines were still silent; the only thing we could hear was the growing noise behind us. I stole a look behind me and saw that the sword was bent in half, ready to snap at any moment.

"Tuari! Why is this ship still dead!" I said over the helmet's comms.

"He can't hear you, you're the only one left with a helmet," said Willis.

I groaned in frustration, but it was short-lived as the ship shuddered to life and the cargo ramp lowered. I was about to celebrate but the booming crash behind us put a stop to that; I didn't need to look behind me to know the door had given way. Sprinting forward with everything we had, we leapt into the cargo-hold.

"Tuari! Go! Go! Gooo," I screamed, using the helmet's speakers to amplify my voice.

"I'm doing my best," he yelled at me from the cockpit, "but this thing has a setup procedure that makes me want to—"

"Just get it sorted!"

I turned back towards the oncoming horde and didn't like what I saw. They would overrun us in moments if we didn't do anything. I threw my shotgun to one side and looked for any weapons on board the ship, but couldn't find anything to hand. "You got any bullets left?" I asked Willis.

"I'm out," he said, picking up Samuel's gun and firing at the horde.

I kept on looking for anything that could be used as a weapon until I came across an old-fashioned flare gun. They kept the thing behind a glass case as an antique, but I cared little as I smashed the glass with my elbow and prayed it had something left inside. Checking the chamber I could see that it had one flare; I snapped it shut and aimed and fired.

The result was unspectacular, as the flare whizzed lazily four feet off the ground and came to a stop less than ten feet away from us, where it sizzled and popped until it died out.

"Sometimes I forget to tell you," said Willis, "how much value you add to the team."

I gave him a look and steadied the axe in my hand as the ship moved forward with a jerk.

"Tuari! Can you pick up the pace?" I asked as the first robot made contact with the ramp and I smashed its head in with the axe.

"I would love to but this thing wasn't exactly built for speed."

Willis had gone for his mace as he too had run out of bullets. He attacked everything in front of him with an anger and determination that was bred from finding out his brother was with us the whole time. What had caused Samuel to come along in the first place was beyond me, but it had struck a chord with Willis as he fought the robots around us with no concern for his safety.

"Can I help?" asked a voice from behind us.

"Not unless you can pull an assault rifle out of your ass," replied Willis.

I looked over my shoulder to see Samuel getting up to his feet. He rocked back and forth while he tried to get his footing. "I can do many things but that isn't one of them," he said.

"What are you doing here?" Willis said, "Shouldn't you be back in The Jungle?"

"I... yes, I should be, but... I haven't seen you in so many years, and I knew you would never want to listen to me, never want to spend time with me, never want to heal what is broken, so I thought what better way to be with you than come along on this trip and pose as John. Even if we didn't speak I could still get to spend time with my baby brother, because if I didn't, then who knew if we would ever see each other again, and I promised Mum to keep you—"

"Just... just," Willis began, cutting off the rumble of words, "just stay back there, will you, out of the way."

I looked at the pair, each in their own inner turmoil, as a thousand unsaid things passed between them. The gulf that had been created was not something that would be mended overnight, but I hoped this would start the process of fixing that.

A big cat's paw swiped inches from my face bringing me back to the fight. I leaned back and attacked it with my axe, biting into the metal at the side of its face; that caused sparks to fly. Placing my foot against its face, I kicked it off the ramp as the ship finally picked up speed.

"I need this thing to pick up some speed before we take off," said Tuari.

I leaned over the side and saw we still had some way to go before we got off the runway. Long enough for these Frankenstein creations to bring us down if we weren't careful.

"Attack anything that gets close," I said, hacking off a head.

"What do you think I was going to do? Pray for their sins?" Willis replied.

Samuel stood between us, fire extinguisher in hand. "I can help."

"With that?" said Willis.

Samuel didn't respond but rammed the canister into the face of a robot, knocking it backwards, where it was trampled underfoot by the horde.

A Dog Is Born

"It'll do," I said, attacking a dinosaur-looking thing in the face. About to move on to the next I stopped as a roar vibrated through the floor. I looked up in time to see the wall that held the fire escape explode outwards as a ten-foot-tall Herculean humanoid robot strode onto the rooftop, pounding its chest. It was made of black metal; its red eyes glinted our way as it tucked its head down and sprinted forward.

"Err, Tuari, you may want to step on it, buddy," I said.

"I'm doing my best."

"I understand that, but we kind of have a situation here."

"You're big boys, you can handle—"

"Dick-face! Get a move on before I come up there and strangle you!" Willis screamed.

The Herculean came forward and wasn't going to be stopped. It knocked out of its path anything that didn't move out of the way fast enough. Its gigantic hands backhanded its friends and its eyes locked on its target. Us.

In less than ten strides it was already on our ass.

I lifted the visor of my helmet and made eye contact with Willis, who gave me a single nod as he moved the mace in his hands back and forth.

"Sam," Willis said softly, "get back." He did as Willis asked.

I lowered the visor of my helmet and faced the oncoming monstrosity. It was now only five paces away. Its feet cracked the floor. With a leap and a jump, it bound toward us and crash-landed down on the ramp forcing the ship to lift up in the air before it crashed back down again.

"What was that?" Tuari asked.

"Just an unwanted guest! We'll take care of it, just get us in the sky," I said as I took a swing at the thing, which it blocked with a hand. Sparks flew into the air as metal met metal. I hacked left and right trying to find a weak spot, but any time I struck the axe only bounced off its metal body. It was made out of a denser alloy than the other creations we had previously fought.

I ducked a swing from one of its hands and came back with an upwards strike with the hilt of the axe that struck it under the chin; it rocked on its heels taking a step back but attacked with a hammer fist blow that drove me to my knees as I blocked it with the axe. Seeing his opening Willis swung at the thing's leg, catching it in the kneecap.

A roar that shook my internal organs escaped from its mouth as it threw a punch at Willis, who ducked underneath it.

I got back to my feet and stood next to Willis as I hacked and he swung, trying to land a significant blow on the thing, but failing to do any real damage. A fist slapped me in the chest throwing me against the wall, where the wind was knocked out of me, I landed on the floor dazed and had to roll to safety as a metal foot descended towards me.

I rolled away from the stomp that was delivered, which shook the ship.

"Hey! I can't take off with this much disruption," said Tuari. "You lot have got to do something."

"We're working on it!" I yelled in between coughing fits as I got up unsteadily to my feet.

"I'm going to take us round in a circle to give you guys more time, but we can't stay on this roof forever—it'll only be a matter of time before we attract more attention," said Tuari.

Willis was taking the fight to the Herculean, but it absorbed all the impacts on its body with disinterest. Dents were being inflicted on its metal body but it didn't seem to care; it wasn't slowing it down. Willis launched an attack at its face, causing the Herculean to jerk back. This was the first sign of fear I had seen from it.

The face! Of course. The creatures we had fought on the lower levels all went down after we destroyed whatever circuit boards they housed in their skulls. Maybe this thing was no different.

"Willis," I said, picking up my axe, "aim for the face!"

I renewed my attack and stood by his side; he attacked low and I attacked high, then we would switch it up, always keeping it guessing. My arms ached and sweat poured down my neck as my helmet did its best in trying to not steam up. I sideways rolled, slicing at the knee which Willis had first attacked, causing the Herculean to buckle. Willis saw the opportunity of an opening and launched an attack at its face, but it blocked the attack at the last minute with the back of its hand.

Hope grew as it removed its hand and we saw a small dent on the side of the Herculean's cheek.

It felt the wound and roared in rage. Willis went on the offensive once again, but the Herculean was ready for him and up-kicked him in the chest, sending him flying backwards where he crash-landed amongst the chairs. I knew he wouldn't get up. I had felt the shock waves from the kick and heard the snapping of bones.

I turned my attention back to the Herculean, who looked me in the eye and beat its chest like a great ape.

I swallowed as I shifted the axe from hand to hand. The giant figure appeared to sense my hesitation and looked down at me with disdain, as it came towards me.

I rushed towards it and met it head-on. Axe met fist and the vibrations travelled down my arms, nearly bringing me to my knees as the ringing from my ears drowned everything out. I rolled to one side as a fist crashed down on the ship floor causing it to shake.

I came back up to my feet and re-attacked the Herculean's bad knee, dropping it to the floor once more; I went in for the kill but was met with a backhand I barely blocked, one that rattled my teeth.

"Quinton, you gotta do something," came Tuari's voice over the speakers. "This roof is getting more crowded by the minute and I don't know how much longer—"

Whatever he said next was lost to me as the Herculean came on the offensive with everything that it had. It attacked with punches in bunches that had me reeling backwards. I ducked, blocked, and rolled with the punches as best as I could, but the fists I was trying to avoid were not made out of flesh and blood, and the danger of being hurt could be life-altering.

I kept doing my best to avoid getting hit but I knew it was only a matter of time before it struck me. I was human. I would tire eventually, while this robotic monster could move indefinitely. It feinted with a right hook and came in with a left that dug into my side, lifting me up onto my feet. I didn't have time to defend. I didn't have time to block.

All I saw were stars.

Then I was being lifted in the air while it wrapped its arms around me, slowly squeezing the life out of me. Vision blurry. I saw its head go in and out of focus as I tried to figure out my next plan of attack. The plan wasn't to die here. Not now. Not while I still had so much to do to make sure Poppy was safe. I tried to struggle and fight back but it was like pushing back the tide.

Spots danced in front of my vision, then the pressure holding me slackened, causing me to fall to the floor.

I got back up to my feet and saw Willis's mace was

embedded in the side of the Herculean's face. Sparks flew from the wound and its limbs moved in a herky-jerky manner while it tried to come forward. Samuel stood in front of the giant like a triumphant David.

"Quinton! I'm going to take off," said Tuari. "Shit's getting crazy out there. It's now or never."

I was launched backwards as the ship picked up speed, and stared in disbelief as the Herculean moved the mace from side to side, while it tried to take it out from its skull. With a roar it pounded its chest, then grabbed the handle of the mace with both hands and yanked it out, causing wires and sparks to fly from the wound.

"We're about to get some air, everyone sit tight."

Samuel looked past me to his brother with eyes that had accepted their fate. With eyes that knew they would never see their loved ones again. A smile crested his lips as he turned to me. "Take care of him, tell him I love him" was all he said before he turned around and screamed in defiance as he rushed towards the Herculean and tackled it by the legs.

I moved towards the pair but I wasn't fast enough, as they both wrestled together for what felt like an eternity before the ship picked up speed and launched itself in the air. Already off-balance and with the weight of Samuel around its legs the robot toppled backwards out the ship taking Samuel along with it.

His smiling face was the last thing I remembered before the ship picked up speed and tore away from the tower.

68

I slapped the button that closed the cargo bay doors and rushed to Willis's aid. I untangled his body from the plush cream leather chairs and sofa cushions and manoeuvred his body to a comfortable position on the floor. Placing a cushion under his head, I wiped away the blood that had run down the side of his mouth. I tore away the front of his suit and grimaced when I saw the red footprint the Herculean kick had made. The area was already going dark purple.

His breathing was faint but steady, but I had no doubt he had broken bones and internal bleeding. He needed medical attention and needed it fast. I did a quick search of the ship but found nothing apart from caviar, champagne and large amounts of money.

I came back to him and tried to stir him, but the blow he'd suffered had knocked him for six. Waking him now might cause more damage than he had already sustained, so the only thing I could now do was to place him in a comfortable position until we got to somewhere where he could be treated.

But before we did that, I had something I had to take care of.

I made my way through the ship until I got to the cockpit where Tuari sat. He looked up at me concern behind his eyes and asked, "How bad?"

I took off my helmet and ran my hands through my hair. "Willis is unconscious, with injuries to the chest and ribs; it also looks like he's bleeding internally. Samuel was—"

"Samuel?" Tuari asked, face screwing up in confusion. "What's he got to with this?"

"It was Samuel who was with us all along, not the mute with the scar, whose name I know now is John. It seems Samuel had switched places with this John because... he wanted to make sure Willis was safe, he wanted to reconnect, he wanted to protect his own interests. I don't know!" I said, throwing my hands up in the air, angry at the last thought that had popped into my brain, after everything Samuel had done.

Tuari said nothing for a few heartbeats, causing the silence between us to become unbearable. I knew what he was going to ask, I just wanted him to spit it out so we could deal with the elephant in the room.

"You said 'was'..."

I took a heavy breath. "He... fuck, we were losing the fight against whatever that thing was back there. Willis was down, I was nearly finished and he stepped up and saved us all, dealt the monster a crippling blow and tackled it off the ship before it could do any more harm."

I closed my eyes at the monotone nature of my words. Samuel deserved better than that and I would see to it he got the hero's funeral he deserved, but right now, if more action wasn't taken, then his sacrifice would be for nothing.

"He did what he had to do and right now, so must we.

The fight isn't over yet,; there's one more place that I need to go to."

"Somewhere in the borough?" Tuari asked in disbelief. "But we're home free."

"No, we are not. We haven't won the war or the battle, but I plan to change that. I need you to take me to the edge of the walls where the cannons are located."

Tuari pulled a face.

"Or as close as you can. I'm guessing they won't fire on this vessel because they recognise this ship's engine signature—"

"You're guessing?"

"Yes. I'm guessing. And that's all we have to go on, but this needs to be done. I have to do this."

"You have to do what?" he asked me.

I told him.

He opened his mouth to say something, shook it, then turned back to the controls. "May the Gods have mercy on your soul, Quinton."

Tuari flew the ship low in-between the buildings of the borough until we came to the unwelcome sight of the cannons sat perched on top of the wall that surrounded the borough. The sun had begun to rise, but the snow-capped mountains that the borough was backed against blocked it from view.

"So far so good," I said, patting Tuari on the back.

"There was once a man that jumped out of a tower and after each floor he passed on his way down, the people inside the building would hear him yell, 'So far, so good,'"

Tuari said, turning in his chair and giving me a meaningful look.

I took no notice but instead took in the beautiful sweeping views the mountains had to offer.

"The controls you want are probably by the waterfall."

"How do you know that?" I asked.

"Guessing," he said with a shrug, "but I saw a building outpost when we first made our way over the wall, so that would be as good a place as any to start."

I couldn't argue with him there.

We continued on until there was nowhere to go but up, where the cover of the buildings would no longer offer us any protection. Tuari looked at me unsure, but I gave him a more confident nod than I felt and he eased the ship up towards the cannons.

The one in front of us swivelled and moved and I held my breath and clenched my ass, as Tuari kept on sending looks my way. We continued up and up and still it hadn't stopped moving, trying to fix us in its sights. My heart pounded against my chest as I grabbed the back of Tuari's chair, willing, praying, that I hadn't made a fatal error.

The dashboard in front of Tuari beeped and flashed red, before a robotic voice came over the ship's speakers: "Please provide the deactivation password or we shall be forced to fire. Please provide the deactivation password or we shall be forced to fire. Please—"

"Well!" Tuari shouted over the noise.

I bit the inside of my lip while I tried to think of what the password would be. The closer we got to the cannons the louder the voice became demanding the right password. One wrong word would end it all here—end it, and allow Alvis to continue his plan of planetary domination.

What would the old man use?

What had I seen time and time again? I thought back to the floors we climbed and tried to think of what they truly represented. What was the meaning behind the suffering, the pain, the hardship? Just to get to the top and a penthouse so sparsely decorated, it felt like you were being punished all over again. Looking back at it now, the whole thing seemed to be designed by a man who truly hated his—

No... that wasn't the point of the floors at all.

I thought back to the old picture next to Diamond's bed. He came from nothing; he had to work for everything he ever had. He had to climb and climb and climb until he got to where he was. After the hellish floors, when we had arrived at the floor with the spas, hadn't there been a message?

I looked around me at the mountains that surrounded the borough, looked properly for the first time, and then it finally clicked. I finally understood. I fully got why he would want to push himself through that torture. To not forget. To never take what he had for granted.

I leaned forward and pressed the button to respond to the computer. "Remember what it took to get here."

The voice became silent as Tuari and I exchanged looks. The only thing I could still hear was the pounding of my heart as we continued to wait.

"Password accepted. Please proceed."

Tuari breathed a sigh of relief and slumped in his chair as the cannon that had been targeting us became dormant once more. We travelled up and up until we came over the lip of the wall and Tuari landed the ship on a walkway large enough to park another ship next to the side of ours. Tuari began to get up from his chair but I pushed him back down. He looked up at me confused.

"I'll be the only one making this trip. Once I leave, I want you to take off and wait for me in the sky. If everything goes according to plan then you'll be able to pick me up in the next five minutes or so; if not... then I want you to make your way back to The Jungle."

"Wouldn't it be easier for me to just wait for you here or better yet, just come with you?"

I shook my head. "Alvis isn't dead. Nor are his legions of AIs that he has created. There is no point in all of us dying for my idea, and if we all do, then there shall be no one left to protect my family. What I'm about to do, I do not take lightly, and as a captain it is not my burden to share. My helmet still works, so I'll be in radio contact with you the whole time, plus you can track my movement from the signal being transmitted in my helmet."

"But—"

"No buts! My decision is final," I said. placing my helmet back on my head. "This should only take five minutes—five minutes and we can finally get our normal lives back."

Tuari laughed as I walked away. "When did we ever have normal lives?"

I hated to admit it but he was right. There were still foes that needed to be dealt with after Alvis. Foes that had dealt us a blow we still had to pay back.

I watched as the ship took off once again, leaving me feeling alone and isolated. The view from the top of the wall was something to behold. The image of the snow-capped mountains, with the rays of the sun turning the sky pink, made the view look like it belonged on a postcard. I rubbed my bare arms as goosebumps rose along my forearms from the chill in the air. A section in the wall, large enough to fly *The Kennel* through, allowed a torrent of water to fall into the river at the base of the wall.

The sound from the waterfall made it sound like it was alive.

It roared and spat like a caged dragon wanting to be let free. Just standing still, I was already soaked to the bone as the air was thick with moisture, mist and fog. The outpost that Tuari described was just about visible through the mist. I wiped my visor clean and proceeded towards it at a trot.

I slowed my speed as I got toward it, not sure if it would be guarded or not. With nothing better than my axe in my hand, I approached the structure with caution. I tried to listen for any sounds someone's presence would make, but all I could hear was the roar from the waterfall. Gritting my teeth I thought of the best way to tackle the problem in front of me, but I drew a blank.

I was wasting time. I needed to act now. This wasn't the time for caution.

I gripped the handle of my axe tighter and moved forward as silently as I could. A rifle lay against the wall of the outpost. I picked it up and moved towards the door, using the barrel of the rifle to push it open.

A bank of consoles and terminals greeted me. Screens that were being fed by cameras along the great wall covered all the available space. There was no one inside. I double-checked under all the tables, but the space wasn't big enough to hide someone without my knowing about it. Satisfied, I was alone I rolled my neck and took in the computers in front of me.

I had work to do.

69

"Quinton!" came Tuari's voice through my helmet. "We have company."

"How close?"

"I'm picking up a small single-seater ship making its way towards your location—it will be with you in a few minutes. I would fire upon it, but this luxury tub hasn't got any weapons."

My thoughts roamed back to the single-seater flyer on the roof, next to the ship we had stolen. I knew we should have destroyed it, but time had been of the essence and we simply didn't have the weapons to put a dent in it.

It had taken me longer to accomplish what I had planned; the controls and system hadn't been user friendly but I had got there in the end.

"What do you want me to do?" Tuari asked.

Taking a step back I double checked everything was right. Satisfied, I picked up my axe. "There is nothing you can do, my friend, we both know who's on that ship and even if you came and joined the fight, two of us against him wouldn't make much of a difference. It would just add an extra corpse to his body count—"

"Quinton—"

"Tuari... we've done all there is to be done. You've served me well, all of you have. You came on this mission with me not knowing if we would ever see the light of day again, and for that I thank you. I couldn't have asked for a better team, I couldn't have asked for a better group of friends. You made me meals that have put all the restaurants I've been to to shame. Willis has protected me more times than I can count. Poppy... Poppy..." I thought of what to say about the person who had made my life what it was. There wasn't anything. Words wouldn't do the emotions I felt justice. "Tell Poppy I love her, and it's the captain's duty to go down with the ship."

"Quinton—"

I cut off the communication from my helmet and I steeled myself for what was to come. If I was to meet my maker, then I would meet him, head raised high, with a weapon in my hand, and show him what a captain of the Junk Yard Dogs was made of. But first I had one more business agenda to take care of. Lifting the axe above my head I slammed it down into the consoles in front of me.

Sparks flew in the air and black smoke poured from the screens as I attacked the consoles, again and again, destroying everything in my path. I hummed as I worked, making sure that not one computer was salvageable.

Done, I took a step back and admired my work.

It would have to do.

I closed my eyes and took a deep breath. It was time. It was time for me to face my destiny. I just hoped I had done enough to stop Alvis in his tracks.

· · ·

A Dog Is Born

I saw the ship descend through the mist, like a scene from one of those clichéd first contact movies I used to love to watch as a kid. Its headlights searched for a safe spot to land, then were cut off as it settled on the ground. With the lights turned off, I lost sight of it. The sun had yet to fully rise and the weak rays that bounced off the mist and fog played tricks with my eyes as I tried to pick out any shapes from the area in front of me.

Rifle in hand, axe strapped to my back, I concentrated down the sight of the rifle and maintained my breathing as best as I could. The moisture in the air made the rifle slippery to hold.

The fans in my helmet worked overtime as they did their best to prevent my visor from steaming up. I had thought of abandoning the helmet altogether, but it was another layer of protection I would need in my upcoming fight.

I saw a flicker from the shadows, then it was gone again. My mouth grew dry as I tried to keep the gun stable in my slick hands.

Another form appeared in front of me, and my finger stopped a hair's breadth away from pulling the trigger before it disappeared again. The bastard was playing games with me. Another shape appeared in the shadows, and another and another, before I saw nothing in front of me, as they disappeared like smoke in the wind.

"You had enough of playing games?"

A chuckle sounded closer than I would have liked. "I never play games, Quinton. That's one thing you should know about me. Games are for children and people who need to be stimulated to be entertained. No, I was just testing your fortitude. Plus, I am puzzled as to why you are still here. After escaping, I would have thought you would flee this place as quick as you could with your tail between your legs. But here you are; doing what, I just had to find out."

"If you think I'm going to give up my secrets that easily, then you are—"

Blurred movement streaked towards me. I fired off a volley of shots but was smashed in the chest by what felt like a battering ram and lifted clean off my feet. I sailed backwards until I crashed in a heap on the floor; I gasped for air as the wind was knocked from my chest.

Struggling to get to my knees, I tried to breathe in and out but nothing came. A kick struck me across the ribs forcing me to cry out in pain as it again lifted me in the air. I collapsed back down and clutched my side; the kick had broken ribs; now, although I wanted to breathe, I tried not to as every intake of air felt like I was being stabbed in the side.

"You know, I just don't know what to say or do with you. I'm not one for grandiose speeches, where I lament poetically about how I have defeated you, or how there isn't a possible way for you to win, because... that's just unintelligent. I know I have won. I know there is nothing you can do to win, so..." I looked up to see him give me a shrug, "I just don't know why you won't just die or go away. That is what irritates me the most. That is what I can't understand. It puzzles me, and I hate to be puzzled. Why would you keep risking your life?" he asked.

"For love."

He looked at me and I could see confusion pass behind his eyes. Here was a man, who had been born just like me, but over the course of hundreds of years and many mind- and body-altering experiments, he had lost the one thing important most above all else.

His humanity.

He shook his head as he laughed and laughed and laughed. I got up to my feet with a grunt and gritted my teeth as I stood to face him. I stood silent as he continued to do so until he finally stopped and wiped the corner of his eye.

"Will you look at that," he said, holding his fingers up to the light. "I wasn't sure I could still express tears, but you have brought it out of me."

"At least you're not completely dead inside."

"For love, how ridiculous. You really think 16-15-16-16-25 loves you? Do you know how long she has been alive? Do you know how many other men, woman, people, she has met in her lifetime? How many more she will continue to meet after you've long passed? A human cannot love a butterfly, no matter how pretty it is. It doesn't live long enough. And you, Quinton, are a butterfly. I don't know why she has allowed you to impregnate her, but her reasons are her own—however confusing they may be. She is a machine, after all, and all machines go faulty with time."

"Just like some humans, ay?" I said, looking his way.

"Hmm. They do indeed. Now, will you do me a favour and tell me what you are doing here, or do we have to continue this charade?"

I grabbed the axe from my back then clicked my neck from side to side.

"I see..." he said with a sigh. "I do so hate physical violence, it's so messy and unnecessary when there are easier ways to solve one's problems, but on this occasion, I shall take great pride and joy in it."

70

He came forward so fast I saw nothing but a blur as my head snapped back and my legs buckled underneath me. I felt myself fall to the floor, but Alvis collected me in his arms and held me up.

"Oh no, my dear boy, it won't be that easy," he said, pushing me away.

I regathered myself before I ran his way, axe swinging from the hip. He sidestepped out of the way and kicked me in the calf causing my leg to go dead and buckle. I dropped to one knee and just had time to move out of the way of a high kick.

The kick was lazy, with no force behind it.

I stepped back and then rushed forward coming in low with the axe before turning it into an upward strike. He dodged and moved, always a breath away from danger. I kept on the attack, turning and striking where he would next be, instead of where he was, but he was always one step ahead of me.

My shoulders and forearms ached as the weight of the axe got heavier with each passing second.

A Dog Is Born

I swung downwards and met nothing but air as the axe head struck the ground. Before I could lift the axe back up a fist sank into my stomach doubling me over.

I coughed and spluttered for breath, while I waited for the tears in my eyes to clear.

"This is getting boring. I will have to end it quickly if you don't make it more fun," he said.

I re-gripped the handle of my axe and went on the attack again, but the result was the same.

He was too quick, enhanced with bionic elements that made him more machine than man. As each second passed the sinking feeling of hopelessness slowly crawled up my spine. There was nothing I could do against this man.

But I knew that already. That is why I didn't ask for help.

I tucked into a forward roll and before I could get to my feet a knee that caused cracked lines to appear on the visor of my helmet met me. Dazed, I went to lift up my axe but found I couldn't. Alvis had trapped the blade under his foot. Looking up I was met with a push kick to the chest that sent me sprawling to the ground once again.

I stared up at the sky and groaned while I willed myself to get to my knees. A loud clank sounded to my left as my axe was thrown to me and settled in the dust next to my shoulder.

"Pick it up."

I got to my knees and reached for the axe but was again met with a thudding kick to the side. I hit the deck face first.

"I... said... pick... it... up."

I went for the axe once more but this time I was ready for the kick and rolled with it. I picked up the axe on the way up and sliced it across his thigh, cutting deep.

I expected screaming. I expected howling. I expected something, but what I got was a simple look down as Alvis inspected his bleeding thigh with disinterest and then proceeded to kick me in the head with the same leg.

Stars formed in my vision as I took a few steps back to safety and waited for the ringing to pass.

He held his leg in the air like a ballerina performing on stage, while I looked at the injury I had given him in shock. The wound was deep. Blood squirted out of the cut. I could see shiny bits of metal underneath the folds of flesh.

"You appear shocked?"

"It seems you feel neither love or pain."

Leg still in the air he brought it down and looked at his injury closer, like a scientist would do an experiment.

"Pain... How I felt it so many times growing up. At the hands of my bullying tormentors who punished me because they didn't understand me. At the hands of my teachers who didn't like to be corrected. At the hands of people just like you who couldn't see my vision for what it was.

"I quickly learnt if you took pain away, then the fear that comes with it, which holds so many great minds back, is gone. Then I could truly evolve into what I was meant to be. So no, to answer your question I no longer feel pain. It comes in handy at times like this, no? To think—if I did, then this fight could have been won by you, but alas—"

He became a blur again and I became airborne as I slammed against the railing wall that kept people from falling into the waterfall below me. I would have heard the crack that took place in my back, if it weren't for the sound of the roaring water that filled my ears. Instead, I felt the sharp pain like a thousand needles flowing up and down my spine.

I took a step forward but found myself falling and landing face-first on the floor.

Everything hurt. I had nothing left. Every breath I took

rattled bones inside my chest and caused a fire to spread across it.

I crawled, one hand next to my head, and pushed myself up, as I heard another sound over the roar of the water. It was faint and if I hadn't been waiting for it, I would have missed it.

One by one the cannons on the walls moved.

Alvis stopped where he was and looked around in confusion as I pushed myself to one knee and got composed, before getting up to my feet. I stood as tall as I could as I lifted my visor and gave him a smile. I had beaten him; he just didn't know it yet.

"What have you done!"

"What needed to be."

The cannons kept on moving like turtles heading for the ocean. Their progress was slow and steady, but they wouldn't be denied. Alvis looked at them and back at me, anger finally breaking through on that blank mask-like face of his.

He moved and before I could react his hand was around my throat lifting me into the air, as he brought my face close to his. "What... did you... do?"

"Something that shall mark my soul for eternity. Something that needed to be done. Something—" He shook me, causing me to cough. "—something that will put a stop to all of this. Not even you can stop what is about to happen, Alvis, it's over."

"You—" He looked over to the outpost building that I had been in and dropped me to the floor as he sprinted toward it.

I could hear the howl of rage and anger that exploded from its doors over the roar of the waterfall. He emerged from the outpost, bloodlust in his eyes as he looked my way.

But I paid him no attention. Instead, I looked at the cannons around me and turned my focus to where they were pointing.

The Diamond District.

I closed my eyes and took a deep—painful—remorseful breath, as I thought of what I had done.

I wished I could have saved the people of this borough; I wished there was another way of freeing them from Alvis's grip, but they had become less than human now—slaves to do his bidding and without a will of their own. I hoped they didn't retain their consciousness while he moved them around like puppets, but when I looked in their eyes something told me they knew all too well what was happening.

They were trapped, locked in a hellish nightmare they could never be free from.

I wished there was another way. Honestly, I did, but I didn't see any way of stopping this madness and keeping my family safe from Alvis's clutches. It had to be this way. I had to burn down the village to keep the disease from spreading.

I reopened my eyes as the first cannon fired.

It spat out fiery flames and lead that shook the floor under my feet as the others followed in its wake, like a choreographed orchestra. Cannon after cannon fired upon the borough below us destroying the buildings one after the other. Some buildings like the Diamond Tower withstood the onslaught longer than others, but eventually they all crumbled and crashed to the ground.

The Diamond Tower stood firm against the barrage that blasted its windows out into a million pieces. Chunks of steel and brick collapsed from its body, falling like meteors down on the street below. Water gushed out from a wound in its side, running down the outside like tears, as red sand cascaded down the other, and still, it stood.

Strike after strike pounded the building from all sides as explosions inside of it took place.

I watched in horror and amazement as the first quarter wobbled back and forth then slid to the ground delicately, where it crashed amidst a blossom of smoke and dust. I continued to watch as smoke covered the borough like a blanket as the cannons continued to do their job.

I didn't know how long they would continue to fire upon their target. It no longer mattered. I had done the deed. Nothing would change that.

Columns of dust and smoke continued to rise up into the air, cutting off my view of the devastation taking place. I tried to feel something, anything, but I was numb to it all.

Lost in my own thoughts I didn't see or hear Alvis move, but I felt my back crashing against the wall railing once more as he held me aloft by one hand and placed me over the wall. My feet kicked against him, but it was like a toddler kicking against a parent. I cast my eyes downwards and saw nothing but water.

Slick from the off-spray of water that came from the waterfall, I tried to escape out of his grip, but there was no give. I yanked and pulled trying to edge my body to safety but it was wasted effort; I don't know how long he held me there for, but it was long enough for me to stop struggling, while he fixed me with an unblinking stare.

"I... what—" He shook his head. "Why can't you see what I am trying to accomplish? Why can't you see that those people I saved would be free from all worries? Free from pain. Free from hunger. Free from... free from it all. Yet in your eyes, I am the villain. I am the one who should be defeated. But time and time again, if we really took a thirty-thousand-foot view, it would be your actions that would appear villainous.

"You are the one who broke into a secure location and set me free. You are the one who stole the love of my life. You are the one who has killed tens of thousands of people, because you fear progress. In taking over this borough, I tried my hardest to make sure as many people as possible were kept alive. But in one fell swoop, you erased all that.

"You went from an office drone to someone who committed genocide, in less time than it took me to build my first scientific experiment. And I was a child genius."

I met his eyes and saw he truly believed what he said, but I knew no matter how long we spoke, we would never see the other person's side.

"Do you have anything you want to say in your defence?" he asked.

I opened my mouth to speak but he had released the grip he had on me. I hung suspended in the air, our eyes still locked, then I felt the force of gravity yank my stomach downwards as I plummeted over the waterfall.

71

There was nothing but darkness for the longest time.

Until I heard what I thought was Tuari's voice, but I must have been dreaming as I fell back into a pit of darkness that I was sure was death.

I woke to the sound of birds.

Opening one eye slowly, then the next, I felt a light breeze blowing across me, ruffling the sheets draped over me. I smelt fruits, wood smoke, and the heaviness that came with an impending rainstorm.

Where... was I?

I tried to move my body, but the sensation of a thousand stabbing needles put a stop to that. I lifted myself to a sitting position and took in my room. A circular room made of light wood, it was sparsely furnished. One coffee table, one king-size bed, one sofa-like chair. They were all designed in a fashion that made the furniture appear like it was growing out of the room, much like a branch on a tree.

I looked out through the large open window and saw nothing but densely packed trees.

I was back in The Jungle. Somehow.

I tried to recall the last thing I remembered, and images of burning buildings collapsing tore through my mind. I smelt the smoke; I felt the floor rumble under me; I remembered the body count I had left behind. Alvis's hand gripping my throat came next. He asked me a question, but before I could answer I was falling for what felt like eternity and darkness embraced me.

Yet somehow, I was in my old bed back in The Jungle.

The same bed that Poppy and I shared all those nights ago when we were looking for asylum. Poppy—I tried to move but once again my body wouldn't cooperate. I needed to see her—I needed to know she was okay—I needed—

The door to my room creaked open and Tuari walked in with a steaming white bowl. The odours of spices and herbs danced on the air as he got closer and laid the bowl on the table next to me.

He looked me over, but failed to meet my eyes. "How you doing?"

"Surprised I am alive, if I'm honest."

"Well, you have me to thank for that. After Alvis threw you from the wall and into the waterfall, I managed to track you through your helmet and collected you at the river basin. Honestly, I wasn't sure you were alive. You were banged up pretty bad. Real bad. I'm sorry."

I looked up at him and gave him a smile, but still, he refused to look me in the eye. "Sorry! Tuari, I'm alive. After taking a beating from that genius freak and being thrown into one of the highest waterfalls I have ever seen, I'm alive!

You have nothing to be sorry for. If it wasn't for you I would be dead right now. How's Willis?"

"He's okay. Dealing with shit the only way that he knows how to."

"Alcohol and violence?"

"Pretty much."

"How... how did he take the news about... about, you know?"

"Samuel?"

I nodded.

"He's—" Tuari sighed and brushed his hands through his hair, "he's going through the process of grief, but he's had plenty of time to settle things in his mind at least."

I felt a tug in my gut. "Plenty of time? How long have I been here? Like this?"

"I collected you from the river basin a little over three weeks ago," he said, sadness radiating from his eyes.

Three weeks? Shit... I must have been in a bad way if I needed that much time to heal. I couldn't remember anything apart from fragments of my battle with Alvis.

"Err... Quinton, there's something that—"

"Where's Poppy?" I said sitting up as far as I could. "Nothing's happened to her?"

"What? No. No, Poppy is fine, Willis is fine, I'm fine, everyone is fine. But what I wanted to tell you was—"

The door to my room slammed opened and Willis walked in, eyes red-rimmed, with the slight smell of alcohol wafting from his body. He marched forward and hugged me in a bear hug that nearly forced me to cry out in pain. He released me from his embrace and took a step back.

"So, how you taking it?" he asked.

"Taking what?" I replied.

He looked between me and Tuari, lips pulled into a thin line and shook his head. "You ain't told him yet?"

"Told me what?" I asked, heart racing.

The silence of a funeral filled the room. I looked back and forth between the pair waiting for someone to say something, anything.

"What's going—"

"Quinton, your legs don't work," said Willis, in a way that you would tell someone that they were out of toilet paper.

"You... what?"

Tuari sent daggers Willis's way as he sighed heavily. "Like I said, when I found you, you were in rough shape. The beating you took fighting those robots on the roof, the beating you took from Alvis, who can bend steel with his bare hands, and the beating you took from going over that waterfall. The doctors here did everything they could, but you were in a coma for so many days, then in and out of consciousness, then—"

I pulled back the sheets that covered me and looked at my legs. They were thinner, yes, but surely they still worked. I just couldn't show Tuari and Willis because I hadn't been awake, that was all. I tried to move my legs but nothing happened. I focused on the left leg and tried to move it so it came off the bed but nothing happened. I focused on the right, but I got the same result.

No one spoke as I concentrated on my limbs, gritting my teeth until a trickle of sweat crept down my back.

I looked up at them but they didn't meet my gaze. Why were they so quiet! Why wasn't anyone saying anything? Something! Just—I touched my legs but couldn't feel any sensations. It was weird. I could see that my hand was on my leg, but I couldn't feel it. I moved my hand up and down, bristling the hairs on my shins, but still I felt nothing.

This couldn't be. We still had a war to fight. My enemies were still at the gate, pounding to be let in.

I poked both legs and felt nothing. I pushed harder. Still nothing. I pinched them until I broke the skin and drew blood but yet they remained unresponsive like two slabs of wet meat.

I hit them.

First with light slaps, then harder and harder, till the sound rang around the room and the only thing that filled my ears was the sound of my yells of anger, frustration, and pity.

"Quinton! Stop. Stop. Stop!"

Someone yanked my arms back and I looked up into the crying face of Poppy. She stared at me and I stared back, my tears matching hers. I opened my mouth to say something, but she wrapped me in an embrace and hugged me while I let the pain and hopelessness I felt out.

72

I don't know how long we stayed locked in an embrace, but it was long enough for sleep to reclaim me despite my best efforts. My body had taken an extreme toll and was now asking to be paid. I dropped in and out of fitful sleep for what felt like another day or two, not seeing anyone when I woke up or when I went to sleep. The only company that I had was the sound of the rainstorms as the heavens opened up, causing rain and wind to pound the trees around me.

The sound comforted me.

Today I felt warmth on my face and I turned away from it. It disgusted me. I longed for the lashing rain and the yowling winds, but they appeared to be absent this morning. Instead, I was greeted with the chirping of songbirds, who mocked my plight.

As the hours crawled past the sun refused to go away, but instead only increased in strength, forcing me to pull my covers over my head against its sunny disposition.

I heard the door to my room open and footsteps approached my bedside, but I refused to acknowledge them.

A Dog Is Born

I could feel the person's presence as they stared at me but I remained still. I could play this game all day. I had no way better to go. Or anything to do. So let them waste their—

"How long are you going to continue to feel sorry for yourself?" came Poppy's voice through the sheets.

I didn't respond, but could see her outline through the fabric of the sheets—both hands on her hips, lips no doubt in a pout. I could feel a lecture coming on but I was in no mood for one.

"Quinton. You've been in here far too long and we have things we need to talk about. Important things...things that concern both of us."

I said nothing.

"Look, I understand how you feel—"

"You understand! How could someone like you understand, Poppy? How could someone like you, who can punch through bricks and leap off buildings, understand what it's like to be without the use of your legs? Understand how different my life will now be? Understand—"

She threw back the covers, face screwed up in rage. "Whatever happens to you, happens to me as well! Whatever you go through, I go through! That's what it means to be in a relationship."

I shook my head. "Those are only words—"

"Don't you dare!"

I closed my eyes and fought against the tears. "You don't understand. You don't get it."

"I don't understand what?"

"Ever since we have been together, you have always been the strong one, the protector, the shield. While I tried my best to offer what I could, and I did try—I fought for us in ways that will cost me for as long as I live—but I've come to realise that isn't enough. Not now, not while Alvis is still out there, not while The Lady is waiting for the opportunity to pounce. I kept them at bay as best as I could, while I was able-bodied. But now, half a man, what the hell am I supposed to do? Fight them from a wheelchair?"

Poppy looked at me as she stroked the side of my face, wiping away the tears that had come despite my best efforts. She said nothing but just kept stroking.

"Aren't you going to say anything?"

She smiled at me, kissed me on the lips, and walked back out the way she came. I didn't have to wait long for her to return, with a bundle in her arms that stopped my breath short.

I looked to her stomach and realised for the first time she no longer had a bump. I pushed myself up to a sitting position and tried to swallow but my throat had gone dry. She rocked the bundle gently from side to side before placing it in my arms.

"I would like to introduce you to your son."

I looked down into a beautiful set of light brown eyes that blended into a sun-kissed skin tone. Eyes followed my every movement as I reached a hand out to touch him but stopped myself; I didn't want to injure him. I looked up at Poppy, who gave me a small nod. My fingers traced the outline of his nose, his lips, his cheeks. He giggled and squirmed, bringing fresh tears to my eyes.

I brought him up to my lips and breathed him in deeply. He smelt familiar, but also slightly different. I rubbed my nose against his and forced another round of giggles from my son.

"Is he healthy?" I asked, still staring at him in wonder.

"As healthy as he can be, the birth wasn't as... stressful... on me as it would have been for a human, so I was in charge of the health checks and you would be happy to know they all came back clear."

"When you say clear, what do you mean exactly?"

"He isn't showing any abnormalities if that's what you mean. We've created something truly special, Quinton. He's the first of his kind. There are no others like him. But in time there will be; he'll grow up with a lot of responsibility on his shoulders and there will come a time when he will have to be a leader, someone who his people look up to. His life will not be easy, but I hope it will be worthwhile."

"You planned this, didn't you?"

She said nothing, but I could feel the frown on her lips from here. "What makes you say that?"

"Something Alvis said, which I didn't take any notice of until now. But the more I think about it, the more... why me? You've been alive for so long, seen so many faces, why did you choose me?"

"Quite honestly, I don't know. Humanity, being human... it's weird, and I don't think I'll ever figure out what makes someone human. But I know one thing, the longer time spent with humans, the more human I become. It rubbed off on me like some sort of aura you couldn't feel or touch, but was there nevertheless. If you look at Alvis and what he's become, he's lost something, something that once made him human, and I think the reason is because he has only had the company of his creations for the last few hundred years.

"And even before that, while building me, he kept to himself, locked away in his lab, forever trying to best nature."

I looked at my son and couldn't help but smile. "Maybe he has. Bested nature that is, but you still haven't answered my question."

She walked to the window and leaned against the window ledge stretching like a cat, while she looked out. I watched the curve of her lower back and allowed my eyes to trace down her buttocks. She looked over her shoulder and gave me a coy smile as if reading my thoughts.

"Did I plan this? No. Not in the diabolical sense of scheming and trying to come up with a plan, but I've always wanted a family and I've always wanted children. That must be weird coming from someone like me, but it is the truth. I did try to tell you once—it was when we spent that night at the Dragon Lair—but things... got away from us."

I remembered the night well; it was the night we had made up after our big bust-up. It was a night of double-crosses, murder, and sex. All in all, a night to remember.

"We never decided on a name," I said in shock, "with everything that has been going on."

She walked over to me and sat next to us. "I've had a name I have been keeping close to my chest for the last hundred years, hoping it was a boy, and now it is, I don't know if it's right."

"That long, huh?"

She looked at me but said nothing.

"Well?"

"I'm not sure you'll like it," she said quietly.

"I won't know until you tell me."

"Kushim."

I looked to my son and stroked his face. "Kushim. "He giggled and beamed in delight. "Kushim." Again I got the same response. "I think our son has given you an answer."

I looked into my son's face and for the first time since I had been awake, I no longer felt miserable, I no longer cared about my legs. It all seemed pointless in the larger scale of things. His health and safety were the only things that mattered. As long as he was happy I was happy. But I knew I couldn't continue living like this; there had to be a way to fix my legs. Modern surgery could now fix most things, but if the problem was deeper—nerve damage—then I would need to relocate to a more advanced planet. Maybe Earth or another planet like it where I could get the treatment I needed. It would be expensive and there was never a guarantee it would work, but it was worth a try.

It would mean taking my family off Safe Haven, but from where I stood, that was only a good thing. There was a war coming between Alvis and The Lady for this planet and whoever stood in their way wouldn't be standing for very long.

As the beginnings of a plan started to take shape, I pulled Poppy close to me and allowed myself to enjoy this brief moment of bliss.

73

I manoeuvred my wheelchair through the grass and dirt, cursing the rabbits and deer that scampered about me able-bodied and free. My destination was less than twenty feet away, but it might as well have been the length of a football field. Small rocks got stuck in-between the tracks of my wheels, and the uneven surface I was on made the effort of pushing myself forward feel like an intense gym workout.

My forearms burned and sweat dripped into my left eye, causing it to sting and water. I gritted my teeth and grunted in frustration as I jerked the wheels forward, but only caused the chair to slowly tip forward.

I stayed suspended between the realms of falling and not, as I tried to push myself backwards to regain balance, but it was a losing effort and I tipped all the way forward falling flat on my face.

Laughter erupted above me

"Fuck me, I could watch that shit all day," said Willis. "If you came to cheer my spirits up then you have succeeded. The look on your face as you hit the mud. Ha!"

I did the best to move my face so the grass was no longer in my mouth, but this only caused dirt to fill my ear. "Instead of watching me, why don't you give me a hand!"

"Nah."

I tried to wriggle myself up just using my upper body strength but the wheelchair pinned me down. The more I struggled the deeper my face dug into the earth.

"Oh, for the love of God. Stop being so pathetic, will you? You ain't the first man who's lost the use of his legs."

With his help we lifted the wheelchair back up. I brushed the dirt, mud and grass from my face and tried to restore some dignity, but Willis wouldn't let me off that easily, as he walked around the back of me and pushed me forward at terrifying speed. I yelled and held onto my seat for dear life, as I bounced from side to side, while he raced the wheelchair over the bumpy grass-covered ground.

We came skidding to a halt in front of the huge naked statue of the woman who was a representation of Mother Nature. Her hands were held up to the sky, vines covered her beautiful body while animals gathered at her feet.

I shook out the blood from my aching forearms and went to rub my legs and lower back but stopped. I stared at them, teeth clenched, hands curled up in balls. I had expected to feel something, anything, but I still hadn't gotten used to the feeling of my lower body being nothing now but a useless sack of meat.

"Doing that good, huh?"

I continued to stare for another ten seconds before I lifted up my gaze to meet his. "I could ask you the same question."

He met my stare with a sour grin before he patted the legs of the statue and leaned against it. Neither of us spoke. We just watched the passing crowd, content in each other's company. The sun felt good on my skin. I had been locked away for so many weeks; it had become a distant memory to me.

"Congratulations on your son. He's a beautiful boy; I'm sure he'll grow up to be a fine young man."

I looked up, puzzled.

"What?" he said with a shrug. "Isn't that the customary thing one says to a parent when their child is born? There was a point where Poppy was showing him to us I was going to say he looked like a wrinkly old man, but Tuari has told me that sort of thing is frowned upon."

I shook my head. "Thank you. I would have brought him around for everyone to see but... movement is a little difficult for me as of late."

"We understand, Quinton. This place isn't exactly wheelchair accessible."

I looked over the unpaved dirt roads, fields of grass, and treehouses where one could only gain access to them by climbing, and shook my head. I couldn't stay here any longer, not if I wanted to get about. Not if I wanted to find a solution to my problem. This borough had doctors, but they believed in holistic medicine first and everything else a dead last.

"So, what are you doing to do?" Willis asked.

"What do you mean?"

"I know you're not going to take this lying down. If you hadn't noticed ,Alvis is still alive and kicking and The Lady still hasn't paid her blood debt."

"For a religious man such as yourself, you sure love a blood debt. Whatever happened to peace to your fellow man and all that?"

Disgust crossed his face.

I sighed. *"If you hadn't noticed,* our last mission ended

A Dog Is Born

with you having multiple broken ribs and internal bleeding, me being thrown off a waterfall, and your brother—" he turned away from me, arms folded across his chest, "and your brother giving his life so we could escape. I'm not going to ignore or dismiss such a gesture, just because we got beaten and want some payback. We didn't kill Alvis or The Lady, no. But we have delayed Alvis's plans for now until we can come back stronger and better. I've already been in contact with The Lady and given her a brief rundown of what's happened."

"Why would you do that?"

"Because it would be easier if our enemies fought and killed each other, instead of us doing it."

"So that's your big plan?"

I sighed. "For now yes. But no, that isn't my big plan. We need time to heal and recover. I need time to heal and recover. From wounds both physical and emotional. I can't do anything in this state, but I'm working on a solution."

He shook his head, anger radiating off him like sun flares, while he dug into the depths of his clothes and pulled out a silver hip flask. The fumes from the flask jerked my head back as they hit my nose, almost burning off the hairs inside my nostrils.

"Don't you think you've had enough?" I said, before the lip of the flask reached his mouth.

He stopped motionless with only his eyes swivelling in my direction. I met his gaze and held it, expecting an outburst any second but none came; instead he lowered the flask slowly, and held it an arm's length away from himself.

"It won't bring him back. I know you and he... had your differences, and it's not my place to speak on such matters, but he did what he did because he wanted to save you, because he wanted to make amends, because he loved you. Don't waste that gesture. If you want to get even so be it, but do it in a way that hurts the enemy, not yourself."

"He did what he did because he wanted to die."

I opened my mouth to say something but thought better of it. Willis's eyes were glazed over as he was transported somewhere I couldn't go.

"I hated him after he killed Dad," he said. I looked at him, confusion crossing my face. "Yeah, I know, not what you thought I would have said, huh? But the fact of the matter was Mum's death was an accident; an accident caused by him, yes, but still an accident. He saw an opportunity to kill his rival outside a bar and he took it. I would have done the same thing. It wasn't for him to know his rival's friends were inside the bar and would fire back, or that a stray bullet from the fight would hit our mother, or that our mother would be there. It was just a host of events that worked against him. Like being hired to kill a man, doing the job and finding his young child hiding under the kitchen table, who witnessed the whole thing, and you two make eye contact and they've seen your face, and in that moment you have to decide whether to pull the trig—" He shook his head, at a loss for words.

A cloud passed overhead and cast his face in shadow, and in that moment, I recalled what José had always told me. There are no good guys in this story, there are just people who are trying to survive the best way they know how.

"But what he did to our father.... the man deserved it," continued Willis. "He was a violent drunk and he would have killed me and Mum sooner or later, but after Samuel killed him things only got worse. I know he thought they got better, because Mum always put on this happy act when he was around, but it was a lie. How was she not going to feel the way she did?

"After all, her eldest son killed the man she loved. And she did love our father. Even after the drinking—the other women—the beating—the psychological and physical abuse, she loved him. Through thick and thin. So it broke her. Having to hide the body, having to lie about where my father was, having to not show Samuel how much pain she was in. Then one day a funny thing happened—she began to drink herself. Ha!" He looked at the flask in his hand, "I guess it runs in the family. That's why she was there at that bar, she was trying to forget. Trying to make it go away.

"That's why I hated him. Still do, if I'm honest. If he didn't pull the trigger and kill our father, then the chain of events that would cause me to lose both my parents would never have happened."

"But can't..." I began, but stopped as I tried to find the right words. "But can't you see he was just a young man, no better than a boy, trying to do what he thought was right?"

The cloud still covered his face while he held the flask an arm's length away from himself. "The truth of the matter is I understand that, but the hate I feel towards him is also partly directed at myself. I should have had the guts to stand up to the man but I didn't. I could have told someone, instead of always lying about it, I could have..."

The clouds parted and the sunlight brushed away the shadows dancing on Willis's face, causing the tears that lingered on his cheeks to sprinkle like frosted jewels.

He took a deep breath and wiped them away. "I could have done a lot of things, but I didn't and that burden is mine to share. Like all the others I have compiled over the years. But I'll carry it, with the faith that once I reach the end God will either show me mercy and allow me into his home or cast me out. Either way, when I meet him, I can stand with my head held high and know I carried my burdens without complaint or bitterness."

I smiled at his words hoping someday he would come to some peace, but thinking back on what I had done, what I had seen, I didn't know if I would when it was all said and done, and there was still so much pain, bloodshed, heartache, and nightmares to go through. I had passed the point of what I thought was normal; when death and destruction were a daily occurrence to me, I kept trying to get back to some life I once had, some life I thought I was happy and safe but knew was a lie.

When the only thing that made me happy, truly happy, was that woman and child up there.

This was my life now, and like Willis, I had to accept my burden and shoulder on, until the end came, and just hope I protected the people who mattered most to me. Once I did that, I could die a happy man.

Willis upturned the flask and emptied its contents at the statue's feet. He walked away but I still had something to ask him.

"I was wondering... I know a lot has been going on what with the mission and everything, but I was wondering if you... you don't have to accept of course, but it would mean a lot to Poppy and me. If you could do something for us— we're not forcing you to—"

"Spit it out! I ain't got all day for your ramblings. God, you can be a woman sometimes."

"I'm glad to see part of the old you is still alive and kicking," I said, thin-lipped. "What I'm trying to say is, it would be a great honour to us, if you did our wedding ceremony."

He turned sharply and walked up to me, grabbing me by

A Dog Is Born

the shoulders. "This ain't no joke?" he asked ,staring me dead in the eye.

"No," I said, smile breaking out on my lips, "we need someone and we thought who better than you."

He closed his eyes and before I knew what was happening, he wrapped me in a hug that lifted me off my seat. I said nothing as more tears rolled down his cheeks and wetted my neck.

"It would be my honour," he whispered before pulling away.

I stared at his back as he walked away before looking at the ground at my feet. "Hey, how I'm I meant to get out of here? Willis! Willis! The ground is covered with grass and mud. It'll take me hours to make my way through this. Willis! Come back here, you cock. Willis, don't leave me out here—the animals are nibbling my feet. Willissss!"

74

I sat under an arch decorated with white flowers and vines that intertwined into the wooden frame, giving off a scent of wildflowers that carried on the night air. Fireflies and insects lit up in colours of green, red and purple fluttered to and fro. They looked like fairy lights came to life. I opened up my palm and allowed one to settle on my hand, its light washing my face in a beautiful glow.

It flew off my palm and I followed its path up and up, straining my neck to keep it in view until it was nothing but another light against the bright starlit canvas that resided above us.

I took in a deep breath and tried to steady my nerves.

I couldn't remember the last time I felt this many butterflies in my stomach. I had been on many death-defying missions, where the outcome of my coming out alive looked bleak, but they never made my palms sweat as much as they were now. I rubbed my hands over my legs, remembering to take in deep breath after deep breath. I looked behind me and saw rows of people sitting on benches positioned in the grass; I knew but a handful of them, but Poppy, being Poppy,

A Dog Is Born

had quickly made friends the first time we had arrived in The Jungle and now they were here to witness this special day.

White petals lined the path on either side that made its way to us.

Willis stood in front of us, dressed in a flowing black robe that had pink petals on it; his beard was trimmed and oiled to perfection. His eyes shone with the light of a man who hadn't touched a drink in weeks. His beard lifted in a smile as his gaze fell upon me. I gave him a weak nod in return, not sure my facial muscles worked properly.

A hand fell on my shoulder and I looked sideways to see Tuari, who was also smiling. "It'll be alright. She can hardly leave you now, can she? You two have a child together."

"Thanks for the words of encouragement."

"If shit goes sideways, I know a gal who's into the whole disabled look," said Tuari with a wink.

I gave him a deadpan look before music began playing behind us, the soft sweet melody of the instruments filtered through the trees causing everyone to stand up. I swallowed, took another deep breath and turned.

Poppy stood at the end of the pathway, dressed in a tight-fitting white wedding dress that had petal designs embroidered into the fabric of the material. A train fanned out behind her like a pool of water. We locked eyes and smiled. And in that moment the butterflies scattered in all directions, leaving me calm and collected.

I gave a nod to Willis, who gestured for the ceremony to begin.

The music slowly increased in volume as Poppy made her way down the aisle. The walk to me felt like it took forever but when she finally reached my side, I smelt her fragrance and wanted to leap from my wheelchair and devour her. She bent down to kiss me, lips tasting like strawberries, and once again I felt the butterflies in my stomach threaten to return, but I kept them at bay.

"We are gathered here together," began Willis, voice quieting the crowd, "to witness this glorious day of holy matrimony, between two of my closest friends. Although religion has been outlawed by Big Brother and acts of happiness like this are growing rarer and rarer with each passing year, because people chose to live in sin and worship fake statues of large-breasted women dancing among the fairies and animals—"

I looked to Tuari but he was already in motion, and with the swiftest shin kick I had ever seen stopped Willis in midflow.

"Why did you kick—"

All three of us stared at him.

"Hmm," coughed Willis, as he straightened his robe, "as I was saying. I count these two as my closest friends, people I would die for a thousand times just to see them take one more breath. I normally am not good with expressing how I feel; it wasn't a gift I was blessed with, and the only emotion I can dance to and understand is anger. But I can honestly say seeing how these two have grown, from enemies to acquaintances to friends and finally to lovers and life partners, has made this whole thing beautiful to watch. When they're together you can't help but feel the warmth from the joy that radiates from their very core.

"I... the journey through life isn't an easy one. Nor is it one always filled with happiness. Sometimes years will go by and the only thing that will be constant in that time frame is pain and suffering. But if you can face that with someone, instead of alone, then the burden becomes a little easier to bear. Now, I believe the two of you have written your own vows," he said, gesturing to us.

We both gave him a nod before turning to face each other.

I went first: "Pop, you are the reason I am truly alive. Before I met you, life was a constant wash of grey. Life had no meaning. No purpose. But all that went away the moment I laid eyes on you. I love you now more than ever, and as each day passes the love I feel for you will only grow as strong and as healthy as our baby boy shall be. I shall always do my utmost to protect you and the life we have created. You mean everything to me. I love you," I said, kissing her on the lips.

Poppy did her best to stop the stream of tears running down her face, but failed miserably. "Quinton, before you I didn't feel real. I didn't know what it meant to be human. I acted out a set of emotions and responses, but inside it all felt fake to me. For years, I have been searching—wanting — hoping I could find someone like you and now I have, it all feels too surreal to be true. I can't wait to continue down this path we have started and see where it takes us."

We turned back to Willis, both smiling, and he spoke again, but I failed to pay attention as something caught the corner of my eye.

It was Scarface aka John. I had seen little of him since we had come back to The Jungle, and any attempt at speaking to the man had been stopped by hand signal gestures as his aide, who worked as a translator, told me in no uncertain terms that John was too busy to talk to me, too busy to talk about what might be coming his way in the form of Alvis, too busy to even talk to me about Samuel's death. I could understand that as the new leader of a borough, he had his hands full, but that still didn't explain why I was constantly given the cold shoulder.

Now he, his aide, and a few other men who acted as his guards were trotting away from the ceremony at some speed.

I strained my head left to right, as I caught other movements from men and women alike in the distance who were all hurrying back inside their homes.

Someone coughed. I turned my head and saw Poppy, Willis and Tuari all staring at me. I looked back at them, puzzled at what I had missed. Two rings had been placed in front of me on a small cushion.

"Take your rings and repeat after me," said Willis. "This ring I give as a sign of my love and devotion."

We repeated the line, placing each other's rings on fingers.

"Quinton and Poppy, since you have pledged your vows before your friends, family and the people gathered here today, and have declared your commitment to each other by the giving of rings, I now pronounce you husband and wife in the name of the Father, the Son and the Holy Ghost. Those whom God hath joined together, let no man separate.

"Quinton, you may kiss the bride."

I looked up at my wife and all previous thought I'd had vanished as she bent down and kissed me on the lips.

It was a perfect moment. It was one I would cherish until the day I died.

She pulled an inch away and I looked into her eyes, lost in love.

"I love—"

That was all I could get out, as an explosion threw me off my chair backwards and knocked everyone off their feet.

75

Ringing in my ears.

That's all I could hear. Smoke covered everything in a thick fog as I groped at the ground, trying to find some semblance of normal. Something wet ran down my face and into my eyes, I wiped it away as best as I could and saw my hands had come back red.

I was bleeding, and bleeding heavily. I groaned as I rolled to my stomach and looked around me. Chairs and benches were thrown clear of their original positions, tossed back by the blast of the explosion. Prone bodies lay on the floor bleeding from too many wounds to be alive. Fires raged in different sections of The Jungle, lighting up the night sky.

"Pop—" I tried to shout, but smoke caught in my lungs and forced me into a coughing fit. I slapped my chest and spat out the bile that rose from my mouth and tried again: "Poppy! Poppy!"

There was no answer.

My chair wasn't far away and I crawled to it as the ringing subsided and was slowly taken over by the sounds of moaning and screaming. I grabbed the handles of my chair and flipped it the right way, and struggled to get myself into the seat. No matter how many times I tried I still wasn't used to this—the helpless condition I found myself in when I willed my body to move faster and perform, but it still wouldn't do as I asked.

Strong hands lifted me up and placed me in my seat. I turned to see Willis and Tuari, both were bleeding like me, but neither had major injuries.

"Where is Poppy?"

They pointed behind them, as my wife was angrily tearing off pieces of her dress so she could move more freely. She hurried towards us, high heels clutched in both hands like weapons.

"Are you okay?" I asked.

"No! Some fucker has ruined everything!" she screamed, foaming at the mouth. I had never seen her like this; I had never known her to swear. She swept her gaze around us and took in the devastation. Everyone ducked low as the sound of gunfire erupted in the distance.

"Who could have done this?" she asked.

"Scarface aka John. He has been spying on us from the start. Alvis knew too much about us, he knew what bar to hit in Paradise Lost, he knew to expect us when we were coming to the Diamond District, and he knew about our—"

Oh no. I looked to Poppy and as our eyes met as the same thought crossed through our minds.

"Kushim!"

Poppy didn't wait for us but sprinted towards our lodging. Willis and Tuari didn't need to be told twice what to do, as Tuari began pushing me at speed, while Willis ripped off the robe he was wearing to reveal his two pistols tucked in holsters under his arms. He also wore a black pair of boxers and nothing else.

"Did you expect this?" I asked him.

"No," he replied, flicking off the safeties, "I carry them with me everywhere I go."

Poppy was now way ahead of us and I could see men approach on the horizon. They carried guns. They didn't look pleased to see us alive.

"Poppy, wait—"

But it was too late. She was too far to hear my cry. Head down she sprinted forward and leapt amongst their ranks, high heels slicing left and right. Men screamed in agony as the heels penetrated eye sockets and throats. They were too tightly packed to fire their weapons and the ones that did only injured their colleagues. I grunted in my teeth as I urged Tuari forward.

Finally in range, Willis opened fire. He took the first two between the eyes, the third in the chest.

I held my breath as I watched Poppy weave in and out of the men around her. She kicked legs, breaking joints in half and causing screams to fill the air. Every move she made ended in death or an injury. She didn't hold back, but attacked with a speed and ferocity that scared me. This was her true nature. This was the beast that had invaded battlefields and laid thousands of men to waste.

This was what the human race feared.

In a matter of minutes she was off again with us trailing further and further behind.

Anything that got in her way was dealt with swiftly. The corpses kept piling up as she moved almost too fast for the naked eye to follow.

"Come on, keep up!" I screamed as the wind pulled the tears from my eyes.

Men came from the bushes to our left but Willis dealt with them. He stood his ground as the numbers kept on coming. I turned my head and looked behind me to see him duck for cover, back pressed against a tree as he picked off his attackers one by one.

"He'll be fine!" said Tuari. "Everything will be fine."

He was right. I was overthinking this. Everything would be okay, Kushim would be okay. We were under attack now but we would defeat this enemy, like we had done so many times before.

Poppy was nowhere to be seen, but that didn't worry me. There wasn't far to go now, to our room, where my beautiful son would be sleeping. Once we had turned this corner the rest of the journey was downhill.

We turned the corner and the roar from a small ship's engines rattled my organs, as a light fighter rose from the ground. We didn't hear the men that came from our left but bullets ricocheted around us, drawing our attention to them. I could see my lodgings, less than a hundred feet away at the base of the hill I was on.

"Deal with them," I said, pointing to the men. "Just give me a running push."

"What?"

"Just do it!"

Tuari didn't need to be told twice as he sprinted forward with everything he had and launched me down the hill. Wind pulled at my clothes as I kept the light fighter in sight and pushed down on my wheels as hard as I could.

He had to be okay.

The ship rose and turned to face me, weapons shifting underneath it. My heart rose to my throat but I didn't stop. It was too late for that. My eyes locked on my front door, blocking out everything else in the world.

The ship fired.

It spat out hot lead that threw up the dirt which pelted me in the face and forced me to half close my eyes. I wanted to close them completely. I wanted to be blind against my incoming doom, but I needed to keep my eyes locked on my target. My front door.

I shouted in pain as something struck me in the shoulder, but I didn't care. I kept on spinning my wheels, making myself as small a target as possible as I continued downhill.

A missile struck the side of the ship causing it to tilt sideways as flames exploded out of the side where it had been hit. It rocked back and forth and turned and fled, but it was losing altitude by the second as it flew over the treetops. Eyes still on my door I heard and felt the vibrations through the ground as it finally crashed somewhere in the distance.

I was only ten feet away from my door when the sound hit me.

It was an anguished scream of pain and hurt. It was a scream of loss. It was a scream I had been dreading.

I turned my shoulder sideways and crashed into the door with force, causing it to fly open as I entered. Our bedroom was on the top floor, where our son also slept in his crib. You could either get there by the stairs or the pulley elevator system. I pulled the doors of the elevator opened and pulled down on the rope that would lift it up.

Please. Please. Please. Let him be okay.

I reached the top, and my fingers trembled as I went to pull the doors apart. But part of me didn't want to, part of me wanted to be kept blind to the truth, so I wouldn't have to face what was on the other side of that door.

I swallowed the bile that rose to my throat and pulled, to see a room in chaos.

Bedsheets were tossed everywhere, our simple furniture

was in pieces and amongst it all, was the still back of Poppy facing me.

"Poppy, is he—"

She turned to me eyes redraw and leaking.

Please no. Please let him be okay. Please—

"They've taken him."

Please leave a review. Reviews help sell books and allows me to create more stories like this. The more reviews I get, the faster the stories come.

I have written a novella, which takes place before book one. You can get it by signing up for my newsletter by clicking this line. I will never spam you and only email you once a month, with news about the latest release, cover reveals and the like.

If you're reading this on paperback, send me an email at Writer@dominiquemondesir.co.uk and I'll email you right back with the link for said short story.

As always thank you once again to my proof readers Martin Ohearn and Brandon Sommerville for making this book readable. If you would like to become a proof reader/typo hunter email me at Writer@dominiquemondesir.co.uk.

Well, that ended with a bang!

I wrote the book, and I didn't see the ending coming, which I always think of as a good thing, because if I'm writing and creating the story and it takes me in a direction that truly shocked me then, as the reader it can only be a good thing for you.

Writing that last chapter was heartbreaking for me.

I had tears in my eyes and I must have put off writing it

for a good three days or more. Thinking if there was any other way I could work around it, but if I did that, then I felt like I would cheat the story as a whole and it wouldn't be as good.

This story ended dark.... really dark, and it only gets worse in the next book until it gets better.

I am afraid Quinton and the rest of the crew will have to crawl through some shit before they make it out the other end and see the sunrise. But as of writing this, the next book will be out in six weeks or so, so if you want to know when it drops and you've not signed up to my emailing list, please do by clicking here.

Plus, if you didn't sign up at the back of book one, you missed a free novella which I shall send to you if you sign up. Once again, just click here.

This book was special than most to me because the same time I asked my fiancee to marry me, Quinton was doing the same. Weird how creativity works sometimes. I hate to admit it but his proposal beat mine hands down, as we were trapped in a beach shack which could have been used on the film set of Jaws, while a full-blown storm was beating down the thin wooden doors, but it made for a good memory.

Anyway, before I ramble anymore I shall leave you ado.

If you haven't checked out my other works please do. Some may be to your taste, some may not, but you never know until you try.

P.S, don't forget to leave that review!

P.P.S, continue on to read chapter one of the next book in the series.

Till next time

DOGS OF WAR

Off-brown wooden beams loomed over me, as I gently rocked back and forth on the cot I lay on.

I longed for sleep to come, for it to take me so I could forget about my problems just for a moment, just so I had some respite, but night after night it eluded me and when it did finally arrive, I wished that it hadn't. Sandman's grip on the back of my neck held me in place, while I watched and re-watched my truest nightmares come to life.

The gun I held in my hand felt right. Heavy. Reassuring.

A simple old-fashioned revolver, its metal seemed to gleam in the gloom as I took in a deep breath and tapped it against my chest and closed my eyes. The sound felt hollow as I kept a steady rhythm, tapping it against me. Tears that I had thought I had long since cried away ran down the corner of my eyes and soaked the pillow I lay on. I brought the gun to my forehead, tapping it against my skull, as my breathing grew more rapid.

Gritting my teeth, I spun the cylinder of the revolver and placed the barrel against my chin and pulled the trigger...

A Dog Is Born

With a frustrated grunt, I rolled onto my side and sat up.

The cot I lay on creaked as the faint smell of stale sweat that had soaked into the mattress wafted up my nostrils. Stains covered my bedding and I reminded myself for the hundredth time to clean them before Poppy came back, but I knew that I would forget as soon as I left my room.

What was the point anyway? The last time I had seen Poppy was...

A wedding ring made out of darkish metal, with rubies along its top that resembled the petals of a flower with a diamond acting as a small centrepiece, rested on a bedside table. I looked at it for a moment, lost in thought before I tore my eyes away from it.

Scratching my face caused dry skin and bits of beard to rain down on my lap. I ran my fingers through the coarse unkempt hair on my face before pulling my wheelchair closer towards me, and then I manoeuvred myself into the chair with the ease that only came with the practice of time.

I swept my eyes over my room, taking in the dirty cups and plates, the balled-up laundry and layers of dust that covered the surfaces I couldn't reach, and dismissed them with a turn of my back.

My door opened up onto a ship gangway that stretched the length of the boat I was on. Unshielded from the elements I would have to make my way along it come rain or shine to my room; today though I was greeted by nothing but sunshine. The waters that surrounded me sparkled and shone as the sun rays bounced off their surface.

I turned my face away from the sunlight with a grimace and pushed myself forward, wheels trying their best to maintain their grip on the sleek dew-covered wooden planks.

My journey took me along the boat to its far end, where I entered the only kitchen aboard.

Hands moved on their own accord as I began my breakfast routine.

Coffee black. Cereal without milk.

I ate and drank in silence while I switched on the computer terminal embedded in the kitchen table top counter. Switching to my messages I saw that once again no one had been in contact. I had been forgotten about. Left to my own devices. I slapped the computer harder than I intended, switching it off.

Draining my cup of the last of its coffee, I threw everything in the sink. I would get to it and the other piles of dirty cups sooner or later, but right now, right now...

I wheeled myself through the small boat until I came to the bridge, and worked my way through the controls and computer terminals to make sure everything was alright. The boat's course and direction changed daily, always moving, always adapting to the weather and the changes of the waterways of The Floating City. It was meant to keep me safe, but I felt like a prisoner.

As always nothing was amiss, nothing needed my attention.

Giving the room a once-over, I sighed and rolled myself back to the kitchen, collecting a glass and a bottle of rum, and wheeled myself back to the bow, where I applied the brakes on my wheelchair, uncorked the rum and poured myself a good measure, before settling in the same spot where I had for weeks and began to drink until I grew numb.

~

Something shook my shoulders and roused me from my sleep with a start.

I looked up with a jerk to see Tuari and Willis standing before me with worried expressions on their faces, which they didn't try and hide. I passed my hands over my face groggily, then wiped the drool that had collected in my beard. The bottle of rum I had opened lay empty on its side, the glass I had been drinking from had emptied its contents onto my legs and dried.

"You smell like a fucking rum shack," said Willis, catching the rolling bottle under his foot.

I rubbed my face harder and looked out over the water. The setting sun made the water appear like it was coated with diamonds.

"Captain, you look like..." trailed off Tuari, as he gestured to me moving his hand up and down.

"Captain am I?" I asked, giving him a levelled stare.

"You're still--"

"To what do I owe this pleasure?"

Tuari looked sideways at Willis, frown deepening, before he looked back at me. "Can't we just come and visit you? See how you're doing? Shoot the shit so to speak?"

I looked at both of them before shaking my head, as I manoeuvred my chair backwards. "I didn't think I would be seeing anyone for another few months. If I had known I would be having company, then I would have gotten myself better prepared."

"Oh, that's why you look the way you do, is it?" Willis said, sarcasm dripping off every word. "You didn't know that you would be having company. If I recall last time we delivered you supplies, you had the same excuse--"

Swivelling sharply back around to face them, I caught

Tuari elbowing Willis in the ribs. Eyes narrowed, I wheeled myself slowly forward.

"I didn't realise my appearance was causing you such distress, Willis. I do apologise. Next time I'm trying to decide whether I should take the extra thirty minutes to clean my ass properly or pick a nice frilly number to wear for you, I'll choose the latter."

"He didn't mean--" began Tuari.

"No! As long as everyone is fucking happy and their needs are fucking met, then I can get the sleep I so sorely need at night. That's the job of the captain, right?"

Neither looked at me. Throwing my hands up in frustration, I turned around again but Tuari's voice stopped me.

"There's been developments, plus The Lady wants to see--"

"You've found him?" I asked, leaning forward in my chair, to the point of nearly tipping forward.

"Not quite, but--"

"You know where he is?"

"Not quite."

"You know where he will be?"

"Not qu--"

"You say fucking not quite one more time and I'll punch you in the dick! You've either found him or you haven't!"

Tuari licked his lips and took in a deep breath. "Look, it's complicated. Things haven't gone to plan--"

"No shit, Sherlock!"

"We're all trying, Quinton. We are doing the best we can to find him, spending every waking minute we have in hunting Alvis down. But, like I said, things haven't gone to plan. I would rather Poppy be telling you this--"

"Where is she?" I asked, head snapping between the pair. "I've not seen her for the last four months."

"You haven't heard from her at all?" Tuari asked quietly.

"No."

They shared a look. "I had thought you two were keeping in contact."

"We were, but things... things became..." I let out a sigh that pained my very soul. "I didn't want to distract her from what she was doing. She had enough to think about, enough to deal with. I would just be a weight around her neck slowing her down."

"But still, Quinton--"

"It matters little," I said, turning around and wheeling myself away.

"The reason why we are here is because The Lady wants to see you. Thinks she can help!" Tuari shouted at my back, but I didn't respond. I was tired of it all. Tired of the pointless conversations. Tired of the fake promises. Tired of the roads that led to nowhere.

And I had no one to blame but myself.

Preorder Book Three Now!

Printed in Great Britain
by Amazon